Hunt weaves a compelling family ~~drama of a 1920s home~~ renovation that sends a brother and sister on a course to discover and confront the painful skeletons in their own closets—and those of their ancestors. Filled with complex characters and buried secrets, *Through Thorny Ways* is a beautiful story of true love, sacrifice, and healing that keeps the pages flying!

—Jamie Ogle, author of *Of Love and Treason*

This book has a bit of everything: mystery, intrigue, romance, family dynamics, and it's impossible to put down! If you love learning about history and immersing yourself in a satisfying love story (perhaps with a tissue box at the ready!), Hunt's writing will not disappoint. *Through Thorny Ways* is a beautiful tale of redemption and healing found in Christ through the prayer and support of the fellowship of believers. It is both refreshing and essential to see stories like this one—where abuse and hurt within the Church are acknowledged and brought to the light, yet where the gift of Church that Jesus gives to each of us is not discounted or minimized.

—Christa Petzold, author of *Gathered by Christ: The Overlooked Gift of Church* and *Male & Female: Embracing Your Role in God's Design.*

Through Thorny Ways

Jennifer Q. Hunt

Blue Springs Books

For all who have chosen to disentangle rather than deconstruct;

To uplift the Church's sanctity rather than her scandals;

To look to Jesus when spiritual leaders disappoint;

Who have seen the ugliest parts of the Bride, but believe her beautiful Bridegroom will make all things new;

To all who have seen the Word twisted, yet relied on the Spirit to make His Sword straight and allowed it to cut away all that is sinful in their own souls—

To you, known and unknown, this book is gratefully dedicated.

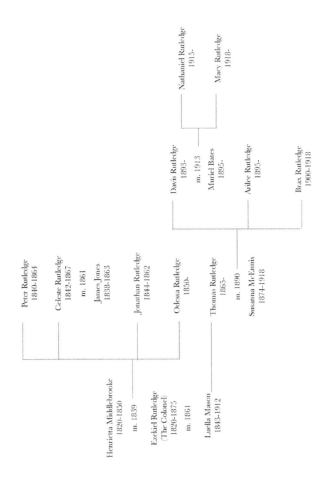

Rutledge Family Tree
1820-1920

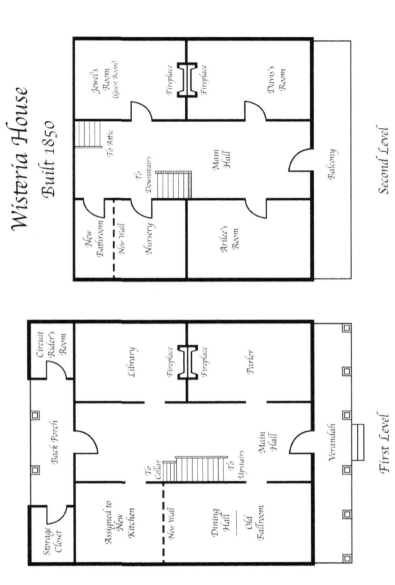

Wisteria House
Built 1850

First Level

- Circuit Rider's Room
- Back Porch
- Storage Closet
- Assigned to New Kitchen
- New Wall
- Library
- Fireplace
- Fireplace
- To Cellar
- To Upstairs
- Dining Hall / Old Ballroom
- Main Hall
- Parlor
- Verandah

Second Level

- Jewel's Room (Guest Room)
- To Attic
- New Bathroom
- New Wall
- Nursery
- To Downstairs
- Fireplace
- Fireplace
- Main Hall
- Arlee's Room
- Davis's Room
- Balcony

PROLOGUE

Thursday, June 19, 1919

Atlanta, Georgia

Her brother Davis was finally coming home, but now she had to figure out a way to tell him his wife had gone mad.

Arilee Rutledge tied little Macy's bonnet under her chin, a sweet cotton and lace creation with satin ribbons. A few of her niece's golden curls peeped out. A prettier baby Arilee had never seen; the child ought to have some compensation in her appearance for having a mother locked up at the State Hospital in Milledgeville.

Arilee knew she should have written to Davis about it. But she couldn't bring herself to put down the whole awful narrative on paper. Instead, she wrote truthfully that Muriel hadn't been well since childbirth and couldn't write to him yet herself. He wrote back asking questions she ignored, their answers too painful on top of all the other losses.

"Aunt Ari, I'm ready!" Nathaniel half-ran, half-tumbled into her room. He looked charming in his little sailor suit and straw hat covering golden hair. His big brown eyes had flecks of gold in them too. "Is it time to find Daddy?"

"It's time, Nat." Glancing in the mirror, she set her own hat—white straw with a wide blue ribbon—firmly over her nut-brown hair done up in a soft chignon. The humidity of the warm evening made the wisps about her face curl. Her face had tanned a little from the days she had wrestled with the overgrowth by the front porch; the scar across her chin stood out more clearly, a white line dividing her life from the carefree days of her childhood to the burdens of adulthood.

"Your daddy will be happy to see what a great big boy you've become."

"I'm four."

"Yes, you are quite grown up now. But it will be crowded at the train station. You must hold my hand to keep me safe, all right?"

"I will." He bounded out of the room and down the stairs. She picked up Macy from the bed, settled the twelve-month-old on her hip, and checked her purse for trolley fare.

The real reason she hadn't written to Davis about Muriel was an unreasonable terror that if he knew the truth, her older brother would never return. He didn't really know his children. Macy had been conceived on a quick leave before the army had sent Davis overseas; Nathaniel had been hardly more than a baby when his father joined the service.

Davis *had* to return.

They'd been abandoned by or bereaved of everyone else but Jewel.

And Aunt Odessa.

Arilee poked her head into the elderly spinster's room. The invalid-when-she-wanted-to-be lay in the bed, propped up by perfectly crisp linen-cased pillows. The heavy drapes were drawn shut against the late afternoon sun, and a candle on the bedside table provided a meager light.

"Come in, girl," she demanded. Aunt Odessa surveyed her from head to toe. "You really think your brother will show up?"

"Of course."

"I'll not have a man living in this house."

Arilee gritted her teeth. "Think how good it would be to have help with the yard work and fixing up the place."

"He won't touch my house." Her shriek made Arilee shiver. "I'll not have him tearing things up, trying to burn the place down with the devil's wires."

"Yes, God forbid we have light in the evening and a refrigerator to keep our food from spoiling," Arilee muttered, shifting Macy to her other hip. To Aunt Odessa she said, "Davis could offer protection."

"He's a soldier. He has blood on his hands and filth in his soul. No man will ever live in this house as long as I'm alive."

Arilee heard Nathaniel shouting downstairs. Odessa considered even this small boy an enemy invader. The woman could have been Dickens's inspiration for Miss Haversham in *Great Expectations*, except Odessa had never been jilted because she'd never been in love. As far as Arilee knew, the woman had never loved anyone, not even her own parents or younger brother. Certainly not her niece or nephews. Maybe she bore some affection for Jewel, who'd been born into slavery in this house and come back here from her life out West to care for Odessa in her "miserable affliction." Jewel would receive a crown in heaven for how much she'd put up with from Odessa over the past few years.

Arilee, however, was *not* a saint, and she'd forfeit any crown to have her brother here.

"Aunt Odessa." She spoke as if to obstinate pupils: "You will not have to see Davis, but he will live here, or else I will leave as well. Jewel is getting too old to do all the work, so you won't have anyone to cook and clean for you and prune back all those overgrown bushes and take care of your errands and wash your clothes."

"As if you have anywhere else to go." Odessa cackled.

Jewel entered the room. Though not much younger than Aunt Odessa, she exuded quiet strength instead of petulant frailty. "You get on to the train station," she said, low, to Arilee. "I'll smooth her over. If Davis don't come poking his head in this room, she'll not know he's around. She's forgetful sometimes."

Arilee nodded. Davis could certainly sacrifice bedside vigils with their cantankerous aunt. He'd have enough problems of his own to worry about. Maybe he'd move them out of Atlanta altogether, though she wouldn't fancy going back to Union Hill. Davis had declared he would never live at Wisteria House as fiercely as Aunt Odessa had declared no Rutledge male would ever abide here.

Maybe he'd blame Arilee for what had happened to Muriel. He'd tell her to go back to teaching, then take the children and leave her here.

No. He'd need someone to care for them till Muriel recovered. The children knew her, trusted her, and depended on her. Muriel's family had rejected these sweet babies completely.

But Arilee needed her niece and nephew as much as they needed her. Dimpled baby hands and downy heads had become her path through the wilderness of grief. She hadn't the luxury of joining Mama and Brax in the grave or Muriel in the asylum; she had to keep the children fed and clothed and clean and loved. Davis mustn't part them, not yet.

She slipped out of Odessa's room and down the once-grand main staircase, dodging the three broken steps. It led to a wide entry hall that ran from the oversized front door to the simple back door. Worn horsehair chairs lined the walls of the hall. A threadbare rug covered scratched hardwoods. The chandelier tapers had not been lit in at least fifty years.

I will never live in Wisteria House.

Davis's adamant pronouncement echoed in her head.

God help me, I didn't want this either.

Life was funny that way. The things you said you would never do, the tragedies you were sure only happened to other people—one day you woke up and you were doing those things and living those tragedies.

Our wills and fates do so contrary run
That our devices still are overthrown;
Our thoughts are ours, their ends none of our own.

Had Shakespeare ever been stuck in a seventy-year-old mansion falling down around his ears with two tiny parentless children and one last desperate hope in life: that Davis would not have changed?

"Fine-a-wee." Nathaniel took her by the hand and practically pulled her out the front door. They crossed the wide front porch with its peeling gray paint on the floorboards and peeling blue paint on the ceiling. Nathaniel hopped down the front steps, stepping on the tail of the tomcat, Woodrow, who scurried away yowling. Macy looked about with interest. The air hung heavy with the fragrance of the mimosa blossoms, and Arilee plucked a fuzzy pink one from a low branch and handed it to the baby to hold.

"Is my daddy tall? Is my daddy good? Does my daddy look like me?" Nathaniel fired off questions faster than she could answer as they walked down Forrest Avenue to the trolley stop.

"He's taller than I am. His eyes are light brown, like yours."

"Will he play with me? Will he like me?"

"I'm sure he will, Nat. He's the best man in the world. You don't need to be afraid about him."

Davis was the best man in the world when he left. But since she'd last seen him, he'd stared death in the face a thousand times. He'd shot and killed those the politicians declared the enemy. Men came back from this war altered. And not just the ones with missing arms or prosthetic legs or who stared straight ahead instead of meeting your gaze.

She thought of how *her* daddy had changed from the devoted, upright man who raised her to the cruel stranger who tore apart their family. And *he* hadn't faced war. If Davis had followed in his footsteps—her insides churned thinking of the possibilities.

Oh, God, she breathed as they climbed onto the trolley. *I know—how painfully I know—better than to place my trust in the arm of flesh. I know there is none righteous, no not one, and it is better to trust in the Lord than to put confidence in princes. I know. But the children and I have lost so much, and if Davis could still be Davis, steady and dependable, it would be enough. I won't ask for anything more, oh, please, please . . .*

Her rambling prayer didn't make sense, but she couldn't think how to compose it with Macy brushing the feathery mimosa blossom in her face and Nathaniel still firing away questions about his daddy without giving her time to answer. How had her taciturn brother sired this loquacious son?

They arrived at Terminal Station. Nathaniel looked around in blessedly silent awe at the massive building and bustling crowds but jumped up and down upon sight of the incoming train. They approached the platform in the shed concourse where the southbound locomotive still chuffed and hissed.

"Trains go fast, Aunt Ari," he shouted above the crowd and the engine noises. "But my daddy flies a'planes, and they go faster."

She nodded, holding tight to his hand in the throng. He kept pulling at her till she was of half a mind to let go, let him land on his bottom, and see how he liked it.

"Where's my daddy?" Nathaniel kept pulling her hand as passengers disembarked from the *Piedmont Limited.* Arilee was thankful Davis had already been discharged and wasn't returning with a full carload of soldiers. If she heard one more jaunty army band rendition of "Over There," she would throw a rock into the tuba and beat the drummer with his sticks.

Macy began putting the flower in her mouth, and Arilee let go of Nathaniel's hand for a second to take it away. He took advantage of his momentary freedom to wriggle through the sea of legs obstructing his view.

"Nathaniel." She hastened after him, the baby still clutched on her left hip. "Nathaniel."

In a split second, she envisioned him hiding in a train car or falling down onto the tracks. She couldn't keep these babies safe. She'd not protected them from losing their mother and not protected their mother from the all-seeing eye of Aunt Odessa. And Davis, if he really was on this train, if he really did come back, would observe at once that she had lost his child even as she'd lost his wife—

"Nathaniel!"

She used to teach her students how to speak in a carefully modulated voice in every situation. Now she shrieked hysterically into a crowded depot.

A khaki-clad soldier emerged out of the press of passengers, holding Nathaniel in one arm and a bag in the other hand.

Davis.

He was twenty-six now; she was nearing twenty-four. There were a few lines around his eyes, a few gray hairs around his temples. He didn't look old, but he looked as if more than two years had passed since the war had taken him away. She reckoned she did too.

"Don't worry, Arilee," he said, and she burst into tears at that easy drawl she hadn't known she missed. "We're both here."

CHAPTER 1

Two Years Later: Friday, June 10, 1921

That a freak summer thunderstorm should coincide with Aunt Odessa's burial made perfect sense. Oakland Cemetery, so parklike that families would picnic here in the sunshine, was as miserable a place today as Odessa Rutledge's soul.

Only Arilee, Davis, Jewel, and the children stood at the grave as the minister-they-did-not-know read aloud a brief service. The reverend from the Presbyterian church Odessa had not attended in twenty years had bailed on them at the last minute when the heavens opened, and Davis had called his attorney, remembering the man had a brother or brother-in-law in ministry. Thus it happened that a clergyman from the denomination she had most despised, and one who was notably *not* reading from a prescribed liturgy or using "thees" and "thous," said the final words over their unhappy aunt.

"Lord, we thank You for the life of Odessa Carolina Rutledge and pray You would comfort these who mourn her passing."

Their large black umbrellas could not keep out the blowing rain. A deafening clap of thunder made Arilee jump.

"She curses us still from the grave," Davis muttered. Macy clung to his neck and looked around with big blue eyes.

"Hush," Arilee said. "She can't control the weather."

"No, probably not, from hell."

Arilee tried to feign shock at her brother's sacrilege. Her acting skills were not up to par between ringing water out of her black skirt and pulling Nathaniel back from the puddles. A streak of lightning lit the

7

gloom, followed immediately by a clap of thunder. Reverend Alexander rushed the closing "one God, now and forever, Amen," till it sounded like "nowenfevvermen."

They picked up muddy clods to drop on the coffin. Jewel threw a nosegay of roses on top of it. "Rest in peace," the older woman murmured gently.

Arilee tried to feel something, anything, other than the most overwhelming relief she'd ever experienced since the day Davis returned from the service.

Aunt Odessa had paid for her college education. She ought to feel gratitude.

Aunt Odessa had given them a place to stay when they had been homeless. Why couldn't she dredge up appreciation?

They left the burial to Barclay & Brandon Funeral Directors and hurried back to where the automobiles were parked—Davis's Stutz touring car and the young minister's tin lizzie. Davis dug into his pocket and handed the tall man a bill. "We appreciate you being available last minute," he said with a nod.

"Glad to help," the minister replied, with much greater sincerity than Arilee's or Davis's feigned grief. "By the way, our church is having a summer Bible school starting on Monday. Religious instruction and uplifting activities for the children. Your boy would be welcome to come."

"Thank you," Davis replied woodenly and opened the car doors for Arilee and Jewel.

About the time they returned to Wisteria House, the rain slacked off. Steam rose from the ground as the sun tried to force its way around the heavy gray clouds. Arilee couldn't wait to shed her black cambric dress, which she'd worn for Brax's memorial service and Mama's burial, and return it to the back of her wardrobe to be smashed behind the pretty teaching clothes she never wore anymore.

Instead of changing, though, they all stood in the wide hall of Wisteria House with the life-sized portrait of Colonel Rutledge in his full-dress uniform looking down on them. They'd just buried the daughter of this famed hero of the Mexican-American War and the War Between the States, and there had been no wake. In this great house, there were no relatives dabbing at their eyes and sharing memories over deviled eggs and pimento cheese sandwiches.

There was silence.

Even if Aunt Odessa had distanced herself from humanity, Arilee knew she and Davis ought to have friends themselves. She knew people from her college years, from her two years of teaching, and from volunteering with the Library War Service. But she hadn't had a conversation with any of them since the 'flu pandemic had altered all social interactions and since her own life fell to pieces.

The children looked about with wide eyes and pale faces. Jewel sighed from the depths of her soul and sat down on the faded settee by the dining room doorway. The elderly woman removed her black straw hat from silver hair that was pulled back into a neat bun at the nape of her neck.

"Aunt Ari—" At six, Nathaniel's questions hadn't slowed down. "Will Aunt 'Dessa ever come back?"

"No, Nat. That's what it is to be dead."

"Is she in heaven?"

"I hope so," Arilee said absently.

"But Jesus is in heaven, and He's a man, and Aunt 'Dessa hates men, so she won't be happy there."

"When you get to heaven, Jesus fixes anything still wrong with you."

"If I see Aunt 'Dessa in heaven, will she like me?"

"Yes, I'm sure she will."

"Aunt Ari, now can my mama come home? Since we ain't gotta take care of sick Aunt 'Dessa, we could take care of my mama, couldn't we?"

Davis made the smallest sound in his throat. It reminded her of a raccoon in a trap. She'd always hated when the boys went hunting.

"You know what I think? I think we've had enough hard, sad questions for one day. Come with me." Arilee took Nathaniel by the hand and led him to the top of the stairs. She situated him on the handrail and then climbed up behind him, gave him a little push, and they took off together, squealing all the way down and dissolving with laughter at the bottom.

"Me too. Me too." Three-year-old Macy would not be left out. Up and down, over and over, for ten minutes, the three of them slid the banister, Davis catching them at the end. At last, Arilee collapsed on the bottom step, panting and laughing.

"I've wanted to do that my whole life," she confessed, wiping at her eyes, noting Davis's rare grin.

"Y'all are naughty children," Jewel protested, but her mouth twisted to hide a smile.

"Run along and play with your sister," Arilee told Nathaniel, and the kids headed to the library where a toy box and basket of children's books were kept.

"I guess now we can do all the improvements we've talked about." Davis surveyed the dim room with its peeling paint. He'd fixed the broken steps, but the new treads had yet to be stained to match the old. "Jewel, how much do you get paid?"

"Paid for what?"

"For working here."

"Gracious, Davis boy, I've never been paid."

Arilee and Davis stared at the colored woman. Davis cleared his throat. "You've never been paid? Not ever?"

"I was born a slave in this house."

"I know. But slavery ended fifty-something years ago."

"After the war, Odessa, Celeste, Luella, and I worked together to try to keep the Colonel alive, to give him hope. His well-being was all that united us. Once he died, Odessa and Luella like to have torn each other to pieces."

Arilee believed it. She had fond memories of Grandma Luella visiting them in Union Hill, but all her memories of coming to this house to see her grandmother were tainted with Aunt Odessa's hostility.

Sometime after the Colonel died, Jewel had journeyed West as a mail-order bride and lived for decades in Kansas. She'd had one child, though she never spoke of him. Her husband had died. Arilee had first met Jewel briefly at Grandma Luella's funeral. Then in the fall of '18, after Mama died and Muriel was sent away, Odessa had written to Jewel that she was dying and to please come care for her till the end. Though Jewel had seen through the lie right off, she had also seen Arilee's desperation and graciously stayed, keeping Odessa at bay while Arilee cared for Nathaniel and Macy.

"You ought to have been paid for caring for Odessa these past few years."

"You don't charge family for loving them, Davey Rutledge, as you well know."

"What will you do now?" Arilee asked, marveling at how Jewel could still refer to Odessa in such terms as "family" and "love." Surely Jewel would stay, wouldn't she? How could Arilee manage life in Wisteria House without her? She needed the wise woman's impromptu grabbing of her hands to pray aloud; she depended on her whispered encouragement: "You know what's best for these children; don't be afraid to do it." Now with Odessa gone, perhaps Jewel would finally answer some of their questions about the family's past.

"Odessa may have been family," Jewel said, "but I wasn't blind to her faults. Her soul was rotted out from a lifetime of bitterness. She sinned against me greatly in keeping some information from me, which she confessed the day before she died. Now I have to see to some matters that should have been attended to long before now, and I pray I'm not too late."

"You're leaving?" cried Arilee, more distraught over Jewel's impending absence than Odessa's permanent one. "Where are you going? When will you return?"

"I don't know when or if. If y'all want to make this place all modernized now that Odessa is gone, that's your doings. It woulda been yours before now except for how she played her hand."

"What do you mean?" Davis raised one eyebrow, his signature expression of interest.

"Your daddy and Odessa made a deal with Luella before she died. She wanted to leave the house to your daddy, but Odessa insisted it be left to her. They finally agreed the house would go to Odessa for the remainder of her life as long as she kept her mouth shut about family secrets. It would go to Thomas and his heirs afterward, though your daddy kindly promised me I'd always have a home here if needed."

The last fact did not surprise Arilee, who had heard plenty about Jewel in Daddy's stories of growing up at Wisteria House; he bore her the brotherly affection he'd never felt toward Odessa.

"You *will* always have a home here, Jewel," Davis said, "as far as we're concerned. We appreciate what you've done." He pulled several bills from his wallet and knelt to hand them to her.

Jewel started to refuse them, but Davis pressed them into her hand. "This ain't payment. This is family looking out for each other. For your trip."

She kissed his forehead before he rose.

"I wish I could stay on to help y'all, but I've got closer kin to see to first. There's things I promised long ago to never say, but you may find out what you'd rather not know if you go poking around too much. On the other hand, the truth might set you free. Well, I've said enough. I'm wrung out as a wet dishrag. I've got to rest and pack."

Arilee stood watching her disappear up the stairs, and for the first time that day encountered the intimately familiar sense of losing someone she loved. Softly, she quoted:

"And whether we shall meet again, I know not.
Therefore our everlasting farewell take."

"You and the Bard." Davis shook his head. "Find yourself a living crush, would you?"

Macy's giggle and Nathaniel's airplane imitation sounds came from the library.

"I wish Jewel'd give us a bit more information." Arilee knew better than to hope they could wheedle it out of the older woman. "*I* didn't think she said nearly enough."

Davis's light brown eyes squinted in thought. "Dad always said she was his older sister, you know. The daughter of the Colonel and one of his slaves that he loved as a wife after his first wife died and before he married Grandma."

"If Grandma's will left the house to *Daddy*, can *we* legally stay here? Isn't it going to be a grand old legal mess?"

"Of course it is. Another *gift* from our father. I'm already due over at the attorney's office to talk about Muriel's case again. We can add this to the list of things nobody can solve."

He stared ahead, lost in thought. In the two years he'd been back, he'd visited Muriel nearly every Sunday. The judge would not even consider letting her out of the asylum unless the doctors declared her mentally sound. Davis continued looking for ways to get her released, but his belief in his wife would have to overcome the hopeless system in which she was trapped.

"You think even if it's in Daddy's name we can make the changes we want?"

"You ever heard 'possession is nine-tenths of the law'? We'll use Mama's life insurance money from Brax and add electricity and plumbing and get the danged yard cleared. Unless God has mercy, and a strong wind blows the whole place down first."

Arilee didn't admit she'd prayed for such a thing a time or two. Inheriting an antebellum mansion was not all one might hope for it to be.

"What will we do first?"

"I think our best bet is to start with an upstairs kitchen and get you out of the basement. And then a bathroom."

"Those will be the best things that ever happened here."

"I've sketched out some plans, but we'll see about hiring it all done."

"Maybe when we're tearing up the walls, we'll find the long-lost treasure."

Davis rolled his eyes. "Sis, don't you think if there was a treasure to be found, Aunt Odessa or Grandma Luella woulda found it ages ago?"

"Grandma Luella always said the Colonel hid it and only he knew where it was, but when he came back home from the war, he couldn't remember."

"Didn't he think his family would need the money if he got killed in the war?"

"I always wondered if Grandma Luella *did* know, but she didn't want it to be found. For fear it would make Daddy and Aunt Odessa fight even more."

Davis shrugged. "This house is as much a wreck as this family. And I, for one, would just as soon not uncover any more surprises from either."

Arilee nodded, but she doubted they had scratched the surface of all the surprises that awaited.

CHAPTER 2

"**A**unt Ari, are we heathens?"

Nathaniel's big brown puppy dog eyes looked up expectantly. His spoon, laden with oatmeal, had stopped midair. It was Monday morning at 7:00, and Arilee wasn't quite awake enough for a theology discussion.

"Of course not, Nat. Whatever gave you such an idea?" She reached for napkins from the buffet and set a stack in the middle of the dining room table. Next to her, Macy stirred her spoon around in her porcelain bowl and spilled her cup of milk.

"You and Daddy were talking about the church Bible school, and he said me and Macy shouldn't grow up to be heathens. I don't wanna be a heathen and burn in hell."

"Nat, wherever did you hear such a thing? We aren't heathens, and going to church isn't what makes a soul go to heaven, but believing in Jesus." Deftly, she wiped up the milk and poured Macy more from the bottle the milkman had left this morning.

"Well, could I go?"

"To heaven?"

"To the church school."

Arilee sighed. Her brother had decided that the summer Bible school the young minister had invited Nathaniel to might be a good idea since he "ought to have religious instruction." Arilee didn't disagree, but she thought a better place to start would have been for Davis himself to occasionally talk to his son about God and read the Bible to him. As it was,

14

he left all of that to her.

Still, Nathaniel desperately needed to be around other children more, and such an activity would help prepare him for his entrance into elementary school this September. With a mixture of trepidation and curiosity, she dropped him off at the two-story brick church on Greenwood Avenue, kissing him on the cheek and promising to be back to pick him up at 3:00. He didn't even glance back as he eagerly entered the sanctuary where several dozen children of all ages were singing "I Love to Tell the Story."

The empty house echoed with Davis gone on his mail flights for the week, Odessa dead, and Jewel departed to unnamed places out West. Restless, Arilee tried to make a list of all the work that needed to be done on the place. She tried not to think that tonight, and every night till Friday, she'd have to sleep here alone with the kids. Should she get a dog? The protection sounded good, but trying to keep something else fed and happy didn't. Woodrow, the cat, lived outside and mostly caught his own food, protecting them from the rodent population that hid in the abundant shrubbery.

She wondered endlessly how Nathaniel was getting along. Were they being kind to him? Was he behaving himself? Would he go blabbing all their family secrets in the first hour? Would he know how to make a friend? She'd already taught him to read, so at least she knew he wouldn't be behind the other children academically.

By 2:45, she was back at Grace Baptist Church. A middle-aged woman with remarkable red hair greeted her.

"I'm here to pick up Nathaniel Rutledge," Arilee said. "I'm his aunt."

"Oh, Nathaniel," the woman exclaimed. "He's in the class with my youngest, Johnson. They've become fast friends. I'm Alannah Macdonald. Pleased to meet you."

"I'm glad to hear he's made a friend." Arilee exhaled. "Arilee Rutledge." She didn't want to give these people her name, but she couldn't be rude in exchange for such friendliness.

"Oh, the children had a lovely day. And Nathaniel is such a bright boy. Feel free to go down the hall and peek in the classroom. They are finishing up now."

"Thank you," Arilee said. "I'd love to see how he's doing."

Macy began pulling against Arilee's hold. "I want Nat. I want Nat!" The three-year-old's nap had been interrupted, and she would be fractious till bedtime. Halfway down the hallway, she began whining. "Carry me, carry me."

"For shame, Macy, a big girl like you." But to get down the hall, Arilee obliged.

At the classroom of five-, six-, and seven-year-olds, Arilee set Macy down and peered in the open top of the wooden Dutch door. The children had painted pictures and currently sat in a semicircle on the floor, reciting the seven days of creation with hand motions. Nathaniel appeared entranced by the teacher, a young woman with curly black hair and a kind expression. Arilee turned to pick up Macy again so the girl could see the brightly colored Bible story cards the teacher held. Macy was gone.

"Macy," she called softly, but the child was nowhere in sight. Arilee hurried around the corner to see Macy heading straight for the steep steps to the lower level.

"Macy, come back!"

The toddler took off running away from Arilee faster than her dimpled toddler legs should have allowed. Arilee couldn't get to her in time, but a young man who was jogging up the stairs effortlessly scooped her up in one arm while holding a mesh bag of jump ropes and rubber balls in the other. Arilee reached Macy a second later and held out her arms for her, looking up to meet the eyes of her rescuer.

"Miss Rutledge?"

"Adam Harrison?"

It would be hard to say which of them was more astonished, but he recovered first. "It's sure swell to see you. Have you been here before?"

Yes, this tall young man was indeed her former student from her first year of teaching.

"We came today for the first time. For the Bible school."

"Your little girl is darling," he said as he handed the squirming runaway back to her.

"Macy's my niece, actually. I take care of my brother Davis's children."

Something in his countenance shifted at this information. Wishing to avoid anything more personal, she hastily asked him, "How are you? Have you been in Atlanta since the war?"

"Mostly. I've been a student at Emory since '19 if you can believe it."

"Of course I can. Adam, that's wonderful. What year are you? What are you studying?" Mentally she worked out he had recently turned twenty-two.

"I entered as a sophomore because I did some classes while I was in France waiting for transport home. So, I just finished my junior year, but this fall, I'll combine the senior year of my B.S. with my first year of medical school."

"Medical school? A doctor? Oh, Adam, I'm so proud."

"You inspired me, you know."

"Me? Surely not."

"Yes, ma'am. I never even considered college till you pushed me to work harder. 'We know what we are but know not what we may be' and all that."

"He still quotes Shakespeare. I knew your brilliant mind could be put to better use than playing tricks on your teacher." She had lost count of how many times Adam and his identical twin brother had tried to confuse her about who was who, or hidden a lizard in her lunch basket, or switched all the dust jackets of the reference books, or . . . well, the list was long.

He laughed. His big, easy smile revealed the one crooked molar she'd used to tell him apart from his twin. That smile. All the girls in her English and speech classes at Canton High School had justifiably had a crush on one or both of the easy-on-the-eyes Harrison twins, with their dark, wavy hair, tall, lanky frames, and fine singing voices. Adam had flirted effortlessly with all of them while showing a preference for none.

"Would you call my bluff if I said those were all Joshua's ideas?"

"I know better. You were the rascal, and you pulled him into your schemes."

He nodded. "You're right. I'm sorry, Miss Rutledge, you deserved better from me."

"It's all in the past now, and you're grown up enough to call me Arilee," she answered lightly, surprised when his olive-tinged gray eyes lit up.

"That's a rite of passage I'll gladly accept."

"I'm not as much older than you as you probably believed." She readjusted Macy on her hip, and the girl pulled a strand of Arilee's hair out of its chignon and began twisting it in her pudgy fingers, whining about Nat.

"Oh, we never thought you were some 'Rock of Ages,'" he said with a wink. "We played all those tricks to try to help age you to a more teacherly appearance. Thankfully, we failed."

Was he flirting with *her* now? "Adam Harrison, I do believe you are as incorrigible as you ever were."

"Yes, ma'am." He said it with such mock solemnity that she found herself laughing too.

"Do you go to church here, then?" she asked.

He nodded. "I met Pastor Andy during the war. Since you didn't get me all sorted out, I had to go learn some things the hard way, you know, and he helped me through a dark time."

"I'm so terribly sorry about Joshua. There are no words for it."

"No, there sure aren't. You've known your losses too." He cleared his throat. "If you're looking for a church, Pastor Andy and his wife are young, but they are no strangers to trouble. He was a hero during the war. Led a charge against a machine gun nest when all the other officers were down. He's the real McCoy."

"I haven't been to church in a while. I, uh, have been through a dark time myself, you could say."

"I understand."

"Best of luck to you with your studies, Adam." If she didn't end this conversation quickly, she'd reveal too much to those empathetic eyes locked on her own.

"Thank you. By the way, if you know of anyone needing carpentry work, I'm looking for a summer job and shamelessly asking every person I meet."

"Oh? What kind of work exactly?"

"I've worked with Dad since I was twelve. I enjoy building and repairing, and it's helped fund my schooling through these shaky economic times. But I'm kind of a jack-of-all-trades-master-of-none."

"My brother and I recently—inherited—an old mansion in disrepair. Davis is gone five days a week with work; he's an airmail pilot. We really need someone to oversee the whole renovation. We've work to fund you all the way through medical school, I imagine."

"It sounds like a project I'd love to tackle."

"Come by the house then. Wisteria House on Randolph between East and Forrest. Saturday evening Davis should be home, and he'd be better than I would at talking to you about it all."

"I'll stop by then."

"Perfect."

"I'm so glad to see you again." He smiled and met her eyes before continuing on his way with the bag of athletic supplies.

She watched him as he strode toward the sanctuary, leaving the faintest hint of citrus and sandalwood in his wake. She heard him singing softly: "What a friend we have in Jesus, all our sins and griefs to bear . . ."

Perhaps her first time back inside a church in four years had not been a complete loss.

CHAPTER 3

Saturday, June 18, to Sunday, June 19, 1921

*A*rilee Rutledge. Sockdolager, she was even prettier than he remembered. Golden brown hair framing her oval face. Aquamarine eyes with long brown lashes. A gentle countenance and melodious voice. Even that thin white scar across her chin still intrigued him, and he had had to restrain himself from reaching out to trace it.

Joshua was the only one who'd ever known he carried a torch for Teacher, a secret his brother had taken to his grave. What would Josh say now to see him turning onto Randolph Street on his way to the home of his unblemished ideal of all that a woman should be, an ideal neither the difference in their ages nor the intervening years had altered?

She'd written to him once, during the war, after Joshua had died. He still had that letter. It had saved his life, and he wanted to tell her that someday.

He wanted to tell her a lot of things someday.

How incredible that she wasn't married yet, he thought, as he turned into the driveway of Wisteria House Saturday evening. She was the sort of woman any man would want for a wife. Maybe she'd lost someone special during the war.

He stood for a moment taking in the yard and the house. She'd not been giving him phonus balonus that it was in disrepair. He gave a low whistle.

Above a brick foundation rose a two-story plantation-style house with a peaked roof. It wasn't palatial, but the simple bungalow he'd grown up in could have fit in it thrice. Six narrow columns lined the front porch like sentinels. A second-floor balcony ran the entire length of the front, and generous windows were parallel on each side of the front and balcony doors.

Doubtless, it had been impressive in its day, but now the whole structure hid in a wilderness of overgrown trees and shrubs. Even a cursory glance revealed rotten wood, loose boards, and a desperate need for fresh paint.

He stepped onto the front porch and lifted his fist to knock, then paused.

He'd been an immature nuisance the last time Arilee Rutledge had known him. It might be impossible for her to see him any other way than as the boy who'd put Coca-Cola syrup in her fountain pen, had talked in Pig Latin on the first of every month, and had written a limerick about her on the blackboard around St. Patrick's Day.

He really hoped she'd never figured out that last one was him.

"You need the job more than the girl," he muttered and tapped on the ornate leaded-glass front door. He noted that the rose vines, though unpruned and wildly climbing over the house and into the dogwood trees, were blooming in abundance and filling the air with perfume.

Arilee herself answered the door and smiled at him, revealing her dimples. He momentarily forgot why he was standing there.

"Hello, Adam, we were just sitting down for popcorn and ice cream, our Saturday night tradition. Do you want to join us?"

"I make it a principle to never turn down ice cream."

"Very wise. You got here, so you've seen the disaster of the yard." A black cat tried to sneak past them into the house, but Arilee pushed it back with her foot. "Woodrow, out."

"How much acreage do you have?" he asked, stepping inside so she could shut the door.

"Almost two."

He nodded, taking in the craftsmanship in the wide front hall: hand-carved crown molding in a design resembling an unending row of birthday cake candles and a long, intricate banister down the main staircase.

A man with coloring and features similar to Arilee's sat at the long but scratched dining room table. A little girl hung off his neck, the same child he'd seen with Arilee this past Monday. Macy, as he recalled. Nathaniel, whom he recognized from his week helping at summer Bible school, jumped up at the sight of him.

"Mr. Adam, you came to my house!"

"Adam, you've already met Nathaniel and Macy," Arilee said. "This is their father, my brother, Davis."

Davis shook his hand, and then Adam extended his hand to Nathaniel, who beamed and shook it enthusiastically.

"We're going to build Aunt Ari a real kitchen," Nathaniel offered.

"Where's the kitchen now? An outbuilding?"

"In the basement," Arilee answered. "The floor is brick, and there's a long fireplace and a coal-burning stove. All from 1850."

"That's nertz."

"Still using words that aren't really words, I see." With a lift of her eyebrows at his slang, Arilee gave him a large bowl of strawberry ice cream straight out of the wooden churn. As he ate, he looked over Davis's drawings and explained about his father's profession as a builder and his own years of working for Dad right up until he and Joshua joined the army.

"Which division did you serve in?" Davis asked.

"82nd."

"Sergeant York?"

"Met him. Man of principle and integrity, never met finer."

"Where were you before the Meuse-Argonne? St. Mihiel?"

"Yeah. My brother was killed there."

"I'm sorry to hear that."

"My Uncle Brax died in the war." Nathaniel, eager to find a way into the conversation, interrupted. "I don't a-member him, but Aunt Ari does, and she cries when it's Memory Day."

"Memorial Day," Arilee corrected gently, reaching to wipe Macy's sticky mouth.

Davis steered the conversation back to the topic at hand. "Our elderly aunt, who passed away last week, refused to allow a man in her house or to do any sort of updates; for two years, I've been living out in the carriage house and doing what little I could between flying all week and visiting my wife every Sunday."

"Aunt 'Dessa died. Our mama is at the xylem," Nathaniel offered.

A shadow crossed Davis's face, but he said nothing, and Adam thought it best to ask Arilee privately. She shooed the children outside to play, kissing the tops of their heads and warning: "First one back inside will be the first one to bed." They ran out, shouting; Macy fell on the way, but unharmed, continued trying to catch up to her big brother.

Davis proceeded to show him a list of the primary work they wanted done: clearing away the overgrowth outside, repairing all the rotten wood, repainting the house, creating a kitchen on the main level, creating a bathroom on the second story, and adding radiators and electricity to the entire house.

Arilee's face lit up as she showed him pictures and ads she'd collected from magazines of Frigidaire refrigerators, built-in tables and china cabinets, checkerboard floors, and ceramic-tiled countertops. She'd drawn sketches of how she wanted the new kitchen arranged.

"What do you think, Harrison?" asked Davis, leaning back in his chair and finishing off his ice cream. "You won't hurt our feelings if you tell us lighting a match would be better than trying to fix this mess."

"I've got three months before school starts back. I could get quite a lot done by then. And if you wouldn't mind me bringing my dad and some outside workers in for a few weeks, we could knock out a lot of the construction and the plumbing and wiring quickly."

"There's money for that," Davis replied. "How soon could you start?"

"Monday, if I can find somewhere to stay by then. I'm supposed to be out of my dorm already."

"If you're interested, you can stay in the carriage house," Davis said. "Don't worry, it's nicer than the main house. Since Aunt Odessa kept me out there, I had it fixed up with electricity and a tiny bathroom. There's no kitchen, but you could take your meals here."

"I certainly don't expect Arilee to cook for me." He looked at her uncertainly. The thought of seeing her every day and living near a family sounded swell. For far too long, at war and at college, he'd been around only men.

"I'm cooking anyway for myself and the kids and Davis, when he's here. Our meals are simple, especially with the current kitchen situation."

"I already got a character reference on you from Rev. Alexander and my attorney Billy Sweet," said Davis. "We're offering you the job if you're willing to take it. One hundred a month, if that sounds fair. Feel free to ask questions or look over the whole house first."

One hundred a month for three months would cover his tuition for the coming year, and his room and board were a generous addition to his wages. But there were always incidentals; he needed some new clothes and shoes, and he would tithe on his earnings, of course.

"How about one hundred for the first month, and if you're pleased with my work, then we'll negotiate for the second month? I'm sure the old house has a few surprises in store, but I would be delighted to take the job." Adam extended his hand, and he and Davis shook on it.

"It'd be a relief to me, for sure," Davis said. "I can do a thing or two when I'm here, but that's one day a week. And to be honest, I'd feel better about Arilee having someone around she can call on if there's an emergency."

"Mr. Rutledge—"

"If Sis has said you can call her Arilee, you can drop the 'Mr.'"

"All right. I do think Arilee's about the prettiest name I ever heard, and I'm honored to use it." Adam looked at her. "Is it a family name?"

Davis began to choke with held-back laughter. Arilee stamped her foot and shot her brother a warning look.

"If he's going to work and live here, he ought to know the truth of it," Davis insisted.

"No!" Arilee shouted, almost jumping on her brother to shut his mouth. He swatted her away and kept talking, while Arilee stood with arms crossed and a stormy expression. Her eyes flashed in a way that Adam found quite alluring.

"Now, Adam, our father's name is Thomas Jackson Rutledge; he went by Tommy or T. J., but our grandfather called him 'Stonewall.' I'm Jefferson Davis Rutledge, and our baby brother Brax was Braxton Bragg Rutledge. Our grandfather served with General Bragg in the Mexican-American War. We always said the reason Brax was so ornery was because he was named after a fellow nobody liked. But Arilee. Sweet, pretty Ar-ri-lee. She got the prize name of us all."

"No," breathed Adam, realization dawning.

"Yes, sir, this here is Roberta Edwarda Lee Rutledge. *R. E. Lee.* Mama never cared for 'Roberta' and called her 'R.E.' as oft as not. A new teacher came to school when Arilee was about nine and asked her name. She told her 'R. E. Lee' and the teacher wrote it down as 'A-R-I-L-E-E,' and Sis never corrected her. It stuck and then morphed to sound more like 'Ar-*uh*-lee'— you know, like the song 'Aura Lee'—and eventually everyone forgot she'd ever been Roberta."

"Roberta." Adam did not try to hold back a wicked grin.

"That's Arilee or Miss Rutledge to you!"

"Still using names that aren't really names, I see." He returned her jab from earlier, much to Davis's delight.

"I'll remind you that I'm cooking your meals and have tricks of my own." But even in her sternest tone, she wasn't a bit scary.

"Yes, ma'am, Miss Rutledge, I wouldn't dream of taking liberties," he replied, knowing full well he *would* use *Roberta* when he wanted to see sparks flash in those pretty aqua eyes.

∞∞∞∞

Nathaniel came downstairs the next morning dressed in his best clothes.

"They have church on Sunday mornings," he announced to Arilee as if he had come into new information. "An' Sunday School. It's like summer Bible school. Johnson told me."

"It's different on Sunday mornings." Arilee grumbled as she portioned out the oatmeal. "You'd probably be bored, and I'm sure your sister would."

"How come you don't want to go?"

She looked at him sharply. "I never said I didn't."

Nathaniel gave her a look. If even a six-year-old could read the truth, it must be blatant.

"We'll try it once, Nat. Then you'll see it's not what you think."

Davis came in on this and raised one eyebrow. "You don't have to," he said. "Nat, don't pester your Aunt Ari."

"The week there was good for him." For some reason, she felt the need to defend Nathaniel. "And he made a friend. Who will also be going into first grade at Forrest Avenue School. We should keep up the acquaintance."

"Suit yourself." Davis shrugged, soon lost in the Sunday edition of the *Journal*. He would go to see Muriel, and Arilee would have to finagle both children alone. Dread pressed on her chest, though the folks had been nothing but pleasant this past week. And why not? They didn't know her family's shameful tale. And for the kids' sake, she hoped she could slip in and out, and no one would ever have to know.

An hour and a half later, they sat down in the second-to-last pew as the pianist, the young woman who had taught Nathaniel's summer Bible school class, played the prelude.

Arilee recognized it.

As if there would be any hymn she wouldn't recognize. Or any verse of any hymn she wouldn't know.

"It Is Well with My Soul."

Her soul was a train wreck.

When Rev. Alexander stood to begin the service, he smiled tenderly at the pianist, and Arilee thought she would burst into tears. She shouldn't be here. If she got one kid in each hand, she could turn and run out quickly before anyone spoke to her . . .

"Let's open our hymnals to 480 and begin with 'How Firm a Foundation.'"

She looked at her bulletin. The pianist was listed as "Mrs. Andrew Alexander." The pastor's wife. That's why he had looked at her familiarly. Arilee exhaled. "'Cowards die many times before their deaths,'" she muttered to herself.

She began to sing. Nathaniel looked at her curiously, no doubt surprised she knew the words. He didn't know them, nor could he read them fast enough to keep up, but he didn't seem to mind as he listened to the others.

Fear not, I am with thee, O be not dismayed,
For I am thy God, I will still give thee aid;
I'll strengthen thee, help thee, and cause thee to stand,
Upheld by My righteous, omnipotent hand.

The song restored her heart rate to something like normal. They hadn't sung this one often growing up, but she'd loved it in college. It brought back memories that weren't as painful, and the words themselves were a balm.

The congregation, mostly young families, sang with feeling. When the pastor got up to preach, she told herself she wouldn't listen, but she did. He was painfully earnest.

Macy sat on the pew with a tablet and crayons, occasionally looking up and around, then returning to her coloring. Nathaniel drew with a pencil on paper next to her but paused to listen to the pastor as he told the story of Paul singing in the Philippian jail, an example of choosing joy amid suffering.

As soon as the service concluded, Nathaniel leapt up, for he had easily spotted the flame-haired Johnson. He ran back briefly to ask permission to join him in Sunday School, and Arilee nodded her consent. Mrs. Macdonald came over to her with a friendly smile.

"I'm glad you came," she said. "Your nephew will have a fine time, I'm sure. What about the little one here? Would she like to go?"

"She's only three."

"She can go to the Little Lambs class, if you like. Katie Sweet teaches them, and she's a wonder with children."

Arilee thought it might do Macy good to get around other children for a bit and followed Mrs. Macdonald to a brightly decorated classroom where children played with a few toys or sat in diminutive chairs listening to a story. Unlike her brother, however, Macy would have none of it. She cried and clung to Arilee. "I stay you, Aun'Ari, I stay you."

"Shh, baby, it's OK." Arilee rubbed a hand over her niece's curls and looked apologetically at Mrs. Macdonald. "She's scarcely been separated from me for an hour in her life," she explained, then steeled herself for a lecture from this experienced mother.

"Ah, that's all right, she'll get there soon enough, and you'll love the freedom and miss those baby arms clinging to you all at the same time. Would you like to join me in the ladies' class?"

Arilee would *not*, but as the men were in the sanctuary, and she didn't know where else to go, she followed Mrs. Macdonald to a large room where the women were assembled. She sat in the back, Macy on her lap, and nodded briefly when Mrs. Macdonald introduced her to the group. As soon as the final prayer had been said, she hurried out, collected Nathaniel, waved quickly to Adam who stood talking with a group of men on the front steps, and mostly succeeded in not having to speak to anyone.

All the way home, both as they walked and on the trolley, Nathaniel told her all about his class, his friend Johnson, the game the children had played, and how he would get a prize if he learned his memory verse by next week. Arilee nodded at him and said, "Lovely, Nat," and tried to still her trembling. At nearly twenty-six years old, rather than sharing her nephew's enthusiasm about church, she understood her niece's terror at the whole idea.

CHAPTER 4

Monday, June 20, 1921, and Remainder of the Week

On Monday afternoon, his clothing in a suitcase and his books and tools in two wooden peach crates, Adam stood before Wisteria House, more excited about a summer construction job than he'd dreamed possible.

This place reminded him of the picture of Sleeping Beauty's castle in the old fairy tale book his mother had read to him and Joshua when they were boys. Overgrown trees and thorny rose vines and hawthorn shrubs, not to mention a jungle of wisteria, obscured most of the house from street view.

He imagined himself the prince, coming to cut through all the thorns and rescue the sleeping princess from her spell. There were a lot of thorns in the way of Arilee's heart. He'd seen glimpses of that in the two conversations he'd had with her over this past week. Not to mention the way she'd nearly run out of church yesterday. Someone needed to cut through all the grief and ghosts of the past and break the curse, end the spell.

"I'm assuming, God, I might be a little outta my mind to think *I'm* the man You have for the job. And yet . . ."

"Mr. Adam." Nathaniel jumped up from where he and Macy were playing in a sandbox on the front porch. "Aunt Ari says you're going to live here now and fix up our house."

"Yep. I expect you're going to help me?"

"Yes, sir." His face lit up.

"Good. Where's your Aunt Arilee now?"

"I'll get her." He ran inside, calling her name at the top of his lungs. She appeared after a moment, wearing a blue checked housedress and wiping her hands on a cheerful apple-green apron.

"Hello, there." She greeted him with a warm smile. "You want to see the carriage house and put your things away?"

"Sure, or since I'm already up here, you could give me a tour of the house, and I can start making notes."

"OK, if you like."

He set his things down on the porch.

"The front porch, as you see, needs paint and a few boards replaced." She smoothed her hair, making him dream of touching it. "It's not too bad. Davis has done a lot with it. You may not believe it, but Davis has already cleared out a mountain of brush."

"Had nothing been done here since Sherman came through?"

"Some things were kept up when my Grandma Luella lived here. My father would come periodically and work on the place, and she paid for some upkeep. After Grandma died in 1912, the house went to Aunt Odessa, who refused to do a thing."

"So, we're looking at about nine years of complete neglect, plus a lot out of date."

"Right."

He grabbed a tape measure and notepad from one of his crates, and they went inside, leaving the kids playing on the porch.

"The hall, of course." Arilee waved her hand. "I'd kill to get that chandelier wired and lit, but I don't know if such a thing is even possible."

"Maybe. I'd have to take it down and examine it. I'm surprised that gaslight was never installed here."

"Prepare yourself for many surprises. This is the parlor." She stepped through a doorway into a room on their right.

"If the king and queen ever come to visit, you'll be all set."

"I know, isn't it atrocious? This room was Aunt Odessa's pride and reflects her disposition admirably."

"Plenty of chairs though."

"Yes. There had to be seats enough for every lady and gentleman to have their own. Were a man to rise and give his chair to a lady, she might feel his residual body heat on the cushion and have unchaste thoughts." She arched her eyebrows with feigned horror.

"How could she even feel the cushion through her eighteen petticoats?"

"Ah, he so easily dismisses the lust of the flesh caused by warm seat cushions." She threw up her hands in mock horror, and he winked back.

Above the fireplace hung a framed copy of *The Burial of Latané*, a melancholy old print of a Confederate soldier being buried far from home by a family of strangers.

"She lost both her brothers in the war," Arilee explained, following his gaze. "Aunt Odessa did, I mean. In the War Between the States. And her brother-in-law. Her father—the Colonel whose portrait stares at us in the hall—came back very altered, they say, a broken man who never could rebuild his life. I try to have sympathy for her, since I'll probably end up a bitter old spinster too."

"You? Naw. 'The fault, dear Brutus, is not in our stars, But in ourselves . . .' Circumstances reveal the true character, they don't make it. See, I listened. Once or twice."

"I'm glad to know all my breath wasn't wasted," she replied lightly as she led him to the room behind the parlor, a sort of library and office area. He glanced over at the kids' toy box and the cushions arranged on the floor by a basket of picture books.

"I know it's not any of my business," he asked hesitantly, "but is their mother still alive? I thought she musta died with the 'flu, but Nathaniel and Davis each said something . . ."

"She's in Milledgeville at the State Hospital."

Arilee turned away, so Adam asked no more. Obviously, such a thing would not be something the family would want to discuss with anyone but their closest friends. He wondered if Arilee and Davis *had* any friends.

They stepped across the hall to the enormous dining room.

"I guess they expected to do a lot of entertaining," Adam remarked.

"It doubled as a ballroom, or it was meant to. Grandma Luella said they held a ball here when she married the Colonel. She was his second wife and considerably younger than he. But then the war started, and I don't think there were any celebrations after that."

"I'm thinking here between these windows we'll add the wall to make the kitchen." Adam drew a wall in the air. "Would that leave a large enough dining room for you?"

"Certainly. And maybe we can have a small banquette table in the kitchen for when it's just me and the kids eating."

"I've been thinking. If we knocked out the back wall here to connect the new kitchen with the current storage room on the porch, that could become your eating area."

"Oh, what a wonderful idea."

Adam measured and made notes, then checked out the back porch. The storage closet was locked. "I can look at it later. What's that?" He nodded at a door on the opposite side of the porch.

"Circuit rider's room. From the old days. Has a bed and washstand and a little desk in it. Separate from the house and kept unlocked for any travelers needing a place."

He nodded, having seen the feature before. The cat came rubbing up against Arilee's legs, purring, and she bent to pick him up.

"There's always an outside cat at Wisteria House, always named after whoever is President when it comes to us. This is Woodrow."

"My feelings about cats and the former President are one and the same," he replied, leaving her to guess his stance on both. They headed back inside and upstairs to the second floor, where another wide hallway with chairs and settees provided what could be a comfortable workspace with a cross breeze when the windows and doors were opened.

"My room," Arilee said, pointing to the closed door on the front left of the house. "Across from it is Davis's room. It was Odessa's until recently, and we fully appreciate the irony of a man sleeping in her room now. The nursery is the one behind my room, and the back room behind Davis's is Jewel's."

"Who's Jewel?"

"She's not here now. She cared for Aunt Odessa in her last years. She had to take care of some family business, and we don't know if or when she'll be back."

Adam spent some time measuring in the nursery, for Davis's plans included turning part of it into the common bathroom which would open into the hallway.

He walked to a small door at the back end of the hall. "Is this a closet?"

"No, the stairs to the attic."

"Do I need a flashlight, or do the windows light it fairly well?"

"I don't know. I've never been up there."

"What do you mean you've never been up there?"

"My person has not walked up those steps and entered that space. Although, if I'm ever going to find the treasure, I know I'll have to. But Aunt Odessa said it was haunted."

"You believe in ghosts? And what treasure?"

"No, I don't believe in ghosts. But she made it sound so creepy. And she forbade me to go up. Said if I did, she'd lock me up there for the night to teach me a lesson. She would have too. She claimed to be an invalid, but she could still get up and around when she wanted. I'm sure the attic's full of a bunch of junk I'll have to sort through."

"Likely, but I need to check it out."

"I'll go grab you a flashlight."

While he waited for her to return, he opened the door and walked up the narrow attic stairs. The ceiling, though sloped, went to a high peak, and the large space could eventually accommodate more bedrooms or—

"What the devil?" he exclaimed, as his eyes adjusted to the dimness. With a shudder, he jogged back down the stairs and slammed the door shut behind him.

Arilee stood in the library pulling a flashlight out of a drawer when Adam came pounding back down the steps.

"You got a shotgun?"

"*What?*"

"The attic is full of bats. Probably two dozen of 'em, sleeping right now. Nasty things, like rats with wings. You weren't too off on the haunted part."

She shuddered. The thought of an attic full of bats right over where she and the children slept unnerved her. Still. "Adam Harrison, you are not going to shoot the bats. You'll make holes in the roof. And then we'll have to clean up guts and blood."

"There are already holes in the roof, or at least in the soffit, for them to get in. And as far as a mess, there is quite a generous amount of their droppings all over the stuff stored up there."

"'Double, double toil and trouble,'" she muttered.

"But I think you're right that shooting them isn't the best way to expel them from the attic." He thought for a minute. "Let me go down to the hardware store; I bet they'll know."

An hour later, Arilee was mending in the main hall while the kids played nearby. Adam returned with multiple cans of Purity Crown Sulphur. From his crates still on the front porch, he pulled out his army-issued gas mask. Nathaniel watched, awed.

"All right, now we're on the trolley," Adam announced.

"What exactly are you going to do?" Arilee asked.

"I'm going to open the attic window on the south side of the house. Then I'll light these cans of sulphur and fumigate them out. The bats hate the smell of it."

"Can't say I disagree with them."

"Yeah, sorry, I know it's going to stink up the house."

"Can I watch? I want to see a bat." Nathaniel dropped his train engine with a clatter.

"'Fraid not," Adam said. "It's going to be hard to breathe up there with all the sulphur smoke. I'm going to wear my gas mask." He put it on and showed Nathaniel, then took the hideous thing off when it made Macy cry.

"Did you have to wear that in the war?" the boy asked.

"Yep. The Germans tried to poison us with their mustard gas. I got some burns from it once."

Arilee put her hands on Nathaniel's shoulders.

"I might need a broom to shoo them in the right direction in case they're stupid," Adam said. "I don't know a lot about bat intelligence. Y'all could go stand in the yard and count how many come out."

Arilee shuddered, but Nathaniel cheered for this idea. She brought Adam the broom and then helped Macy buckle her shoes. As she lifted the girl, she saluted Adam.

"Good luck or Godspeed or whatever one says to someone going to chase bats out of an attic."

She and the children stood below and off to the side of the specified attic window, by an azalea bush that needed to be trimmed down to a third of its current size. After a moment they heard noises at the window, and then Adam's face appeared. He waved at them. After several minutes she saw yellowish smoke begin to emerge, followed a few moments later by bats.

Nathaniel counted eagerly, skipping over the number sixteen and unsure what came after twenty. Macy, still on Arilee's hip, asked, "Birds, Aun'Ari?"

"No, baby, those are bats."

"I don't want 'em in our house."

"Me, neither. That's why Mr. Adam is getting them out for us."

Several minutes later Adam appeared. He had taken off the mask, but he looked pale, and his eyes were watering.

"Are you all right?" Arilee studied him closely. He didn't have the flush of success or jubilant expressions of slang she had expected since his plan had worked.

"Huh? Yeah. Gotta repair where the gaps are to keep them from coming back."

"OK. I'll make some supper and we'll eat outside where the air is clear. I appreciate you taking care of the bats so quickly and thoroughly."

He was still staring into the distance.

"Adam?"

"Huh?"

"It's the mask and the yellow smoke, isn't it?"

He nodded and looked away, but not before she saw the misery in his expression. She didn't know what to say. Her heart ached for all the young men who'd gone to war. "Make the world safe for democracy," indeed. Fine for the politicians to send boys to die for their stupid promises. As though any of it had made any sense or had any purpose.

She laid her hand on his arm. "Sometimes it takes more courage to face the memories than the actual thing that made them, doesn't it?"

A look of surprise flashed in his eyes. He nodded again and shook himself. "C'mon, Nathaniel, help me find the ladder and tools in the shed." The two of them went that direction, Adam whistling and Nathaniel firing off questions about bats.

Adam had changed significantly from the boy who'd sat in her classroom. She hoped she could be an encouragement to him while he worked here at Wisteria House. Perhaps she could do for him what she'd failed to do for Brax and would now never have the chance to do again.

All that week, Adam worked in and about the house, preparing for the major work to be done the following week when his father and several hired workers came. The back porch storage room, when finally unlocked, contained decades' worth of discarded household items.

"I don't know what to do with all this." Arilee threw up her hands as she stood before the open doorway on Wednesday morning. There were canned goods of uncertain age, an old mattress, a cracked butter churn, a broken table and chairs, and a set of Keeling & Co. *Asiatic Pheasants* chinaware wrapped in yellowed newspaper from the 1890s. "Most of this needs to disappear. Those dishes are pretty, and I could wash and sterilize them, but unless you unearth something else you think is valuable, please get rid of it all."

"I take it you don't frequent this place any more than you do the attic," Adam remarked.

"You'll laugh."

"Oh, good. Now you have to tell me."

"I saw an enormous cockroach in here one time when Jewel sent me in to find something. And then I never would come back."

He didn't laugh. He backed out of the room and closed the door. "I'm going to go grab something from the carriage house," he said. "And then I'm going to see about burning as much of this as possible."

"There's an old well behind the tool shed you can throw trash down," Arilee offered. "I'm scared one of the kids may fall in one day, so I'd be glad for it to be filled in."

Adam worked on emptying the storage room all morning. He left the dishes, unwrapped, in a neat stack by the back door. After the well was filled in, he began a fire in a hard-packed dirt section of the backyard. Nathaniel chafed at having to be indoors where he missed all the excitement. Arilee was about to start lunch when she heard a gunshot from the direction of the storage room.

"Stay right there," she ordered the children and hurried to the back porch. "Adam?"

He stood in the doorway of the room and held up an enormous rat by the tail. It dripped blood. She screamed.

"Was that *in* there?"

"Living the high life, I'd say. He'd knocked over some of the jars of canned goods and was getting fat and happy. I have a distinct hatred for rodents after living amongst them in the trenches of France; if you were wanting me to find him a new home, I'm afraid I'm the wrong man for the job."

Arilee shuddered. "Thank you for dispatching him without hesitation. I'm worried about what else is in there."

"Several dozen cockroaches. I wish I was exaggerating."

"Let's just burn the house down."

"No, but I'd feel better if you and the kids were maybe away till this is all cleaned up."

"OK. I'll take them on a picnic to the park. I can leave you some lunch."

"No. I can't eat when I'm dirty. Let me get all this done, and then I'll get myself cleaned up."

"All right. Do you like Coca-Cola?"

"Yep."

"I'll pick you up some to have on hand."

"Sounds good. Thanks."

She took the kids on the trolley to Piedmont Park, and they waded and splashed in Clara Mere to cool off from the heat. She thought of Adam killing all the pests and burning and burying the trash. If the whole month continued like these first couple of days, he'd earn a bonus for sure—if he didn't quit on them.

It was nearly evening by the time she got back with the kids. Outside, Adam watched over the burn pile, face streaked with sweat and soot, but jauntily singing "The Last Long Mile." The smoke filling the yard was a better smell than the sulphur stench still lingering in the house but not by much. The storage room door stood wide open, the room completely clear.

She fixed the kids a quick supper of toasted bread and cheese and Campbell's tomato soup. It was 8:30 and they were asleep before Adam came in for his supper, clean and smelling of aftershave, but eyes bloodshot from the smoke. Arilee brought up two bowls of soup and a platter of toasted bread and cheese from the basement kitchen, and she and Adam sat at the dining room table.

"I waited to eat with you," she said. "I hope you don't mind."

"I'm glad for the company," he replied. "I locked the storage room back since I doused it in poison to discourage a comeback from the creatures."

She shuddered. "You must think I'm a terrible housekeeper, what with bats in the attic and rats and roaches in the porch room."

"No, to be honest, all I've wondered is how can you possibly take care of the children *and* the house. You give your niece and nephew priority, which is admirable. They're swell kids, and it's obviously due to you."

"Thank you. Davis says I coddle them too much, and it's true I'm not the disciplinarian. He was gone, and then their mother was gone, and there was no one else. But it never felt like I had to do it because it was my duty. It felt like we all needed each other."

"Kids who have been through so much loss need love and security more than anything. You've given them that, and it'll be the foundation for them respecting your instruction and learning self-discipline."

"I hope you're right. I appreciate the encouragement. Jewel used to say things like that. She was my only friend the past few years, and I really miss her."

Adam opened his mouth and shut it again. She looked at him curiously. He met her eyes and his voice was soft as he said, "I'm glad to be your friend, Arilee, and I hope I always can be."

"Thank you. I obviously need a friend who can protect me from the horrors in my own house."

He answered with that grin. Goodness, a girl could get turned inside out with too many of those smiles.

He was just a kid, who doubtless still thought of her as his teacher.

That's how it would remain.

Of course.

CHAPTER 5

Sunday, June 26, 1921

A dam paced the length of the front porch. At breakfast, he'd casually asked Arilee if she and the children were going to church again this Sunday. Nathaniel had shouted with enthusiasm, but Arilee had looked as if he'd asked her to go to the trenches of France. Davis had raised one eyebrow, muttered something unintelligible, and gone back to his coffee and newspaper.

Arilee's older brother was friendly enough, but Adam thought it would take an investigative journalist to get inside the man's head. He'd come home from his air mail route late Friday. Yesterday they'd worked together on purchasing supplies for the upcoming construction. And this morning he'd left for Milledgeville right after breakfast.

Afraid of being late, Adam almost gave up waiting on Arilee. But his long-suffering was rewarded when she opened the front door and ushered the children out, all of them clearly in Sunday garb. Instead of her usual print or checked housedress, she wore a stylish dark green number with a satin sash at her small waist and a straw hat adorned with a matching green ribbon. All the deep green brought out the green hints in her aquamarine eyes. She looked stunning, and he forgot why he was waiting there.

"You, uh, want me to walk with you and help you with the kids on the trolley?" he finally stammered, feeling like he was seventeen again and his voice might crack.

"You don't have to, but it certainly would be appreciated. Unless you know how to drive?"

"Yes. You don't mean the Bulldog in the carriage house, do you?" He'd admired the Stutz Model K Touring car every night as he entered his living quarters.

"Davis bought it earlier this year, and he taught me to drive it, but it's hard with Macy still small. I'm always afraid she'll open the door and fall out or slide all around the back. If you drive, I could hold her in my lap and sit Nathaniel between us."

"I'm all for that." He was used to driving his parents' flivver. Getting to escort Arilee *and* drive her brother's roadster? Sockdolager! He'd really have to pull himself in check to focus on the Lord this morning rather than how and with whom he'd gotten to church.

The steering wheel on the right side of this automobile was opposite what he knew, but he adjusted easily. Beside him, Nathaniel asked about every button on the dash till Arilee told him he had reached the end of his allotted questions for the day.

At church, Adam wasn't sure what to say to Arilee. He knew almost everyone here; she was new and uneasy. Would she want to avoid sitting with him lest people assume they were a couple? Not that he would mind them assuming such a thing, but it could be awkward if they were called on to explain. As they climbed up the front steps, he said, "I can come in after you and sit on the other side if you want."

"Oh goodness, Adam, this doesn't strike me as a church where people would think anything of a lady sitting with her brother's hired man."

He hoped he kept his face impassive. "No, of course not."

Her brother's hired man.

She didn't think anything of them walking in together with two kids because she couldn't imagine someone possibly mistaking that *they* were together.

He threw open the church door with a little more force than necessary and filed into the pew with the two kids between them. He held his hymnal down where Nathaniel could see it since he didn't need the words to "God Leads Us Along" anyway, but his singing sounded mumbled and distracted, not like Arilee's sweet soprano floating over to him.

Stewing, he couldn't concentrate on the message. When the service ended, he said, "I have a meeting. I'll be outside after Sunday School to chauffeur you home."

"OK. You don't have to. I mean, I'm not expecting you to add chauffeur to all your other duties."

"I don't mind," he answered so curtly she probably thought he did mind. Flustered, he walked off toward the back. He ought to point out to her where the ladies' class met and help her get the kids to their classrooms, but he wanted to be away from her. After all, her feelings about church weren't his problem. He was just her brother's hired man.

Adam hadn't joined them for Sunday dinner. He'd said he needed to take care of some personal business and then he intended to go back up and clean out the attic when the temperature had cooled. Maybe he planned to eat with friends from church or school. Maybe he didn't care for her simple cooking, though he'd seemed pleased enough the past week.

Had something happened at church that put him into a bad mood? He'd hardly said two words all the drive home. If there were major underlying problems at this church, she couldn't keep going there and expose the kids to that hurt. Davis would say, "I told you so." *She* wouldn't be hurt, not really. She would never open her heart to any of the people there. She would attend only because God and society expected it and the children needed it.

The women at Grace Baptist seemed to take turns leading the ladies' Bible class, and this Sunday it had been Mrs. Sweet, the pastor's mother-in-law. She reminded Arilee of her own mother, sincere and godly in a way Arilee knew she could never be. After the talk from the book of Proverbs, they had shared prayer requests, although Violet Alexander had prefaced this time by reminding the women to be careful to avoid gossip. As each woman who wanted to do so shared her burden, several other women would surround her, place hands on her shoulders, and pray over her right then. Arilee had felt a lump rise in her throat several times. She had tried again to slip out the back as soon as the class ended, but persistent Alannah Macdonald had seen her.

"I'm delighted you're back, Miss Rutledge. Did Pastor and Mrs. Alexander call on you this past week?"

"No, I'm sure they don't know where I live, and I, uh, the house is all torn up with the remodeling we're doing, and I'd rather not receive visitors right now, you understand."

Alannah nodded and smoothed a strand of red hair behind her ear. "Of course, if you'd prefer. They are delightful. I've known Violet—that's Mrs. Alexander—her whole life, and she's best friends with my daughter Cornelia, who is married to Violet's brother Billy."

"Billy Sweet? He goes to church here?"

"Yes, one of the deacons."

"Oh. He is acquainted with my brother." She'd forgotten Davis's attorney went here; that was how they'd initially made this connection. Seeing the man who knew all their family secrets would certainly be disconcerting. Not to mention what he might tell everyone.

"I better get my niece and nephew." Today, Macy had gone into the Little Lambs class, drawn in by a lively song and the exuberance of "Miss Katie," the teacher.

"I'll walk with you," said Mrs. Macdonald.

Arilee's pulse raced, and her palms grew sweaty. Would there be personal questions about where the children's parents were? What might Billy Sweet have already told her? If he told even half of what he knew, would they still be welcome? But the walk back to the nursery to get Macy had been full of Mrs. Macdonald's friendly chatter, not interrogation.

Still, sitting on the back porch now, shelling peas and watching the kids play in the yard, Arilee wondered if she was making a horrible mistake. Sooner or later these church people would want to know her story. Probably sooner. Maybe folks were already talking. Perhaps that explained why Adam had been distant ever since church. Maybe he already wished he hadn't rearranged his life to work for such a messed-up family.

Adam appeared then, picking Macy up and swinging her high, making her shriek with laughter, then chasing Nathaniel with Macy bumping along on his broad shoulders. He took a few minutes to play catch with the kids, then promised to find them a treasure in the attic. They pulled at his pants legs and asked to come with him.

"Not yet, not till I make it safe and clean."

"Adam," she said, rising and scattering pea pods all over the porch floor. "You don't have to work on a Sunday. You ought to have a day off."

"I want the attic cleaned up before Dad and all the workmen arrive tomorrow so we can get as much done as possible while they're here."

"Oh, OK."

He still wasn't making eye contact with her.

"Did something happen at church?" she asked abruptly, desperate.

He turned on his way inside. "What do you mean?"

"You seem—different. I found out our attorney goes to church there, and I think it's a terrible mistake for me to go, because he knows all our secrets, and no one will want us there if they know, and maybe you don't want to be here either and associated with us . . ."

He crossed back over to her on the porch.

"Arilee, I know going to church is hard for you. The folks there aren't perfect, but they are people of the Word, who love the Lord and want to follow Him. Pastor Andy and his wife were deeply hurt by some false rumors at their last church, and they do not tolerate gossip. If your attorney is Billy Sweet or Sam Harris—they both go there and are the only attorneys I know—you don't need to worry. Talking about clients or cases is a violation of their code of ethics as professionals, and they are both fine men of integrity."

"OK." She wished her voice carried more confidence, and that his carried a bit more warmth.

He turned to go inside and up to the attic, then paused. "And all your secrets are safe with me, *Roberta*." He stuck out his tongue at her and strode away.

"You palooka, Harrison," Adam muttered as he entered the dim attic. "You don't want her to think of you as a schoolboy, so you stick out your tongue and stomp away. Use your noodle, for Pete's sake."

He took his cleaning supplies and worked out his frustration. He'd found some old burlap sacks in the carriage house and scooped up the bat guano into them, then used rags and bleach to clean it off the rafters and floor as needed. Though he wore work gloves and a simple cloth mask, and the bleach fumes were potent, the familiar panic over germs soon churned in his stomach, another way the war had addled him.

"Lord," he muttered. "I'm such a blockhead."

Mere days ago, he'd prayed to be the one to fight through the thorns and win the princess. And now he sulked over a thoughtless comment she'd made when she was terrified of walking into a church.

What *had* happened to her family? He wished he could remember, but he and Joshua had left for basic training around that time. He hadn't thought to add the question to his latest weekly letter home. He carried a pencil and paper around with him everywhere he went; as thoughts came to him, he'd jot them down to his mother. Even if he asked his father a question—last week's letter held quite a few regarding construction—his mother was the one who always answered or took dictation for his father's advice. At any rate, Mother and Dad were coming tomorrow, so he'd ask her in person. She would remember.

Two hours later, the attic was clean. There were several ancient-looking trunks along one outside wall, and a few random large pieces, such as an old hoop skirt, an enormous gilt-framed mirror, and some old portraits. Arilee would have to look through and determine what she wanted to do with all this, but he'd find out if she preferred for him to bring it down or to come up and see it for herself.

Gathering up all the rags and bags and the two flashlights he'd needed, he headed back downstairs. The children were nowhere to be seen, and the nursery door was shut. No doubt in the morning they'd be anxiously looking for their treasure, and thankfully, he'd found an old stick horse they would enjoy.

Arilee sat in the library, curled up in a plush armchair, feet tucked under her, reading. She started to rise when she saw him, but he motioned for her to stay seated.

"I need to ask you a few things, but I gotta get cleaned up first."

"OK. Bring me back those clothes, and I'll wash them for you."

"You don't have to do that."

"You didn't have to clean bat crap out of my attic, either, but you did."

Had Miss Arilee Rutledge, the eternal corrector of his slang, just said *crap*? He couldn't stop his grin.

"Aunt Odessa would've washed my mouth out with lavender soap," she said wryly and waved him on his way.

He went back to the carriage house where he scrubbed down, changed into clean clothes, and doused himself with aftershave. Despite her offer, he put his dirty clothes with the rest of his laundry, which he hired done rather than add to her workload.

When he returned to the house, she sat on the back porch with her bare feet hanging off the edge, staring out into the darkening sky. He lowered himself next to her, and she handed him a mug of tea and a generous slice of pound cake.

"Thank you," he said. "About earlier, I'm sorry I was short with you. It had nothing to do with church."

She nodded. "How bad is it in the attic?"

He appreciated the way she moved on and didn't have to know why he'd been in a bad mood.

"It's decontaminated now. What I wanted to ask you is if you want me to bring the stuff down for you to examine, or if you want to go up? I guess I could have asked you earlier, but all I could think about was getting cleaned up myself."

She laughed softly. "You've gone above and beyond the call of duty all week, so I'm happy to feed you and talk for a minute if you're not anxious to get away."

"I guess it's pretty quiet here for you in the evenings when Davis is gone."

"And when Davis is here. While you were in the attic, he got back from Milledgeville, ate, and went to bed because he'll leave at five tomorrow morning. Davis has never been chatty, but since the war, he's pulled even more inside himself. I never know what he's thinking."

Adam nodded. "It's hard to know how to talk to people now, especially women. I've been on exactly two dates since I got back. The first girl wanted me to tell her every detail of my time in the service, hounded me with questions as if I were being court-martialed. And the second girl acted as if the war had never happened. Everything was shallow. This movie, that fashion, the latest dance craze."

"Ah, what's two more broken hearts?" Arilee teased. "As I recall, you and Joshua left behind a whole string of them in high school. Did you serve together?"

"Yes. I wanted to join, and he didn't. Mostly because he was a good son and didn't want to make Mother cry. But the preachers and the politicians were telling us what a great service to God and country we would be doing, and I couldn't stand to miss it. He joined so I wouldn't have to go alone."

He'd come back alone though.

"We'd always done everything together." He fiddled with the empty fork. "I don't think either of us knew how to be adults and lead separate lives."

He looked out across the charcoal sky. Clouds covered the moon, and the air hung heavy with the smell and feel of coming rain.

"Brax ran away from home and joined the 22nd Aero Squadron in Texas to be a pilot." She began explaining slowly. "Daddy'd just left us. Mama was distraught. Davis joined up too, to try to look out for Brax. Davis's wife, Muriel, never forgave him, for with family to support, he'd not likely have been drafted. But he did make better money as a pilot than he made as a postman at home.

"While he was overseas, Muriel lived in terror every moment of every day that there would be a knock on the door with the fateful telegram. The day it came, and it was Brax instead of Davis killed in action, rather than being relieved, she spiraled deeper into her fears."

Arilee looked at him, appraisingly, before giving him the next piece. "After Mama died in the pandemic, Muriel's parents wouldn't help her, wouldn't take her in, because of Daddy and the scandal. I should've realized how fragile Muriel was—"

"You'd just lost your mother and your brother. I think all 'should'ves' were off the table at that point."

She met his eyes. Even in the dim light, he saw the struggle, the uncertainty. "Still. If only I had. Macy was four months old and colicky. One evening, she would not stop crying for anything. Muriel took a pillow and put it over the baby's face."

Adam gasped.

"Odessa saw it and snatched Macy away from her. I was putting Nathaniel to bed, and Odessa ran in and thrust the baby at me, shrieking about a murderer among us. Macy wasn't breathing, but she wasn't blue. I blew in her mouth and nose, and she startled and cried. Odessa summoned the police, and they arrested Muriel. The judge sent her to the asylum instead of prison.

"I'm grateful Odessa saved the baby, but I wish she'd let me talk to the doctor rather than turning Muriel in. She had a hard time after both her children's births, to say nothing of the stress and loss weighing on us all that fall."

Arilee didn't speak for several moments. She looked out over the backyard, but Adam knew she wasn't seeing the huge magnolia or the scattered outbuildings. "Davis blames himself for it all because that's how he is. A man of greater integrity you'll not find, but joy's in short supply. He and I say 'the war' to refer to everything from the summer of '17 through the summer of '19. Everything is 'before the war' or 'after the war' or 'during the war,' and we don't talk about it."

That was the way of things. Adam doubted it was the right way, but neither did he want to bare his soul about the living hell of 1918. Though with Arilee he felt different. Maybe because of what she'd been through herself, he felt he could tell her anything. Well, almost.

"What book were you absorbed in?" He changed back to neutral ground.

"A mystery by a new British author, Agatha Christie. It's intriguing so far. I'm afraid I'm not doing the kind of serious reading you've been doing with your studies."

He shrugged. "You put in your time. Do you think you'll ever go back to teaching?"

"When Macy is school age, I suppose I will. I did enjoy it, despite the orneriness of some of my pupils." Her smile revealed those two adorable dimples.

"Will I ever live that down?"

She absently traced the scar across her chin. "You may find it hard to believe, but I pulled some adolescent stunts I'd rather forget. I know what it is to be judged on your past mistakes, and believe me, Adam, I may tease you, but I don't hold anything against you."

He cleared his throat. Lightning flashed in the distance and thunder rumbled low. "We've got our work cut out for us this next week. I don't know if I mentioned it, but my mother decided to come too. I think she just wants to see me. Both my parents will stay with me in the carriage house."

Arilee nodded. "I'm sorry I haven't better accommodations for them at the moment, but they are certainly welcome."

Another crash of thunder and flash of lightning. Woodrow came running from the yard, meowing warnings at them. "Guess I'll turn in. Thank you." He waved at the empty cake plate, but he meant more. He appreciated *her*, but he didn't know how to say it. Raindrops began pelting the tin roof, making it necessary for him to shout his good night. He jogged across the yard to the carriage house. When he looked back, she stood on the porch and gave him a salute and a smile before turning and heading inside.

He didn't mind getting drenched to see that smile.

CHAPTER 6

Monday, June 27, 1921

By noon Monday, Arilee wished they had made good on all the threats to burn down the house.

The interior side of the back wall was torn apart from attic to cellar, and she couldn't go anywhere without encountering a sweaty man with tools. She dared not take her eyes off Macy lest the child be electrocuted, hit with a hammer, have a board or a pipe dropped upon her, or any other of the dozens of disasters she had imagined. Meanwhile, Nathaniel followed Adam with endless questions, which he answered with more patience than Arilee had given him credit for.

It all reminded her of when she'd directed *Merchant of Venice* in her first year of teaching. Sets to be built, costumes to be fitted, props to obtain, actors to train, stagehands to find, tickets and concessions and programs and advertising. For weeks, she'd barely eaten or slept. Though she'd been pleased with the performance, she'd sworn off directing. Forever. So much so that she'd taught elementary school her next and only other year of teaching. A small skit about the first Thanksgiving had definitely been enough drama.

But Adam was in his element. He had men here from McCray Refrigerator Company, Acme Electric Company, Cromer & Thornton Building Materials, S.S. Shepard Plumbing and Heating Co., and Price & Thomas Woodworkers. All at the same time. He stood amidst the chaos, directing the whole dismantling and re-mantling of Wisteria House with absurd aplomb for his age and experience.

Trailed by Macy, Arilee came tramping up the basement steps with two platters of food for the workmen and saw a couple she vaguely recognized standing in her front hall. They looked to be in their mid-fifties, both with graying brown hair and dressed simply. The man was quite tall, his wife nearly a foot shorter.

"Hello." She felt she ought to know who they were and why they were here. The woman stepped forward and took one of the heavy platters. "Miss Rutledge, it's wonderful to see you again. I do apologize for intruding."

Oh, yes, Adam's parents. He'd told her they were coming in on the morning train.

"Hello, Mrs. Harrison, Mr. Harrison. Thank you for coming, and I apologize that the house is in a bit of an uproar." She had to speak at an uncomfortable volume to be heard over the shouting and hammering coming from the direction of the back porch.

"That's why we've come," Mrs. Harrison returned lightly.

"Where's Adam?" Mr. Harrison asked.

"Adam is—" Arilee blinked. "He appears to be sort of everywhere. I can't say exactly."

Both of the Harrisons laughed. "Sounds about right," said Mrs. Harrison, while Adam's father went to find him. "Now, how can I help *you*?" the older woman asked.

"I'm not sure. Everything is topsy-turvy, and I'd leave, but it seems Adam has continuous questions for me about what way I want something or the other done. I am trying to get together some lunch for the workmen, but I certainly don't expect you to work."

"Nonsense. Once my husband finds Adam, I will be quite abandoned by them both as they talk over every detail of the building forty-three times backward and forward. It would be a delight to have some female company. And what is your name?" The older woman knelt and beamed at Macy. Arilee's heart constricted thinking how this child would never have a grandma and how much Mama would have cherished her.

"Macy Jane Rut-wedge."

"How old are you?"

Macy held up three fingers, carefully positioning her thumb to hold back her pinkie.

"Aun'Ari made me a cake when it was my birfday."

"I like cake too," Mrs. Harrison confided. "Birthdays are exciting, especially when you turn three."

Macy rewarded the woman with a smile and holding her hand.

Arilee started thinking out loud. "It's sweltering out. I thought maybe if everyone came in and rested a minute and had cold lemonade and roast beef sandwiches and pickles and canned peaches—do you think that's OK? I haven't hosted anything in ages, and the dining room is torn up with the new kitchen wall, so it will have to be here in the hall."

"I think that sounds delightful. Workmen don't expect to get lunch at the job site, as a rule, so they'll be tickled pink. I'll set out the plates and glasses if you'll point me in the right direction."

Arilee almost couldn't speak. She had missed this. Dreadfully. Working alongside another woman. It had been three years this fall. Three years since Mama and Muriel were taken from her. There had been no companionship with Aunt Odessa. Faithful Jewel had been kept busy caring for the crotchety old woman's demands, unable to offer Arilee more than a passing word of encouragement or helping hand with the never-ending work; rarely had they had the opportunity to work *together*.

Arilee and Mrs. Harrison set up the food and plates on the dining room table, which had been moved into the hallway. When the workmen came in, they offered sincere gratitude for the food and the break. Mr. Harrison said a blessing over the meal, and talking and laughter filled the hallway and the parlor. Macy hung back, clinging to Arilee, till Adam walked over. Then she ran to him, and he picked the child up without a thought as he leaned forward to greet his mother and kiss her cheek.

"Have you got Arilee all straightened out yet?" he teased.

"We're hoping she can get you all straightened out, rather," his mother replied with an arch smile.

"Wouldn't count on it," he replied around a mouthful of sandwich. He swung Macy onto his back and took her running up and down the stairs on a "wild horsey ride" while she screeched with joy.

"It relieves me to see him like this," Mrs. Harrison said to Arilee as the two of them went back to the basement for a pitcher of sweet iced tea and more cans of peaches. "When he returned from the war, he was solemn all the time, distant. Not in a cruel way, but it broke my heart for him. He threw himself into his studies, determined to make up for the lost time and work as hard and fast as possible. I thought college life would bring back something of the boy I remembered, but he didn't seem able to make deep friendships with the other fellows who hadn't been over there. Don't get me wrong, I'm glad he's matured, but . . ."

Arilee nodded as the woman's voice trailed off. "My brother Davis has never spoken a word to me about the war. Not even about our younger brother dying there. I've given up on him ever opening up about it."

She had missed this also. Talking with other women about their complicated menfolk. It soothed something deep in her soul, even as it made her physically ache for her mother.

After lunch, Arilee tried to coax Nathaniel to go play quietly in the library. Mr. Harrison, seeing the boy's crestfallen face, said, "If you don't mind, I'll be responsible for him. He just wants to see what's going on, same as me."

Arilee smiled. "If he won't be a bother to you?"

"Course not," Mr. Harrison said. "He's going to be my helper."

The man had the easy grin of his sons, though his quiet demeanor reminded her more of Joshua than Adam. "Sounds good," she said. "Thank you."

"Arilee." Adam came running up to her a few moments later.

"Please, not another decision."

"No, well, sort of, yes. Did you ever decide about the stuff in the attic? They'll be up there running wiring and some of it's in the way."

"Oh, I forgot."

"You got a minute now?"

"Your dad has Nathaniel and your mother has Macy. If you think they don't mind?"

"My parents are probably thrilled. They always wanted more kids, but I guess I wore them out."

"That I can believe."

Adam grabbed a flashlight, and they walked up to the attic. The lingering odors of sulphur and bleach nearly made Arilee gag.

"You want me to bring the stuff downstairs instead?" Adam offered.

"I don't know. It's at least not as much as I feared. And the attic is bigger than I imagined."

"Yeah, this is a great space up here. You could turn this into a few extra bedrooms or a playroom for the kids or whatever."

She nodded. Perhaps if the windows let in a cross breeze, it would be bearable. Currently, her brow was beading with sweat, and her drawers were sticking to her legs.

"I don't think I'll be needing a broken hoop skirt to attend any balls," she said, pushing it out of the way. "And I don't fancy that mirror."

"I'll start carrying down what you don't want and adding it to the trash pile."

Arilee settled the flashlight on a small side table she thought she might commandeer for her bedroom and knelt before an old leather and wood trunk. Turning the key already in the lock, she opened it and gasped. Two Confederate cavalry uniforms were there, along with military horse tack and some old tintypes and letters. As Adam returned up the steps, she handed him a perfect officer's sword.

He whistled low and pulled it out of its sheath. "Show this to a marine," he exclaimed. "You ought to hang this beauty over your fireplace or something."

"Yes, good idea. Way out of Nathaniel's reach. I imagine it belonged to my grandfather, Colonel Rutledge, although he had two sons who died in the war; it could be one of theirs."

"Are the letters from them?"

She nodded, putting the letters and tintypes aside. "I will look at those later. The rest can stay in the trunk for now, till I figure out what to do with it." She closed the lid and locked it, pocketing the key to keep in her own dresser.

Another trunk was full of antebellum-era gowns: silk ballgowns, cotton day dresses, woolen capes, and linen church dresses. What exactly she would do with them, she had no idea. "These belonged to Aunt Odessa, or maybe her older sister Celeste. Or maybe my Grandma Luella, or all three of them," she mused, more to herself than to him. "There's no letters or anything here to give any clues."

The remaining items in the attic were old furniture. Some pieces Arilee thought she could reuse elsewhere in the house, and a few were too broken to be much good. As Adam scooted an elegant dressing table missing its mirror across the wooden floor of the attic, Arilee spied a large open hatbox that had been partially obscured underneath. It was stuffed with letters and seemed to have been rifled through, perhaps by someone looking for something. Or perhaps by bats. Guano appeared sprinkled throughout the box like three-syllable words on a page of Shakespeare.

"Ugh!" She drew back her hand.

"Disgusting. You want me to throw it out?"

"No, not yet. Some of these letters look like they are from the War Between the States. Might be some kind of important family history there or a clue about the treasure, so I'll have to actually go through all of this."

"That would give me the heebie-jeebies."

"'The web of our life is of a mingled yarn, good and ill together.'"

"Is there any event you don't have a Shakespeare quote for?"

"Is there any event for which you don't have a crazy slang expression?" She raised her eyebrows at him, then set the hatbox over on an old credenza she hoped to refinish for the front hall. She'd deal with both later.

"OK." Adam wiped his hands on his shirt front. "I think I've moved everything out you don't want and everything out of the way that you do."

Arilee nodded. "I think I've breathed in enough stench for one day."

"Yeah, let's dust out."

She grabbed the letters and tintypes from the first trunk, and he grabbed the flashlight and lit the staircase for her. She set the letters on her own dresser, promising herself she'd look over them later. When Wisteria House wasn't torn to pieces.

Adam hadn't expected supper to be so much fun. Arilee and Mother had made a chicken pie, and they all ate at an old worktable in the basement kitchen—him and his parents, Arilee and the kids. Normally this mostly underground space, with its brick floor and walls, reminded him of a dungeon. Tonight, he welcomed its coolness after the heat of the day and the coziness of all of them gathered around the table, illuminated with the flickering flame of a kerosene lamp.

They finished off the meal with strawberries and whipped cream and sat talking while the kids drew with chalk on the brick floor. Of course, Mother and Dad put everyone at ease, but watching them work their spell on Arilee made him appreciate their unfailing graciousness more than ever.

Arilee smiled and even laughed a few times. Her posture grew less stiff. He considered how much stress she lived under on a daily basis, even aside from remodeling the whole house.

She still filled his thoughts when he and his parents walked back over to the carriage house later. "Mother," he asked when they were inside the small but comfortable space. "What was it Arilee's father did? I think she thinks I know, but I don't. Whatever it is, it's made her not want to go to church. She only recently has visited a few times at Grace Baptist, and it seems to scare her to death."

"You know how I feel about talebearing," his mother said slowly. "But given the circumstances, and the fact that it's commonly known, I think it best to tell you.

"Her father, Thomas Rutledge, was a well-established pastor in the Union Hill area for decades. I think they had two or three hundred members in their church. He was the charismatic sort who could build and hold a loyal following. In the summer of '17, it came out that he'd been having an affair with the pianist for several years. The woman was much younger than him, but married too, with a school-age son."

"Di mi!" Adam rose and leaned against the windowsill. He looked at his parents. Their love for each other and for him and Joshua was the foundation of his life. He couldn't even imagine the devastation of finding out his good, honorable father had been living a lie for years.

"Right before the congregation discovered the truth," Mother continued, "Rev. Rutledge and this woman stole all the church's money and ran off together, never to be heard from again."

"What a sharper."

"Mrs. Rutledge had to leave the parsonage, destitute and homeless. The church blamed her and the children, insisted they'd known about or even participated in the deception. Arilee and her mother moved here to the city, and Arilee taught school again. That's the last I heard."

"The younger son, Brax, ran away and became a pilot in the war," Adam filled in, "and then the older son, Davis, joined too." He explained about Davis, Muriel, and the kids. "Brax was killed, though," he added, "and Arilee's mama died right after. Muriel couldn't handle it all and was sent to the state hospital, and the children and everything fell on Arilee."

"She wrote to me when Joshua died," his mother said. "She sent me the kindest letter of condolence of any I received."

"She sent one to me too," Adam answered, lost in thought.

"You care for her, don't you, son?"

"Mother, honestly. She's four years older than me."

"The fact you know that is enough of an answer right there. I've got eyes in my head, Adam James. I see how you're always looking at her."

"Well, she ain't looking at me. I'm just 'her brother's hired man.' That's what she called me."

Dad, who'd been listening silently from behind his book, gave a short laugh. "Keep moping over it, and I can guarantee that's all she'll ever see."

Adam scowled, and his mother stared him down till he wanted to squirm.

"She's been through a lot," Mother said quietly. "Enough sorrow for a lifetime. We lost Joshua, and it's the hardest, worst thing to ever happen to us. But she lost both her parents and her brother. And her church and her family's reputation. Don't you think maybe she just needs a friend right now?"

He nodded. "I *would* like it to be more than friendship," he admitted in a mutter.

Mother clasped her hands over his. "Then start by being her friend. Be someone she can depend on and trust. Let things unfold slowly and naturally. Pray God will heal her hurts and bring her back into fellowship with His people."

Long after his parents had gone to sleep in the room's one bed, Adam shifted in the chair, tired, but unable to sleep as he pieced everything together in his mind. He could see Arilee's face, smell her lavender scent, hear her gentle laughter at supper tonight. All the betrayal and losses she had faced explained the differences between his idolized teacher and the haunted young lady whom he'd observed over the past two weeks, the one who kept on with a dogged determination for the ones she loved, even as her own heart was still broken to pieces.

Gradually his impressions grew to a conviction.

Some things a man *knew* in his soul.

He might be merely her brother's hired man, but *she* was the woman for him.

CHAPTER 7

Saturday, July 2, to Sunday, July 3, 1921

Saturday night, after that long week, Arilee held herself back from bouncing.

"All right," announced Adam. "It's the moment of truth."

She and Adam, his parents, Davis, and the kids were all assembled in the front hall. For all that remained to be done, Arilee was pleased with the progress the men had made in one week.

The new kitchen had begun to take shape. A wall had been erected in the dining room, and the outside wall had been opened into a large archway that connected the room with the former storage closet on the back porch. The newly created kitchen had pipes and wiring, a large gas stove, a refrigerator, and some shelving and cabinetry.

Upstairs, part of the nursery had been taken to make the new bathroom, which also had pipes and wiring, a toilet, and a huge white clawfoot tub. The sink would be next.

A boiler had been installed in the basement to provide hot water to both new rooms and eventually steam heat to the entire house. For now, radiators had been placed in the kitchen and bathroom. The surrounding rooms—the nursery and upstairs hall, the dining room and downstairs hall —also had piping for future radiators.

Adam and Mr. Harrison had extended the kitchen wiring into the dining room and front hall while everything was torn up. Mr. Harrison had taken down and wired the ancient candelabra chandelier in the front hall, and he and Adam had rehung it this evening.

Georgia Power had installed a meter, and each of the wired rooms had outlets and a light fixture or lamps. Slowly, the whole house would be electrified, and there would be no more incessant worry over knocked-over candles sending the whole house up in smoke. No more endless cleaning of lamp chimneys and filling of lamp bases. Adam had put *four* outlets in the new kitchen; even with the refrigerator taking one, she'd always have plenty available for the small appliances she planned to acquire: a toaster, an electric iron, and maybe even a mixer.

Adam scooped up Macy and told her to press the button by the front door. She poked out her little finger, Adam helped her give it some strength, and light flooded the front hall. A cheer rose from the group.

"Sockdolager!" Nathaniel said it with Adam's exact inflection. Arilee rolled her eyes at Adam, who grinned back without the least remorse. The kids ran around the house, shouting, Nathaniel turning on every light and lamp available, and Macy clapping and cheering each time he did.

"This calls for a celebration," Arilee announced. She'd bought ice cream at Belmont Dairy that afternoon; with her new shiny, white refrigerator, they could have ice cream on hand whenever they wanted, not a few hours in the making. She began dishing up large bowls of vanilla, while Mrs. Harrison poured warm caramel sauce over each.

"I like living here," Adam teased. "We have ice cream a lot."

"You still have your hollow leg, I see," Mrs. Harrison returned playfully.

Arilee watched him with his parents, as he and his father discussed the next project, and his mother served them both ice cream. A familiar ache rose in her chest. Would it never ease? Would she ever feel peace over Mama's untimely death, ever stop hearing her tortured last words as she cried deliriously for Daddy and Brax? Would she ever stop looking for Daddy in every crowd, ever cease hoping that every car turning into the driveway might be him coming to make things right?

Arilee slipped back down to the basement to get some napkins; Mrs. Harrison followed her.

"We'd like to join you for church tomorrow if you don't mind," the older woman said. "We are planning to stay for the festivities on the Fourth and then head back home."

"I have loved having you here. It has been a while since I worked alongside another woman. I didn't know how much I missed it."

"I have prayed often for you, Arilee, over the past few years. I know it must be difficult to attend church and allow yourself to open up to another group of believers, but I have met many of the folks at Grace Baptist, and they are kind, gracious people. The ladies there would gladly befriend you."

Arilee busied herself stacking up more pots and pans to be transported from the old kitchen to the new. At last, she blurted out, "I don't really have friends anymore. Ever since what happened with Daddy . . . and losing Mama . . . I guess I needed friends more than ever, but I felt I had nothing to give to a friendship. I was trying to survive. I didn't know how to host someone coming here with the house falling down around us and Aunt Odessa controlling my every move. I didn't know how to go out with the children or how to explain to all my college friends with their husbands and babies why I was single and raising my niece and nephew. You're right, I *ought* to have been at church, but even now it still scares me to death."

To her surprise, Mrs. Harrison hugged and held her, tears in the older woman's hazel eyes. "God has a plan for *you*, Arilee. He's been there all along, and He's not forgotten you."

She said it with such conviction that Arilee discovered a frightful inability to speak around the burning lump in her throat.

"I guess we'd better get Adam some more ice cream," she said at last. "He's earned it."

Davis stepped off the passenger car at the small Milledgeville asylum depot, as he did every Sunday afternoon following his morning trip from Atlanta. Today, he glanced once behind him, to see the young man he'd observed on the journey. Still in his teens, the boy was led by the arms between two sturdy officers. His eyes were downcast, his countenance withdrawn, yet he trembled hard in his final moments before being committed to the Georgia State Sanitarium. Wildly, he looked up and around, taking in the cloudless blue sky. A sob escaped him.

In all likelihood, the boy would never leave this place. Not many did anymore. For the past few decades, rather than a hospital to restore broken souls, it had become a prison to hide the unwanted. Thousands and thousands of them. With the war, several doctors and numerous staff had left, the nurses deciding even the battlefront offered greater reward than endless shifts from 5 a.m. to 9 p.m. working a thankless, futureless job where they had to be locked in their own rooms at night to protect them from their patients housed a floor below.

The Powell Building, one of several overcrowded wards for women on this enormous campus, stood with majestic exterior, featuring Ionic columns and a dome like a statehouse. Inside, the cramped spaces, worn-out furniture, and listless fatigue of the place made Davis feel *he* was going out of his mind.

Each week he brought Muriel something to eat and something pretty to look at. Flowers. A photograph of the children. A magazine with colorful pictures and interesting stories. Today, he had a paper bag of oranges and a picture Nathaniel had drawn of Wisteria House and "my family"—in his mind, Davis, Nat, Macy, and Arilee. But Davis would let Muriel think her boy had drawn *her*.

"Hello, Mrs. Barker." He nodded at one of the senior nurses as he stepped into the Powell Building. He tried not to wrinkle his nose at the familiar but nauseating mixture of odors: Lysol, water closets that could never be kept clean enough, and the black-eyed peas served for lunch. Removing his straw hat, he used it to fan his damp forehead, then handed the kind matron one of the large, fragrant oranges.

"Thank you, Mr. Rutledge. It's good to see you. Your wife brushed her hair earlier and put on a clean dress. I hope she's in good spirits today. Why don't you get a shady spot in the garden, and I'll have one of the nurses bring her out for your visit?"

"Thank you, ma'am." A sudden shriek from down the hall reminded him of why he'd always choose outdoors, even when the temperature made him sweat after the short walk from the depot to the Powell Building. Outside, a breeze might relieve the sticky heat, and birdsong might cover the screams of inmates.

The nurse smiled at him. "Mrs. Rutledge is quite blessed to have such frequent visits by such a devoted husband."

He nodded and looked down, shifting his weight from one foot to another, twisting the top of the paper bag. He hated the stares and the whisperings from the staff here. Many folks were enthralled with the "romance" of flight, and his occupation as a pilot was well known. Everyone also knew he came weekly to visit his wife, while some families came but once a year or less. If only Muriel still looked at him with a fraction of the admiration with which these nurses did.

He selected a bench in the shade of a pecan tree. Last week had been one of the best in months. She'd been happy to see him, clinging to his arm, chattering away, promising him soon she'd be well and could come home. If they could manage two good weeks in a row . . .

In a few minutes, Muriel joined him outside, and the nurse left her to his care for the visit. Though they were surrounded by ten-foot-high brick walls, he tried to pretend they were like any other young couple on a Sunday date in the park.

"You look lovely," he said, rising from the bench and kissing Muriel's cheek. The nearly three years at the asylum had aged her noticeably, but she remained pretty, with the blonde hair and blue eyes Macy had inherited. "I brought you some oranges."

"If I don't eat them here, the others will get them, or the staff will take them away," she sighed.

"Eat them here, then," he said and nodded at the bench. Stiffly, she sat down, and he settled beside her.

How he dreaded initiating the conversation. When they'd courted, in what now seemed another lifetime, it had always been Muriel who filled the silences, and he'd been able to get away with occasional remarks, certainly never needing to discuss anything difficult or deep.

"Are you well?" he asked her.

She shrugged and began peeling an orange. "How do you think I can ever be well here?"

He didn't know what bothered him more, this cold distance or her frantic tears. He was well-versed in both and thought either preferable to her fury.

"I'm doing all I can to get you a hearing with the judge."

"They'll never let me out of here."

"Is anyone harming you, Muriel?"

She stared ahead in stony silence.

"Please, I need to know."

"They don't hurt me if I do what they want."

"What do you mean, 'do what they want'? What is it they want you to do? Who are 'they'?"

Another long silence, while his mind raced ahead with possibilities; he'd experienced this when flying through a storm, wondering if there would be a place for an emergency landing, or if he would have to try to make it through, battered and banged-up.

"What do you care, Davis? You left me for your airplanes and your brother. If you had stayed home where you belonged, I would still be home too."

They were back here again. Like a stuck phonograph record repeating the same phrase endlessly.

"I think, Muriel," he said slowly, "You would be happier if you didn't allow all this bitterness to consume you. I've asked your forgiveness for joining the army. I made what I thought was the right decision at the time, and it has had both good and bad consequences. But it can't be undone. No matter how much I regret it, or how much you resent me for it, we can't go back in time."

He picked up her hand, slightly sticky from the orange, and held it. "Is anyone here hurting you, Muriel?"

She shook her head and refused to meet his eyes. Something closed in her countenance, a subtle change, like window shades being drawn on a house. After two years of these visits, he knew to expect nothing else from her today.

So, he told her about Wisteria House getting electricity and Nathaniel making a friend at Sunday School. When he pulled Nathaniel's picture out of his coat jacket and showed it to her, she crumpled it.

"You keep him from me. You took my boy away and gave him to your sister. You won't even let him come see me."

"Think now, would you want him to see you here? It would frighten him if you had an outburst and upset him if he had to see you restrained."

"I want my son."

She never wanted Macy. Never spoke of Macy. Never acknowledged Macy when he spoke of her.

"I want you to try to be very calm every day. If Superintendent Jones could see that you are restored, we could get you released with the new governor's permission. Please, Muriel. I am doing all I can, but you have to do your part too. Be composed and cheerful, even if you don't feel like it.

Please."

He felt the weight of his own hypocrisy. *He* wouldn't be composed or cheerful if he were here, locked away from his family and his career. But he still believed she could be well again if they could somehow get her home. He had to believe it, or he would crash with the utter hopelessness of the situation.

"What have you done this week?" he asked, reaching again for her hand, desperate for some connection with her.

Patients who were quiet and behaved were given meaningful work at the asylum and allowed to participate in the dwindling diversions the institution still offered, such as a dance or movie. Sometimes she took interest in these activities.

She pulled her hand away. They took a silent stroll around the grounds. She refused to look at him as they walked back toward the Powell Building at the end of the two hours allowed for visiting. Other patients were gathering for the weekly chapel service; he urged her to go, but she shook her head.

As they stepped inside, she clung to him, screaming. "Take me out of here. If you really loved me, you would get me out of here. I hate you, Davis Rutledge; I hate you for this!"

Two nurses came and peeled her off him and forced her back toward the wards even as she fought against them, turning her head to shriek and spit at him. One nurse spoke soothingly, the way he'd seen Arilee respond to Macy having a tantrum. The other snapped, "Settle down or it'll be the restraining chair or the cold pack for you."

Oh, God, how will I ever fly through this storm? But where's the landing? He pulled out his handkerchief and wiped her spit off his face as they led her away. Maybe they'd just give her Luminal; he didn't like them using the sedative on her, but Muriel had told him about being wrapped in steamy or ice-cold sheets, and the terror that being physically restrained brought to her.

"Please—" he called after the nurses.

What could he say?

Please, it's my fault. Then they'd tell him to stop visiting so much.

Please, she can't help it. Yeah, that was the point. The reason she was here.

Please, I love her.

They would pity him, but they couldn't help him. No one could.

Yet if he did manage to get her released and she hurt one of the children or Arilee, how could he ever forgive himself for that?

How many regrets could a man carry?

CHAPTER 8

Thursday, July 21, 1921

After another few weeks, Arilee's kitchen had a navy and white checkerboard floor, an enormous Hoosier cabinet, and a walk-in pantry lined with shelves. A smaller broom closet held the cleaning supplies, the ironing board, and her new electric iron. Adam was almost done building the "banquette" seating in the former storage room area. He'd painted the whole kitchen the cheery lemon color she had chosen.

On this evening, Arilee stood pressing the azure curtains she'd sewn for the window over her new white porcelain sink. She'd chosen blue as an accent color with the yellow, and Adam kept the cobalt blue vase on the counter filled with roses cut from the yard.

Macy played with her baby doll nearby. Like Arilee, she seemed unable to get enough of this bright, clean new room. That this dreary old house could have a spot of such color and comfort seemed nothing short of miraculous.

Nathaniel had wandered outside to watch Adam work. Arilee planned to speak to Davis about giving Adam a raise. He'd not worked less than a twelve-hour day in the month he'd been here. And while the scope of the work needed meant there remained much still to do, everywhere she looked she saw how much he had done. For the first time, she started to believe Wisteria House might be *her home.*

Her reverie was broken by Nathaniel racing inside, yelling. "Aunt Ari, Aunt Ari, come quick. Mr. Adam has bees stinging him all over!"

Arilee unplugged the iron quickly and moved it out of Macy's reach. She met Adam as he burst in the back door, out of breath, face flushed.

"Bees?"

"Yellow jackets," he panted. "Cursed little sons of—"

"Watch your tongue, Adam Harrison," she interrupted, nodding toward the children, who were watching wide-eyed. "Come in the kitchen, and let's get some ice and have a look."

"I was going to say, 'of the devil,'" he protested, following her.

"Where'd they get you?"

"Arms, chest, back. Hands. They have a nest under the porch, and the little huns came out and flew down my shirt."

"Sit down on the stool and take it off then."

He hesitated. "It's so hot out that I don't have on an undershirt."

"I have two brothers, a father, and a nephew. I've seen a male chest before. We need to put cold compresses on those stings, and then I'll mix up a paste of baking soda and aspirin."

He nodded and shrugged out of his suspenders, then began to unbutton his loose cotton work shirt—stiffly, as there were at least two stings on his right hand. The kids stood gaping, entertained by the drama.

"Back up." Arilee bumped them out of the way. "Good heavens, Adam, you're covered. Did you jump in their hole for a glass of lemonade?"

"You would think," he muttered, looking pale. Quickly, she went to the refrigerator and pulled out a Coca-Cola.

"Drink this," she instructed. "And press the cold bottle on some of your stings."

She filled a bowl with ice water and grabbed a clean but old cotton dish towel. She cut this into strips, then dipped each in the water. She wrapped the strips around his swelling hand, then began placing them as compresses on his right side. The muscles of his arms and chest were *more* than she had expected.

Under his right arm she noticed a large patch of discolored skin, like a burn scar. She stood pondering it for a moment.

"That's from mustard gas," he explained. "You don't have to touch it if it disgusts you."

"No, but I don't want to hurt you."

"It doesn't hurt anymore. Except where I got stung right there." He pointed to a rapidly swelling spot. She pressed a cold compress to it, then moved to the stings on his back. She told herself she had to do this; he couldn't reach these himself and they needed attention. All of that was true. But why must she be so acutely *aware* of him?

When she moved around to his left side, she gasped slightly. "You have a tattoo!"

"It didn't just happen," he said through gritted teeth.

A circle, filled in with blue ink except for the thin, flesh-colored lines of two A's, marked his left upper arm. Studying it a moment, she recognized it as the 82nd's emblem, the double A's standing for "All American." Under the symbol was the name *Joshua*.

"How'd you make that there?" asked Nathaniel incredulously. "Did you draw it?"

"That's a 'A'," announced Macy, proud of knowing her letters.

"No questions now, Nat," Arilee said. "You take your sister outside, and I'll bring you some ice cream."

"Stay away from the front porch," Adam called after them. "Those yellow jackets are still mad."

"The front porch? You came in the back door."

"I ran around the house trying to shake them off before I came in."

Arilee began mixing up baking soda, crushed aspirin, and cool water into a paste to put on the stings.

"Keep drinking," she urged.

"I gotta get back out there and pour gasoline down their hole."

"Not tonight. You're done for tonight."

She worked in silence for a few minutes, laying cool compresses over each sting. After a bit, he muttered, "Sorry about the tattoo."

"You don't have to apologize to me for it."

"I meant the kids seeing and having to explain it to them. I was rip-roaring drunk the night I got it."

"Hmm. I'm glad they didn't see *that*. I didn't know you drank."

"I don't. Now. After Joshua, I didn't handle it as well as you did losing your brother."

"What makes you think I handled it well?"

"Do you have a tattoo?"

She burst out laughing, and he joined her, albeit with a bit of groaning.

"No," she finally answered. "I don't have any tattoos, and I haven't ever tried alcohol. But maybe it would have been better for me to do those things than what I did do, which was to hide from God and everyone else. Here, take some aspirin for the pain."

She handed him a few of the white pills, and he swallowed them with the rest of the Coca-Cola.

Then she got out the ice cream and spooned out a bowl for him. She dished out a bowl for each of the kids, which she took to the backyard. Nathaniel stood on the board swing Adam had somehow taken time to put up for the kids last week. Unaccountably, Macy sat against the tree holding the cat who would not allow anyone else to even pet him. His deep rumbling purr suggested he was not merely humoring the girl.

"Is Mr. Adam gonna be OK?" asked Nat.

"He is, but he got stung up pretty bad. Stay away from the front porch till he can get rid of the rest of the yellow jackets."

"It was my fault." Nathaniel's voice wavered. "He told me to stay away from there, but I started throwing rocks at those nasty 'jackets, and they came out, and he pushed me outta the way and said to come get you."

"Nathaniel. You aren't going to be allowed to watch Mr. Adam if you can't obey."

The boy hung his head. "I'm sorry, Aunt Ari."

"Maybe you ought to tell Mr. Adam you're sorry," she scolded and went back inside to coat Adam in the medicinal paste she'd created. He sat on the kitchen stool, trying to eat his ice cream with his left hand while his right remained wrapped in a cold compress.

"Nat confessed. You're a good man, Adam Harrison, even if you pretend not to be."

He shrugged. "It was the kind of stupid thing I woulda done myself as a kid."

She began removing the cool cloths and coating his stings in the paste. Desperate to relieve the awkwardness of the moment, she pretended she was Florence Nightingale on the battlefield. She pondered an apropos Shakespearean quote. When neither helped, she started chattering.

"I appreciate you letting him shadow you, Adam. It's been so good for him. Davis is a kind father, but he's gone all the time. Nat worships the ground he walks on, but Davis doesn't always see it; he's worried he's going to mess up. Of course, he's never told me any such thing, but I can read him."

"He doesn't say much, for sure." Adam shifted, a grimace on his face as he pressed the cold Coca-Cola bottle to a large swollen place on his neck.

"Right. I've learned to pay attention to his actions. The Chattahoochee would freeze before Davis would ever say he loves or appreciates me or tell me something in his heart. But when it came time to plan the kitchen, he insisted I pick out whatever I wanted, regardless of price."

"You did a good job planning it."

"You did a good job executing the plan. It's better than I even imagined. I want to stay in this room all day long."

"We'll get the rest of the house just as nice for you."

"You and Davis are spoiling me."

"I'm trying." He winked at her and flashed that signature smile.

Completely undone, she began babbling again. "I feel guilty Davis and I are spending so much money on all this luxury. It's the life insurance money from Brax's death, you know. He left it to Mama, and Davis and I thought fixing up the house was the best use for it. But the house isn't really ours. It's our father's. Billy Sweet told us if we pay the taxes and do the updates, it will make the case stronger for us to claim ownership in the future, but if Daddy comes back, it would probably come down to a judge's decision, if we couldn't work it out among ourselves."

Why couldn't she talk about normal things? Or shut up? He didn't need or want to know all about their family mess. He was doing a job to earn money for medical school. Count on her to make an awkward situation more awkward.

She finished coating the twenty-third and final yellow jacket sting in her baking soda paste.

"Are you OK? You aren't going to stop breathing, are you?"

"Never have before. Josh and I both used to get a few stings every summer. This is a new record for me, though."

"Bats, rats, roaches, yellow jackets. These weren't exactly the treasures I hoped we'd find."

He gave a short laugh and rose stiffly. "Going to put away the tools outside," he said, his shirt draped over his arm. She looked at him and flushed, then quickly busied herself with washing up the dishes.

God help her, she might have seen her brothers with their shirts off a hundred times and thought nothing about it, but an encyclopedia's worth of thoughts was stacked in her head right now, and not a one of them was motherly or sisterly or teacherly.

CHAPTER 9

Tuesday, August 16, 1921

A rilee had her hair back in a kerchief as she stood on the step stool, arranging painted baskets on the higher shelves of her kitchen. Adam had helped her bring the last of the kitchen supplies up from the basement last week, and everything finally had a place. She'd framed and hung favorite recipes handwritten by her mother and Grandma Luella, as well as by herself and Muriel. Seeing her neatly scripted "Lemon Cream Pie" recipe on the wall had led to daily teasing from Adam as to when she was going to make it and how much work did a fellow have to do to get a pie anyway?

He'd been up laying tile in the bathroom this evening, but after she'd put the kids to bed, he had disappeared down to the basement to see to something with the pipes. Presently, she heard pounding up the steps, and he appeared, out of breath and so pale she thought he might faint.

"Adam, what's wrong? You look as if you'd seen a ghost."

He nodded. "I—sort of—yes—come."

She set down a cobalt blue bottle, wiped her hands on her apron, and stepped down.

"What is it?"

"Another case of the heebie-jeebies."

"I certainly hope you haven't found any more creatures or pests."

"Uh . . ."

She followed Adam down the basement steps, descending into the cool but dank dungeon that she had gladly abandoned for her cheerful new kitchen. As much time as she'd spent down here, parts of it still gave her the creeps. Adam had run the BX cable across the ceiling and down one wall, allowing single bulbs to be hung in a few select spots and making one outlet into which he had plugged her new Maytag washing machine and wringer.

"See that wall," he pointed, standing away from it as if a monster might appear from the other side. "The one with the bricks removed? I couldn't figure out why it was there. It wasn't supporting anything, and it's not the outside wall. So, I knocked out a few of the looser bricks."

On the underside of the stairs there was a space about two feet wide, between the edge of the wooden staircase wall and the outside wall. The space had been bricked in.

"Why did you start breaking down a wall for no reason?" She crossed her arms.

"Because I couldn't see any reason for it to be there. If I'd found the treasure in there, I don't guess you would've minded my curiosity."

"But you didn't find the treasure, did you?"

He nodded toward the space and handed her a flashlight from his toolbox. She switched it on, then went over and peeked through the hole he had made in the brick wall, shining the light in.

A scream escaped before she clamped her hand over her mouth, dropping the flashlight. A skeleton lay stretched out in the spot. She picked up the flashlight and studied the remains. A bit of short hair clung to the skull. A row of metal buttons between the ribs and spine, as well as disintegrating blue fabric and a brass US belt buckle, suggested an identity. Adam came up next to her, and for a long moment they both stood silently staring.

"Do you think it's been there since—?"

"No doubt." Adam rubbed his hands on his trousers.

"Maybe Jewel would know. If we could get her to tell. And if we knew where she was. What do you think we should do about it?"

He shrugged. "I guess we have to finish tearing down the wall enough to get in there and see if he has any identification. Maybe he still has kids or grandkids who never knew what happened to him."

"Maybe we should call the police," Arilee suggested.

"And say what? 'We found the skeleton of a Union soldier in our basement and were wondering if y'all wanted to figure out who put him there fifty-odd years ago in the middle of a war?'"

"Well, maybe not the police. The army?"

"Maybe. He should be given a proper burial. I'll have to take the bricks out one at a time. I accidentally dropped one in already, and I think it cracked his skull."

"Might change his view of Southern hospitality," she replied drily.

Adam laughed, and they exchanged smiles. Then he began chiseling away at the bricks, while Arilee held the flashlight. "'Blest be the man that spares these stones, And curst be he that moves my bones,'" she murmured, taking a brick Adam handed her.

"It's Billy Yank in there, not William Shakespeare."

"I know. I wish we could put the bricks back and pretend we didn't see this. But you're right. He could have family who never knew what happened to him. I wonder all the time about Daddy."

He paused in his brick removal to rest his hand on her shoulder and look at her compassionately. "That's really hard. I'm praying you get answers someday."

"Thank you," she murmured. She held the light, and Adam removed bricks for the next several minutes. She missed a pleasant evening together, each with a book and a cup of tea, yet often finding themselves in conversation instead.

"I think I can get in now," Adam said, and nimbly for his height, he scaled the remaining half wall and went feet first through the opening, then dropped down to the other side.

"Do you think we'll get in trouble for examining him?" Arilee held the flashlight shining down into the opening.

"I think this fellow croaked too long ago for anyone to figure out what killed him. There's no sign of a bullet. It obviously happened during the war. So, it's not really like disturbing a crime scene."

The uniform crumbled at Adam's touch. "They called that fabric 'shoddy,'" Arilee recalled from something she'd read or heard. "It didn't last the war, let alone the half-century since, and now the word means anything cheap and inferior."

"Yeah. If we assume our friend here came through in 1864 with the Battle of Atlanta, that would mean he's been here roughly 57 years." Adam looked over the remains but found no papers or personal effects of any kind. "Bone structure confirms a man," he noted. Looking at the bottom of the

71

boots, he added, "Here's some initials. VT."

"Do you think those stand for his name or mean he was from Vermont?"

"Could go either way." He looked at the skeleton again. "What's your name? Victor Townsend? Vincent Thomas?"

"Valentine Thurgood," Arilee suggested.

"Vance Trueblood."

"Virgil Thompson"

"Vernon Taylor."

"I like that one." Arilee stood on tiptoe, staring at the body. "Wonder what his rank was."

Adam studied the decaying uniform. "Can't tell. He had lots of buttons. Maybe an officer? I don't want him to outrank me, so we'll make him a corporal."

"I didn't know you made sergeant. That's commendable, Adam. As for you, Corporal Vernon Taylor, we sure wish you could tell us how you came to be buried in our basement."

"You might rather not know." Adam stood up, wiping his hands on his trousers again. "He's in a private house, not a battlefield. He maybe wasn't an honorable man . . ."

"True. How do we notify the army about it?"

"I know a fellow at Fort McPherson. I can make a call."

"I would appreciate that."

She shone the flashlight to the brick wall behind Adam, the actual outer wall of the basement. And then she noticed—

"Adam." Her voice lowered to a whisper. "Look."

He turned to see where her light had landed on a wooden board, a little over two feet square, at the bottom of the wall.

"Hand me the hammer."

She did so, and he used the claw end to remove the board easily. A scent of musty earth followed.

"Flashlight." He held out his hand, and reluctantly she gave him the light. She still had the dim glow of one bulb behind her, but between the skeleton before her and the banging of the pipes beyond, she longed to get back up to her cheerful kitchen.

He shone the light into the space that had been boarded up.

"Well, sockdolager. It looks like some kind of tunnel."

"I wonder if it's the Underground Railroad tunnel?"

"What?"

"There's an old family story. Daddy said there was a tunnel under the house to help slaves escape. See, my grandfather, the Colonel, had slaves. After his first wife died in childbirth, he—found comfort—with the woman who cared for Baby Odessa. They had a child together. Jewel, whom you've heard me refer to. Jewel's mother died of a fever, and her dying request was for the Colonel to treat their daughter the same as his other children. That was his intention, and he married again. My Grandma Luella, who was quite young and an abolitionist. She started helping the Colonel's slaves and then others also to go north. He knew about it and just looked the other way."

Now that she said it all, she could only imagine what he must think of another sensational story from her family tree.

"Do you think the rumored treasure could be in the tunnel?" he asked.

"Possibly. But I don't want to crawl in there. You?"

"Not for love or money."

"Then why don't you put the board back and we go upstairs and have tea and gingersnaps and play a few rounds of *Rook*?"

"Add washing my hands, and I'd say that's a swell plan," he answered with a wink.

She handed him his hammer and fresh nails for the preexisting holes. He boarded up the tunnel entrance for the time being, then vaulted himself up onto the ledge of the partial brick wall and over, landing back down beside her, a little closer than they would normally stand.

She didn't back up. She looked up and met his eyes. "I'm really not sure whether to laugh or cry at this new discovery."

"Will I be forgiven for tearing down the wall?"

"Not on your life. But if I ever want to go grave-digging or mystery-solving, I'm definitely taking you along."

That Saturday, Davis removed the board, widened the entry a bit, and squeezed through it to investigate the tunnel. Adam waited outside the broken brick wall and peered at "Vernon Taylor" (as he and Arilee continued to call the skeleton). Arilee had the kids upstairs, as she wisely did not want Nathaniel, in particular, to know about the body or the tunnel.

"It's caved in a few yards out from the house, though not impassable," Davis announced, crawling back out and brushing dirt off himself. "It appears well supported up to that point, but I would be curious to get your opinion, Harrison, as to whether or not we need to fill it in for safety's sake."

"OK." Adam did not wish to tell Davis *no*, but the thought of going in there made his chest start to compress. Davis hadn't served in the trenches. He didn't know.

"I called a fellow I know at McPherson." Adam deflected. "He said they'll send someone out when they can. Do you want me to show them the tunnel?"

Davis scowled. "Last thing I want is government people poking their noses around this house. There's no known connection between the body and the tunnel. Least you and Arilee say to those folks, the best."

"I take it you don't know anything about it?"

"No, and I don't want to. I don't know how much Arilee's told you, but most of our family stories aren't good."

"She's told me some," Adam said vaguely. "You want me to finish removing this wall?" he asked as Davis climbed out from behind it.

"When you get to it. I'm much more interested in you extending the electricity and steam heat to the rest of the house. You've done good work. Are you satisfied with your wages?"

"Yes." After the first month, Davis had raised his compensation to $150 a month.

"And you start school when?"

"A little over a month."

Davis screwed up his mouth in thought. "I don't like the idea of Sis being here alone all the time. Any chance you'd be willing to stay and board here for the school year?"

"I'd be glad to and would continue on with the remodeling and yard work in my free time around classes and studying."

"I'd like that, for Arilee. But there is a possibility I'll need the carriage house for my wife at some point. I would hate for you to have to move after you start school."

"Oh." It *would* be a problem trying to get a room in the dorm or find a room to rent partway through the year.

But it would be unthinkable to leave when his term at Emory began. Unbearable to know Arilee remained here with no one to help or protect her.

He wanted to see her every day.

For the rest of his life.

"If needed, I could always take the circuit rider's room." He spoke as casually as he could.

Davis studied him for such a long time that Adam almost squirmed. He had the feeling Davis could see right through his motives.

"OK. I'll talk to Sis and see if she wants you to stay on or if she's tired of you." A glint of amusement lit Davis's eyes. Adam did squirm then. "And if she's agreeable, we'll negotiate a salary for the school year beyond your room and board. You're a hard worker and a skilled one, and you've done wonders with this place in a short time."

$$\infty \infty \infty$$

Arilee was swirling the whipped cream on Adam's lemon cream pie when Davis came into the kitchen.

"Looks like you're making good use of your new stove." He leaned against the sink.

"It's marvelous. This whole room is. I'm thankful for it, Davis, to you and Adam both."

"Speaking of the devil, how would you feel about him staying on and boarding here after he starts back to school? I'm hoping to use the carriage house for Muriel, depending on if we get the hearing and how it goes. But Adam said he'd take the room on the porch if the carriage house isn't available later."

"The circuit rider's room? Davis, it isn't nice at all. I don't want him out there freezing to death all winter."

"All right, I'll tell him it won't work then." Davis ran a finger around the remains in the whipped cream bowl and popped it into his mouth.

"Wait a minute. I mean, if he *offered* to take it . . ."

"It was his idea. I just need to know if you want him around or not. He said he'll keep working on the house and yard as he can in exchange for his room and board. I'll give him a little salary too. So, do you?"

"Do I?"

"Want him around after this next month?"

Arilee rested her hand over her mouth and chin. The thought of being here alone with the kids day after day, week after week, sounded so dismal and depressing, especially after Adam's effervescent presence, she could feel the heaviness of it.

"Sure I do, but I can't imagine he'd want to give up dorm life and all the goings on at Emory to be here."

"He didn't seem to see it that way. Maybe he could study better here away from all the 'goings on.' Or maybe he finds the company here more to his liking."

"If you think he really doesn't mind, it would be wonderful."

"Adam strikes me as a man who knows what he wants in life and isn't likely to be coerced into anything he doesn't want to do." Davis arched his eyebrow. "Besides, you bake a man a pie, and there's no telling how long he'll stick around."

CHAPTER 10

Monday, August 29,1921

On the last Monday of August, a steady rain and a gray sky cooled the stifling heat and increased the unending humidity. Arilee sat at the kitchen table with needle and thread, preparing Nathaniel's clothes for his impending entrance into school. Hems on his short pants needed letting down, and buttons on his overalls should be reinforced. Macy sat beside her, stringing wooden beads on a shoelace and stirring her finger through the button basket with its decades of interesting notions.

Upstairs, Adam worked on adding a radiator to the hallway. She heard Nathaniel's little voice keeping up a steady stream of questions, and Adam's deep voice patiently answering. She appreciated his ability to not only work under the six-year-old's interrogation, but to give the boy small tasks so he would think he was helping.

The cozy afternoon filled Arilee's soul with peace, and from that, hope for the future, something she hadn't had much of in recent years. Unbidden, she thought of Pastor Andy's sermon yesterday. He had spoken of God as a "good Father." She had almost stopped listening until he said, "Some of you find this concept foreign or troubling. You hadn't a father growing up, or the man whom you called your father was unkind or neglectful. I urge you, if this is your case, to find an example on earth to redefine what a father is. Or, if you are a parent, become such an example. Start measuring the Father's love for you with the deep love you feel for your own children and know that it is exponentially greater."

She snipped the thread from where she'd sewed a button back on one of Nathaniel's good shirts. She loved these children and would do anything to protect and provide for them. She wanted to believe God loved her similarly, but she didn't understand how He could care yet allow Daddy to leave and Brax and Mama to die. God's love felt distant and His kindness cold. Doubtless the fault lay with her, but she didn't know how to make herself believe that God's *goodness* hedged all this heartache. Like the lost Confederate treasure, His goodness was real, but something she'd never find.

Another thing bothered her. Davis's proclamation about Adam: "Maybe he finds the company here more to his liking." Surely Davis didn't think—? It was too fantastical. Adam couldn't possibly have feelings for *her* beyond friendship, could he? And if he did, how could she discern and discourage such a thing? Surely a nice single girl, eighteen or nineteen, attended their church. Someone from a good family, with parents as loving and stable as Adam's own. Arilee would pay more attention. Look around at the women's Bible class. She could find someone for him and befriend the girl, then invite her over and gush about all of Adam's incredible work on the house. It would be easy enough for this imagined young woman to fall in love with him. Yeah, that part wouldn't be hard at all.

As she pondered these things, a buzzing sound came from the front of the house. Macy looked up. "What dat noise?" she asked.

"It's the doorbell Mr. Adam put in." Arilee hadn't heard it since the day he tested it. She took off her apron, smoothed the curling wisps of hair back from her face, and shook the wrinkles out of her blue skirt.

She opened the front door to two men in full dress uniform.

"Hello, ma'am." A tall, handsome officer doffed his hat. "I'm First Lieutenant Everett and this is Second Lieutenant Smith. We've come from Fort McPherson to collect the body of the soldier you found here."

"Oh, yes, come in." She held open the door. Lieutenant Everett shook the water off his umbrella and left it on the porch.

"I'm Miss Rutledge," she said. "It's, uh, the body is down in the basement. But my niece and nephew live here, and we don't really want them to know about, well, any of this. Could you give me a moment?"

"Certainly."

She picked up Macy, who'd followed her, and started up the stairs. Adam and Nathaniel were heading down, and they met halfway, out of sight of their guests. She looked her questions at him.

"Why don't I take these gentlemen downstairs?" Adam suggested. "You settle the kids in the library and close the doors, and then we can talk to the officers in the parlor."

Arilee nodded, grateful for his quick plan. Grateful *he* was here to help her navigate this strange situation that had broken up her cozy afternoon with reminders of the grim past. Grateful this whole odd discovery would soon be behind them.

∞ ∞ ∞

Adam started to tease Arilee that if she kept acting nervous, they'd think *she'd* put the body in the basement, but he rounded the curve in the staircase and took a good look at the two officers from McPherson. The first lieutenant, as tall as Adam himself, boasted an impossibly Herculean chest and the looks of Nils Ashter, the "Prettiest Actor in Hollywood." He even had the same stupid thin mustache as the actor.

"Aunt Ari, why are those soldiers here?" asked Nat. "What body are they talking about?"

"No questions, Nat. I haven't time to explain, and it's not something for a child to hear anyway. I want you and Macy to stay in the library."

Nat looked so crushed that Adam piped up. "You obey Aunt Ari, and I'll tell you about it after, OK?"

"OK," he muttered. "I just wanna know." Nathaniel took Macy by the hand and headed to the library with many looks back to see what he might be missing.

"Adam Harrison." Adam extended his hand to the officers who stood dripping in the front hall. "How do you do?" He didn't actually care a fig how they did. But his mother had taught him manners, and he wouldn't embarrass Arilee for the world.

Pretty-Boy Lieutenant introduced himself and the mute patsy beside him, then Adam took the men down into the basement and showed them the skeleton.

"Has anyone messed with the body?" Everett asked.

"No," Adam said. "I checked it for some identification, but there's nothing left but what you see."

"Are you the one who broke the wall and discovered the body?"

"Yes."

"Please meet us upstairs for questioning."

Adam rolled his eyes. "I assure you, I'm not a suspect; he was dead long before I was alive."

Lieutenant Everett didn't find this amusing. "Please leave the scene to allow us to get photographs and remove the deceased."

The scene? The deceased? Glad to leave them to their business, especially as a crack of thunder shook the house, he muttered, "Y'all have fun," and stomped upstairs.

Arilee fussed in the kitchen, fixing a tray with teacups and cookies. Nathaniel, arms crossed, pestered her, while Macy cried in the library.

"Come on, Nat," Adam said. "I've got a game for you and Mace."

In the library, he hid all the Noah's ark animals for the kids to find and promised them each a cookie if they stayed put till the soldiers left.

"Tea parties with grown-ups are very dull," Adam assured them. "There's a lot of talking and you have to sit completely still. It will be much more fun in here."

At last the soldiers came tramping up the stairs carrying the remains on a field stretcher covered with a sheet. Adam opened the door, and they headed out through the rain to put the stretcher in the back of the covered army-green truck.

Arilee stood beside him, watching them, then checked her hair in the hall glass. He started to tell her she looked fine, then remembered the lieutenant and decided to keep his opinion to himself. The soldiers returned, and they all arranged themselves in the too-small parlor chairs. Adam sat next to Arilee, close enough he caught a whiff of lavender. She served tea and cookies and chewed on her bottom lip.

Everett droned about how they needed to get as much information as possible but "Miss Rutledge need not be frightened" at this mere formality. Then he looked at Adam as though he hadn't been sitting there for a full three minutes—or spoken to him in the basement—and asked Arilee, "Is this your hired boy who found the skeleton?"

Adam almost slammed down his cup and walked out, but Arilee answered sweetly, "Sergeant Harrison is the one who found the body and contacted Fort McPherson about it."

"Mr. Harrison, please tell us the circumstances around the discovery."

So, he didn't get the honor of "sergeant" since he was but a lowly non-com, huh? Horsefeathers. He could tell this man a thing or two about real warfare, he reckoned. Had *the lieutenant* kept at his post after getting mustard gas burns, or run up a hill being fired on by machine guns, or gone endless days in a row with barely any food or sleep?

Everett began scratching notes on a small tablet. To Adam, he fired off his inquiries as if he were standing court-martial. To Arilee, he stammered and simpered as if she were a delicate bloom ready to wilt away at the mere mention of something so vulgar as "remains." The contrast was so comical, and his treatment of them both so condescending, though in opposite ways, that Adam already anticipated the fun they could have at his expense when he left.

"It's clear to me neither of you has any information about who the deceased could have been or how he came to be here. But should you find out anything, please do your duty and inform me right away, as there could be descendants remaining who would like the comfort of knowing their ancestor's final resting place."

"If my ancestor was found buried in the enemy's basement during wartime, I wouldn't be too comforted pondering what the heck he was doing there or why," Adam remarked drily.

"Mr. Harrison, I remind you we are in the presence of a lady," Everett scolded.

"I'm sorry to disturb your sensibilities," Adam muttered at Arilee with a lift of his eyebrows. "I should have my mouth washed out with lavender soap."

She bit back a smile, but her dimples still showed.

Everett cleared his throat. "The body will be buried in the National Cemetery in Marietta. I will let you know when we have concluded our investigation and arranged for the burial. You are welcome to attend if you wish."

"Thank you," said Arilee. "I'm relieved to have the remains removed from my home, to be honest."

"Of course. You have withstood the shock with courage equal to your beauty, Miss Rutledge."

Adam nearly choked, the lieutenant was laying it on so thick. Arilee flushed a little and said a demure "thank you." Really? To Pretty Boy? Everyone rose, and Adam rolled his eyes behind the lieutenant's back as Arilee walked him to the front door.

"Until Marietta then," Everett said and kissed her hand.

Adam balled his fists and exhaled.

Arilee gave their guests a smile that revealed her dimples again. "Thank you, Lieutenant Everett, Lieutenant Smith," she said. Smith merely touched his hat and said, "Ma'am." Adam stood in the doorway of the parlor, ignored by the two officers and trying not to grind his teeth.

Arilee shut the door and let out a sigh. "That wasn't as bad as I feared. He took us at our word and was surprisingly friendly."

"Conceited little whiskbroom," Adam muttered, relieved her anxiety had been over the situation and not what personal impression she made on Everett.

"What did you have against him?"

"He was too pretty and polished."

She laughed softly. "I don't know about that. He *was* rather rude to you."

"What about you? You weren't at all insulted that he talked to you as if you were a fragile creature scarcely able of withstanding the least stress?"

"I guess you're right. Sometimes, though, everyone's belief in my ability to handle everything gets exhausting. A little harmless flirting and someone seeing me as a woman and not just a caretaker felt nice for a change."

She stepped past him to the library to see about the children who were arguing. When she was out of sight, Adam banged his head against the doorframe. Then he had to bite his tongue to keep from yelping, as he hit it a little harder than he meant.

What was he doing wrong? *He* certainly saw her *as a woman*. What on earth would it take for her to see him as a man?

CHAPTER 11

Friday, September 2, 1921

When Davis arrived home late on Friday nights from his mail run, he had but two goals: a bowl of ice cream and his own bed. Saturday would be devoted to the kids and whatever work he needed to do around the house; all of Sunday would be taken up with the trip to Milledgeville and back and the visit with Muriel. And before daybreak Monday morning, he would leave for another week of flights on the transcontinental mail route from New York to San Francisco.

The changes and improvements at the house pleased him immensely. Hiring Adam had been a good move; the young man was a capable manager of the workmen and a hard worker in his own right. The kids adored him, and he and Arilee seemed to get along companionably. It relieved Davis considerably to have a man about the place during his absences and to know he didn't have to figure out this crazy house himself any longer.

This Friday evening, he arrived home in time to say goodnight to the kids as Arilee tucked them into bed. He tickled their tummies, relaxing in the therapeutic sound of childish giggles, and promised them they'd have fun tomorrow.

"And Aunt Ari says if you say *yes*, we can go to May-retta tomorrow and have a picnic." Nathaniel bounced up and down in the bed.

"And why do we have to go all the way to Marietta for a picnic?" he asked, looking up at Arilee.

"'Cause the soldiers are going to bury the skeleton Mr. Adam found in the basement!" Nathaniel's bouncing escalated. "It was real old and dead and had on a Yankee uniform."

"The men from McPherson came," Arilee explained. "I'll tell you about it while you eat your ice cream."

He settled Nathaniel and kissed both kids goodnight, then he and Arilee headed downstairs. "Why on earth do you want to go to the funeral of some unknown Yankee?"

"I don't know how to explain it, Davis. It's like *The Burial of Latané*. He died far from home, and his family never knew what happened to him. We've also been through a war, and our brother died far from home, and I like to think someone was there for him at the end."

Davis's chest tightened. He prayed Arilee never learned how Brax had perished. "Your mystery skeleton died half a century ago. The people 'there for him at the end' were likely some of our relatives killing him as he broke into the house."

"We don't know that. Maybe he tried to help them and was killed by his own side for offering aid and comfort to the enemy."

Davis snorted. As they stepped into the kitchen, he heard tires crunching wildly on the gravel driveway and the drone of an automobile engine.

"Who is racing in here this late?" Davis groused as a car door slammed shut. "Does Adam have people over often?"

"Adam never has people over, except his parents this summer. He's getting cleaned up from mowing, and then he's coming back over here for cider."

A moment later, a decided knock sounded on the front door.

"Then who is this?"

"I don't know, Davis, but you can open the door and be polite, can't you?"

He walked back through the hall and opened the door to a woman who appeared to have stepped out of the pages of *Vogue*. She had golden hair, bobbed to just slightly below her chin. Everything from her ridiculous hat adorned with enough pheasant feathers that she ought to be able to fly, to her high-heeled pumps trying to add inches to her petite frame, bespoke a carefully curated *perfection*. She carried a tablet and pencil in one hand and her pocketbook on the opposite shoulder.

"Good evening. I am looking for Mr. Rutledge."

"I'm Davis Rutledge."

"I am Margaret Rose Woodhouse, a reporter for the Atlanta *Journal*. I wanted to talk to you about the skeleton found in your cellar recently."

"I don't know anything about it," he barked and closed the door.

"Who was it?" Arilee asked when he reentered the kitchen.

"Some reporter woman about your mystery skeleton."

"Well, where is she?"

"I told her I didn't know anything about it. Which is true."

"But I do."

"She didn't ask for you, she asked for me."

"Obviously you can't open the door *and* be polite." Arilee rolled her eyes.

"It will be a cold day in Hades when I willingly allow any part of our lives to be published in the newspaper."

A moment later there came a rap on the back door. Arilee went to answer; Davis listened to the exchange from his seat in the kitchen.

"Are you Mrs. Rutledge?" the woman reporter asked.

"I am *Miss* Rutledge, Davis's sister," Arilee answered.

How nice of her to give away more information than asked. Next, she'll be inviting the woman in for tea.

"I am Margaret Rose Woodhouse," the stranger repeated. "I write for the *Journal.* I wanted to talk to someone in the household about the skeleton found here."

"Oh, sure. Adam found it. He works here. He and I talked to the officers from McPherson on Monday. Davis has just gotten back from a week of flying, so don't mind him. You go sit in the kitchen, and let me get Adam, and we'll tell you all about it."

Arilee disappeared out the back door, and the woman he'd all but slammed the front door on wandered into the kitchen and stood facing him.

"Sis is the friendly one," he muttered.

"So I see."

The smile playing about the corners of her mouth almost made Davis leave the room. However, he did want to make sure that Adam and Arilee—great talkers both of them—didn't tell their whole family story to this nosy woman.

"You are a pilot then?" she asked when the silence had stretched to awkward proportions.

Why in the Sam Hill must Adam take so long? Why couldn't he sit at the

85

table smelling of dirt and grass like any normal man? Davis still smelled of airplane fuel and engine grease. And why had Arilee hurried out to fetch him? Davis should've gone instead.

"Yes."

"Barnstorming?"

"Certainly not. Airmail."

"You don't approve of barnstorming?"

"Like female reporters, I find it an unnecessary occupation."

As he'd anticipated, that got her dander up. Her eyes, large and soft chocolate brown, lit with fire. She stood up taller (which still wasn't very tall) and opened her mouth to let him have it he guessed. He started laughing.

She shut her mouth. "You're trying to rile me, aren't you?"

He shrugged innocently. "I think people should ride in airplanes and transport cargo in airplanes, not be out doing tricks risking their lives for other folks' entertainment. There's plenty of real reasons and ways to die without creating new ones."

"You were in the war then?"

He nodded. *What* was taking Adam and Arilee so long?

"And your disapproval of female reporters?"

"Miss Woodhouse—"

"*Mrs.* Woodhouse. I am a war widow."

"I'm sorry, ma'am. Truly."

Dang it all, she had him seeing her as a person now instead of her job, and look at all she'd finagled out of him already.

Arilee and Adam waltzed in the back door and moseyed into the kitchen.

"Did you count all the stars in the sky?" Davis asked irritably.

"Were those three minutes too long for you to have to be civil, Davis?" Arilee retorted.

Mrs. Woodhouse choked with laughter. Arilee shot daggers at him with her eyes, then did exactly what he knew she would. She served up food—warm cider and gingersnaps, not ice cream, to everyone. Davis moved the meeting into the dining room where they could all sit in separate chairs and be spared the embarrassment of having to crowd beside each other on the bench seating of the banquette.

Arilee and Adam enthusiastically launched into the tale of their discovery of the skeleton in the basement. Mrs. Woodhouse took notes on her tablet in precise shorthand.

"And will you be at the funeral tomorrow?" Mrs. Woodhouse asked.

"Oh, I thought it might be kind of interesting," Arilee replied. "I hate for someone to be buried with no one there. I told the kids we'd drive out there and have a picnic in Marietta."

"The kids?"

Davis made a noise in his throat.

"My niece and nephew, Davis's children," Arilee answered, ignoring the looks he shot her. "I am their caretaker."

Mrs. Woodhouse nodded and to her credit and his relief did not ask after the children's mother.

"I'm coming too," Adam put in. Mrs. Woodhouse did not write this down. She had not even written down Adam's name. Even though the kid had found the dead guy, she apparently didn't find that worth noting.

"Have you any idea, Miss Rutledge, why the body might have been there? Or why this house was spared in the burning of Atlanta?"

"No. I asked my Grandma Luella once about when the Yankees came through, and she said some things were better left in the past. We did find an old stash of family letters from the war when Adam cleaned out the attic."

"May I see them?" Woodhouse asked eagerly.

At last Arilee's forthcomingness found a limit. "Actually, the letters were somewhat damaged, and I need to sort through them myself."

Woodhouse set her lips into a tight line to suppress her frustration. Davis bit back his own smile. Arilee had given her a motherlode of information, yet it wasn't enough. With her perfect posture, perfect style, and perfect diction, the woman no doubt lived in a continual state of disappointment.

"Would you do that for me, Miss Rutledge? Do you think if I came back in a month or two, you might have had a chance to look through the letters for clues about the remains found in your basement?"

Davis cleared his throat. "We've provided you with quite a bit of information already, Mrs. Woodhouse. If we find out something else, I'm sure we'll need to take it to the authorities, not the press."

"I'll see what I can do about the letters," Arilee promised, trying to smooth over the situation before Woodhouse had a chance to respond to his curt reply.

Arilee had spent her whole life trying to smooth over situations.

It was the best and worst thing about her.

"Excellent." Mrs. Woodhouse rose and gathered her things. "If you have nothing further to add, I will let you all get back to your evening. Thank you for your time. And for the cookies. Thank you for your help, Miss Rutledge, Mr. Rutledge." Her voice sounded strained at his name. At least she'd gotten the message.

"It was a pleasure to meet you," Arilee said. "Davis will see you to the door and walk you safely to your automobile."

"There's no need," she hastened to say.

She didn't *want* him to walk her to her car. Then, by cotton, he would. Davis rose and led her back through the hall to the front door. They stepped out into the muggy night. Cicadas screeched at a volume louder than he'd ever played a phonograph record.

"Good night for flying," he remarked at the sight of the clear sky and bright moon.

"I'm going to fly an airplane someday."

He studied her. "Yeah, you probably will." They walked down the front walkway.

"I'm sure you don't approve of women pilots any more than you approve of women reporters."

"Nope. But I reckon my disapproval will only fuel your desire to do it."

She laughed, and he bit back his own chuckle. He stopped when he saw her car. Not a steady Buick or even a Packard. A Rolls Royce Silver Ghost Tourer. He let out a low whistle.

"You like it?" she asked.

"It's the cat's pajamas," he acknowledged gruffly.

"Someday you take me up in your airplane, and I'll take you for a spin in the Ghost. Or don't you approve of women drivers, either?"

"I taught my sister to drive."

He wondered why a woman who clearly didn't need the money was working. Maybe she needed something to do. There were worse things for a pretty woman to be than a journalist. Maybe.

She climbed into the car, started it, turned on the headlamps, and then backed up so fast that she ran over an azalea bush and nearly hit the fence. Apparently, *every* area of her life wasn't perfect and precise.

"I don't approve of *that* woman driver," he muttered, hoping they had seen the last of the crazy female reporter.

CHAPTER 12

Saturday, September 3, to Sunday, September 4, 1921

Adam glared at Lieutenant Everett behind the man's back. There he stood, all fancy in those dress blues, holding Arilee's elbow and whispering explanations of the military funeral service to her.

Adam and Davis, as discharged civilians, were not permitted to wear their uniforms. When he'd returned home in '19, Adam had stuffed that khaki into the back of his closet at his parents' house, behind all of Joshua's old clothes, which his mother insisted Adam could still wear. His medal his mother had on display in her front room; it made her proud while he tried to forget.

The reporter woman, Mrs. Woodhouse, had come for the burial. She jotted down notes furiously, stopping periodically to look around. On the other side of the open grave, Davis watched with his characteristic unreadable expression. The kids stood on either side of him, each holding one of his hands.

The army chaplain welcomed them on behalf of the United States government, then read the twenty-third Psalm. With the soldier being unknown, there was little to be said. The chaplain led them all in reciting the Lord's Prayer, then gave the committal.

"... I commit his body to the ground in this sacred place; earth to earth, ashes to ashes, dust to dust. For his faithful service, our nation today bestows full military honors. In life, he honored the flag, and in death, the flag honors him."

A trumpeter played "Taps." Adam watched Lieutenant Everett speaking into Arilee's ear, needing the distraction of jealousy to keep him from focusing on "dust to dust," "in life he honored the flag," and the mournful call of the bugle, all things that immediately began to pull him back to the Aire Valley in France, where Joshua lay, one of the many thousands.

He'd wanted his parents to request Joshua's body be returned to the States, but his mother had decided otherwise. Secretly, he feared that Mother pretended Josh was still away, that he merely hadn't come home yet. He didn't want to make their burden heavier; uncertain, he said nothing, though he longed to tell them about his brother's final moments and final resting place.

He'd thought surely he could attend the funeral of this long-dead stranger to whom he had no personal connection. But instead, he felt a familiar strangling tightness in his throat and nausea churning his gut. Images began flashing through his mind at breakneck speed. Bodies and body parts and blood and stacks of caskets. The moving pictures in his mind landed on a helmet. One lone helmet, half-buried in the mud of no man's land, with a bullet hole through it.

Adam moved to stand under an enormous oak and took slow, deep breaths as he stared out at the thousands upon thousands buried here from another war as senseless as the one he'd survived. The military band played "The Battle Hymn of the Republic." He gritted his teeth. It was almost over. He had to make it through the twenty-one-gun salute and the smell of gunpowder. Then he'd talk with Arilee and run around with the kids, and he'd be OK again.

Lieutenant Everett offered Arilee his arm to help her walk in her pumps over the uneven ground of the cemetery back to where the cars were parked. Mrs. Woodhouse moved to a bench to continue with her notes. Davis, hands in his pockets, ambled over to Adam.

"You're not going to win by staring him down."

"What are you talking about?"

Davis rolled his eyes. "You think I don't know you're carrying a torch for my sister?"

"She thinks I'm just the pain in the neck kid she taught in high school."

"Maybe, maybe not."

"She hasn't given me any encouragement."

"She probably won't. You might have to man up and tell her how you feel."

"I would if I had any idea she cared about me *like that . . .*"

"Guess you didn't earn your Distinguished Service Cross being a coward."

"How do you know about my medal?"

"I told you, I checked with Rev. Alexander before I hired you. You think I'd let any old palooka around my sister and kids?"

He raised one eyebrow and bore into Adam with a look. After a moment, Adam strode away, eventually catching up to walk at a distance behind Arilee and Lieutenant Everett. The officer droned on about the history of the cemetery, a sorry tale about how the rebels and Yanks couldn't agree to allow even their dead to be buried on the same field. Then Everett turned and took Arilee's hand. "Duty calls, and I must take my leave. Might I call on you, Miss Rutledge? I'd be delighted to see you again."

Arilee chewed on her bottom lip. "Oh, I appreciate the honor of you asking me, but I'm, that is, well, I don't date. I am the caregiver for my niece and nephew, you see, and I can't think about anything more."

Everett hid the sting of rejection smoothly. He smiled, tipped his hat to her, and rejoined the men from McPherson. Adam glanced back at where Davis stood with the children. Did he realize his sister was putting off having her own life to raise his kids? Or was this merely Arilee's way of giving Everett the icy mitt less icily?

Once the lieutenant had walked away, Adam decided to pry. Arilee stood watching the children now playing tag with their father, a look of contentment on her countenance. He strolled over to her.

"Lieutenant Everett seems quite taken with your charms," Adam remarked as offhandedly as he could.

She waved a hand dismissively. "He's pleasant enough, and I will admit I've enjoyed his attention, but it would be wrong to let him think it could be anything more."

"Why not? I mean, why couldn't it be anything more?"

"I can't leave Davis and the kids. I don't expect any man would understand my position, let alone be OK with it."

"Davis doesn't strike me as so selfish he wouldn't want you to be happy and have your own life."

"He isn't selfish, and don't you dare repeat to him what I said, you hear? It's just—we lost everything and everyone. All in about a year. Maybe it's wrong, but I couldn't love the children more if I had birthed them, and I won't leave them until they have a mother again. And if Davis can't get Muriel out, he would never divorce her to remarry, and the kids might never have a mother again."

"You don't have to defend it to me."

"But you see what I'm saying? No man wants a wife who comes with her brother and his kids and a house with buried skeletons."

"'*No* man' is a bit broad. I think the *right* man would find those—appendages—to your life fascinating. And your loyalty to them admirable."

Her face brightened into that dimpled smile that warmed him. "You are thoughtful to your old teacher, Adam," she said lightly, "even if I find your opinion entirely unrealistic."

"Arilee."

She met his eyes.

"I don't think you're old, and I don't think life has passed you by. I, for one, am praying for God to 'restore . . . the years that the locust hath eaten' in your family."

"Thank you." Her aqua eyes shone with unshed tears under those long brown lashes. Their hands brushed, then she briefly squeezed his. "You've been a godsend at a time when I had about given up on God remembering we even existed."

"Aunt Ari, let's have our picnic." Nathaniel came running, and she followed him. Adam held back, observing.

Arilee Rutledge was the best woman he'd ever known. But wooing her wouldn't mean flowers and chocolates and kisses in the moonlight to sweep her off her feet, though a bit of romance might help her feel appreciated. The true path to her heart lay in loving the ones she loved and accepting the brokenness in her life, not trying to fix everything and move on to some imaginary happily ever after.

Loving Arilee the way she needed to be loved might be the hardest, best thing he'd ever done.

∞ ∞ ∞

Sunday morning, Arilee read aloud from the Atlanta *Journal* to Davis and Adam over a breakfast of eggs and cinnamon toast.

The Fascinating History and Ongoing Mystery of Wisteria House
by M. R. Woodhouse

You've heard of the proverbial "skeleton in the closet" when studying one's family tree. But for one Atlanta family, this saying took quite a literal turn this past month.

During the recent modernization of their antebellum home, the Rutledge family uncovered a shocking surprise in the form of a complete human skeleton in a Union uniform. No identification other than "VT" on the sole of a boot gave any indication as to whom this lost soldier might have been.

In 1838, Ezekiel Rutledge of Rutledge, Georgia, married Henrietta Middlebrooke. The couple settled in nearby Madison, where they had two sons and a daughter. Ten years later, better business prospects brought Mr. Rutledge to Atlanta. His wife agreed to the move if she could have a home in Atlanta identical to the one she left behind. Her obliging husband built the home she desired, with the addition of a full second-floor porch. This home stands on Randolph Street and is commonly known as "Wisteria House" for the large wisteria vines growing around it.

The house was completed in 1850, but tragedy struck soon after. Mrs. Rutledge died giving birth to her youngest daughter, Odessa. The home Ezekiel Rutledge had built for his beloved wife was now a constant reminder of her absence. In 1860, he was wed to Miss Luella Mason, some twenty years his junior.

In 1864, when Sherman's Army came through Atlanta, only Odessa, the young second Mrs. Rutledge, and a few servants were living in the home. Colonel Rutledge was away fighting under General Lee, his two sons already killed in action. He returned home a broken man, grieving his lost sons, destroyed business, and desolated hometown. Colonel Rutledge had one son by his second wife, and the current occupants of the home are this son's children and grandchildren.

Yesterday the unknown soldier's remains were respectfully interred at Marietta National Cemetery, with military honors being presided over by personnel from Fort McPherson. Davis Rutledge, his two children, and his sister Arilee Rutledge were in attendance. Neither Mr. Rutledge nor Miss Rutledge has any knowledge of the identity of the skeleton, how it came to be in their basement, nor how it might be connected to their family. A former slaves who was at the home at the time of the War Between the States is still living, but her whereabouts are currently unknown.

When asked for comment about the skeleton, Mr. Rutledge, an army pilot in the recent war, stated: "We don't expect he was a good man, since he came to be buried in our basement rather than with his fellow soldiers. But then again, we have some questions about our own ancestors, and I can't say as we've made all the best choices ourselves, either."

"That's what you had to say to her?" Arilee asked as she set down the paper.

"I found the skeleton, I called McPherson, and I attended old Vernon's funeral, and I didn't even get my name in the paper?" Adam complained.

"I'd gladly give you the honor," Davis snapped. "Meddlesome woman reporter. I couldn't tell when she was just talking to me and when she was interviewing me. I didn't know that was my official statement."

"Still, it could've been worse. Whatever she did to uncover all this, she didn't include anything about Daddy or Muriel; either she didn't find out, or she was kind to us." Arilee thought in a different setting she could probably have been friends with Margaret Rose Woodhouse, though the woman did intimidate her.

Davis snorted at the idea of Mrs. Woodhouse's kindness. "Make sure I'm gone whenever she comes back to harass you about those letters, OK?"

"I don't think anyone tells Mrs. Woodhouse when to come. I think she simply appears."

"It reminds me of what Shakespeare once wrote," Adam inserted drolly. "Methinks that lady wilt not accept nay for an answer."

Davis laughed and Arilee rolled her eyes and swatted Adam as he rose to take his plate to the sink.

"I'm off to Milledgeville," Davis said. "Y'all try not to make any more notable discoveries around here this week, OK?"

CHAPTER 13

Week of September 18, 1921

With one week left till his classes began at Emory, Adam went to Davis and asked him where he would like him to devote his time. Though the work seemed endless, Adam was pleased with all that had been accomplished in the past three months. Besides the vast changes to the interior, the exterior of the house had gotten a fresh coat of paint last week. And he had cleared away undergrowth and overgrowth till his arms were so scratched up he appeared to have fought with wildcats.

"Sis won't ask for herself, but I'd say getting wiring to her room, and then mine if you get the chance," Davis said. "I know it takes time to do it right, and I appreciate you not doing a shoddy job of it."

Monday morning at breakfast, Adam asked Arilee when he might work in her bedroom.

Flustered with getting Nathaniel off to his first day of school, she huffed a bit. "Whenever you want, I guess. I don't want an overhead light, just an outlet by the bedside table for a lamp."

"You're going to have a great day at school, Nat." Adam clapped him on the shoulder. "Your Aunt Ari's already taught you so much, you'll be ready for whatever the teacher throws at you."

"She's going to throw things at me?"

"Naw. That just means whatever new things you learn."

"I wanna go to school." Macy, next to him, spoke up. "I know my wetters."

"You're going to be so smart when you start school, they'll ask you to be the teacher."

She giggled and looked up at him with large, adoring blue eyes. "Sugar?" she asked as he dropped two cubes in his coffee. He took a third cube out of the dish with the tongs, then dunked it in his coffee long enough for it to get soft and popped it into her waiting open mouth.

"Tank 'oo, Mr. Adam."

Arilee shook her head at their morning routine. "Come on, Nat, eat up, you've got a big day ahead."

"I'm gonna see Johnson every day now," he said. "And his lunch box has trains, but mine gots airplanes. Mr. Adam, are you really going to school next week?"

"Yep."

"But you're a grown-up."

"Mr. Adam's going to be a doctor." Arilee set a basket of hot biscuits on the table. "You have to be smart and go to lots of extra school to do that."

"I'm gonna fly airplanes like Daddy when I'm a grown-up." Nathaniel flew his spoon over the breakfast table. "And go far away and fight bad guys."

"Flying is one thing, but fighting is another, and one you don't need to hope for," Arilee said.

"Did you fight bad guys in the war, Mr. Adam?"

"Yep."

"Did you win any medals?"

"One."

"Can I see it?"

"Some time. It's at my parents' house. Remember my mother and father who came to help us a while back?"

Nathaniel nodded. "I like them a lot. They need to come back. Maybe—"

"Nathaniel Greene Rutledge, stop bumping gums with Mr. Adam and eat your breakfast or you'll be late for the first day of school."

Adam rose from the banquette table and went over to where Arilee stood pouring orange juice into small empty jelly jars she used as drinking glasses for the kids.

"Arilee," he said low, so Nathaniel couldn't hear, standing close enough that he could smell her clean lavender scent. "He's gonna do fine. And you're gonna do fine." He placed his hand on her arm until she finally met his eyes. "He's going to love school, and the teacher will love him, and he'll have lots of friends, and he'll learn everything he needs to know. And, yes, there will be some rough moments, but those'll help him learn too. And you'll be here to guide him."

She wiped her eyes on her apron.

"It's OK for it to be hard," he murmured. "It's a big change for both of you. But I promise, he's going to do swell because you've prepared him for this."

She nodded but didn't sit down to eat and checked and rechecked Nathaniel's tin lunch box. Once she and the kids were out the door for the walk to school, Adam hesitantly headed up to her bedroom to survey the work needed.

With enough curiosity to spell the demise of a whole litter of cats, Adam turned the brass knob of the always-closed door, stood in the doorway, and looked inside.

The far wall was lined with bookshelves and books, nearly as many as were in the library downstairs. Some appeared to be sets of commentaries, and he supposed she might have acquired her father's theological library upon his disappearance. He saw a beautiful set of Shakespeare's complete works, as well as many other classics and some newer fiction.

The four-poster bed, dresser with mirror, and deep wardrobe were old Victorian styles, intricately turned and carved oak pieces. The walls displayed framed pictures of Doré's Bible illustrations and illustrations from Shakespeare in a similar style. The bed, spread over with a pink and green quilt, was neatly made. The table beside it, burdened with more books, would be where she wanted the outlet. This room was wallpapered, and if he did it right, they wouldn't have to open up the whole wall, make a big mess, and repaper.

Pulling out his tape measure, Adam began making notes. He stopped as a breeze whistled through the large window that faced the second-story porch. He'd been out on the balcony several times, replacing rotten wood and fixing broken soffit; he'd seen Arilee's spot, but he hadn't thought about it. Now he stepped back into the hall and out the door onto the wide balcony, enjoying the hint of fall in the air on this perfect 70-degree day.

On the balcony in front of Arilee's room sat a wicker settee with gingham cushions and floral pillows. A crocheted blanket lay folded on it and a small table sat before it. A leather-bound journal, a used coffee mug, a magazine turned open to a picture of a living room, Shakespeare's *Sonnets*, and the second volume of Matthew Henry's *Commentary on the Whole Bible* all littered the table. Several potted plants, including a large basket of lavender, adorned the space, which was secluded behind the thick wisteria vines growing up the porch. He stood in Arilee's personal sanctuary, as much an intruder here as in her bedroom.

An oil lamp perched on the table. What if . . . ? He measured and evaluated.

Yes, it could be done.

Especially for her.

On Wednesdays, Arilee typically did her marketing. The new refrigerator had transformed this from a chore of every other day to twice a week. After walking Nathaniel to school for his third day, she and Macy took the trolley down to the Piggly Wiggly.

Adam had been right, of course. Nathaniel adored his teacher and being around other children. He ranked top of the class in reading, and whatever she'd failed to teach him about arithmetic, he was picking up easily.

She returned in time to make lunch. After a quick sandwich, Adam announced, "I should have that outlet in your bedroom done by this afternoon."

"Guess I should get a lamp."

"I had to go to Dixie Electrical anyway, so I picked out one there. If you don't like it, then I reckon they'll let you exchange it."

"I'm sure you made a very practical choice," she stated, trying to hide her disappointment, for she had been dreaming of pretty lamps. She couldn't quite decipher his expression, but he said only:

"I ran the BX wiring down from the attic through the wall and only had to cut the opening in the baseboard for the outlet. I think I got all the dust cleaned up."

"You mean you didn't have to take the whole wall apart?"

"Nope. No new plaster and lathe and wallpaper for you."

"Oh, that's wonderful. I can't wait to see it."

Though that was true, by the time she dealt with laundry in the basement, ironing in the kitchen, picking up Nathaniel, and then the usual rush of supper, dishes, and getting the children bathed and to bed, she'd forgotten all about her bedroom. As she stepped out of the children's room into the hallway after the final requests for water, songs, stories, and prayers, she noticed that a light shone from beyond her open door.

She stepped to the doorway and sucked in her breath a little. There on the bedside table sat not the practical lamp she expected, but a beautifully curved and molded brass base with a reverse-painted glass shade of greens and pinks, the same colors as her quilt. Even though her and Davis's money had paid for all this, it still felt like a gift.

As she stood taking it in, she realized light was also coming through the window, and it wasn't moonlight. *A light shone on the balcony.*

"'What light through yonder window breaks?'" she murmured.

She stepped outside and took in a light fixture over the door and another matching fixture over her reading nook. Adam stood in the shadows, watching for her reaction.

"Oh," she breathed. "Adam."

"The button by the door is for both lights," he explained. "I'll add one on Davis's side of the porch later to make it all symmetrical."

"Adam—this, and the beautiful lamp—thank you." She gave him a quick hug. Like she'd give to her brother. "Was the porch light your idea or Davis's?"

"Mine."

"It's perfect." She wasn't sure how to tell him what it meant to have a safe and steady light for her little hideaway. "Do you want some cider and popcorn? We could sit out here, especially as the night is so pleasant."

"Sounds great. Let me put away my tools, and I'll meet you back here."

"Thank you again," she said, meeting his eyes.

"Glad to do it for you." He smiled, his easy grin that made her all fluttery. Why he didn't have a sweetheart remained a mystery.

Ten minutes later, they sat on the balcony settee. She hadn't considered how close it would be for two; her skirt kept brushing up against his leg. Pretending she wasn't the least flustered by his nearness, she picked up *The Black Moth*, another novel by a new British author, Georgette Heyer. She attempted to read, while he munched popcorn and jotted down some sentences on what she'd learned was his weekly letter to his mother.

A thoughtful gesture, she pondered. *Thoughtful* described him in both his work and relationships. She would never have guessed it of him when they hired him a few months ago. Now after this week, she would never have Adam around again all day. He would be at school or studying. He'd told Davis he'd work 12-15 hours a week on the house and yard. She'd still see him, but it wouldn't be the same.

Another loss. She felt the sharp stab of grief and the ache of dread, no matter how silly she told herself such feelings were.

She was staring into space when he cleared his throat and said, "I hope you're still going to feed me snacks every evening and let me bring all my books over here to study."

Had he read her mind, or did he have the same feelings she did?

"I hope you will. I'm certainly going to miss having another adult around all day. Even though we're both busy with our separate work, it's been nice knowing you're here. Won't you miss dorm life with the other fellows, though?"

He snorted. "I've had my fill of that. Besides, this is medical school. Serious stuff. I don't plan to rejoin my fraternity, and not living on campus gives me a great excuse."

"I don't want to be the reason you miss out on the fun parts of school."

"I'll probably stay in the literary society. I enjoy debating, and there's plenty of topics to discuss these days. I'm going to push that, this year, we have a true debate on the validity of this so-called science of eugenics."

She closed her book, the opportunity of conversation a greater enticement. "You don't believe in it, then?"

"I believe it's horsefeathers. You cannot hold a literal view of the Bible and simultaneously embrace a teaching that some people are more worthy than others. It goes against God as the Creator who made man in His own image. It goes against the Gospel that 'God so loved the world.' And it makes it impossible to obey the command to love one's neighbor as oneself."

She nodded. "Do you know anything about the Klan?"

"I know enough. One or another of their members tries to recruit me every few months. It's something I'm never going to be part of. They use violence and lawlessness to try to effect political and societal change. Not only are their methods wrong, their goals are misguided. And it galls me that they try to parade as a Christian organization when the spirit of antichrist permeates the essence of who they are."

"I don't really understand it," Arilee admitted. "Daddy supported the Klan, so I thought it was something good. But then when it came out about him committing adultery, the Klan turned on him and threatened him, and I've wondered if that's part of why he ran off like he did without another word or way to contact him. Muriel's father was pretty high up in the local group, and a huge proponent of eugenics, and he turned nasty on Davis after Daddy left us.

"When Muriel was sent to Milledgeville, I thought her parents would want the children, at least till Davis came home. And instead, they said no, that the kids came from bad blood and would grow up to be criminals like their grandfather or crazy like their mother. Then they said the kids would be better off in an orphanage than with me or Davis. They've never gone to visit Muriel or had anything to do with the children."

"I'm sorry they are that way, but since they are, I'm glad they aren't in the children's lives. I've seen it over and over with this poison. Once you ingest it, it consumes you till you turn against neighbors, friends, and even family. I certainly understand folks being distraught over the direction the country is going, the decay in morals, and how the world is rearranging following the war. But it's crazy to think the problems are caused by immigrants or blacks or Catholics or Jews, as the Klan purports, when white Protestants were bigger players in the danged war than anyone else."

"I'm ashamed that it took me so long to see how wrong it is. How can we live surrounded by these lies and not absorb them, though?"

"It's hard. I didn't start to *think* till I got into the Word of God and began to study it for myself. There in France. Before that, it was the 'Good Book' to me, something for church and funerals. It wasn't living and active in my life."

"Daddy always preached from the Bible, always quoted it, but I've come to see that he sometimes made it say what he wanted it to."

Adam nodded. "I know what you mean. Before Josh and I and some of the other boys left for the war, the pastor at my parents' church preached a sermon about how we were going to defeat the forces of darkness and spread the light of Christ's kingdom around the world. Later, when it was all over, I talked to some German boys whose churches told them the same thing. We weren't *any* of us fighting for some righteous cause. After the

Armistice, no one knew what it was about or why it happened."

"Shakespeare noted that 'The devil can cite Scripture for his purpose!' So how much more the teachers of eugenics, the Klan, the warmongers can. But how do I know that *I'm* not doing the same thing myself on a smaller scale? How is it possible to discern *what* is true amidst overwhelming deception when even the Bible can be mishandled so easily?"

Adam munched more popcorn. She hadn't meant her question rhetorically, but maybe he didn't have an answer either, for she'd never known him to take this long to have something to say. Yet when he did speak, his deep voice was more contemplative than usual, his gray-green eyes focused on something beyond this cozy spot.

"There's a verse in the Old Testament where God says, 'Not by might, nor by power, but by my spirit.' I think . . . I think when we really want to know what is true, when we are walking in fellowship with God and depending on His Spirit, when we are truly taking up our cross, dying to our own ideas, and following Him . . . then He reveals truth to us, gives us discernment. Certainly, we need to be in the Word. Studying it more and not less. But the Pharisees had memorized all the prophecies about the Messiah yet couldn't see when He lived among them because they only cared about their own might and power, their own kingdom and not God's."

Arilee sipped the rest of her cider. "Jewel knew the Scriptures as well as Daddy, but it was different. Daddy spouted off verses to make you do what he wanted or to show you he was right. But Jewel . . . she spoke the truth in love, as it says in Ephesians. She became like a mother to me after Mama died. She protected me from Odessa's wrath. She kept telling me verses of hope and praying over me when I was too overcome with grief to read my Bible or talk to God. Because of her beautiful faith and forgiveness in contrast with Odessa's bitterness, I realized I had a choice. I hope and pray I will be like her.

"For almost three years, we shared this house, the table, the burdens. And it's because of her, I cannot agree with the laws and customs of segregation. I cannot believe they are biblical or helpful to our society, but I don't know how or what I can ever do to change things so engrained in our culture."

"Raising two youngins who know what's right is certainly a start," Adam returned. "I know Pastor Andy and his wife and her family all think like us. He told me he believes his church will always be small because he won't accept money or support from the Klan or bow to their intimidation. He needs folks who will stand with him even when it gets tough."

"I said I would never care about a church again," she murmured. "But I find it happening in spite of my resistance."

"Jesus cares about the church too, Arilee. Even when we get it wrong and break His heart."

A shadow passed over his face, an unspoken pain. Sometimes, with his natural cheerfulness, she forgot he had experienced tremendous loss and difficulty of his own. Yet he'd come through it with a humility and integrity that awed her.

She was forever thankful God had sent him to Wisteria House. And that he'd be here a while longer.

CHAPTER 14

Thursday, October 13, 1921

In the excitement of remodeling and getting "her boys" back to school, Arilee had given little thought to her promise to Mrs. Woodhouse to look through the family letters. One evening, after putting the children to bed, she trudged up to the attic.

Adam had installed light bulbs on the stairs and in the open attic. Arilee pulled the chains and cowered till light flooded the space and she could verify nothing creepy lived up here. She thought about the trunk of old dresses and wondered about remaking the aging fabric into crazy quilts or donating them to a museum. As interesting as that project sounded, getting the children's winter clothes sewn or purchased must come first.

Autumn wind moaned around the eaves; she shivered, grabbed the polluted hatbox of old papers, and scurried out of the shadowy attic. From her dresser, she picked up the war letters from the old trunk, which had been sitting untouched since their discovery. She took it all downstairs and fixed cocoa for herself and Adam, who was doing some work in the basement and would be up to study soon.

She sat at the desk in the library with her warm drink; he came in whistling "St. Louis Blues" and carrying his physiological chemistry textbook.

"Whatya doing?"

"Sorting through the secrets of the past, I guess. There's some cocoa." She nodded in the direction of the mug on the end table. "We'll see which of us has more success."

"Yours looks more interesting."

"I won't argue with you there."

She started with the letters from the trunk. They were mainly correspondence from the Rutledge men to the women at home during the War Between the States. The brothers' infrequent letters were short and gave vague accounts of army life, no doubt their attempt to shield their sisters from the horrors they were experiencing.

"Oh," she exclaimed softly.

Adam looked up. "What did you find?"

"Jonathan was just killed, and Peter is writing to Celeste with the news."

"Who are these people?"

"Let me draw it out," Arilee suggested. She pulled out the huge Rutledge Family Bible from the bookshelves, sat back down at the desk, and sketched out a family tree. Adding in the dates of everyone's birth and death helped her to get a better perspective on the tragedy of it all. "Jonathan was eighteen," she whispered.

Brax had been eighteen.

"Colonel Rutledge married Henrietta Middlebrooke and they had Peter, Celeste, and Jonathan. Two boys and a sister in the middle, like my family." She showed Adam the chart, pointing to each in turn. "But then they had a fourth child. Henrietta died giving birth to Odessa. I don't know if the others spoiled or neglected the girl for her to turn out like she did. Listen to this though. This is what Peter wrote to his sister Celeste when their younger brother was killed."

Aloud she read:

My dearest sister,

It is with heavy heart that I write to tell you that our brother has passed from this life to the glories of heaven and the arms of the Savior. I do not know if you have received the news already, but since I remained with him at the end, I promised him I would tell you. He is with our mother again, the first to be reunited with her in eternity. A man of greater honor and kindness I have never known, except for our own father, of course.

With all my heart I wish Papa, or your husband, or I could be there with you now, to offer our comfort and strength as our family faces yet

again the unraveling of our tapestry in this second great loss. I pray our
stepmother, though she is young herself, will not be insensible to the loss of
a brother, and that you and she can tell Odessa these sad tidings in such a
way as to protect her delicate heart.

I cannot help but think of our summers running wild and barefoot, picking
blackberries and catching fireflies, building tepees, and looking for buried
treasure. I do not know how I will go through this life without my friend
and brother.

Arilee's voice broke, and she began to cry. Not a few stray tears, but deep sobs that shocked her with their force.

"Hey, hey," Adam rose and rested his hands comfortingly on her shoulders and rubbed gently. "Shh, it's OK, it's OK."

She pulled away after a minute, face red and eyes averted. "I'm sorry," she mumbled, "I don't know what's wrong with me."

He pulled the armchair close to her desk chair, sat on its arm, and made her look at him.

"Did you really ever have a chance to grieve your mother and brother?"

"I just went on. Because I had a newborn and a toddler needing me to keep them alive, and a bitter old aunt, and this crazy house and—" The tears kept coming.

He handed her a handkerchief.

"Thank you. I ought not to be crying to you. You lost your brother too, your only one."

"That's exactly why you should be talking to me. And it's not a competition over whose losses were worse or more or whatever. I know what it is to not have a chance—or know how—to grieve."

"If only I knew Brax was in heaven, like in the letter," she mourned, "it would be easier to bear. He wasn't a man of 'honor and kindness,' second only to our father. He was an angry, hurting boy who ran away because he had a dishonorable, cruel father. And as far as I know, he never found the forgiveness and salvation offered to him by our Heavenly Father."

"You don't know what God may have been doing in his heart overseas, facing death. War changes everyone who experiences it. God may have used it to draw Brax to Himself. I'm sure you all were praying."

"I tried to, but I—" She met his gray-green eyes. Why could she speak to *him* about things she'd shut inside for years? Shakespeare had written:

Give sorrow words. The grief that does not speak
Whispers the o'erfraught heart and bids it break.

Adam had given her such a gift in listening to her grief, a gift she hadn't even known she needed.

"I'm keeping you from your studies."

"Hang physiological chemistry."

"I didn't pray. After Daddy left us, I never went to church, and I didn't pray. It wasn't until over a year later in the wee hours of the morning. Muriel had been taken away, and Macy wouldn't stop crying, and she wouldn't take a bottle. Jewel had the 'flu, and I had no one to turn to. I broke down and begged God for help. Out there on the balcony in fact. And He met me there, even though I'd turned my back on Him for all those months. But trying to understand who He is, trying to separate the truth of Him from all that my father did and taught, has been a long struggle."

"I can't imagine that it wouldn't be. I was angry with God after Joshua died, did a lot of things I regret now, and I wasn't dealing with other people's betrayal or judgment." He gently squeezed her shoulder again.

His sweet concern and thinking about what he'd faced, also alone, almost made her start crying again. "You can tell me about it," she invited, searching his face.

For a minute, he looked as if he might. She saw the conflict on his countenance before something closed.

"I appreciate the offer. I will some time," he said. "But I'd better study now."

∞ ∞ ∞

Monday, October 17, 1921

Davis was dressed in his best suit, thankful for his attorney next to him. He'd met Billy Sweet when he went to the practice of Sam Harris and

Associates shortly after returning from the war. The senior attorney had referred Muriel's case to his new young assistant.

Not one to like most people, Davis had a grudging respect for Sweet, a fellow veteran who, despite life-altering injuries, still managed to work hard and be hopeful. A hearing such as they had finally arranged for today was unheard of; Billy had worked tirelessly to get the case reopened, contending that Davis, Muriel's legal guardian, had been overseas and at war at the time of the original sentencing.

Muriel came in, escorted by a nurse and a doctor from Milledgeville. Davis stepped over to greet her and bring her to sit in the wooden chair beside his. Dressed in clean clothes, her hair combed, she looked well, but he saw the fear in her eyes.

"It's OK," he whispered to her, squeezing her hand. "We're going to talk to the judge about why we want you to come home. This is a good thing." He preferred this small, spartan hearing room to an imposing courtroom.

The judge stepped in and greeted them. "I have reviewed the details of Mrs. Rutledge's case. I understand that you do not challenge the accusations, nor do you claim that the accused is now recovered, but that you still wish to petition for your wife's release, Mr. Rutledge?"

"Yes, sir," said Davis uneasily. Put that way, it sounded foolish.

"Your Honor," stated Billy, "it is our opinion that Mrs. Rutledge is *unable* to recover in the overcrowded and impersonal conditions of the state sanitarium. Mr. Rutledge is prepared to bring her to a safe environment where she will have personal, twenty-four-hour supervision and care."

"Describe what you have in mind," Judge White requested.

"I have a carriage house on my property that's been fixed up to be a suitable cottage for one or two people to live in. It is well-ventilated, heated in the winter, and has both plumbing and electricity. It's a small but comfortable apartment. My wife could stay there under the supervision of qualified nurses."

"She is under the supervision of qualified nurses now. Why will being alone in a cottage be better than in an institution designed for the care of the insane?"

"Her care would be more personalized and regulated."

"And would she have access to your children? Would they be safe around her?"

Davis cleared his throat. "My children live at the main house under the care of their aunt, my sister, Miss Arilee Rutledge. My sister would ensure—"

"I hate Arilee. I won't live with her." Muriel's tone bordered on a screech.

"You won't be living with her," Davis replied calmly. "You won't see her at all."

"She took my son away. She locked me up so she could steal my boy."

Davis cleared his throat. His gut churned with the same feeling he had when he knew the plane was going down, but he had to keep flying.

The judge looked at the doctor and nurse. "Is this behavior typical for Mrs. Rutledge?"

"Her official diagnosis is schizophrenia. Her behavior is erratic," said the doctor, a tired-looking fellow named Ross. "Unpredictable. She has moments of great lucidity and calm, followed by outbursts that can be both physically and emotionally violent. It is unclear what is causing these dramatic swings."

Davis didn't agree with the diagnosis, used broadly for any behavior psychiatrists couldn't understand. But he wasn't a doctor. "She is given Luminal on occasion. The administration of sedatives may aggravate her condition."

"Sedatives are necessary to keep the patient from harming herself or others," the doctor returned. "It is my opinion, and that of Superintendent Jones, as he states in his letter to Your Honor, that Mrs. Rutledge is best served by remaining where she is. In a situation such as you describe, she could go in search of her children, or they in search of her, and she could harm them. Seeing them with their aunt could agitate her further. And of course, if Mr. Rutledge chose to exercise his husbandly prerogatives, a further pregnancy would certainly do irreparable harm to his wife's fragile state."

"I am not going to have relations with my wife," Davis snapped. "I want her to be well. She is never going to get better at the asylum, stripped of all dignity and humanity, treated like a prisoner."

"I remind you, Mr. Rutledge," the judge interjected, "that your wife could have been sentenced to prison for attempted murder. Surely you value the safety of your children?"

"Your Honor, nothing is more important to me than protecting and providing for *all* of my family. My children. My sister. But also, my wife."

"I hate your sister." Once Muriel became fixated on a thing, she would speak of nothing else.

The judge cleared his throat. "Mr. Rutledge, conditions are quite favorable toward you being granted a divorce."

Davis looked at Muriel. He had been twenty, she eighteen, when they'd wed after a courtship of two years. He'd loved her spiritedness to his steadiness. She'd been sunshine and laughter and color and music. She made their simple house pretty. And she'd always been happy, like a little bird flitting about, glad to be alive. A year and a half after their marriage, she'd had Nathaniel. He'd noticed some melancholy after the birth, but gradually, surrounded by her family and his, she'd come back. They'd been terribly proud of their baby, but he'd tried to be careful about her having another one too soon, as his mother had cautioned him.

He hadn't known she was pregnant when he headed overseas. She had conceived on his last leave before shipping out. One more way he'd failed to protect her. She'd been angry when she wrote to tell him about the pregnancy. Angry he'd left her for the army. Angry she'd had to move to Wisteria House with his mother and sister. Angry he'd sold their house to pay back what his father had stolen so the church wouldn't come after his mother.

He'd failed her as a husband in countless ways. Perhaps the blame for her present condition lay as much with him as with her.

"For better, for worse, in sickness and in health." He spoke the words quietly but clearly. Said them for the judge but looked at Muriel.

"I am sorry for you, then," the judge replied. "For I cannot rule in favor of her release."

Undeterred, for the next ten minutes, Billy Sweet argued eloquently and logically against the asylum itself, contending that while the staff there were well-meaning, they were too overworked and the institution too overcrowded for Muriel to receive care that would lead to her restoration. The Georgia State Sanitarium had become a dead end, with patients no longer receiving help and returning home. Billy had the numbers to back up his arguments, and the judge listened, interjecting occasionally with questions, all of which Billy answered thoroughly.

At last, Judge White looked at Muriel and asked, "Mrs. Rutledge, do you want to return home?"

"I want my own house in Union Hill," she declared. "The one *he* sold."
Here she pointed at Davis.

The tail was on fire, and the airplane was about to spin out of control.

"He put his family before me," she continued. "His brother, his mother,
his sister, all of them. Even his planes. I lost everything. He hates me, and I
hate him. I hope he burns in hell."

"Mr. Rutledge, the circumstances of your wife's committal to the asylum
during your absence are indeed pitiable," Judge White said somberly. "If
she had made a normal recovery in the years following childbirth, I would
indeed recommend appealing to the governor for her release and acquittal.
I do sympathize with your frustrations over our worthy institution at
Milledgeville. I have friends who are part of the board of trustees, and I
know that the oversight of the asylum is never an easy task.

"However, as neither the doctor, nor the superintendent, nor you, nor
Mrs. Rutledge's behavior itself can give me full assurance that she will
not harm herself or others, I cannot in good conscience advocate for her
release. Until there is clear improvement, Mrs. Rutledge will remain at the
institution."

Muriel gave a shriek and tried to run out of the courtroom. The doctor
and nurse caught her and put restraints on her, then gave her a dose of
Luminal. Davis stepped over to where she stood sobbing.

"I love you, Muriel. I'll visit you on Sunday."

He should say more, but spent, he sank to the nearest chair. The judge
spoke to Billy for a moment, then filed out of the courtroom, and the doctor
and the nurse took Muriel away. Her shrieks echoed in his mind long after
she left.

They said things weren't the same as in the old days, like when Nellie
Bly went undercover at Blackwell and discovered torture and deprivation,
concluding that life in an asylum would drive a sane woman to insanity. But
the people who assured him it was all right now were the same people who
stood to be in trouble if it was not.

The hand on his shoulder startled him. He glanced up at Billy Sweet.

"I'm terribly sorry," the young attorney said, shaking his head. "I really
thought the judge would hear us out."

"I think he did. Muriel sabotaged herself. I know she's not ready to rejoin
society. I just don't think she ever will be, not while she's stuck there."

"Do you think it would help her for your sister to visit?"

"I've considered it, but I think it would make matters worse. Arilee is unfailingly tenderhearted. *She* would never have turned Muriel in. That was all Aunt Odessa's doing. Arilee loved Muriel as the sister she never had. I think seeing Muriel there, seeing what it's done to her, would about kill Arilee."

Billy nodded in understanding, but as he limped ahead out of the hearing room, Davis muttered under his breath, "I'm pretty sure it's killing me."

CHAPTER 15

Sunday, October 23, to Monday, October 24, 1921

Arilee had found the perfect girl for Adam. Ida Cantrell at church was a friend of the pastor's wife, a wholesome young lady with good parents. She was helping them raise her cousins who had been orphaned during the pandemic. Pretty and petite and about a year younger than Adam, she would make a perfect match for him.

A fellowship dinner followed this morning's service, and Arilee asked the Cantrell family to sit with them at one of the rectangular tables in the church hall. As she had expected, Adam came to sit with her and the kids, though he certainly could have sat with anyone, since he seemed to be on a first-name basis with the entire church. Laughter echoed around the room and plentiful food filled every plate.

Nathaniel knew the Cantrells' young nephew, and their eight-year-old niece took a sisterly interest in Macy. The adults chatted companionably, but rather than talking to Ida, whom Arilee had artfully managed to get sitting next to him, Adam began talking with Mr. Cantrell. No man could make his best impression on a woman while droning on about football. Yet on and on they went, deep into the ins and outs of the rivalry between Georgia Technical Institute and the University of Georgia, which seemed to center around Tech, a training school for soldiers, continuing to play football during the war years and UGA questioning their patriotism because of it.

"Ida, tell me about yourself," Arilee quickly interjected in a lull in the conversation.

The young woman blushed and fidgeted with her napkin. Arilee had not counted on Ida being painfully shy and tried to guide the conversation. Had Ida gone to high school? Where? What were her interests?

When Adam excused himself to get some pie, Arilee mentioned, "Adam's about your age, Ida. He's in his first year of medical school at Emory."

"I heard he's been fixing up your house?" Mrs. Cantrell questioned.

"Yes. I knew Adam and his brother from when I taught in Canton, where they are from." Somehow it was too painful to admit to young, dainty Ida that she had taught *them*. "My brother hired Adam this summer to fix up the old house we inherited. He has exceeded our expectations in the quality and speed of his work."

Mrs. Cantrell asked how Nathaniel liked school, and Ida slipped away to talk to a group of girls her age. Arilee sighed, even as she wondered why she felt so relieved that her plan had failed.

On the drive home, she mentally chided herself for being silly, as if Adam were hers to keep. Taking a deep breath, she attempted to salvage her attempt. "Nice family, the Cantrells."

"Yep. Took in those kids and have given them a good home."

"Nice girl, Ida."

"Sure."

"Pretty too, don't you think?"

Now he looked at her. "She's fine. What is this?"

"What is what?"

"Are you matchmaking?"

She felt heat creep over her cheeks. "What if I am?"

He came to a stop sign at Angier Avenue and Randolph and did not go on but turned his head and looked at her. "Listen to me, Roberta Rutledge. I don't need your help finding a girl, and if I did, I'd jolly well ask for it."

She put a hand over her chin, absently tracing the scar. He still wasn't driving; his eyes bored into her. "OK. Sorry," she murmured. "That was inappropriate on my part."

He grunted and drove home. Awkward silence settled over the car, and back at the house, he locked himself away to study.

116

Adam grabbed his histology book, lay on his back on his bed, and stared at the ceiling. He blew out a long breath of air.

He'd seen her every day for four months.

He'd taken a few hundred meals with her.

He'd gone out of his way to make things in her house especially suited to her needs and wishes.

And she still couldn't see he was crazy about her.

What was it going to take to win this woman? He didn't think the difference in their ages even slightly significant. But the fact that she had first known him as her student, was that an impediment they could never overcome?

He thought about just asking her to go on a date with him. But since she wanted to match him with someone else, she'd likely give him the icy mitt, and then things would be strange between them and even more hopeless.

Mother had said to be her friend and be patient. Swell, but for *how long*? He could tell she valued their conversations and time together. Their friendship meant more to him than any other he'd ever had besides Joshua's, which he wouldn't classify the same at all.

"Lord, you've brought her back into my life and given me this tremendous love for her. But I don't know how to make her see it. Please show me what to do, how to approach this with her. Or if I'm not worthy of her, and it would all end in disappointment for both of us, protect her. She doesn't need more heartache, Lord. Give me the strength to walk away if that's what's best for her."

∞∞∞

That evening, Adam felt the tension between Arilee and himself but didn't know how to ease back into their usual camaraderie. He forced himself to focus on studying for his upcoming exam and hoped things would be better the next day. When he got back from school Monday afternoon, he changed into his work clothes and started to read his letter from Mother; presently a knock on his door interrupted him. He opened to a tearful Arilee.

She had no idea how beautiful she was, standing there hugging a red sweater around herself as brisk autumn wind teased the newly fallen leaves and sent the smell of woodsmoke in their direction. Wisps of her golden-brown hair curled softly around her face; he longed to caress those tresses.

"I'm sorry to bother you. I know you're still mad at me." She sniffled.

"Darlin', I'm not mad at you."

The pet name slipped out unintentionally. She blinked those blue-green eyes and froze.

"What's the matter?" he asked, deciding this wasn't the moment to make the conversation about *them*, unless by some miracle that's what she'd come to talk to him about.

"It's Nathaniel. He got in trouble at school today. He started fighting with another boy on the playground. The boy called his mother crazy, and Nat pushed him down and started pummeling him. He was taken to the principal's office and paddled. And when I tried to ask him about it to figure out what happened, he yelled at me, 'You're not my mama.' He's never talked to me that way before."

Adam exhaled. "Where is he now?"

"He and Macy are outside on the swing. Could you talk to him? He looks up to you so much. I don't know what to do, Adam. I feared this would happen. I can't protect them from the truth about Muriel, and it's too much for a little kid to carry. I shouldn't even have sent him to school yet."

"Arilee." He paused until she looked up at him. "I know you're hurting for him. But love doesn't mean shielding the one you love from all pain and heartache and hardship. It means being there with them when you can and trusting them to God when you can't."

She bit her bottom lip.

"But I'll talk to him if you want."

"It would mean the world to me. He needs a man to speak to, and Davis won't be home for days yet."

"You're doing a good job," he offered. "I know it's tough trying to be both mother and father to them. You're doing good."

She started getting teary again. He gave her a brief hug, wishing he could just hold her, then went toward Nathaniel.

"Macy," Arilee called. "Come, let's get snacks."

Macy ran to follow, nearly tripping over Woodrow in her haste, leaving Nathaniel on the swing.

"Hey, can you help me in the toolshed for a minute?" Adam faced Nathaniel.

The boy squinted at him. "Are you going to whip me?"

"No. Why would you think such a thing?"

"Travis says when he gets paddled at school, his daddy gives him a worse whipping when he gets home."

"Well, I'm not your daddy, am I? I hoped you'd help me for a bit."

"OK."

Nathaniel hopped along beside him. For several minutes there was no conversation except Adam's directions for straightening the shed. Then Nathaniel asked, "Did you ever get paddled at school, Mr. Adam?"

"More times than I can count."

"Really?"

"I wasn't a good boy. If I got bored, I'd think up trouble. Sometimes I'd blame my twin brother, and since we looked alike, he'd get punished instead of me."

"Did your brother die in the war?"

"Yes. He's in heaven now."

Nathaniel thought for a while. "I'm sorry that happened," he offered with more simple sincerity than Adam had received from most adults. Adam went and sat down on the leaf-covered ground, his back to the toolshed. He picked up a red maple leaf, twirling the stem in his fingers, admiring its simple perfection. The color reminded him of Arilee's sweater.

Nathaniel came and sat beside him.

"It's hard when you can't be with someone you love, isn't it?" Adam asked the boy.

Tears filled Nathaniel's eyes and his chin wobbled. "At school, everyone has a mama but me. I don't remember her. I don't know if she loves me or not. Sometimes I wish Aunt Ari was my mama 'stead, but it feels wicked to think that."

"It's not wicked. It's hard for a boy to be separated from his mother. It's hard not knowing if you'll see her again or when."

"*Is* my mama crazy?"

Nathaniel's big amber eyes pled for truth. Adam prayed silently for wisdom.

"You know I'm studying to be a doctor, right?"

Nathaniel nodded.

"I'm going to answer you as best I can. You know how sometimes you get sick? You get a fever, or sneeze, or cough, or feel weak?"

"Yes."

"Sometimes things happen that make a person get sick in their mind, to where they can't think right. Your mama had a lot of hard things happen to her, and it made her so sad she tried to harm other people and herself. Some folks took her to the state hospital, and she has to stay there until their doctors say she is better."

"But will she ever get better?"

"I don't know, Nat. I wish I could tell you."

"Could *you* be her doctor and make her well?"

"I'm not a doctor yet. Not for almost four more years."

"I hate Travis."

"Is he the boy you beat up?"

"Yes."

"Did hitting him make your mama better?"

"No-o," Nathaniel answered at last.

"Did hitting him make *you* better?"

"I'm not sorry."

"That's not what I asked. And I didn't ask if it made you *feel* better to hit him, 'cause I reckon it did for a while. But did it make you a better boy to beat up another boy?"

Nathaniel shook his head.

"Did hitting him make things better for Aunt Ari or your daddy?"

"No."

"OK then. Were you acting with wisdom?"

He shook his head.

"Listen, you know about the war. And how lots of people got killed like my brother and your Uncle Brax. Do you know what started the war?"

"Not really."

"A whole lot of grown-ups were unhappy with how their lives and their countries were. Instead of trying to fix those things, they decided to say mean things to each other and beat each other up. And it didn't make anything better, it made everything much worse and hurt lots of people who weren't even part of the fight."

120

"I was kinda mean to Aunt Ari."

"I heard something about snacks. Suppose we go check that out, and you give your Aunt Ari a hug?"

"OK." Nathaniel smiled for the first time. They rose and Adam tousled the boy's hair. Nathaniel ran ahead for the promised treat, but Adam walked more slowly, praying that each of them in Nathaniel's life would know how to train and direct his tender young heart.

CHAPTER 16

Friday, October 28, to Saturday, October 29,1921

"There's something I'm a little concerned about." Adam pulled Davis aside one Friday evening toward the end of October. "I haven't wanted to say anything to Arilee to worry her, but something's not right around here."

"What do you mean?"

"First, I noticed things in the toolshed look rifled through, even though I straightened it up Monday. I thought maybe Nat messed around, but I asked him, and he said he hasn't been in. I've not known him to be dishonest. And some of the things that were moved were too high up for him to reach anyway.

"I didn't think too much more about it, but then the next day, I noticed some bushes by the basement window had been trampled through. It could have been an animal or that danged cat. But there was a large boot print right by the window.

"I decided to check out the basement, and there, behind what's left of the broken brick wall, I found a bottle of hooch."

"What the devil?"

"Arilee knows I drank some in the war, but I haven't touched a drop in three years, and I made a vow to God I never would again. I didn't figure it was yours, either. But it got there somehow. I have a feeling someone's been snooping about the place. Maybe a vagrant now that the weather's getting cooler?"

Davis cussed and set his lips into a grim line. "This is why I didn't want the newspapers involved when y'all found that skeleton. Now we've been in the news, and we're a target for strange goings-on. You have a firearm?"

"Of course."

"Keep it handy. I assume you'd use it if needed?"

"If I ever catch anyone in the house who's not supposed to be, I'd certainly knock him off before he lays a finger on Arilee or the kids."

"I'm glad you're here and they aren't alone when I'm gone."

Adam nodded. That night he studied till his eyes were nearly glued shut but flipping off the light and flipping himself over in the bed, he still couldn't sleep. He thought maybe they ought to call the police, but he knew Davis would hate any more publicity, especially since news of the skeleton had hardly died down.

A noise outside startled him. Quickly, he pulled his trousers on, suspenders still attached, and padded silently out the carriage house door, met by cool evening air and a distant chorus of frogs. Flashlight in hand, he began walking the property, but he didn't see anyone or find anything amiss. He stood on the front porch, considering if he should go back to bed, when Davis opened the door.

"More trouble?"

"I don't know. Not that I can see, but I can't shake this sense I have about it."

"I'll check inside the house before I go back to bed."

"OK. Good night." Adam headed back to the carriage house. He hated the feeling of adrenaline shooting through his veins, the wild pounding of his heart. He'd lived in this exhausted state of hypervigilance in the trenches for weeks on end. For hours, he tossed and turned before finally falling into a nightmare-ridden sleep.

The next morning being Saturday, he didn't *have* to get up, but he felt lazy for not dragging himself out of bed till eight. Arilee always made a wonderful Saturday morning breakfast, usually bacon and eggs with grits and biscuits. Most Saturdays, he'd already put in a few hours of work by then. This morning he didn't even take time to shave. A thought had come to him sometime in the night. Dressing quickly, he headed to the house and met Davis in the hall.

"Have you checked the tunnel?" he asked.

"No, you?"

He shook his head. "I know you asked me to look at the structure and safety, but I've been busy with other projects. I wonder if it's being used."

Without another word, Davis started for the stairs. Adam tramped after him.

Davis didn't need the hammer to remove the board covering the tunnel entrance. It practically fell off when touched. Someone had already been messing with it. Adam climbed up and over the broken brick wall to join Davis in the small space and peer inside the tunnel.

The smell of lingering cigarette smoke met his nostrils. Davis shined his flashlight to reveal a bedroll, a few apples, and another bottle of whiskey.

Davis muttered words he wouldn't have said upstairs.

Adam grunted. "Should we call the police?"

"I'm home tonight. We'll see if we can catch this guy. If not, I guess we have no choice."

"No choice about what?" Arilee came down the steps, a basket of laundry on her hip. "Why aren't you boys up eating breakfast?"

"We seem to have another guest or pest in the house," Davis said. "Someone's using the tunnel."

"What? Someone's been *in* there?"

Davis grunted.

"Do you think it could be Daddy?"

Adam's heart constricted at the hope mixed with trepidation in her voice.

"It's possible." Davis exhaled. "Maybe he saw the article in the paper, learned Odessa is dead, and decided he wants the house now."

Davis turned back to Adam. "Let's go eat breakfast. We'll set a watch tonight. Probably your next project needs to be filling in this stupid tunnel once and for all. Take a look at it sometime today, would you?"

Adam froze. He didn't know which would be worse: going in there or admitting to them he couldn't.

"Let's check it out while we're down here," he suggested. "Then we can talk about it while we eat."

"Suit yourself." Davis handed him the flashlight and headed upstairs, not at all what he'd had in mind. Meanwhile, Arilee stood watching him. Adam took a deep breath and pushed his body through the narrow opening. He could look quickly. Make an assessment and get out. He wasn't a coward.

The tunnel wasn't nearly tall enough for his 6' 2" to stand up inside.

Beams lined the walls and ceiling at regular intervals, but the smell of damp earth permeated. He had crawled a few yards when his hand brushed something. It was a tree root, but for a moment, it sent him back to slogging through a muddy trench and hitting a corpse's rotting finger.

The images and sensations were back, pulsing through his mind faster than the wild beating of his heart. Filthy water up to his ankles or higher. Rats as large as cats scurrying from corpse to corpse, gorging on the bodies of the fallen. Lice. His scalp began to tingle. The gagging stench of human filth and death. The whistling of shells coming in. A bullet splintering a skull and the man next to him falling dead mid-sentence.

He couldn't breathe.

He couldn't get out of there fast enough.

"Adam, are you OK?" Arilee's sweet inquiry couldn't drive the shadows away. He hated that she stood witnessing his frailty.

"I need to wash my hands." He bolted up the stairs and stood at the kitchen sink, gulping deep breaths of air as he washed his hands and scrubbed his face. If he'd had anything in his stomach, he would have lost it.

What kind of man feared a tunnel?

And what kind of man *lived* in a tunnel like a phantom?

He still stood at the sink shaking when Arilee came up. She rested a hand lightly on his back, and even her touch made him flinch. She withdrew her hand.

"War memories?" she asked quietly.

He nodded.

"Sit down and let me get you some coffee. I heard you and Davis talking late last night, though I didn't know what about. If you been on high alert all night, no wonder you're tense now."

He exhaled. Her ability to connect the dots when his own brain was too muddled to sort it out impressed him. He'd had the heebie-jeebies over signs of an intruder, anxiety over danger to people he cared about, and then he'd discovered a vivid reminder of trench warfare right where it should never have been.

He took the black coffee gratefully and drank it even though it scalded his tongue and burned all down his throat. Upstairs, Davis and the children were romping; Macy's squeals of laughter and infectious giggles released some of the tension. He rubbed the back of his neck.

Arilee put bacon on the cast iron griddle. He watched her mixing up waffle batter. Her cheerful apron, bright blue with yellow flowers, the sunshine coming through the windows, the scents of breakfast, and the bitter taste of the coffee slowly worked to ease his heart rate back to normal. Arilee came over and took his empty cup, then refilled it, adding sugar and cream this time. She set it down before him, then stood behind him and gently rested her hands on his shoulders.

"You're tight as a new fiddle string," she commented and began kneading the knots out of his neck and shoulders. Did she have any idea what her touch did to him? Even as his muscles relaxed, his skin blazed with the feel of her soft but strong fingers.

It lasted but a minute, and his gruff "thanks" didn't convey half of what he wanted to say. But Davis and the kids entered, and Macy clambered up in his lap for her morning "lump of sugar" dipped in his coffee, followed by a kiss on his cheek.

"Scratchy," she said and made a face, causing the adults to chuckle.

The breakfast was refreshingly normal and familial, and by the time they were done Adam announced: "I'm going to start on trimming the rose bushes. Need to work outside a bit to clear my head. I'll see about taking down the rest of the brick wall after lunch."

Once certain Adam was out of earshot, Arilee turned on Davis. "I'm pretty sure crawling in creepy old tunnels is well outside Adam's job description."

"What's your beef?"

"It's too much like the trenches, Davis. He looked absolutely sick when he came out of there after a couple minutes."

Davis shrugged. "It's hard the first few times you have to relive war memories. Flying was that way for me for a while. He'll work through it."

"I don't think it's right."

"He'll resent you if you try to interfere, Sis."

This gave her pause. Adam certainly hadn't been happy with her matchmaking attempts. Still, the thought of him having to go in there alone and face tormenting memories unsettled her.

What had he told her the other day? "Love doesn't mean shielding the one you love from all pain and heartache and hardship. It means being there with them when you can, and trusting them to God when you can't."

Of course, she didn't *love* Adam. But she cared about him. That was OK. Wasn't it?

∞ ∞ ∞

With the brick wall removed, they had easy access to the tunnel entrance. Adam was worn out by supper and filled with dread over trying to nab the intruder tonight and having to fill in the tunnel next week.

The simple supper at the kitchen table lightened his mood with easy conversation, but once the kids were tucked in bed, the three adults met back in the kitchen to discuss a strategy. The men would take turns having one man watching in the dark basement and the other outside, scanning the yard for signs of a trespasser.

"Please tell me I have some purpose other than making coffee?" Arilee sighed as Davis and Adam went over every scenario they could think of and their imaginary response to it.

"Sis, if you hear gunshots or things get out of hand, call the police."

She rolled her eyes. "I could—"

"No." Davis stood and shoved his hands in his pockets. "Arilee, don't you go down in the basement, and don't you go outside. I need you safe and keeping the kids safe."

"Jefferson Davis Rutledge."

"Please, Arilee," Adam interjected. "I couldn't stand it if something happened to you. How rattled I felt this morning would be a hundred times worse."

"Fine," she huffed. "I can't fight the both of you and a ruffian too."

Davis rolled his eyes. "Ruffian? Really? For your sake, I hope we find a man in tights and doublet spouting sonnets."

"At least maybe he'd have something to say worth listening to." She turned to wash the dishes.

Adam and Davis stepped out onto the porch together to confirm their plans for the outside.

"We think the tunnel leads north?" Adam gazed out into the dark yard.

"Yeah. I'll focus my efforts over there. I'll take the first shift outside, now till midnight, then we can switch."

Adam nodded and absently fingered his Colt pistol.

"Don't shoot unless you have no choice," Davis warned.

"Have a little faith in me, would you?"

"OK, right, sorry. I appreciate you helping me with this."

They parted and Adam headed for the basement after stopping back by the kitchen first. Arilee gave him half a dozen large chewy gingersnaps, and he went down. Alone in the dark, he heard every noise of the old house. The simple sounds of Arilee moving about the kitchen, singing softly, soothed his frayed nerves.

Again, he wondered about the sort of man who would willingly live in a tunnel. If it was Mr. Rutledge, would the reunion with his children be a peaceful reconciliation or would he continue to wreak havoc in their lives?

After a while, Arilee fell silent upstairs, and in the pitch black, his mind began to go back to that other darkness. Bile rose in his throat as guilt and regret and fear began their assault. By the grace of God, he'd use the rest of his time on earth repairing bodies rather than maiming them, but could all the doctoring in the world ever absolve him from the knowledge he'd doubtless taken someone else's brother as surely as they had taken his?

He wasn't a warrior, but he'd shot men so close he'd seen their faces crumple in death. He wasn't a warrior, but he had a medal for things he could remember only in nightmares now. How could he, Adam Harrison, a man who was terrified of sitting in a cellar alone, be the same man who had been declared a hero of the Meuse-Argonne Offensive?

Alone. That was why. He hadn't been alone. Even after Joshua's death, when he'd started to unravel, he'd still been surrounded by brothers-in-arms. Some had pulled him to the darkness, others to the light, but he'd never actually been *alone*.

Nothing scared him as much as being alone.

Ready to escape so much self-revelation, he began murmuring aloud Psalm 27, the constant prayer of his heart.

"The LORD is my light and my salvation; whom shall I fear?

The LORD is the strength of my life; of whom shall I be afraid?"

all the way to

"Wait on the LORD: be of good courage, and He shall strengthen thine heart: wait, I say, on the LORD."

Rain hit the high, narrow basement window. The door opened above, momentarily flooding the space with light before it was closed again. He smelled apple cider and heard soft footfalls. The glow of a flashlight grew closer.

"Thought you might need something," Arilee whispered, holding out a warm mug to him. Their hands brushed in the dark.

He sat down with his back to the wall. She sat beside him; their shoulders touched.

"Davis'll throw a conniption you're down here." He kept his voice low.

She shrugged. "He'll get over it. He never really gets angry."

"You're not supposed to be here."

"I know."

"Shouldn't have a light."

"Nope."

"And we shouldn't be talking."

"Definitely not."

A flash of lightning outside momentarily lit the basement. A low rumble of thunder followed.

"I thought Davis unkind, making you take the basement first, but he's got to stand out in a storm, so I guess it's about fair. I finished reading the letters from the war trunk, and now I have to go through the hatbox the bats got into. I grew uneasy being by myself in the library, so I decided I'd see how you were faring."

"I was growing uneasy being by myself in the basement," he admitted.

"I bet. I hate this place in the day, especially since you discovered the skeleton. And now this." She sighed.

"You do have to wonder about the stories that tunnel could tell. I wish it was the entrance to the cave in *Tom Sawyer.* You and me could go exploring in there together and find your lost Confederate treasure."

"Sounds fun. I'd gladly be Becky Thatcher to your Tom Sawyer."

He sipped the drink. The comfortable silence and stillness made him acutely aware of her breathing, of her nearness. The cider wasn't the only thing warming him.

He heard a sound from the direction of the tunnel. She heard it too, for she tensed at the same time he did and switched off the flashlight. He set down his mug, rose, and stepped silently forward.

"Stay back," he whispered at her.

She scooted back a few inches, but he didn't have time to worry over it, for the sounds were growing louder. The board was pushed from within and out crawled a man.

Adam jumped on him in the dark. The intruder gave a shout and then promptly fell to the ground and rolled on top of Adam, punching him in the eye, the jaw. Adam reached for his gun. Arilee turned on the flashlight, shone it right at them, and then began screaming for them to stop. The attacker rolled off Adam and stood staring at Arilee.

Adam struggled to his feet, trying to make sense of what was happening. He brushed past the dirt-covered young man who had just bashed his face and hurried over to Arilee who had gone white and started hyperventilating.

"It's my brother. Brax."

Adam caught her before she hit the brick floor in a dead faint.

CHAPTER 17

Saturday, October 29, 1921

Arilee came to upstairs lying on the small library sofa. Adam, with a bleeding lip and swollen-shut eye, knelt beside her, wiping her face with a cool, damp cloth.

Davis paced the room, hands fisted, veins popping, shocked eyes staring at—Brax? Dirty and disheveled, her younger brother sprawled across the armchair. Arilee bolted upright, but, still lightheaded, sank back down.

"Hey, hey, take it easy. Are you ok?" Adam rested his hands lightly on her shoulders.

She nodded and wondered how she'd gotten up the basement steps, even though it wasn't important at the moment.

"Brax," she whispered, trembling. "How did this happen?"

Davis spun on his heel. "Yes, Braxton, tell her," he spat out. "*You* tell her what you just told me."

Brax studied her; his deep blue eyes were bloodshot. Instead of explaining the confusion over his death, he muttered, "There wasn't anything to come back for, so I didn't." His gravelly voice couldn't cloak the awfulness of his admission.

"You mean you—you *chose* not to come back? But we thought you were dead."

"That was the point."

Arilee sat up slowly. She fished for a handkerchief in her pocket.

"Tell her, Brax," Davis demanded. When Brax said nothing, Davis swung to Arilee. "Turns out he faked his death. No concern that he destroyed all our lives and killed our mama."

"Mama's dead?" A note of regret registered in Brax's slurred voice.

"Yeah. A few weeks after she got the telegram about *your* death. Influenza. And a broken heart."

"Look, I—"

He ran a hand through his brown hair, and Arilee noted a fancy watch on his wrist. So many questions. She couldn't even think them all in words. Brax. Brax was alive. Brax had been alive all this time letting them think he was dead?

Adam cleared his throat. "If you're OK, Arilee, maybe I should go."

At the same moment Davis said, "No, you deserve to be here," Arilee said, "Wait, I'll get ice for your eye," and Brax asked, "Who the devil is he?"

"Adam Harrison," Arilee answered. "He's been helping us with fixing up the place."

"Adam Harrison? 'The evil twin' Adam Harrison?"

Heat crept up Arilee's face; she dared not look at Adam, who made a sound in his throat. But Davis replied, "Yes, Brax. The war matured some of us."

"You're just like Dad, always thinking you know everything."

Davis leaned into Brax's face. "Seems to me *you're* the one like Dad, walking out on everyone and leaving us to sort through the disaster you left behind."

Arilee sobbed aloud and fled across the hall to the kitchen. Adam followed her, while Davis and Brax continued yelling at each other. She wrapped up ice in a towel for Adam's black eye and busted lip and handed it to him. He took her trembling hands and held them a moment, looking at her compassionately through his one good eye.

"I'm sorry my brother hit you," she said awkwardly.

"I'm sorry—well, shoot, Arilee, I don't know what to say. I'm sorry he did this to y'all. The war messed up a lot of men real bad."

She nodded, wiping her wet cheeks in vain. She took the loaf of bread off the counter and sliced thick wedges, wielding the knife with greater force than needed.

"Brax, Davis, stop fighting and come in here," she called weakly.

They came, the hostility between them tangible.

She studied Brax. He'd always been roguishly good-looking, but there was an edge to him now that left her feeling wary. He smelled of cigarette smoke, alcohol, and cheap perfume. She walked over to him and gave him a hug. Stiffly, he hugged her back.

"Brax, you broke my heart. I have mourned for you every day for three years. But you *are* alive, and I love and forgive you, regardless of how you came to be standing in my kitchen tonight. Now sit down and eat and tell us why you've been hiding in our basement and what you plan to do with yourself."

No one sat.

"Your kitchen and your basement? Didn't the house go to Dad when Odessa died? Is Dad dead?"

"We don't know," Davis muttered. "No one's been able to find him. We kept living here because there's no one else to."

"I saw in the newspaper about you finding the skeleton. That's how I knew y'all were here. We can finally find the treasure now."

How many times had she and Brax dreamed together about finding the treasure and all that they would do when they did?

Davis pushed away the bread with apple butter she offered him. An hour ago, she'd whispered to Adam, "Davis never really gets angry," and now he spoke through clenched teeth.

"So, it's money, is it? You're back because you want money."

"I want what's coming to me."

"I'll gladly give you what's coming to you!" Davis threw himself at Brax, and when Adam tried to step between them, he got knocked to the floor.

"Would you both stop beating up Adam?" Arilee stamped her foot. "He's the only sane one here."

Brax took a swing at Davis, but Adam caught his arm at the same time that Davis lunged for it, knocking Adam off balance and nearly to the ground again.

Adam cleared his throat and spoke with authority such as Arilee had never heard from him.

"Listen here. I don't care who did who wrong, *your sister* deserves better than this from both of you. Brax, you're loaded to the gills, and you reek. Davis, he's a thieving and conniving piece of trash for what he did, but he's your brother. And before God, if I had even one more chance to see my brother, I'd for sure deck him for a trick like this, but I'd hug his neck and thank God he was alive too."

Silently her brothers stared at each other.

"Every night, Brax." Davis's hard tone covered a wretched desperation. "Every night for two years I dreamed about your plane going down. I was flying that day. I watched you lose control and begged God to help you. I had two aces on my tail who shot my propeller to Swiss cheese and put a couple bullets through my arm with their Lugers. As soon as I landed, I took off running through the woods to where I thought you were. And when I got there and saw the inferno engulfing your plane and what I thought was your body, I stood there and screamed at God and nearly bled to death. Then I relived it over and over, night after night—"

"It wasn't against you, Davis."

"No? I came home to find our family gone to pieces over what happened to you. I lost Mama and Muriel over what you did. And now for you to waltz in here making demands and saying you had nothin' to come back for. Good God, Brax, that's the nastiest thing I ever heard. You did worse than anything Dad ever thought of, to put another man's corpse in your cockpit and set it ablaze. It's a lie conjured up from the pit of hell—"

Arilee gasped and recoiled at the awfulness of Davis's revelations, still piecing together the story that must have been explained while she lay passed out. Brax hadn't just run off, he'd premeditated making Davis and everyone else think he was dead.

Brax let out a string of profanity, and Davis pinned him to the wall.

"I swear to heaven," Adam hissed, pushing them apart, "if either of you makes Arilee cry again, I will call the police and my pastor too. Brax, go outside to the room on the back porch and sleep it off. Davis, go to bed!"

Without another word, Brax stumbled out of the kitchen. Arilee ran upstairs to get fresh linens for the bed, but by the time she returned, Brax was nearly asleep on the bare mattress of the circuit rider's room. Inside, the air was stale but the space, clean. She stepped forward and covered him with a blanket and kissed his forehead.

"I didn't know about Mama," he murmured. "I didn't know, Arilee."

"Go to sleep, Brax. We'll talk in the morning."

She shut the door behind her and went back inside. Davis had gone. Turning to Adam, who still stood in the kitchen she said, "Why don't you go get some rest too?"

He nodded. She followed him out the back door. The rain had stopped, but the air remained heavy, and a stiff breeze blew. She wrapped her arms around herself.

"Are you OK?" He studied her in the dim light of the cloud-covered moon.

"I could ask you the same."

"I got a little chin music," he said, waving at his face. "You received quite a shock. And it isn't exactly the joyful reunion we could hope for. If things get out of hand between your brothers, or if you just need to talk about it, come get me, all right?"

She nodded. "Thank you, Adam. For everything."

He shrugged. "It appears I have a lot of making up to do for all those months of being 'the evil twin' if Brax still remembered that the minute he heard my name."

"I'm so sorry. I should never have said such a thing. I was completely inexperienced and didn't know how to manage a classroom at all."

"I'm pretty sure I was the bane of every one of my teachers' existence, experienced or not. At least till college."

She laughed softly. "You've improved significantly."

"That's high praise, Miss Rutledge, ma'am."

She reached for him, to playfully push him on his way, but instead, he caught her hand and pulled her close. She rested her head against his firm chest, and his strong arms moved around her protectively yet tenderly. His embrace warmed her against the cool of the night, shielded her against the disturbing revelations she still hadn't wholly comprehended.

Several minutes passed. The rhythm of his heartbeat, the methodic dripping of water off the trees onto the tin roof above, and the familiar scent of his aftershave were like salve on the raw wounds of her heart. She wanted to *stay* right here.

At last, he whispered fiercely: "Arilee, you *are* worth coming back for." He kissed the top of her head, and then strode off into the night, whistling "How 'Ya Gonna Keep 'Em Down on the Farm?" on his way to the carriage house.

Undeniably, whatever stirred inside her at the voice and face and touch of Adam Harrison was not at all the same thing she felt toward either of those brothers of hers ready to tear each other to pieces.

CHAPTER 18

Sunday, October 30, 1921

A s sunlight poured through a thinly curtained window, Brax rolled over and fell off the bed onto the floor. Cursing, he flopped back onto the mattress and squinted, trying to remember where he was and why. No woman lay tangled up in his sheets. He moved his arm in all directions, but no empty bottle of giggle juice hit his hand. Dirt streaked his clothes.

Oh, right. The tunnel and the fight. Wisteria House.

He hadn't planned to meet up with his siblings, per se, but at least his sleeping quarters had improved from a blanket on the basement floor to an old rope bed with quilts.

He swung his legs over the side and rested his head in his hands. What to do? If he stayed here, Davis might turn him in, and Arilee would preach at him. And what of that Adam fellow? He'd mentioned calling the police.

He needed to get back to Cuba and Bazán. See if his boss had cooled down and was ready to take him on again. But he should at least talk to Arilee about the treasure. She'd always believed in the legend. Perhaps in the remodeling she'd found some clues.

He shuffled inside the house, following the scents of coffee and fried ham. The new kitchen, though too cheery for his taste, suited his sister. Her face brightened like the sunlight streaming through the window when she saw him. She was alone except for a small girl who sat on the floor, pretending to feed a doll with a silver baby spoon.

"Good morning." Arilee stepped over to hug him and kiss his cheek. Dangit, she looked and acted so much like Mama that his heart ached more than his head.

"Where is everyone?"

"Davis has gone to visit Muriel, as he does every Sunday. Adam took Nathaniel to church."

"How's he going to explain that black eye and swollen lip? He gonna snitch on me?"

"Davis asked him to keep quiet about you being here. Bath or food first?"

"Coffee."

"Sit down." She waved to the built-in kitchen table. "I've got coffee and homemade donuts, but you'll have to answer some of my questions to get them." She set a large, steaming mug in front of him.

"Where's Muriel?"

"Milledgeville. After we got the telegram about you, she was convinced Davis would die. She wasn't right after giving birth." Arilee nodded her head in the direction of the little girl with the doll. "Then Mama died, and Muriel spiraled out of control. Odessa got her arrested, and the judge ordered her committed." Arilee looked over at the child, who had stopped playing and was staring at Brax. "I can tell you the rest later."

"You wook wike Daddy," the girl said, coming to stand before Brax.

"You look prettier than your daddy," he replied. "What's your name?"

"Macy Jane Rut-wedge. Who are you?"

"I'm your Uncle Brax."

Macy looked at Arilee for confirmation as to whether or not this was true. "Uncle Brax is my brother, like Nat is your brother." Arilee attempted to explain.

"You raised her then?" Brax asked. It didn't surprise him. Arilee would care for her people or die in the attempt.

Arilee nodded, setting donuts and ham before him. "But it's my turn for a question. Where have you been for the past three years?"

"'On a hill far away.' Europe. France mostly. A bit in Monaco and Italy. I went to Northern Africa for a while. Russia for a stint."

"Doing what?"

"Ah, no, that's two questions. It's my turn. How'd you end up here?" He spoke around a mouthful of donut.

She briefly explained about moving to Wisteria House with Mama and Muriel. "Aunt Odessa finally died this past June," she concluded. "And Jewel left on some mysterious errand immediately afterward. We used the life insurance from your death to fix up the house. I don't know how you being alive changes our claim on the money."

"I have no desire to have a legal status again. As far as Uncle Sam's concerned, I'm still dead."

"Didn't you have to have papers to come back?"

"Not the way I came in."

"What way was that?"

"Too many questions. Way past my turn." He pulled a cigarette and matchbook out of his pocket, but Arilee shook her head at him.

"Not in the house. Adam told me the smell makes him relive the trenches."

"You and this Adam fellow sweet on each other?" He might have been a bit plastered last night, but he hadn't missed the way the once so-called "evil twin" had been looking at Arilee.

Arilee flushed and took too long to say, "He's just a good friend. He's done a marvelous job restoring and updating the house."

"I don't care if he built the house. He sure seems like more than a faithful employee. Swept you right up in his arms when you fainted and carried you up the stairs like he'd been planning to do that his whole life."

Her blush deepened. "He's a medical student at Emory. He lives in the carriage house, and Davis pays him to do all the work of upkeep plus oversee the renovation. As you can see, we now have electricity and running water."

Brax nodded. "It's a sight improved from when I last saw it."

"My turn. What have you been doing?"

"'Sinking deep in sin, far from the peaceful shore.'"

"You still speak in hymns, I see."

"I have a job flying. My boss and I had a falling out, so I'm giving him some time to miss his best pilot."

"Why here? Why now?" She chewed on her bottom lip, trying to hide the hopeful look in her eyes.

He grabbed another donut and took a bite, the hot cinnamon-sugar crusted pastry melting in his mouth.

"I propose an arrangement. Let me land in the porch room occasionally. I'll take care of myself, though I'm not going to turn down food. You won't concern yourself with my comings and goings, and I won't concern myself with yours. In exchange, I'll stay legally dead and out of everybody's way."

"I don't know, Brax. Is it even moral to hide that you're alive? And probably we owe the government your life insurance money."

"Please don't tell me you plan to repay the government that got us into the fool war in the first place."

"What do you have against Davis and me?"

"Nothing. But I'm not interested in being part of family life. I'm not the little boy you remember, Arilee. I know you. You'll want to mother me, and Davis'll want to fix me. Pretty soon, you'll be trying to drag me to church or talk to me about repenting of my sins and all that garbage."

"Oh, Brax." She sat down opposite him in the kitchen banquette; the little girl came over and climbed into her lap.

"Did you *ever* hear from Dad?" he asked after a while.

"No. Never. We don't know if he knows about Mama dying and you."

"Don't guess he really cares if any of us are dead or alive."

"I can't believe that."

"You're still like Mama. Always hoping the best about everybody. Well, you can believe me: I've seen the world, and everyone is out for themselves. Trying to have a moment of happiness before they die and it's all over."

"You can't believe it's all so meaningless."

"I can, and it is."

"I know many selfless people," Arilee said, apparently oblivious that she should be at the top of the list. "Davis goes to visit Muriel every Sunday. He could divorce her and remarry, but he won't."

"Yeah, but he's not happy, is he?"

"Happiness isn't everything. He's at peace. He can sleep at night knowing he's acting in integrity."

"Know what else helps you sleep at night? Booze."

"Brax!"

"You're good, Arilee. And I admire it. If 'trust and obey, for there's no other way' makes you happy, then I'm glad for you. What makes me happy is indeed another way—doing whatever the heck I want."

She studied him for a long moment. There wasn't condemnation there, rather a sorrow smarting worse than if she'd chewed him up and spit him out as he knew he deserved.

Arilee had been his best friend growing up. She had made his boyhood so much *fun* with her big imagination, ready stories, and fearless participation in his grand schemes. They'd built a tree house together. They'd climbed up on the roof to watch Halley's comet in 1910. They'd raced Dad's old horses bareback down to the swimming hole and jumped in.

Now that he'd feasted amply on the pleasures of sin himself, maybe he could someday forgive Dad for adultery, stealing, even abandonment. He'd done plenty of all three himself.

But what their father had done to sixteen-year-old Arilee? No. Brax would *never* forgive that.

"Eat up and go take a bath," his sister said now. "Bring me all your dirty clothes to wash."

"I have others. You don't have to."

"I'm going to try to keep you in my debt as much as I can," she teased.

He looked away from her smile as fast as he could. Her goodness and kindness were too painful a contrast to his own festering soul and too painful a reminder of the past he could never quite outrun.

∞ ∞ ∞

Adam couldn't concentrate in church for worrying about Arilee's interactions with Brax. He received plenty of comments about his black eye and busted lip and made up several entertaining versions of how he'd come by them, each so ridiculous it would be clear he didn't want to talk about it.

"Are you in some kind of trouble?" Pastor Andy asked him, pulling him aside after the service.

"No. First honest black eye I've gotten in my life," Adam assured him. "There was a little, uh, *incident*, last night, where the family appeared to be in danger, but everything's under control now."

He hoped that last part was true.

On the drive home, he broke the news to Nathaniel as simply as he could.

"He was hiding all along?" Nathaniel asked, dumbfounded at Adam's tale.

"Yeah. Pretty sockdolager game of hide-and-seek, huh?"

"Wow, I want to see him. Is he going to hide again?"

"Don't know."

Back at the house, he and Nathaniel stepped inside to the aroma of roast

140

and potatoes for Sunday dinner. In the kitchen, Arilee stood at the stove, stirring gravy and staring into space with red-rimmed eyes.

"Where's Macy?" Nathaniel came in loud and oblivious to the undercurrent of tension.

"Upstairs in the hall playing with the blocks." Arilee hugged the boy and sent him on his way.

"How are you?" Adam asked when Nathaniel ran out of earshot.

Arilee pulled the gravy off the heat and turned to him. "Oh, Adam, he's such a mess. A lost, angry mess." She told him about their conversations from the morning.

"There's one thing he hasn't answered," Adam said slowly. "Why is he back *here*? Is it really just to find the treasure? He may say he doesn't care about family, but he can 'tell that to Sweeney'; I think there's more going on."

"I hope you're right."

"There's a difference between numbing your pain and being *happy*."

"He doesn't have any interest in doing what's right. I don't think he even believes God exists anymore."

"Arilee."

She finally met his eyes.

"Love 'hopeth all things.' You're the most loving person I've ever met. *You've* got to hope for Brax if anybody will. Davis is too angry. Your parents are gone. But whatever the reason, and however it happened, God saved Brax's life and brought him back here."

She pulled rolls out of the oven. "Thanks, Adam. I knew you'd listen and help me know how I should see it. I think you're the best friend I've ever had."

She said it with her everlasting sincerity, as if she'd never had any doubt in his ability to help her handle this. She stepped over and lightly touched his bruised chin and lip.

"Does it hurt much?"

He shook his head.

"Your eye?

"It'll be fine."

His eye still stung like blazes, truthfully, but her gentle fingers touching his face, and the memory of holding her close last night, made it not only the first honest black eye he'd ever had, but the only one he'd do over again without a second thought.

CHAPTER 19

Thursday, November 10, to Friday, November 11, 1921

"**A**fternoon, Rutledge." Billy Sweet greeted Davis as he stepped into the attorney's private office at Harris and Associates on Edgewood and Ivy. "Come in. I hope you didn't have to take off work for our meeting."

Davis took the seat Billy waved him toward, and the young attorney came around from his desk to sit in the leather chair opposite, foregoing his cane but limping noticeably from his war injury.

"I already had a few days off, and your request to meet actually mirrored my own. Apparently, I've inherited a new legal dilemma." Davis leaned forward in the chair and spun his fedora in his hands. Between Muriel's case and the Wisteria House estate, he was already here every few months; Billy's sound advice kept Davis from complete despair over the two thorny situations.

"Please tell me you don't have anything more complicated than a house where the inheritor has disappeared, or a wife sentenced to the state asylum."

"How about a brother raised from the dead?"

For the next few minutes, Davis told the story of how they had discovered Brax and what Brax had told them about staging his own death. The star young attorney listened slack-jawed.

"Rutledge, if I were giving out awards for the most unbelievable situations, you would win every year. What do you plan to do?"

"I don't know. He apparently has a job flying cargo for a private company and wants us to let him use the guest room off the porch whenever he's passing through town."

"But he doesn't plan for that to be his primary residence?"

"No. He hung around a week or so after we found him. He looked for the family's mythical lost Confederate treasure. Then he left, and we haven't heard from him since, though he promised he'd be back through occasionally."

"What was his demeanor while he was here?"

Davis shrugged. "He drinks and smokes and swears and generally is a pain in the rear to have around. But my sister holds illusions that our mother's prayers will finally be answered, that he's going to get right with Jesus. In reality, he's going to break Sis's heart again."

"And Adam Harrison and the kids are the only other ones who know he's there? Would Adam turn him in as a deserter, do you think?"

"Naw. Adam's sweet on Arilee. He ain't goin' to do nothing to upset her. It doesn't seem like his way, anyhow. He lost his brother in the war, so he wants us to reconcile with ours now that we got him back. But do I have a moral or legal obligation to notify the authorities?"

Billy coughed into his fist. "I can't say I've ever encountered anything like this."

"Here's the other thing: when he was reported killed in action, Mama got his insurance money. After she died, Arilee and I used it to fix up the house. You know, the house we don't legally own and that our father could come and take from us at any time. Do we have an obligation to repay all the money to the government now?"

Billy coughed again and rubbed his right knee. "That's sticky. My guess is that the obligation would be on your brother, not you."

"But to complicate it even more, *I'm* the one who found Brax's downed plane and reported him killed. I will swear on the Bible that I believed him dead, but it doesn't look good on me, you know. Some might think I participated in a scheme to collect the money. I want to be careful to be aboveboard here, but honestly, I don't want to turn in my brother for a crime that potentially carries the death penalty."

"I'm going to have to make some discreet inquiries." Billy stretched out his bad leg and circled his jaw in thought. Outside an automobile horn honked and two drivers started yelling at each other. "This will fall under military law because his crime was desertion, and there may possibly be other charges for faking his death. What kind of service record did he have?"

"Lied about his age. Joined at seventeen years old. Made ace at eighteen. Shot down a total of seven planes."

"His record will help his case. I doubt he'd get the death penalty under any circumstances, but he could definitely be sentenced to Leavenworth. It would also go in his favor if he would turn himself in rather than being caught. Any chance of that?"

Davis shook his head and spun his hat again. "He's been running away from God and the family for the past four years."

"Let me see what I can find out for you," Billy said, coughing again. The young attorney had residual effects from mustard gas poisoning in the war. "The war's done and the soldiers discharged, so it's not as if anyone is looking for him. We have a bit of time to figure out the best approach. Now, tell me about Muriel."

Davis shifted. "She's about the same. The staff assure me she is being treated well and that they are doing all they can for her. I don't believe things will ever improve where she is, but what can I do?"

"Legally, we're at a bit of a dead end, but with your permission, I'd like to write to Dr. Adolph Meyer at Johns Hopkins. He's one of the leading psychiatrists in the nation. If you could secure a copy of Muriel's medical file from Milledgeville, we'll include it in our letter. I want to see if Dr. Meyer can make any recommendations, or even if he or one of his associates would be willing to travel here to make their own assessment and diagnosis. A report from a man of his standing would surely be of value in negotiating with the Milledgeville staff as well as the judge."

"Thank you," Davis stammered, at a loss for words over Billy's above-and-beyond help with his case. "This is a top-notch idea."

"I'm afraid it's my only one at the moment, but as long as you're willing to fight for Muriel, I'll be here alongside you."

A tiny spark of hope kindled in Davis's heart for the first time since the hearing. His daily awareness of his wife's confinement in that dehumanizing, demoralizing place weighed him down like an overloaded plane flying through a headwind. The burden felt a bit lighter as he shook Billy's hand and headed back to Wisteria House.

∞ ∞ ∞

Thursday afternoon, persistent knocking sent Arilee to the door in the midst of rolling out biscuits for supper. Instantly aware of her flour-dusted and grease-spattered apron, she greeted Margaret Rose Woodhouse, the epitome of style and sophistication in an embroidered dress of green velveteen with a fur collar.

"Mrs. Woodhouse. Come in. Would you care for some tea?"

"Please, don't trouble yourself. I know this is rather an inconvenient time of day and tomorrow's the holiday. I happened to be near the area, and wondered if you might have a quick update for me about the letters."

"Oh, yes, hmm." Stalling for time, Arilee said, "If you don't mind sitting in the kitchen to talk, I've a pot of vegetable soup on the stove I need to finish assembling."

"Certainly." Mrs. Woodhouse followed Arilee into the kitchen and looked around the house appraisingly. "You've done a lot since I last visited. Your hired man has done a good job."

"Adam? Why he's practically a member of the family now."

Margaret Woodhouse sat across from Nathaniel at the table while Arilee stirred the soup and continued peeling potatoes. The boy looked up from his page of sums.

"We have a new member of the family now," he informed Mrs. Woodhouse. "My Uncle Brax was hiding in the tunnel, and he wasn't dead at all."

"That'll keep, Nat," Arilee gave him her sternest look which, if her brothers' typical reception of it were any indication, wasn't frightening at all.

"Mrs. Woodhouse, this is my nephew, Nathaniel. Davis's son. Nat, you can finish your homework later. I need to talk about grown-up things with Mrs. Woodhouse. Please go play with Macy."

"Yes'm." Glancing back at Mrs. Woodhouse, he added, "Mr. Adam is filling in the tunnel now because Uncle Brax said the treasure isn't there."

"Go on now, Nat," Arilee urged. "Macy's in the library."

"Yes'm."

Arilee tried to keep her face impassive as she turned to face Mrs. Woodhouse. Which, again, if her brothers' usual reaction were any indication, probably wasn't impassive at all.

"Tunnel? Treasure? Brax not dead at all?"

Arilee exhaled. "What do you want? If it's money, I've got a few pieces of antique jewelry I'll give you to leave us in peace."

"I want a story. Your nephew gave me the headlines for three. You decide which one you want to tell me, and I'll forget I heard the others."

Obviously, Arilee couldn't tell the woman about Brax. And Mrs. Woodhouse reporting about a missing treasure might send all sorts of other fortune-seekers around to cause trouble.

"All right. I have an old letter to show you. Wait here."

Arilee stepped across to the library and went to the desk. Now a third of the way through the polluted hatbox, this letter proved her most interesting find thus far. It answered the mystery of the tunnel and would surely prove a compelling story for Mrs. Woodhouse.

Returning to the kitchen, she smoothed the brittle page before the reporter. "There's a tunnel in the basement. The entrance was behind the brick wall, there where we found the skeleton. The tunnel is quite old; Adam is filling it in to make sure it's not a structural liability and so the kids don't go in there and get hurt."

"And what was the purpose of this tunnel?"

"It's in the letter."

While Arilee went back to chopping vegetables, Mrs. Woodhouse read aloud:

My dearest Luella,

I received several letters from you yesterday and cannot thank you enough for them. They were a flash of color in a world hopelessly gray, from the uniforms around me, to the skies above me, to the haze of smoke covering the battlefields. Indeed, even our cause is gray to me, for I cannot feel confident that we are entirely in the right, nor condemnation that we are completely in the wrong. I fight to defend my home and my liberties, but I cannot defend that institution that has so defined my home and deprived other men of those liberties. Your ardor in our secret cause has been a balm to me. You are a worthy woman, and the hope that I shall return to spend my latter days with you and the children at Wisteria House is the only earthly consolation left me.

You will forgive the melancholy tone of my letter. The deaths of my sons and son-in-law weigh upon me at every hour. They say Sherman shall march upon Georgia. I beg of you to keep yourselves safe. Cease the courageous operation that drew us together. Make Wisteria House your fortress, secure against attacks by the enemy. Above all, I beg of you, keep <u>all</u> my girls safe.

Your most affectionate husband,
Ezekiel

"The 'secret cause' and 'courageous operation'—am I correct that this tunnel was part of the Underground Railroad?"

"Yes. My grandfather, Colonel Rutledge, went from being a slaveholder to an abolitionist. His second wife, my grandmother Luella, was also an abolitionist, and they met at some sort of secret meeting."

"I should like to copy this letter, if I may," Mrs. Woodhouse asked. "I may reprint parts of it in my story."

"That's fine. As long as it doesn't bring the Klan to our door because my grandparents helped slaves escape."

Mrs. Woodhouse gave a slight shrug. "Surely you are not afraid of a little opposition over what is right, Miss Rutledge. Not after having such stalwart grandparents as these."

"To be honest, I should prefer not to have *anyone* come to our door at present," Arilee replied wearily enough for Mrs. Woodhouse to back off with her sermon. The journalist copied the letter in silence, and Arilee seasoned the soup. Adam came in the back door in his work clothes, singing "'Round Her Neck She Wears a Yeller Ribbon."

"I'm going to work in the tunnel," he called before Arilee could warn him to be quiet. He glanced into the kitchen and saw Mrs. Woodhouse.

The woman practically jumped up at his announcement. "I should like to observe."

Adam's eyes widened. "I must say, ma'am, it's rather a mess down there.

148

Every day I mix up a batch of mortar and fill in another section with rocks and concrete. It's quite a ways from being finished yet."

"Good. I want to go in and see the tunnel for myself. Perhaps take a photograph."

Adam looked at Arilee. She gave a helpless shrug.

"It, uh, it's a very small opening; you would have to crawl through." Adam measured the air with his hands.

"And you crawl through there?"

"Yes."

"Well, since you are a good foot taller than I, and quite a bit broader, I am sure I can manage."

"It's creepy inside." Adam tried one last time. "Reminds me of the trenches."

"I am sorry to hear that, but as I was not a participant in trench warfare, I am sure it will not disturb *me*. Lead the way, please."

Arilee watched them disappear downstairs. Mrs. Woodhouse's smart heels tapped on the wooden steps all the way down. Arilee checked on the bubbling soup and decided this was a good time to carry some laundry to the basement. By the time she got there, Mrs. Woodhouse had disappeared into the tunnel, and Adam stood by the entrance.

"She's got the flashlight," he told Arilee, voice low, "and I turned on the big work light inside."

"She's got gumption, I'll give her that. Nat started telling her about Brax, the tunnel, and the treasure. She said if I'd give her one story, she'd leave the others be. I figured this was the least harmful."

"You really think she'll leave the others be?"

"Maybe if you brick her inside the tunnel quick."

"Davis'd give me a raise."

Their eyes met with the shared joke, and Arilee went to check on her laundry drying across the basement clothesline.

When Mrs. Woodhouse took her leave, she looked none the worse for her adventures. How the woman could be so impeccable at all times mystified Arilee who struggled to paint her own nails or pin her hair in a different style.

"I shall check back with you in a few months to see if you've discovered anything else about the skeleton or the tunnel," she announced upon her departure.

Thankful Davis had missed Mrs. Woodhouse's visit, Arilee nearly forgot about it by the next day, the newly established federal holiday of Armistice Day. But that evening, Davis picked up the latest *Journal* while he was eating his dessert. The paper gave detailed reports about the dedication of the Tomb of the Unknown Soldier at Arlington. Arilee hoped this would be enough to satisfy Davis's itch for news, but he scanned over the paper and lighted on Mrs. Woodhouse's article quickly.

The Mysterious Wisteria House Reveals New Secret
by M. R. Woodhouse

When a skeleton was found behind a brick wall in the basement of Wisteria House on Randolph Street, the Rutledge family began to investigate further. They soon discovered the entrance to an old tunnel believed to have been used by their grandparents as part of the Underground Railroad, helping slaves escape to freedom.

The article went on to describe the letter and Arilee's search for more information and concluded with:

A hired workman has been filling in the tunnel for safety reasons and said it reminds him of the trenches of the late war. The author traversed as much of the tunnel as is still accessible and found it quite neat and compact. If walls could talk, these could tell us much of human suffering and heroism.

Davis nearly spit out his buttermilk pie in annoyance.

"Arilee, what were you thinking, telling that woman—*showing* that woman—the tunnel?"

"It was the tunnel or Brax. Or the treasure. Nat spilled all our secrets in the first thirty seconds of meeting her."

"Nathaniel," Davis said sternly. "You are not to tell anyone Uncle Brax was here, do you understand me?"

"Yes, Daddy," Nathaniel said, voice wobbly. "I thought we were happy he was alive again."

"Of course, we're happy. And he's not alive *again*, he wasn't ever dead. He was hiding. But he did some things he shouldn't have, and the police might take him away if they find him. No one can know but our family."

"Mr. Adam knows."

"Mr. Adam who finally got mentioned as the illustrious 'hired workman,'" Adam muttered.

"I told her you were practically family now," Arilee said, resting a hand on his arm. "She's pretty highbrow for us Cherokee County folk, isn't she?"

He smiled at her, not his big grin, but a look of shared connection. "Honestly, Mrs. Woodhouse does scare me a little."

"She intimidates me. I can't imagine being so perfect."

Davis scowled. "She *annoys* me. I don't want her around here. And that explains why the hedge looks run over again. Arilee, next time she comes— because like the plague she will—for the love of Mike, don't let her in."

"You try telling her no, Davis. Margaret Rose Woodhouse does whatever she pleases, and I for one, aim to stay on her good side."

CHAPTER 20

Wednesday, December 21, to Friday, December 23, 1921

A rilee fastened Nathaniel's coat over his shepherd's costume and handed him his wooden crook with a stern: "Your sister is not a sheep."

"Mr. Adam said he would come. Can I go out to the carriage house and get him?"

"'May I?' Mr. Adam has serious tests this week. Exams. I know you want him to see your program, but it's not a good time for him."

Nathaniel's face fell. "Could Uncle Brax come?"

"Honey, Uncle Brax isn't even here right now." She'd lied to Davis and Adam at Thanksgiving, claimed her teary eyes had nothing to do with Brax's absence. Since his initial appearance, her younger brother had been by only once, for a day and a night the first week of December. He'd eaten a few meals with them, poked around for the treasure again, and given her a bag of oranges, which he said were what his employer had him flying across the country right now.

"But Daddy's flying, so who's gonna come see me?"

Arilee tried to keep her tone bright. "I'll be there, Nat, with Macy."

"I'm tired," Macy whined. "I don't wanna walk to school."

Arilee buttoned the girl's red wool coat and put her mittens on her hands. "You'll like it once you're there, Macy. It's a pageant about Baby Jesus."

Macy stared at the creche set up on the old credenza Adam had carried down from the attic. She liked to play with the ceramic figures when she thought Arilee wasn't watching.

"What if we pulled you in the wagon?"

"OK." Macy still sounded tired, and Arilee went to grab a blanket to wrap around her. By the time she returned to the hall, she saw headlamps outside. Adam opened the front door with its huge holly wreath.

"You ready?" he asked Nathaniel.

"Baa-baa," Nathaniel replied and giggled.

"I know it's not far, but it's pretty cold out," Adam said to her. "I thought we'd drive?"

"You're coming?"

"I promised Nat I would."

"Don't you have to study?"

He shrugged. "I'll finish later."

"OK. I'm glad you're coming. For Nat's sake," she hastened to add.

He raised his eyebrows and said no more as they walked out to the driveway. He helped her into the car, tossed Macy into the air and caught her, making her squeal, then handed her to Arilee.

The school auditorium was crowded, and Arilee had to hold Macy on her lap, which put her sitting directly next to Adam. Closely so. Of course, she also sat closely next to an unnamed mother of a wise man on her other side, but Arilee barely noticed her. Adam was so tall and broad-shouldered he took up a bit more than his own seat. The citrus and sandalwood of his aftershave teased her.

The program began, various classes singing carols and taking their place in the nativity. Macy fidgeted and Arilee resettled herself, trying to find a more comfortable way of holding the restless child on the hard wooden chair. She bumped against Adam's shoulder, and thought about the day he'd been stung by the yellow jackets and wished he'd put his arm around her.

What is wrong with you, Arilee? You've not thought about a man like this since—

The shepherds and sheep entered. She glanced up at Adam's profile and sucked in her breath as reality hit her.

I am in love with Adam Harrison!

"*I do love nothing in the world so well as you. Is not that strange?*" she muttered the Shakespearean quote under her breath, drowned out by the persistent bleating of the first-grade boys.

Yet her face flamed as if everyone in the auditorium could read her thoughts. What had happened? How had he gone from being her student, to her friend, to—what? What was he to her?

He was the man she loved. And it put her girlhood crush on Walter Wickler to shame.

But did *he*—?

No, surely not. He flirted with her some, but with his temperament, that didn't mean anything.

The time he'd called her *darlin'*. His fierce declaration: "You are worth coming back for" as he held her protectively, possessively. The look on his face when she'd said he was practically family now. *Could* it be more than friendship to him?

How could she possibly be in love with Adam Harrison? She was lonely, that's all. As she made more friends at church, she'd soon forget all about—

What? She'd forget about a tall, strong man who'd carried her up the basement steps after she passed out and stepped in between her fighting brothers to protect her shattered heart? She'd forget about the extra touches he'd done around the house simply to please her, while always smiling and singing and patiently answering Nathaniel's endless questions? She'd forget about evenings together talking and studying and laughing? Other than the children, no one else had made her laugh since—

She didn't even know.

The final strains of "Joy to the World" were ending. The parents were clapping. In a few moments, children came bounding off stage to rejoin their families.

"Did you see me Aunt Ari? Did I do good?"

She'd hardly paid attention to anything other than the man sitting next to her. "Yes, Nat, you were a fine shepherd. I'd trust you with my sheep anytime."

"Great job, kid," Adam encouraged him. "You all right, Arilee? You look a little flushed."

"I'm fine."

He studied her a moment, then swung Macy up onto his shoulders; Arilee took Nathaniel by the hand, and they walked out to the car together, as if they were a couple and these were their kids. *He'll be a great father someday.* The thought came, unbidden, making her blush all over again.

At the house, they all drank cocoa. "I've got one more exam tomorrow morning, and then I'm done with this quarter," Adam explained to Nathaniel. "To celebrate, maybe I'll get a Christmas tree on the way home."

Nathaniel cheered. "Honest? A real Christmas tree for our house? And we can decorate it, Aunt Ari, right?"

"Of course."

"Hooray! Will you help us decorate, Mr. Adam?"

"I'll be here through Friday morning. Then I'm going to see my parents for Christmas."

"You won't be here for Christmas?" Nathaniel cried, aghast. Arilee felt the same, but she said nothing. Of course he would be with his family for Christmas. Why would she imagine otherwise?

The same thing was going to happen this Christmas that happened every Christmas. She was going to make it a special day for the kids and Davis. This year, add Brax if he showed up. After all the shopping, wrapping, cleaning, and baking, she would have a few new books or a hat from Davis and a mumbled thank you. And a glaring reminder that she was unattached and always would be.

Unless.

No, it was too crazy.

Yet . . .

She mustn't think this way.

Still—

"Arilee?"

"I'm sorry, did you say something to me?"

She noticed, startled, that the kids had run off, and she and Adam were alone in the kitchen.

"You OK? You seem kinda distracted tonight."

You have no idea.

She chewed on her bottom lip. "Just a lot to think about for the holiday."

"I bet. You work hard to give them a great life. Let me know how I can help you."

"Thanks for coming tonight. Nat really appreciated having you there. I did too."

That smile. "Sure thing, darlin'." He winked at her roguishly and headed to the carriage house to get his books.

Did he have any clue what he was doing to her?

∞ ∞ ∞

Adam grabbed his embryology notes and his copy of the script for the upcoming play. He didn't remember one thing about Nathaniel's pageant, only the feel of Arilee's shoulder brushing his, the charming color in her cheeks, and the way she'd looked at him as if she'd never seen him before. Did his attending the school play mean so much to her? The difficulty of her role as the children's mother figure, yet not their mother, must be wearing. Especially when Davis seemed to leave almost all of the *parenting* to her.

He strolled back over to the main house to study, pausing to first build a fire in the library fireplace for an ambiance the radiators could never give.

He didn't want to go home for Christmas. He wanted to stay here with her and help her with what he knew would be a difficult day. He couldn't disappoint his mother, of course, but he wished . . .

He wished she was his. That they would spend every Christmas together forever.

He settled on the library sofa and had finished his studies for tomorrow's exam by the time Arilee came down from putting the kids to bed.

"What are you studying?" she asked, pulling a book off the shelf.

"The literary society decided to put on a play next month, with the thought we'd all have nothing to do but learn our parts over Christmas break."

"What play?"

"*Julius Caesar.*"

"My favorite." She beamed. "What part do you have? Can I help you learn your lines? You know, read the other parts?" She dropped *A Christmas Carol* and came to sit beside him on the sofa.

This was working out exactly as he'd hoped. When the opportunity to act in a Shakespearean production presented itself, he hadn't been able to turn it down. Not when he knew it would command Arilee's interest and attention.

"I'm Brutus," he informed her. "And I'd certainly appreciate your help and coaching."

"Oh, you'll be perfect for that. When is the performance? May I come?"

"First Friday of January. I'm counting on you to be there."

She clapped her hands. "Let me be Caesar and the rest. I'll go get my copy."

"Hail, Caesar!" He gave a mock Roman salute, rewarded by her giggle.

For the next hour, while the fire crackled and cast a warm glow, they read and acted and laughed. He loved watching Arilee lose herself in the words and their cadence. He loved seeing her happy.

∞∞∞

On Friday, Arilee fixed a lunch of potato soup, gingerbread, and pecan pie for their last meal with Adam before he left for Christmas in Canton.

"That was swell," he told her when they finished, then turned to the kids. "Who thinks they've been good enough to get one present early?"

They cheered and went running to the hall where the twelve-foot fir stood by the main staircase. She and Adam followed. The evergreen scent mingled with popcorn strings, dried orange slice garlands, and cinnamon stick bundles to create a heavenly aroma. Arilee had hung a few dozen crocheted angels and the Christmas cards from the church folks as ornaments. Though the decorations were all homemade, the children were enchanted. As was she. No Christmas tree had ever adorned Wisteria House before, Aunt Odessa being opposed to "such heathenishness."

"We got something for you, Mr. Adam," Nathaniel announced and handed Adam the small box. He unwrapped and admired the gold-stamped, green leather wallet Arilee had picked out as a gift from the family to him.

Macy's present was almost more than she could carry, but she unwrapped the brown paper tied with red ribbon to find a handmade doll cradle the perfect size for her beloved "Small Baby." For Nathaniel, Adam had bought a set of real but miniature tools "for when you help me." Thrilled, the children hugged him and ran off to play.

"Those are such thoughtful gifts, Adam." Arilee hoped her tone conveyed her thanks. "You mean a lot to them."

"I uh—got something for you too," Adam said, shifting from one foot to the next. "It's a little unconventional . . ." He handed her a heavy hatbox.

"I'm going to assume it's not a hat in here unless you're giving me the crown," she teased. "And hopefully not any more letters the bats have been through."

She lifted the lid and unwrapped something in red tissue.

"Oh," she breathed.

It was a blue and white china plate with a beautiful scalloped border and a partially raised design along the edge. A scene of an old-fashioned man and woman in a field graced the middle. The reverse was marked with Royal Doulton, England, and a quote from *Much Ado About Nothing,* Beatrice telling Benedick, "Against my will I am sent to bid you come in to dinner." Eagerly, Arilee unwrapped the next plate, which matched the first, but with a scene from *Romeo and Juliet:* "To smooth that rough touch with a tender kiss." On the final plate was a scene of Bassanio and Portia from *The Merchant of Venice*, the back marked with the phrase, "Gentle lady, When I did first impart my love to you."

"I, uh, thought maybe you'd like to hang them in your new kitchen since you were using a lot of blue accents." He fidgeted with the new wallet, studying her for a response.

"These are incredible, Adam. What an absolutely perfect gift."

"There were other ones," Adam explained, "but I, uh, liked these scenes for you. Especially the last one."

Because they'd studied *The Merchant of Venice* when she was his teacher or because of what the plate *said*? She put her hand over her mouth and chin as she stared at the plates, trying to figure out if the gift reflected platonic friendship or something more.

"Adam—"

His eyes met hers. Watching, waiting, even hopeful?

If she was completely misinterpreting his actions based on her own wishes, how embarrassing for them both.

"Have a wonderful time with your family, and please give your parents my love," she finished feebly. He smiled at her, wished her a merry Christmas, and headed out to catch his train home. Afterward, she sat on the stairs, staring at *"When I did first impart my love to you"* far longer than a woman responsible for making Christmas for two kids and two brothers had any right to sit.

CHAPTER 21

Saturday, Christmas Eve, to Sunday, Christmas Day, 1921

B rax entered the back door of Wisteria House on Christmas Eve to the savory aroma of cloves and roasting meat and the excited voices of his niece and nephew.

"Merry Christmas, Sis," he said, coming over to hug her and kiss her cheek.

"Brax! Are you going to have Christmas with us?"

"Sure thing. Can't miss the pies. Where's Davis?"

"He went to see Muriel today instead of tomorrow so he can be with the kids for Christmas. He should be back soon."

"You aren't going to try to drag me to church, are you?"

"The children are singing tomorrow morning." Her voice carried a hopeful note, but he had his limits.

"Nope. But I have some things for them for Christmas morning, and I'd be excited about a good home-cooked dinner."

"All right," she returned brightly. "Having you here is gift enough."

Arilee, still Mama remade. Welcoming him as warmly as if the festivities had been planned for him alone.

"Where's Harrison?"

"Adam told us goodbye yesterday and went to visit his parents for Christmas."

"'No farewell word shall e'er be heard, Beyond the vaulted sky,'" Brax sang idly. The hymns would never let him be.

"He gave me a gift before he left. Do you think—" She showed him three plates. "Do you think it means anything that every scene he chose is a love scene?"

"I think he's been carrying a torch for you for quite a while. Has he said anything?"

"No. Yes. I'm not sure. He's called me *darlin'* a couple of times."

"That's not what any man calls his employer or his schoolmarm in my experience."

"He always comes back over to spend the evening together, even if he's studying."

"I think he just needs a bit of encouragement. Have you given him any?"

"I don't know how, really."

Brax laughed. His sister's naiveté, though endearing, worried him. How easily she could fall prey to a broken heart again. Dad and then Davis had kept her life confined, to say nothing of her own persistent religious beliefs. She'd be shocked to know his own transformation over the past few years from small-town preacher's kid to full-fledged Casanova.

Fortunately, this Adam wasn't a fool, and a pinch of persuasion about Arilee's feelings ought to have him declaring his own. He was steady and devoted, still not deserving of Arilee, but probably as close as she'd find.

"I dunno, Sis. You're both so infernally *nice* that one of you may have to actually *say* something to the other, you know."

She laughed and his romantic advice was interrupted by Davis entering and Arilee calling everyone to the table for Christmas Eve supper.

"Uncle Brax, what do you want for Christmas?" Nathaniel asked him.

"Hard to say," said Brax, who figured his wish for "a choice bit of calico" might elicit a reaction from Davis he could do without. "Maybe some new goggles for flying."

"Who you working for, Brax?" Davis's tone held a note of challenge.

"Company out of Florida. I fly oranges and stuff up north." If Davis started probing, there'd be fireworks for sure. Brax clenched his fists, tired of being questioned. He'd had to put up with a regular interrogation to get back into Bazán's good graces, and it had come at the cost of cutting ties with all other organizations. Brax preferred to keep his options open, and being owned by one boss already felt suffocating.

"Can't they use a truck? Flying produce seems like it would make it unreasonably expensive."

"Rich people don't always make sense. Guess they could send the mail in a truck too, couldn't they?"

Davis opened his mouth to say something, but Arilee gave him a look and said, "Let's have some carols on the Victrola while we eat."

Whether she was really this innocent and trusting, or merely afraid to too deep into his business lest she not like what she saw, Brax wasn't sure. He had no intention of paining her with the more unsavory side of his lifestyle, and if it made her happy for him to be here and alive, he'd put up with her Christian devotion. One thing he could say about his sister: she wasn't a hypocrite.

∞ ∞ ∞

Christmas could have been worse, Arilee decided that night, as she tucked the children into their beds long after their bedtime.

In the morning, added to the gifts she'd bought with Davis's money were others labeled "from Santa," in Brax's scrawl. He rose uncharacteristically early to see the kids' faces. For Nathaniel, he'd bought a pedal car, complete with spare tire and electric headlamps. For Macy, a wheeled riding horse with a structure much like a tricycle but in the shape of a fine, brightly-painted steed. These grand gifts made the Lincoln Logs for Nathaniel and Raggedy Ann doll and book for Macy seem paltry, and of course, she didn't really expect the children to be impressed with their new coats or shoes. Davis had one final surprise in an airplane toy that excited both children, and while the three of them played with it, Brax gathered up the wrappings, and she made breakfast.

"What does he mean coming here and spending that kind of money on the kids?" Davis muttered, coming into the kitchen.

"What a fine Christmas spirit," Arilee snapped. "Why not thank him for making it special for them? They think it's all from Santa Claus anyway."

"Hmph."

"Davis Rutledge, if you're going to be a Scrooge—"

"I have a present for you. And Brax."

"What about me?" he asked entering, his hair still tousled, still wearing his pajamas.

"I bought a radio."

"Let heaven and nature sing," Brax exclaimed.

"But there's nothing to hear," Arilee protested.

"Yet. This year, Atlanta is getting her first stations. Believe me, you will thank me."

After breakfast, she took the kids to church for the Christmas morni. service. She begged Davis to attend, but he deferred. As she and the kids came through the church doors, they were greeted by one person after another with "Merry Christmas." Alannah Macdonald and Violet Alexander each gave her a hug, and Violet's younger sister Katie, teacher of the Little Lambs class, gave Macy a felt book with activities to keep her hands and attention busy during the service. The familiar carols led by Pastor Andy brought her both comfort and heartache. "Hark! The Herald Angels Sing" had been her mother's favorite, "The First Noel" her father's. She found herself wondering which carol was Adam's favorite and desperately missing his baritone blending with their voices.

Over Christmas dinner that afternoon, Davis and Brax talked about radio and airplanes; other than Brax's smug, "One of us at this table made ace" comment, the tension from earlier seemed to have dissolved. The children ran off to play with their new toys, and her brothers fiddled with the radio, finding a heavily static-laden station out of Charlotte. Giving up, they went outside to throw a football, leaving her with the dishes.

She tried to imagine Christmas at Adam's house. Her mental list of all they'd talk about when he got back grew by the hour. And he'd been gone only two days.

When she came down from putting the kids to bed, Brax had gone out for the night, and Davis sat in the library reading the latest Zane Grey novel that she'd given him. She started to pick up A Christmas Carol but asked first if he wanted anything to eat.

"Naw, I'm still full from dinner. Thank you for everything, Sis. It was a good day."

"You're welcome."

"You heard from Adam?"

"He just left Friday. I don't expect to hear from him."

"Don't you?"

"He gave the kids and me gifts before he left."

"So I saw. He likes you, you know."

She squirmed.

"Well?" he persisted.

"I always said I would never fall in love again."

"I always knew you would. You aren't bound to stay here, Arilee, or to take care of the kids. You can have your own life. Or if you want the house, the kids and I will find somewhere else."

This house, ever an albatross around their necks. They couldn't sell it and split the money because it wasn't legally theirs. They couldn't even buy out each other's interest in it because it didn't belong to any of them.

"Is it too inconceivable that Adam could live here?" she murmured.

"A man wants his own castle. If you have a chance at your own life and happiness, take it. The children will be OK. If they've made it this far without their mother, they'll be fine without their aunt."

How easily he dismissed her role in their lives, as if all she'd done could be replaced by a housekeeper he hired. She blinked back the tears stinging her eyes. Rather than feeling released from a burden, the potential decision weighed upon her. She would have to choose between Adam and the children. Davis said she couldn't have both.

Davis went up to bed, and she sat alone staring at the cold fireplace. Now that she knew what it meant to have Adam here, *alone* felt emptier than it ever had before.

Feeling sorry for herself, she wandered to the desk and picked up the next hatbox letter, written by Celeste in 1864.

"I thought Celeste lived at Wisteria House then," she mused aloud to the empty room. "When the Colonel wrote to Luella to take care of all his girls, he must have meant Jewel as well as Odessa. He really did love and acknowledge Jewel as his daughter, and apparently, the rest of the family did too."

Dearest Sisters,

I have heard with great trepidation that the Yankees have come to Atlanta. I do not know if this letter will even get through to you or how long it will take. But I want you to know you have my constant prayers on your behalf that God will see you through this affliction of living in an occupied city. In all your fear, run to Him. His name is a strong tower, the righteous runs to it and is safe.

If you can get away, please come here, and I will receive you, though I cannot promise that you will be safer here than you are there. The days are uncertain, and truly He must be the stability of our times for there is none other. Be strong and courageous. Do not fear or be afraid. The LORD your God is with you wherever you go.

Our losses have indeed been heavy. Our sorrows have been many. I confess it is in my sinful heart to doubt the goodness of the Only One Who Is Good. When such doubts arise, borne along in such swells of grief that I think my heart shall break, I remind myself that in His compassion, He is ever with me. Emmanuel, God with us. He is a husband to the widow. A friend Who sticketh closer than a brother. He is with you all when I cannot be. And though He slay me, or all whom I love, yet will I praise Him. I pray you will find your consolation in Him during this time of trial.

Hope in God, for I shall yet praise Him, the psalmist says. I would have lost hope unless I had believed to see the goodness of the Lord in the land of the living. Wait on the Lord. But remember, His goodness is Who He is, not merely a gift He gives or a miracle He performs.

You will say I have written to you only Scriptures you could have read yourselves, and so I have. But my own words have given out, and I go to the words of life which alone have the power to sustain you.

Most affectionately yours,
Celeste

Arilee read over the letter again. She remembered her offhanded comment to Adam that she'd probably end up a bitter old maid like Odessa. But no one simply ended up hateful, as though they had no choice. Celeste and Jewel and Odessa had all lost brothers and mothers. Celeste had lost her husband. Their father, the Colonel, had returned broken and feeble. Celeste had died young but loving and loved by all. Jewel had courageously made a new life for herself out West. But Odessa had clung to the past. Allowed self-pity to shut her off from everyone else.

164

Tonight, long dead, another woman of Wisteria House reminded Arilee that she must make these choices also. She could cling to her grief and fear and end up bitter and alone. Or she could cling to Jesus and choose courage and love.

She loved Adam.

She loved the children too.

She loved her brothers, even when they made her crazy.

What would it mean, and what would it cost, to choose a life of love?

CHAPTER 22

Friday, December 30, 1921

"**M**r. Adam is back!" The kids ran through the hall and out the back door.

Arilee was washing the supper dishes, and her heart leapt as high as their voices. "Give him a chance to put his things down," she called after them, but they were assaulting him with hugs and eager explanations of all Santa Claus had brought them, trying to show him everything at once. She dried her hands and went to watch from the door as he patiently admired Nathaniel's car and Macy's horse and looked at the box Nathaniel had been building with his new tools.

He stepped onto the back porch, and she caught the familiar scent of his aftershave.

"Hello, Arilee."

Why did she feel so tongue-tied when for the past week she'd made endless mental lists of everything she wanted to talk to him about? And argued endlessly with herself about whether or not Davis was right, and she would have to choose between Adam and the children?

"I missed you," she blurted out.

He stepped closer. "I mighta thought about you too, darlin'," he said, that easy grin lighting his face. "I was thinking—"

Whatever he'd been thinking was interrupted by Nathaniel chasing a shrieking Macy up the porch steps and Woodrow the cat trying to dash in to avoid them. She caught Nathaniel. "Upstairs. Bath. Now."

He started to protest, but Adam gave him a look that changed his mind. Grumbling, he went upstairs.

"Mr. Adam, I wanna have coffee wif you." Macy grabbed his hand and stared up adoringly.

"Sounds like a good plan for tomorrow morning," he said.

"Let me get them to bed, and maybe we can catch up in the library?" Arilee grabbed the cat and set him back outside.

"OK. Either of your brothers here?"

"Davis should be home soon. Who knows about Brax? Did you have a nice visit with your parents?"

"Yes. It was—"

From upstairs, Nathaniel yelled for her.

"It was quiet." He raised his eyebrows.

She nodded. Sometimes these two children felt like two hundred.

She got them into clean pajamas and tucked under the quilts, then read aloud a chapter from *Winnie-the-Pooh* and one from the Bible storybook. Davis finally got home and took over, and she kissed the children goodnight and headed to her own room.

She checked her reflection in the glass and put on a bit of fresh powder and rosy pink lipstick. Her hair was coming loose, and the wisps around her face were curling. She put another few pins in the messy chignon but didn't want to wait any longer. She needed to see Adam with an intensity that startled her.

In the library, Adam studied his part for *Julius Caesar*. She closed the pocket doors and sat down next to him on the sofa.

"How was your week?" she asked.

"I worried about you. If Brax would come. If your brothers would fight and make it hard."

"They behaved. Brax joined us for Christmas Eve and Day. He's the one who gave the kids the riding toys. He went out and got drunk that night, but he celebrated with us at least."

Adam nodded. "The kids sound like they had a happy day."

"They did." She chewed on her bottom lip. "Davis and I were talking Christmas night. And he said the children have been fine this long without their mother, and they'd be fine without me too. Do you think that's true?" Her heart pounded as if her life depended on his answer.

"Not only is it not true, but Davis is a fool to think it."

She exhaled.

Adam studied her a moment and then said slowly, "Davis isn't around most of the time. When he is, I try to stay out of the way so the kids will look to him. He probably worries he's keeping you from having your own life and wanted you to understand you don't have to stay here. But he doesn't really understand how it is with you and me in the daily interactions with the children. Don't pay him any mind. *I* would never make you choose. Besides not being fair to you or them," he concluded with a chuckle, "I'd probably lose anyway."

She sucked in her breath. Was he merely being theoretical, explaining that if he were Davis, he wouldn't make her choose between having her own life and caring for the children? Or was he truly saying that she didn't have to pick between *him* and the children? Unbidden, tears filled her eyes and trailed down her cheeks.

"Hey, now," he reached to brush the tears away with his thumbs. "Darlin', I aim to make your life better, not harder, OK?"

She nodded because she couldn't speak. *What was happening?*

"If I—" he took a deep breath and fiddled with the sofa cushion fringe. "If I asked you out on a date, would you accept?"

She couldn't really say yes, could she? Yet the thought of refusing and losing him—! She nodded.

"Sockdolager." He momentarily stopped attacking the cushion to smile at her. How long had he been wanting to ask?

"I want to know you outside of Wisteria House," he said. "Your roles here are integral to who you are, and you're amazing at them, but I want to see the real you beyond all this."

"Sometimes I'm not sure who the real me is anymore since the war and things."

"Then let's figure it out together."

They sat in companionable silence for a few minutes while he crumpled the fringe again and she noted the ticking of the mantle clock. Needing to lessen the intensity of the moment with some normalcy, she said, "What if we go over your lines?"

"Sounds good."

For the next half hour, they went over Act 1, then came to Act 2 and the scene with Brutus and Portia.

"Who's going to play the part of your wife?"

Adam made a face. "Some gal from one of the girl colleges. You know, maybe one of those snooty Scotties."

She swatted him. "This Scottie will do it tonight."

"The director wants me to kiss Portia's forehead at this part," he said, pointing to the line. "It's embarrassing."

"Haven't you ever kissed your mother on the forehead?"

"That's not the same."

"I'm sure they'll pick someone pretty, and then you'll be sorry it's only her forehead. For now, you can practice on me."

They read through the lines a few times. "All right, script down," Arilee instructed. "Let's act the scene and try to sound convincing that you like me this time."

"I'd like to have a wife who calls me 'my lord,'" he teased.

"Ha!" Arilee began imploring: "'Dear my lord, Make me acquainted with your cause of grief.'"

"'I am not well in health, and that is all.'" Adam put the right hint of annoyance in his voice, and two lines later at "'Good Portia, go to bed,'" he sounded exasperated.

For Portia's next line, she had to get down on her knees and plead.

"I charm you, by my once commended beauty,
By all your vows of love, and that great vow
Which did incorporate and make us one,
That you unfold to me, your self, your half . . ."

The lines of acting began to blur. She wanted him to unfold his own self to her. She longed for more glimpses into even the painful parts of his past. For courage to give the same.

As Adam stepped closer to lift her, his "'Kneel not, gentle Portia,'" came out huskily. He did not release her, but held her gently, his arms around her, and searched her face as she quoted her next line. Which she almost forgot as his gray-green eyes studied her. Being in his arms felt so safe, so right. She fit here, in every way, from his height, wonderfully superior to her own too-tall-for-a-girl inches, to the way his muscular arms encircled and supported her, to the sincerity in his unwavering gaze.

Transfixed, she almost startled when he declared, quietly yet strongly,

"You are my true and honorable wife,
As dear to me as are the ruddy drops
That visit my sad heart."

He pressed his lips to her forehead, but instead of stepping back, he kissed her cheek, and then, ever so lightly, her lips. Her hands rested behind his neck as she responded to his kiss, wanting him.

They weren't acting anymore, were they?

He gave a grunt of pleasure and pulled her closer, and his lips sealed on hers, wonderfully soft in contrast to the wee bit of scratchiness of his day-old whiskers.

Yeah, they definitely weren't acting.

For ten full, delicious seconds, she was perfectly happy as she breathed in his aftershave and explored his lips, fingered his hair, and knew she was completely cherished while their shared kiss went deeper and surer.

And then it came back.

All of it.

Every humiliating detail, even the ones she'd forgotten.

The barn.

The feel of straw boring into her palms.

The terror.

The shame and rejection.

She stepped—almost jumped—back from Adam's embrace, trembling, tears pooling in her eyes and sobs rising. She could never have this. How cruel to let him believe they could ever be more than friends. *What had she been thinking?*

"Arilee? What's wrong, darlin'?"

"I can't. I'm sorry."

"But you did. We did. Kiss. And it was pure heaven." He stepped toward her, reaching out a hand in comfort.

But she backed away. The confusion and concern on his face—now she'd hurt him too. Would her pain never end?

"Please, would you tell me what's wrong?" he asked tenderly.

She had to tell him. She couldn't let him think he'd done something wrong or she was angry at him. But she opened her mouth and couldn't form words. Her hand flew to cover her chin, her scar. That scar always there to proclaim—

"I can't," she choked out, barely able to catch her breath. "Please, it's not you. I wish I could tell you. I'm so sorry."

"Darlin', who has hurt you?" His eyes pled for the truth more convincingly than her Portia had pled with Brutus.

He probably thought from her reaction that she'd been raped or seduced at some point in the past, and she didn't want him to believe that. She didn't really want him to know the truth, either.

Faintly, she heard the refrigerator door open in the kitchen. Davis. He would rescue her.

"Ask Davis. Tell Davis I said to tell you."

She turned and fled.

CHAPTER 23

Friday, December 30, 1921

Adam stared after Arilee's retreating form. Sweet mercy, that kiss had been the singular best moment of his life thus far.

But her reaction. For her to go from ardently pulling him closer and eagerly responding to his cautious peck with a clear desire for more, to suddenly backing away with a look of panic . . . ? A few scenarios ran through his mind, each worse than the last. Someone had hurt her, and without knowing who or how, he already wanted to kill whoever was responsible for her anguish.

He found Davis in the kitchen, eating a dish of vanilla ice cream with canned peaches on top and reading the *Journal*.

"Can I talk to you?"

"Sure. Want any?" Davis gestured to his bowl.

Adam shook his head. He didn't want anything right now except answers.

"Arilee told me to ask you . . . that is, things between us, maybe you've noticed—"

Davis snorted. "Helen Keller coulda noticed by now."

"I wasn't sure how she felt, but this past week when we were apart, it seemed to make everything clearer. But, well, we kissed tonight for the first time, and it made her real upset. Crying and saying, 'I'm sorry,' and when I tried to get her to explain, she said to ask you."

Davis heaved a sigh and narrowed his eyes.

Adam gestured helplessly. "I love her. I would never do anything to hurt her."

"I'm glad to hear it, because if you did, I'd put you in the ground. But this ain't about you at all."

Davis pushed the unfinished ice cream away and threw the paper to the stack on the floor. "I'm surprised she wants me to tell you. She never talks about it."

A sick feeling spread through Adam's stomach, as his imagination continued to run ahead. He picked up the glass saltshaker off the table and began turning it over and over in his hands.

"When Arilee was about sixteen, she had her first suitor. Walter Wickler. He was a year or two older than her. He'd come to the parsonage for supper or take her for a drive on a Sunday or walk her home from church. Dad gave them strict rules, a lot more than he did for me courting Muriel.

"It was spring, I think. Yeah, Grandma Luella had recently died, but it was before Arilee's birthday. Dad caught her and Walter kissing behind the barn. I didn't see what happened, but from what Walter told me after, he got a little carried away, put his hands where they didn't belong, and Arilee went along with it all. Dad pushed them apart, then instead of confronting Walter, he hauled Arilee inside the barn and barred the door. The next thing we knew she was sobbing and begging for mercy while Dad took the buggy whip to her backside."

Adam dropped the saltshaker with a tremendous clatter against the table.

"Brax and I came running to the barn door. We'd both experienced that whip a few times. Brax maybe more than a few. But Dad always stopped after five or so licks, 'cause it cut like a knife. And that was on our rear ends. But this time Dad didn't stop. He made her strip down to her chemise, and he flogged her back like a sailor, the whole time calling her a whore and a jezebel and trash, while she sobbed and whimpered and begged for mercy."

He'd misunderstood. He *had* to have misunderstood. How anyone could hurt sweet Arilee baffled him, but her own father? Beating her? Adam got up from the table and paced to the sink. "Had he abused her before this?"

"No. She idolized Daddy, and he treated her like a princess. Never even raised his voice at her."

"It doesn't make sense."

Davis's jaw hardened, as did his voice. "Brax and I banged on the door, tried to get it open. We yelled to Dad we'd take her place, but if he heard us, it didn't slow him down none. At some point, she must've turned her head toward him, because the whip hit her face, which is how she got that scar across her chin."

Adam sucked in his breath. Her scar wasn't a reminder of some grand childhood adventure, but of a horrific betrayal by her own father. Adam fisted his hands.

"What happened?" he asked hoarsely.

Davis exhaled slowly. "She'd passed out by the time Dad finally opened the barn door. Brax rushed in swearing, and Dad hit him and knocked him out. Dad told me to carry Arilee to the house. She roused as I laid her on her bed. She was shaking uncontrollably from the pain. Dad let Mama put salve on her blistered, bleeding back and told her she'd better be ready for church in the morning. I left to find Walter."

"She had to go to *church*?"

"The next day was Sunday. We always had to go unless we were on our deathbed. Dad had her stand up before the congregation, and she had to read a confession he'd written. Out loud, and loud enough for all to hear, she had to beg forgiveness for her spirit of fornication and being overcome by 'the lusts of the flesh.' Had to praise her father's kindness in delivering her soul from hell by beating her with a rod of correction."

"Of all the deceptions and misuses of Scripture straight from the mouth of Satan!"

"That afternoon Dad sent her away. Put her on a train with a letter to Odessa."

"Couldn't your mother intervene during any of this?"

Davis shrugged. "She didn't know what to do, I reckon. Daddy changed so much after his mother died, none of us understood him."

"Wait, was this when your father—"

"Yeah. He horsewhipped his daughter for kissing and petting the same time he had started a torrid affair with a married woman."

Nausea compelled Adam to sit back down. He picked up the saltshaker again.

"The only good thing to come out of it was that Aunt Odessa saw Arilee's potential and put her into college right off. But Arilee's never talked about what Dad did, not ever."

"Did you ever ask her? Maybe she needs to talk about it, and no one will listen to her." Adam exhaled. Getting irritated with Davis and his reticent near neglect of Arilee as a person wouldn't help anything. "What happened to the boy who kissed her?"

"He left town for a while, more scared of Dad than in love with Arilee. He never tried to check on her or contact her or nothing. Killed in the war. At Soissons, if I remember. Arilee's never let herself care for any man since, till you."

They were silent for a moment as Adam tried to comprehend the horrible story.

"It destroyed Brax," Davis added with uncharacteristic forthcomingness. "He adored Arilee. And her being sent away . . . he got real sullen afterward. Then he was the one who found Dad and that woman together. During his formative years, he didn't have the kind of father Arilee and I had had, but a mean, hypocritical bully. I tried to step in for him, but too little, too late.

"This family is complicated, and we have a lot more skeletons than the one you found behind the brick wall. You need to be sure you want this bad enough to put up with all the trouble. I won't see Arilee hurt for anything or anyone. If this is more than you want to take on, Harrison, not a soul would blame you, but I'd ask you to disappear and not drag her feelings along. She's been abandoned by so many people she trusted. Don't you be one of them."

Adam exhaled. "I wouldn't respect you if you said anything different. I love her, Davis, and I'll do everything in my power to protect her."

"She's probably up on her balcony spot crying. Maybe you know better what to do with crying women than I do."

Adam doubted that entirely, but he had spent a lot of time these past several months studying this one woman and trying to figure her out. He walked outside. In the cold December night, a few stars shone through the haze of the city.

He remembered one day in high school, about the middle of his senior year. It had been raining for a week, cold winter rain that never turned to snow. All the students were restless, and when Arilee's back had been turned to write on the blackboard, Adam had thrown a ball across the classroom to where Joshua stood at the pencil sharpener. The principal had walked in right as he'd released his pitch, making him throw too high.

Joshua hadn't caught it, and instead, the ball had knocked the picture of George Washington off the wall, shattering the glass in the frame.

"Mr. Harrison," the principal had demanded. "What is the meaning of this?"

"I-I'm sorry, sir."

"You're sorry? Indeed you are. A sorry excuse for a pupil and a young man. Miss Rutledge, at the end of class, send this unruly boy to my office for corporal punishment."

The principal left, and Adam sat at his desk, head lowered, face flushed, feeling the stares of the other students. Pity, disgust, a few smirks of satisfaction.

"I don't believe this concerns any of you," Arilee had announced to the whispering class. "Adam, would you please get the broom and dustpan and clean up the broken glass? Everyone else, back to outlining *The Merchant of Venice*, please."

Adam had moved to obey, carefully sweeping up the pieces. He'd taken Washington's picture down and removed the shards remaining in the frame. Walking over to Arilee's desk, he'd whispered, "Miss Rutledge, may I take this home and get another piece of glass for it?"

"Yes, Adam, I think that would be an excellent way to take responsibility for your actions. In fact, I would like you to go straight home right now and take care of the picture, and I'll see you tomorrow."

She'd locked eyes with him then, those exquisite aqua eyes filled with her meaning.

"Yes, ma'am. Thank you, ma'am."

"Be sure you have the sonnet memorized by then."

"Yes, ma'am."

He had it memorized still.

The lattice creaked and cracked and Adam sounded like an animal crashing through the wisteria vines. He climbed until his head appeared over the porch railing. Arilee sat on the small wicker settee, upright and at attention to determine the source of this invasion of her sanctuary. He ungracefully vaulted himself onto the porch, landed on his backside, and scrambled up. She laughed despite everything, and he smiled sheepishly.

"That seemed a lot more romantic in my mind than when I tried it," he admitted, brushing himself off. "May I sit beside you?"

She nodded and scooted over on the settee. He sat next to her, and she shared the large old quilts she had brought out for the cold night.

"Did—did Davis—tell you?" She looked up at him and he saw the tear stains all over her face.

"Yes." He reached and ran his fingers softly the length of her scar, then quoted:

"The quality of mercy is not strained.
It droppeth as the gentle rain from heaven
Upon the place beneath. It is twice blest:
It blesseth him that gives and him that takes."

He saw the recognition of their shared memory on her face as he continued quoting.

". . . It is an attribute to God Himself;
And earthly power doth then show likest God's
When mercy seasons justice."

"That was the day I knew I loved you. Maybe it was a schoolboy crush, then, but I told Josh, and he believed me."

He stretched his arm around her shoulders, expecting her to stiffen. Instead, she melded into his side, and he moved his arm to pull her closer. They sat together for several minutes. At last, he forced himself to speak.

"There's so much I need to tell you. But tonight, right now, I just want you to know I love you with all my being, Arilee Rutledge, and I'm not going anywhere."

He heard her soft intake of breath and plowed ahead. "I'm not looking for a way out or an easier story. I don't know what that means. I know what I want it to mean, but I'm not going to push you. But however it all shakes out, I want you for my friend always."

She nodded, her soft hair rubbing against his cheek.

"I'm sorry," she whispered.

"No. Let's start with no longer apologizing for what other people did wrong or for things you aren't comfortable with. You don't have to make everyone happy, Arilee. You can't. And what your father did to you was *wrong*. I hope you know you didn't deserve that."

She didn't answer or even nod, as he wanted her to. Could she really consider her father justified in his rage and abuse? What did she need most right now, he wondered.

"You are safe with me, darlin'. And I won't kiss you again unless you tell me you're ready. Do you want to talk through all the shadows?"

"I don't know if I can."

"Some memories you shouldn't have to bear alone."

He sat holding her, the winter night quiet compared to the cacophony of insect noises the rest of the year. In the distance, a train whistle blew. The sounds of the city were far away, her voice beside him small and hesitant.

"It wasn't him beating me. Or making me stand before the church. Davis and Brax, they couldn't ever forgive Daddy for those things, or for sending me away after. And that was all awful, of course. But it wasn't what hurt the most. It was—I never knew him after that. I lost him. We never had a deep conversation again. Never talked about books or sat on the porch singing or painted the farmhouse together again. He sent me away, and he never wrote me a letter or came to see me. He let Mama visit only a few times. At holidays, when I came back, he avoided me. Looked at me as though I was tainted. I was desperately homesick at college and the year teaching in Canton. But when I did finally get to come back home to live, it was to the family he'd abandoned and all the disaster."

She shifted a little, and he ran a hand over her soft hair. "It's OK that you loved your daddy," he offered.

"I know he did awful things and hurt a lot of people. But I did love him. He was my hero, and he made my childhood magical. And I still love him. Even knowing the truth and seeing him with all his sins exposed. If I knew where he was, or if he ever came back, I would welcome him. Davis says that's not very smart. But then he still loves Muriel and wants to get her back, so I guess love isn't always smart, is it?"

"'Tis mightiest in the mightiest; it becomes the throned monarch better than his crown,'" he murmured. "You wear mercy and love like a jeweled crown. You aren't denying the truth about your father, but you can still extend mercy to him. Maybe it's not smart by the world's standards, but it's Christlike; He is 'full of grace and truth.' There sure wasn't anything smart in Him extending mercy and grace to me, but He did."

"Thank you," she whispered, and he sensed she was too spent to say more. He sat holding her and praying God would give him wisdom to navigate her past and his own and help them find a future in all of it.

They sat for a while longer, silent. A barred owl called out insistently. A few automobiles drove past, and inside the house, a door opened and shut. After a while, Adam realized Arilee had fallen asleep snuggled against him. He eased her into his arms and carried her into her bedroom. She stirred as he gently lowered her onto the bed, the quilts from the porch still covering her.

Her eyes fluttered open.

"Shh." He kissed the top of her head. "Good night, my love."

She gave the shudder of a leftover sob and a sad smile and drifted back to sleep.

CHAPTER 24

New Year's Eve 1921

A rilee stirred, confused, memories of that dreadful night almost a decade ago mixed up in her dreams and startling her awake. For a moment, it had all been real again—the pain and Daddy's anger, the fear, and the horrible, burning shame.

She had vowed as a new teacher never to use shame as a weapon against any of her students. When their "tight ship" principal had caught Adam in one of his many rambunctious moments, she had almost caved to the desire to teach her most trying student a lesson. Maybe if he got what he had coming, he would settle down and be more respectful.

But she hadn't been able to do it. Not when he sat at his desk with his head down, all eyes on him. It had hit too close to home. She knew how it felt to have your sin paraded before everyone, to be made an example of. She'd wondered if she would regret her leniency, but she hadn't. For the rest of the school year, she'd never had another minute of trouble from Adam Harrison. In fact, he'd started participating in class, making straight A's, and generally caring. He'd built all the sets for their school play.

There had been the anonymous limerick scrawled across the blackboard right before St. Patrick's Day. She smiled now recalling it:

There once was a teacher so pretty
We can't believe she came to our city
From sonnets to plays
And grammar for days
She was as kind as she was witty.

She hadn't been sure who had written it then, and embarrassed, had erased it. But Adam's confession now confirmed her suspicion. What had he said last night? *That was the day I knew I loved you.*

But he wasn't a schoolboy anymore, and this wasn't a crush. He had kissed her, and she had kissed him back.

And she had enjoyed it.

Nothing bad had followed his kiss. Sitting on the balcony with his arm around her had filled her tattered heart with peace. He'd listened when she tried to explain about Daddy, and maybe he'd understood a little. Certainly more than her brothers. She wasn't sure when she'd drifted off to sleep, but he'd considerately brought her inside and honorably left.

He loved her.

That was a problem.

Her hand reached up and traced the scar across her chin.

She heard Aunt Odessa on a tirade against men. "Marriage is bondage. What woman in her right mind would choose to be the slave of a husband?"

She thought of Mama. She'd loved Daddy with all her heart, and he'd broken it so completely she'd never recovered. Arilee had never seen grief like her mother's when Daddy left them.

And what of Davis and Muriel? Had the few years of happiness they'd had together been worth the ongoing pain of the present?

Yes, she and Adam were *in love*, but it couldn't stay like this. They would either move toward marriage or break apart. She didn't know which one terrified her more. But it would be better to break his heart now than destroy his life.

She touched her lips, remembering their sweet kiss. How she would treasure the memory of it for the rest of her days. But if she really did care for him, she'd set him free now. Free to find a girl not jaded by years of loss, not tainted with dark family secrets, not scarred inside and out.

She sat up and squinted at the clock. Five in the morning. Her corset chafed, but rather than changing into her night clothes, she went downstairs and put on the kettle. She wouldn't mind a few hours of quiet to think and pray through her confusion before facing this day.

While she waited for the water to boil, her mind replayed the evening again. The feel of his lips, his arms around her.

I love you with all my being, Arilee Rutledge, and I'm not going anywhere . . .

The quality of mercy is not strained . . .

I'm not looking for a way out or an easier story . . .

She groaned in misery. He hadn't run away like Walter. Of course, to be fair to poor Walt, Daddy wasn't around to threaten Adam. She tried to imagine the two of them meeting.

Then it struck her.

Adam reminded her of Daddy.

Fun, confident, intuitive. So like the man she had adored all her growing-up years.

What was she doing? Talk about playing with fire.

How had she let things go this far? All for a big grin and drawled *darlin'* and someone who would *talk* to her. All because for the first time in ages she'd felt seen.

These were all selfish reasons. What about Adam? Surely his parents wouldn't want their only remaining son mixed up in a mess like her family. Surely he wouldn't wish it himself once he was a bit older and trying to establish his career and community standing.

Turning off the tea kettle before it could begin to shriek, she poured the hot water into the china pot, then carried it to the library. The smell of the steeping bergamot in the Earl Grey blend soothed her. Adam's aftershave had a note of bergamot in it.

"Stop it." She hissed the words aloud to the empty room.

Who could refrain
That had a heart to love, and in that heart
Courage to make . . . love known?

But she didn't have Adam's courage.

She clicked on the electric lamp on the desk and went to stand by the warm radiator. Adam had wired and heated this room. He'd . . . God help her. She was twenty-six, not sixteen now, right? Stupid kiss had totally undone her.

She scanned the shelves for a distraction before the whole mess of her feelings dissolved her to tears again over a romantic relationship she must end before it began. Restless, she sat at the desk and pulled the next letter from the stack of rescued bat-crap missives. Silently she scanned another of Odessa's wartime letters to her older sister.

Dear Celeste,

Something has happened so horrible and shameful that part of me wishes not to write a word of it, and part of me wishes to shout it from the rooftops that all might know what a wicked, lying woman Luella Rutledge is.

As you know, we didn't end up with any Yankee officers quartering here, on account of Jewel and I having typhoid fever when they entered the city looking for lodgings. As we did during the siege, we spent most of the bluebelly occupation imprisoned in our home. When we did go out, we went the three of us together, to church or to help with the wounded. Luella insisted that we should care for the wounded of both sides.

On the night of November 11, some of those cursed Yankees, against orders, started burning down houses before their withdrawal from this city to begin their march of destruction across Georgia. About dusk, six of them showed up on our porch and told us to leave. They were going to pillage the house for valuables and burn it to the ground. Luella said no, we would not leave, and they laughed at her and threatened to burn our home down around us. She said, "I'm sure we can work something out," and invited them in. She served them wine and a rum-soaked fruitcake from down cellar. And then she told them that if they promised to leave me and Jewel and the house be, she would see to all their needs.

One said he wouldn't be part of it, but he wouldn't stop them. Celeste, she took those five other Yankees one after the next and prostituted herself to them in exchange for their sworn and signed pledge that our house would not be touched. Afterward Jewel and I heard her crying in her room, such bitter weeping as I have never heard. It was a death, Celeste, of all honor and virtue and decency. For days, I couldn't even look at her.

But here is the worst of it. It is now four months since that sickening night, and Luella is with child. She told me and Jewel, and then she said, "I have written to the Colonel and told him I was raped by a Yankee soldier after the Battle of Atlanta and am now to bear a child. He wrote back to give the baby a good Confederate name and suggested Thomas Jackson Rutledge. He will raise the child as his own. I want you both to know this in case I die in childbirth."

Our father is married to a harlot, Celeste, and does not know. What am I to do? Shall I tell him the truth and further break his heart, which is already carrying unspeakable grief over the death of his sons—and soon the loss of our Cause? He has lost more than any man should. Shall he lose all respectability as well and take back to his bosom a woman who has been grossly unfaithful to him with the very enemies who have taken everything from us? How can I accept as my brother or sister such a cursed child as Luella Rutledge shall bear? I pray she and the babe both perish at the birth.

Odessa

∞ ∞ ∞

Adam slipped in the back door early, trying to walk softly on the creaking wood floor, thinking to get a cup of coffee and a few cookies to tide him over till Arilee's famous Saturday morning breakfast around nine. He hoped to get the wisteria pruned today, a full day's work in the biting wind. Before he could enter the kitchen, he heard sniffling coming from the library and saw a light shining from that direction.

"Arilee?" He stepped in and spoke softly, so as not to startle her. Her head was down in her arms on the desk, her light brown hair mostly fallen out of its pins and cascading around her. His kissing her last night had opened up a slew of bad memories. What was the right next step?

She looked up and began to cry harder. He pulled up an armchair next to her. "What is it, darlin'?" he asked, searching her face for clues.

Instead of answering him, she handed him one of the old letters from the attic and nodded at it. He read it over, trying to piece it together with her family tree.

"But the baby didn't die . . . that was your father, right?"

She nodded and pulled what he believed to be his handkerchief from her dress pocket.

"Now I know why Odessa hated him. Hated us. Davis and Brax and I aren't even really Rutledges. Who knows who our grandfather is? My grandmother was a prostitute, and my family legacy is adultery and lying!"

"Hold on. I don't think that's fair to your grandmother. First of all, this letter was written by Odessa, who you said already had a chip on her shoulder against her stepmother. She glosses over the fact of 'if they promised to leave me and Jewel and the house be.' Luella's actions protected two adolescent girls. Jewel's perspective on this would be helpful."

"I don't know where she is, and when or even if she's coming back."

"A woman wanting to protect her home and family in wartime does not make her a prostitute, Arilee. War is hideous. It's madness. It drives people to do things they would never have dreamed of and might well be ashamed of later."

He stopped himself. This certainly wasn't the right time for him to tell his own secrets.

"I'm just saying don't equate what your Grandma Luella did with what your father did in having an affair. They aren't the same."

She sniffled and sat staring into space. Another thought came to him, slowly, though as usual, he started talking before it was fully developed in his mind.

"Did your father know about this?"

Her breath caught in her throat and her eyes widened as she jumped aboard his train of thought. "Daddy came here right before his mother died. After that he began to change. We thought it was grief. But maybe . . . maybe Odessa told him the truth or forced Grandma Luella to. Jewel said there was a deal. Odessa agreed to keep quiet about family secrets if Grandma Luella agreed for the house to go to her instead of Daddy. But they must have told Daddy those secrets so he wouldn't contest the will . . ."

"It makes sense," Adam said. "You said he was proud of his Rutledge name and heritage. To find out that he not only wasn't the Colonel's son but was conceived in adultery with an unknown Yankee father . . . that would be a tough blow. And then maybe, when he went off the rails and hurt you, maybe it wasn't about *you* at all, but about his anger at his mother and himself."

She sat absolutely still. "It makes sense. Daddy found this out and it destroyed him."

"Should you spill this to your brothers?"

"I don't know. You're a man. What do you think?"

As much as he appreciated her confidence in him, Adam had no idea, either. He weighed the matter. "Brax is so bitter, I don't think it will make much difference to him either way."

Arilee nodded. "I think you're right. But Davis isn't like Daddy. He can handle it."

"I can handle what?" Davis asked suspiciously, stepping in.

Adam glanced at Arilee, and at her small nod, handed Davis the letter. He read it silently.

"You think Dad knew this?"

"I think maybe he learned it when Grandma Luella died, and that's why he changed."

"Explains some things. At least we're not related to Odessa, huh? When's breakfast?"

Adam about fell out of his chair. "Tarnation, Davis. You can fry your own bacon. I'm taking Arilee out to breakfast."

Davis studied them both.

"You two courting or what?"

"No," said Arilee, and "Yes," replied Adam at the same moment.

Davis raised his left eyebrow.

"Guess you'd better go and figure it out then."

"I need to change," Arilee said and fled upstairs.

Davis turned to Adam. "You know what you're doing?"

"Not a clue."

"Good luck, then. You can take the Stutz if you want."

Upstairs, the kids had woken up and run into Arilee's room. An argument appeared to be breaking out between them. "Guess I'd better go corral those Rebels so she can get ready." Davis set the letter back down and headed upstairs.

Adam took the moment alone to pray for wisdom to offer Arilee whatever she needed most. As he did, an idea came to him—maybe a little crazy, but worth a try. In the kitchen, he made a telephone call; as he hung up the receiver, Arilee stepped in.

She wore a rose-colored dress that emphasized her slim figure and beautiful coloring, but his heart hurt to see how her eyes were puffy and bloodshot. In the past twelve hours, she'd had to relive one of the worst experiences of her life, and she'd found out more unwanted information about her family. The last thing she needed was pressure from him.

But encouragement? Surely he could offer that and take her to the most encouraging person he knew.

CHAPTER 25

New Year's Eve 1921

T hey drove in silence for several minutes through downtown. When
Adam turned onto Interstate 3, she asked, "Where are we going?"

"It's a bit of a drive."

"How much is a bit?"

"Depends on how bad the roads are."

"Are you going to tell me?"

"Just relax. We're not getting there till brunch."

"You'll be hungry and grouchy before then."

"Will not."

"Will too."

He sighed. "There's a little bakery up ahead with nice pastries and
coffee."

"Good plan."

Neither of them spoke for another mile other than Adam's occasional
mutterings about "danged Atlanta traffic" until he pulled off the highway
and found the bakery, which bore the quaint name *The Screaming Peach*.
Adam went in to get the pastries, and she sat in the car, not wishing to be
seen with her swollen eyes. Should she demand he tell her where they were
going? What did Adam think of her declaration that they weren't courting?
What if he had planned some special day, and then she still had to tell him
at the end she couldn't be his sweetheart?

He got back to the automobile with two paper cups of coffee and a bag of
donuts.

"I hope you're OK with apple—"

"Adam, I can't date you."

"Wow, if you're that much against apple, I'll see if she can find some other flavor."

Why did he always have to make her laugh?

"No. I don't want you to go to trouble for me. I don't want you to hope. I don't—I can't—I'll break your heart. I won't be able to go through with it, no matter how much I care about you."

"I'm gonna need to eat something to sort through all that," he said and quickly put away a donut and half his cup of coffee as they sat in the parked car.

"First off, this morning isn't very planned," he said. "It's quite spur of the moment, actually. I thought since you had a horrible evening and morning, maybe you needed to get away, somewhere safe.

"Second, I'm not asking you to commit to anything. Would you just let me be your friend?"

"We were friends. Then we kissed, and now it can't be what it was. It has to be complicated."

"OK. Let me simplify it for you. I love you, and I am willing to risk you breaking my heart to see if you can love me in return. Here, have a donut."

She shook her head. Honestly, men could think about food at the strangest times. "You can't do that."

"Why not?"

"It doesn't make any sense. Find a nice girl four years *younger* than you who isn't shackled to a tainted family name and afraid of kissing."

He shrugged and started in on another donut. "If you're actually afraid of it, we could practice regular. You know, like all these Shakespeare practices to overcome stage fright." He gave her a devilish wink and his big, easy grin, and it took everything in her not to fall into his arms and kiss him right there. "As for your supposedly tainted family name, I thought I could give you *mine* by and by."

She grabbed a donut and bit it in frustration. "You're trying to make this too easy," she huffed as he put the car in reverse and headed back to Highway 3.

"Or maybe *you're* making it too hard. I know what I want, Arilee. I've faced a German machine gun nest head-on and spent countless nights sleeping standing up in a muddy trench, and been covered in nasty blisters from mustard gas. I've stuffed four years of college into three and kept up a steady A. You think I'm going to be scared off by your family story or your personal hesitations? Unless you look me in the eye and tell me to go away because you want nothing to do with me for the rest of your life, I'm going to be around."

She ate another donut and wiped her sticky hands on the brown paper sack. She didn't know what to do with Adam Harrison. How could someone be so maddening and so magnetic at the same time?

When they reached Marietta, he turned onto Highway 5. "You're not taking me to your parents' house, are you?" she asked, panic rising.

"Yes, why? I thought you liked my parents."

"I love your parents. But I can't see them right now. I'm too confused and —"

"Darlin', this isn't about us. I'm not taking you there to make some kind of announcement or have them pressure you that I'm a great guy you should consider spending your life with. They're more likely to warn you about what trouble I am anyway. I thought maybe, with everything going through your mind right now, you might find it more encouraging to spend time with my mother than with me."

Since when had he gotten such insight into her needs? Why was he taking his whole Saturday, right before starting the winter quarter, to cheer her up when she had nothing to offer him? She'd run from his sweet kiss, revealed her most humiliating secret, discovered another disgraceful family revelation, and now sat sniveling over the donuts.

"Feed me the last donut, will you?" he asked, one hand guiding the steering wheel, the other shifting gears as he navigated a hill. She obliged, but it felt almost as intimate as a kiss when his lips touched her fingers. Her face heated, and she turned her head to stare out the side window. The silence grew loud, but she didn't know what to say. Adam would say something, she figured. He always did.

He began to sing.

When he had been in her speech and voice class at age seventeen, his voice had barely finished changing; it had been like a pair of shoes a size too large, as if he hadn't fully grown into it. Though she'd enjoyed his singing since then in church and working about Wisteria House, now enclosed in the automobile together, with no other sound to distract or compete, his confident mellow baritone began to unravel something all knotted up inside her.

"Should auld acquaintance be forgot, and never brought to mind?
Should auld acquaintance be forgot, and days of auld lang syne?"

"You ought to be in a chorus or choir," she said when he finished the haunting Scottish song.

He shrugged. "I enjoy singing because I want to more than because I have to. Maybe that's lazy?"

"No. Art often ceases to bring joy when it's a duty. It's not exactly the same, but I used to enjoy embroidery. Then when Daddy left, and we moved to Atlanta, I did some on commission for a fussy client. I'd sit up late, exhausted, trying to make myself do it and hating every minute."

"I'd like to see some of your work. The ones you enjoyed."

"It's nothing much."

"Do you ever admire my handiwork on the house?"

"Daily."

"Well then."

"All right."

"Now you're on the trolley. That's the first time all morning you've agreed with me."

"No, it isn't—" she began and stopped when he started laughing at her. "Stop," she cried and swatted at his arm. His grin settled into a smirk, and he took up singing "Pack Up Your Troubles in Your Old Kit Bag."

About ten that morning, they arrived at the Harrison house, a white two-story bungalow on the outskirts of Canton proper. Adam opened the door to enveloping warmth and the smell of cinnamon. Mrs. Harrison greeted Arilee with an embrace and delighted exclamations of welcome.

"I didn't know Adam was doing this to you," Arilee protested. "I feel we must be imposing terribly."

"Nonsense. I know Adam's ways by now. We are glad to see him any chance we get, even when he was just here. How wonderful of him to bring you along so I can have another woman to talk to while he and his father drone on about construction."

Brunch was stewed apples and tall fluffy biscuits, sugar-cured ham, grits, eggs, and gravy, all the more delicious because she hadn't had to prepare it. After the meal, she helped Mrs. Harrison put the leftovers away, and the men began discussing trim work, which necessitated going out to the tool shed.

Arilee grabbed an apron to start on the dishes, but Mrs. Harrison gently caught hold of her wrist. "Those'll keep," she said. "Let's have a cup of tea in the front room."

Arilee swallowed, feeling a bit closed in. Now the interrogation would begin. But instead, Mrs. Harrison chatted away cheerfully about her neighbors and doings at her church and inquired after Davis, Nathaniel, and Macy.

"And how about *you*?" she asked. "Adam said—"

She paused, and Arilee almost interrupted with a change of subject before Mrs. Harrison added gently, "Well, he didn't say anything, I guess, other than the past few days have been hard for you, pulling up a lot of difficult things from the past. I certainly understand how painful that is. May I pray for you, my dear?"

Arilee nodded stupidly, fearing if she spoke, she would cry. Afterward, she didn't remember what the older woman said, only the feel of her hand on Arilee's own, and that every word soothed her battered heart. At Mrs. Harrison's "amen," Arilee dabbed at her eyes with the same handkerchief in her pocket from earlier. Adam's handkerchief she'd swiped months ago because it smelled of his aftershave.

"Thank you," she whispered in disbelief that she'd been given the gift of compassion without having to bare her soul as to why she needed it. "Adam was thoughtful to bring me to visit you."

"He's changed so much," Mrs. Harrison mused. "When he came back from the war, I almost thought there'd been some confusion over which of my boys had died, for he was as quiet and introspective as Joshua. If it weren't for that one crooked tooth of his, I'd have probably accused him of playing a trick on me."

Arilee smiled. "That was how I always told them apart in school. When it wasn't obvious from their behavior, which it usually was."

Mrs. Harrison nodded. "Exactly. When Adam returned silent, almost as if he'd absorbed Joshua's disposition and identity into his own, it jarred me. I missed *him* as much as I missed Josh. He threw himself into his studies, determined to work himself into forgetting. I know he saw Joshua die, but he's never spoken of it to my husband or me. Has he said anything of it to you?"

Arilee shook her head. "No, I didn't know he witnessed it. He said once he had a rough time afterward." She didn't think it her place to inform Mrs. Harrison about the drinking and the tattoo in case Adam hadn't shared these things with his parents.

"He has that medal, and he won't talk about it, either." She rose and took something from a curio cabinet by the window and brought it back to Arilee.

"Oh my. A Distinguished Service Cross." Her hand covered her chin. "I had no idea. That's incredible."

It was the highest decoration other than a medal of honor. What had he done to earn such an award, and why wouldn't he open up about it?

"I don't need him to tell me, for my sake, but I worry he's burying it all deep within himself. You're so good for him, my dear." Mrs. Harrison patted her arm.

Arilee sputtered. "I—my family has many complications—scandals, really—that I'm sure you don't want your son getting mixed up in." Maybe she could turn Adam's mother against the whole idea, and *she'd* help Adam see he could do a lot better.

"This past Christmas was the happiest I've seen him since the war. He talked again. Mostly about you."

"Only the Lord can give us true and lasting joy," Arilee replied stiffly, fingering the bronze cross with the eagle in its center.

Mrs. Harrison stared at her curiously. "And yet, He saw fit to create not one man to glorify Him and enjoy Him forever, or even a hundred individuals, but a family, for it was not good for the man to be alone."

Arilee nodded, confused. She'd thought herself selfish to lay claim to Adam's affections, but perhaps she was looking at it wrong. Maybe she could do him good, even as he was always doing her good. Maybe they could mutually help each other through the pain of the past and build a future . . .

Adam stepped in then, his smile melting her heart. Yeah, if she even tried to look him in the eye and tell him to leave, he would know it was a lie, that she desperately *did* want him in her life.

"You two solved the problems of the world yet?"

"Forget the world, we haven't even solved yours," Mrs. Harrison replied.

"I hate to end a conversation about y'all's favorite person, but if me and Arilee are going to get back before dark, we'd best be going pretty soon. Dad's loaded me up with more tools and ideas."

"All right. May I use the bathroom?" Arilee asked.

"It's upstairs between the bedrooms," Mrs. Harrison said.

Arilee handed Adam's medal back to his mother and headed up the steps. Framed pictures of the twin brothers from babyhood to their high school graduation lined the way. Joshua had an angelic smile and Adam a mischievous grin, from the time they were toddlers to adults.

She peeked into a closed door and discovered it was not the bathroom but what must have been Adam and Joshua's bedroom. Though four and a half years had passed since they'd left it, nothing appeared to have changed. A bunk bed on one wall. Pennants and posters on another. A crowded bookshelf. A desk with a stack of papers in what she recognized as Joshua's neat handwriting.

How hard it must have been for Adam to return to his boyhood home and be reminded of his brother constantly, even in his own bedroom. No wonder he hadn't lived with his parents again. How could Mrs. Harrison not understand what this shrine to the past must do to Adam?

Arilee exited quickly before she was caught, but it was another clue. Adam Harrison communicated as much by what he didn't say as by what he did.

∞∞∞

"Adam," his mother said after Arilee had gone upstairs. "Do you remember the year our garden and shrubs wouldn't grow because of the drought?"

"If you mean the year Josh and I were slave laborers watering it every day, how could I forget? I'm still hot and sore from it."

"Hush. Halfway through the summer, a tremendous thunderstorm struck, and you boys were all excited. You thought it would end the drought and your watering days would be over. Instead, the ground was so parched and hard that most of the downpour rolled right off. It didn't help the plants one bit. Gentle showers are what starved soil needs."

"This isn't about landscaping, is it?"

"Arilee is starved for love. She's been neglected for so long she's hardened her heart to it. If you come in like a torrent, you'll scare her away. Gentle rain, son. Slow and steady."

"You do know patience is not my strong suit?"

"Yes, and I'm near giddy you've finally found something you want bad enough to learn it."

"Ha! You're right. I hope you're praying for me that I don't mess this up."

"Indeed. You and that sweet girl are covered in prayer."

∞ ∞ ∞

"You and Joshua were tow-heads when you were little," Arilee remarked, looking at his dark locks. "I saw the pictures on the stairs."

They were driving back, but this time the silences were comfortable and contemplative, not charged with emotion.

"Yep. Mother says it's a good thing we were cute because we sure drove her to distraction."

"I believe it. Does it bother you how your bedroom still has so much of Joshua in it?"

He glanced at her sidelong. "Doing a little snooping around, were you, Goldilocks?"

"You've snooped all over my house."

"Because it's my job!"

She laughed softly. "I was curious."

She thought he wasn't going to answer the initial question, but finally he said, "It makes Mother happy to go in there and remember him. She's finally taken his clothes out of the closet and given them away in the past month. That's progress. She had said she was leaving them for me, but none of them fit anymore, as she knew. The years away made me taller and broader."

"Your mother's so intuitive it surprises me she doesn't understand how hard it would be for you to stay there with your brother's belongings everywhere."

"We all have our things we can't see. Or don't want to."

"Thank you for today." She changed the subject, sensing his discomfort. She thought of Mrs. Harrison's concern about Adam's inability to speak of Joshua's death. She thought of his reactions to the sulphur in the attic and the tunnel in the basement. Anything that brought up memories of the war seemed to invoke a strong physical reaction. Maybe he wasn't *unwilling* to talk of Joshua's death; maybe he was *unable*.

"I needed this time," she added. "You know me pretty well."

"I've been studying up on you. Despite all the teasing about the girls in high school and their broken hearts, I've never *really* had a blue serge. I know you're not sure about me—"

"It's more I'm not sure about *me*, Adam. I do like you. Quite a lot."

He appeared to be trying to hold back a smile but not succeeding. "That's progress, anyway."

"I might be older than you and have been courted once ten years ago, but I really don't know how it's supposed to work, either. Especially now with my complicated life and family. This morning I decided I should call off the whole idea. Adam, I'm terrified."

He brought the car to a stop on the side of the road and took her hand. "What if we started praying together? About all the things we don't know and that aren't clear."

"OK."

"What if on Saturdays we try to have a proper date? Dinner out or see a picture show or a walk in the park when the weather is nice?"·

"I would like that." Her voice barely rose above a whisper.

"All right then. I think that's enough to figure out for now. At least for me, it's enough. If you don't think I'm leading things right, I need you to tell me, OK?"

She nodded and ran her fingers along his. His hands were calloused and work hardened, but each nail clean and impeccably trimmed. She thought of all these hands had already done around the house, and recalled them holding her close last night and tenderly tracing her scar.

Fear had grown like thorns surrounding her heart for nearly ten long, lonely years. It would take more than even Adam's ardent love to cut through them. She sucked in her breath as he began singing again, as if he had read her mind:

"No more let sins and sorrows grow
Nor thorns infest the ground;
He comes to make His blessings flow
Far as the curse is found,
Far as the curse is found,
Far as, far as the curse is found."

CHAPTER 26

Sunday, January 8, 1922

Havana, Cuba

Braxton Rutledge swallowed the last of his Bacardi rum and set the glass down on the outdoor table. Havana in January rivaled heaven, with seventy-two degrees and sunshine. Besides the rich scent of the rum, the fragrance of flowers and saltwater helped relax his tension from a hard week. He wished he could stay here, and when Lola came over and refilled his glass, he wished it more. He pulled her into his lap, and she put her arms around his neck, eyes sparkling with promises of what they would do when they were away from the watchful gaze of her boss here at the *Cantina El Durazno Gritón.*

"Yours was—Feliz Navidad?" she asked.

He swallowed the sweet rum. While he rarely drank himself into a stupor anymore as he had in those first days of discovering the long-denied pleasures of alcohol, he also had differing limits for days he had to fly and days he didn't, and he wouldn't be going airborne this afternoon.

He shrugged in answer to her question. "I stayed with my sister and brother, my niece and nephew. I got the kids presents. Sis cooked a good meal. She's happy finally, my sister. In love with a decent fellow who's good to her."

"Ah, Brax, I thought you cared about no one," she teased. She sparkled with a generous display of costume jewelry, as well as sequins sewn in patterns on her knee-length red dress. He ran a hand down the silk stockings on her shapely calves.

"How many presents before you believe I care about you?"

She waved her hand dismissively. "All bribes. You tell me you never marry. What about your sister? She marry?"

"Yeah." He took another swallow of his drink. "She's a good girl. Very religious. They'll get married and have a bunch of kids and be pillars in the community and grow old together."

"So this atheist, he have a religious sister? And this man who say he never going to marry, happy his sister find a husband?" She rolled her beautiful brown eyes.

"I love my sister, and that's the kind of life that will make *her* happy." He toyed with the glass, now empty again. "She's a 'sunshine in my soul' and 'peaceful, happy moments roll' sort of girl. She's never going to drink rum in a Cuban cantina."

Lola looked wistful, as if thinking Arilee's future looked brighter than her own, so Brax hurried to change the subject.

"What of you? Was yours a Feliz Navidad?"

She shrugged. "I paid for the meal for the family. Mamá, Papá, and all the little ones."

Brax couldn't remember if there were eight or nine younger siblings.

"Papá called me a *prostituta*, told me to move home and get married. Apparently my cousin Pedro will have me even though I'm a fallen woman."

Brax stiffened. "Your Papá, will he hurt you? Do I need to pretend to be your husband so he won't be upset?"

She chortled. "Believe me, if I showed up with a gringo husband, Papá would be much more upset about that than about me working in a cantina and living in the city. But you are sweet, Brax, even when you are stubborn."

She cradled his face in her hands, and he ran his own hands up her smooth arms. There might have been kissing, but at that moment Señor Nicho Bazán stepped over. He waved a hand at Lola, and she kissed Brax's forehead and scurried way. Bazán's lean frame straddled the chair diagonal to Brax, and he snapped his fingers. Another girl, whose name Brax couldn't remember, hurried over with a glass and a decanter and set them down with a curtsy.

"There's trouble."

"Always the bearer of good tidings, Nicho. Good afternoon."

"You need to be aware."

"Only you could live in Paradise and find Purgatory."

Nicho's dark eyes bored into him. "If you are caught, I won't rescue you. I won't compromise this empire even for my best pilot."

"Never asked you to." Brax poured himself more rum. He'd been back in Bazán's good graces less than two months. "What is it?"

"The federal agents are changing in a couple of our usual drop spots. And Chicago is out. Torrio and his new right-hand man Capone demand a share of my profits, or they'll have my men arrested or shot."

Brax raised his eyebrows. "We're giving up our clients there?"

"Of course not. But we're moving our midwestern base to Cleveland to throw them off our trail."

"I think Cincinnati or Indianapolis make more sense."

"I'm paying you to fly an airplane, not to think."

"Always the charmer, Nicho, always the charmer."

"My goal is to make money, not control cities or buy off agents. If Torrio and Capone want to run your whole U.S. government, *que sera, sera.*"

"It's not *my* government. They think I'm dead, and it's going to stay that way."

"I heard you met up with your family. They may get careless. Talk to the wrong people."

Brax knew Nicho hadn't risen to the top by indifference, yet the intrusion into his private life still grated on him. He wanted to work for the entrepreneur, not be owned by him.

Nicho Bazán, the son of an American father and a Cuban mother, possessed familiarity with both countries and languages, as well as an uncanny ability to find information and get what he wanted. Over the past two years, he'd built a rumrunning empire, and with it, considerable wealth. Ever ambitious, he'd begun an exclusive service to his wealthiest clients, allowing them to order the alcohol of their choosing with a fulfillment time of mere days. Whether champagne for a lavish wedding or scotch for a high-powered business event, Bazán had a reputation for fast and discreet delivery; while Prohibition agents focused on catching the rumrunners on the sea and the bootleggers on the land, the giggle juice soared over their heads, as often as not to politicians themselves.

"As far as my sister and brother are concerned, I fly oranges and cigars and they see me maybe once a month. Very unpredictable. I sleep in a room off the porch they leave unlocked for me. Eat my sister's home cooking and argue with my brother."

"I'll take care of you as long as you are loyal, Braxton, but if you betray me or you get sloppy, I will remove you."

"I haven't the least doubt of it."

"Don't take any wooden nickels then. Cleveland."

"Cleveland. Right. 'All other ground is sinking sand.'"

Bazán rose as abruptly as he'd come and strode away. Brax stared after him, his peaceful mood from earlier torn asunder. All the choices he'd made for his life were like bullets making holes in his fuselage. Sooner or later, it would all explode and take him down.

Monday, January 9-Thursday, January 12, 1922

All of Adam's plans of officially courting Arilee were derailed, when, during the second week of winter quarter at Emory and three days after a smashing success performing in *Julius Caesar*, he contracted the 'flu. That he should have missed it in '18 when the rest of the world had it and it might have gotten him out of battle, but had it *now* instead when he *really* needed to be in class, drove him batty.

On Monday, a gray, bitter day, he came home early from school with a fever and left a note on the outside door of the carriage house: "Influenza. Don't come in." He fell into bed, pulling all the blankets up over his undershirt and trousers, and slept fitfully.

When he awoke, dusk smudged what remained of the winter sun. He'd heard something, he thought.

The door opened a crack. "Adam?"

"Don't come in, darlin'. I don't want you or the kids to catch this."

"I brought you some chicken soup and tea."

"Thank you," he croaked. "Just leave it at the door."

"Are you clothed?"

"Yes, but don't—"

She came in and turned on the lamp but at least stood back from him.

He tried to smile at her but couldn't quite. His teeth were chattering.

"I think I better call the doctor."

"I had five doctors at school tell me to go home and go to bed."

"I don't like you out here alone. What if things get worse, and you need to go to the hospital?"

"I'm fine." The room whirled around him, and the rest of him shook.

"Should I call your mother?"

"Absolutely not. She'll worry herself sick."

"You're very ill." She wrung her hands.

"It's OK. I won't kick off."

It was the wrong thing to say, which he realized as the words left his mouth, and she recoiled as if he'd hit her. Her mother had died of the 'flu. Naturally, it would scare her. It scared everyone after undetermined tens of millions had died in the pandemic.

"Listen," he said, hoarsely, trying to remember how to use words. "Whatever's going around this winter is neither as contagious nor as deadly as the Spanish Flu. You don't need to worry. But I really don't want anyone else to be miserable, so please let me quarantine."

"I want to help you," she whispered.

"The soup and tea will feel wonderful on my throat. I'll probably sleep all evening."

"OK."

She looked so uncertain that he forced himself to smile and hoped it didn't look as weak as he felt. Blinking back her tears, she returned to the house. He appreciated her concern, he admitted to himself, even as he hated that he'd made her anxious and couldn't even comfort her.

Arilee came several times a day to check on him. After two days, his fever broke and he stopped feeling as if his body were going to fall to pieces. Now his lungs hurt, and he had a deep cough and a congested head.

"Is there anything I can get for you?" she asked on the morning of the fourth day of his illness. "More books?"

He shook his head. She'd brought him the mystery novel she'd read last summer, by the Christie woman. Though interesting enough, he couldn't focus on it for worrying about what he was missing in class.

"I got all A's on last quarter's exams. I could make magna cum laude when I graduate with my bachelor's this year. But if I don't get back to class soon I'm going to get behind and lose that. Which shouldn't matter to me, but—"

"Of course it matters. Who has notes?"

"I don't know, and I can't get them till I get well. I think I could go tomorrow."

"No. You cannot and you know it."

He growled. Why must she be right? His head ached, and he'd need a hundred handkerchiefs to make it through a day. He wouldn't be hitting on all sixes for at least a week yet.

"I could probably get outside and prune a little bit if—"

"Adam Harrison. If you try to leave this carriage house, I'll get a padlock and lock you in here. Rest. Get better. Macy and I are going out and won't be back till this afternoon. There's some lunch for you on the side table here. Allow me to repeat my earlier question: is there anything I can get for you?"

"No." He heard the sulking in his own tone and tempered his statement with an added: "I miss you."

"I miss you too. The *well* you. So stay in bed till he returns, OK?" She arched her eyebrows at him and gently but firmly closed the door on her way out.

∞ ∞ ∞

"Come on, Macy, I need you to be my helper today." Arilee took the child's hand and bundled her in her new coat. The blue velvet highlighted Macy's blueberry eyes. The hood covered but didn't hide her golden ringlets.

"Where we go? We go Pigwee-Wigwee?"

"We're going to get something for Mr. Adam to help him feel better."

"Candy?" Macy had discovered an inordinate love of sweets over Christmas.

"No, baby." Arilee put little white mittens with blue edging on the child's tiny hands. The girl looked less pudgy than she used to, but Arilee wasn't sure if she was growing taller or if she'd actually lost weight. She made a mental note to check on it soon.

They took the trolley out to Emory and made their way to the John P. Scott Laboratory of Anatomy. Nervously, she introduced herself to the red-haired young man at the front desk.

"Ah, the famed Miss Rutledge, Adam Harrison's girlfriend. I'm pleased to meet you. I'm Sam Tate, a friend of Adam's."

She felt her cheeks heat. What had he been telling these folks? And how strange to have her name automatically associated with his, to belong to him after a fashion. After years of hiding her real first name and years of being ashamed of the Rutledge name after what Daddy had done, she gasped considering how Adam in such short order had made her name a ticket to admiration and respect.

"Thank you. Adam is still too ill to come to class, and I wanted to see if I could get notes for him so he can keep up his studies?"

"Certainly. I'll help you go around to his classes, and we'll make photostats for you to take to him."

This took a great deal of walking, as Adam had classes in a few different buildings, and a good deal of waiting, which Macy bore admirably (the peppermint stick she got from Adam's physiological chemistry professor helped). But everywhere they went, Adam's professors praised his hard work and quick mind, and his fellow students spoke warmly of his friendship and helpfulness.

"I must say," Sam drawled, as he handed Arilee an empty file folder in which to carry home her sheaf of papers, "Some fellows get distracted by romance, but Adam's regard for you seems to have motivated him to work even harder."

"Is it true he could make magna cum laude?"

"We all expect him to attain summa cum laude."

She couldn't hold back her smile of pride. "Well then, I best get him these notes."

"You're good for him, Miss Rutledge. He's always been a solid friend to all of us, but he's been a lot happier this year."

The thought that she could be *good* for any man, let alone the one she most admired, still surprised Arilee. As she picked up a tired Macy to head back to the trolley and home to give Adam what would help him most right now, she smiled at strangers and looked folks in the eye. Roberta Rutledge wanted to hide in shame, but Adam Harrison's girlfriend—*she* was glad to be alive.

CHAPTER 27

Late January-February 1922

A fter a week and a half in quarantine, Adam went back to class, still weak and sporting a deep cough. Thanks to Arilee's help by twice going out to Emory to get him notes, as well as her willingness to type up his two papers due (and perhaps clean up his flamboyant punctuation in the process), he kept up his hard-earned A. He also *finally* got the wisteria vines trimmed, though Arilee insisted she wanted the privacy of having the vines still covering her little porch sanctuary. He hoped she truly desired that and wasn't trying to spare him the work, in her worry about his recovery.

Now with January fairly over, he still hadn't taken her on a true date. They'd prayed together only a few times, though he'd prayed plenty *for* her and for their future when he lay miserable in bed for days on end.

"Tell me about this Walter Wickler fellow," Adam said lazily one evening as they sat on the sofa in the library. His arm stretched around her shoulders, and she leaned against him, a bit of mending sitting neglected in her hands. He'd desperately missed these evenings together while he'd been ill. He cherished the feel of her sitting snuggled beside him and prayed he'd never take it for granted.

"Oh, that was ages ago."

"What was he like? Intelligent? Handsome?"

"He didn't hurt to look at."

"Hmph."

"He was about my own height, so I never wore shoes with a heel."

"Score one point for Adam."

"It's not a competition. I don't still have feelings for him."

"*Did* you love him?"

"I loved him like any sixteen-year-old loves, with something akin to blind idolatry. He was the first boy to show interest in me, despite how tall and ungraceful I was. If Daddy hadn't put a stop to it all, I suppose I would've married him and been a farm wife with three or four kids by the time he went to the war. I expected that life. Except for the war, of course. Mama married Daddy at sixteen."

"Do you wish your life had gone that way?"

She contemplated. "My world was so small then. I'd never been anywhere or done anything. I've still never been out of the state of Georgia. It makes me a wee bit jealous of you and my brothers going to France. I'd like to have an adventure someday, though not the death-defying kind."

"Sadly, most of what we saw 'over there' wasn't worth seeing or remembering, and even what was, I wasn't in the right frame of mind to appreciate."

"I reckon not." She met his eyes. "It's hard to imagine my old plans now. We can't ever go back. To how naive we all were before. Something shifted forever with the war, and the world will never be the same. Nor will we."

"I've tried to explain that to my parents, but it's hard for them to understand. Their lives aren't the same, but it's mainly about losing Joshua. They don't realize that even if he had come back, it would've been *different*. I never thought I'd do anything but work with Dad and live in Canton the rest of my life. Over there, I started thinking about medicine, but Josh wanted to go into education. It bothered him how many of the fellows we fought with hadn't had good schooling."

Adam dared one more intrusive question. "Did it hurt you when Walter didn't come after you?"

"I never thought he should. Daddy got angry at me, not him. He called me a 'worthless woman,' and a lot of other things that I believed for a long time."

"Oh, darlin'." He pulled her closer. "Did college help you see how wrong he was?"

"I loved my college classes, as far as the learning went, but I hid in my books, awkward and shy around girls my own age. Aunt Odessa paid extra for me to have a private room instead of sharing with a roommate because she didn't want me 'wasting time in frivolity.'

"I was younger than all the other freshmen and from the country. My clothes weren't stylish, and I'd never been to a dinner party or cotillion. Gradually, I learned those girls were a lot more worldly-wise than I was. The things they read and talked about showed me how sheltered I'd been. I realized that my little story about kissing behind the barn wouldn't shock any of them near as much as Daddy's response to it. So, I never talked about myself; I listened to them and knew the secrets and hurts of every girl in the Class of 1916."

"I've no doubt. But a real friendship has to go both ways."

"I understood Shakespeare because Daddy read it to us growing up. The other girls discovered this and started piling in my room for help with their English assignments. For the first time, I earned my peers' respect, and I discovered that I enjoyed teaching. I hoped it would be enough that I could be content without a family of my own."

He picked up her hand and traced his finger over it. "Have you truly not dated anyone since Walter?"

"The school required written permission from one's parents to receive gentlemen callers, and I wasn't about to ask for that. But I believed anyone who got to know me would reach the same conclusion Daddy had anyway. Teaching, and then Nat and Macy, gave me back a sense of purpose and worth. I didn't ever expect to be courted again. I planned that if I couldn't be a wife and mother like my Mama, at least I'd be a charming old woman like my Grandma Luella."

He touched her soft, lavender-scented hair, running a stray nut-brown lock through his fingers. The desire to kiss her again overpowered him till he thought he might have to get up from the sofa. Adam shifted so they weren't sitting *so* close. She needed to talk, not kiss. He'd promised to be her friend and be patient. Sockdolager, had he ever done anything more difficult?

"Tell me about your grandma. Why you wanted to be like her."

"She was always smiling, always thinking of others. She stayed very involved in her church till she died and encouraged Daddy in his calling. Every morning before breakfast, she read her Bible and prayed, and she taught me to do the same."

"Do you still?"

"Yes, I try. Do you?"

"During the war, I started that habit and have continued. It helped me to get back to a right walk with God when I sort of fell off the rails after Josh died."

"Yeah. For years I did my devotions because I thought if I didn't God would be angry with me. Like Daddy. But when I became responsible for the kids, it shifted to needing His help and strength desperately. I don't know how I lived through the past few years except for His grace day by day."

"Arilee." He waited till she looked at him. "There is no condemnation for us in Christ Jesus. Your purpose and worth are *in Him*. Your daddy should have been an example of the Heavenly Father. But he wasn't, darlin'. He wasn't speaking for or representing God at all when he hurt you and sent you away and left you all."

"I know, and I'm trying to see it right. You're making it easier." She looked down shyly, clueless how endearing her uncertainty was.

"Good. Well, let's pray together, and then I'd best go study till I fall asleep on neuroanatomy."

"Shouldn't take too long."

"Nope." He took her hand and prayed a simple prayer of thanks for their day, that she would always know her worth in Christ, and that the words of their mouths and meditations of their hearts would glorify Him. Since they'd started this habit, sometimes she prayed too, but tonight when she remained silent after his amen, he squeezed her hand and rose, as did she.

"Good night," he said, giving her a quick hug and starting for the main hall.

"Adam?"

"Hmm?"

"You may kiss me goodnight. I know you want to."

He guessed she'd noticed him staring at her lips too often.

"What do *you* want?"

"I want it to feel *right* without any memories of the past. But it may take some practice as you said."

"Darlin', I'm always available. 'Cept when I have the 'flu."

He leaned his arm against the door frame and bent his head. *Keep it short and sweet, Harrison,* he warned himself. Better to leave her wanting more than frighten her by taking too much, too soon.

His lips brushed against hers, and she responded to his kiss, causing him to linger one second, two, three. His heart pounded as he stepped back. She smiled, oblivious to what she did to him.

"This is a better way to say good night, I think," she whispered.

He nodded and backed out the doorway, leaving before he was overcome, glad for the cold breeze on the brisk walk back to the carriage house.

He had meant to tell her tonight, but he'd convinced himself it wasn't the right time, that she needed the chance to talk about the pain from her past. But loving and leading her meant soon he had to tell her the pain from his.

$$\infty\infty\infty$$

Valentine's Day fell on a Tuesday, and Adam informed her they would be celebrating in style. He arranged for the Sweets' middle daughter, Katie, to come watch the kids that evening and told Arilee to be ready around six for dinner at the Georgian Terrace.

Davis had often told her to buy the clothes she needed, but she rarely did. However, on Monday the 13th, she left Macy with Mrs. Macdonald and went downtown to Rich's department store, where she bought a silky black slip and a black net dress that seemed nearly entirely made of beads. Heavy and quite sleeveless, it fell mid-calf in front but almost to her ankles in back.

"You have a cape or fur?" the shop girl asked. "Powder and lipstick?"

"Yes."

"You have a razor? You have to shave your underarms to wear a dress like this."

Some of the girls in college had done this. At the time, Arilee had paid little attention, never imagining she would one day do such a scandalous thing as wearing a sleeveless dress. Now she wondered why she had waited so long. She'd snag one of Davis's Gillettes and give it a try.

Accordingly, on Valentine's afternoon, she got dressed up while Macy stood watching, Small Baby in one arm, book of fairy tales in the other.

"You be a princess, Aun'Ari, like Sweeping Beauty?"

"Sort of." The girl's mispronunciation amused her, for *sweeping* certainly better described her life than *sleeping*.

"You spark-wee dress is bootiful. Who gonna be your prince Aun'Ari?"

"Mr. Adam is taking me to dinner."

Macy digested this information.

"He berry nice. Will you and Mr. Adam get married?"

"Maybe. I don't know yet."

"I think yes."

She smiled at Macy. "I think yes too, but right now we have to keep it a secret, OK?"

"OK," Macy whispered and smiled.

The look on Adam's face when she came down the stairs for their date amply repaid her efforts in getting ready.

"Hotsy totsy," he breathed, but his eyes said much more and couldn't seem to look away.

Adam had asked Pastor and Mrs. Alexander to act as their chaperones for the date. "It's kinda stupid, I guess, after all the time we've spent alone together," he told Arilee while they waited for the Alexanders to arrive at Wisteria House, "but it's different going out in public officially together than me driving you to church with the kids."

"I appreciate that you want to do things right," she replied.

"You would be a good friend for Mrs. Alexander." Adam looked as if he was making a request. "Pastor Andy told me his wife just miscarried again for the third time in their year and a half of marriage. I think they are going to consult with a specialist. But it's been a hard time for them both."

"I'm dreadfully sorry for her," Arilee murmured. "But I can't imagine why you think I would be a good friend. I've never experienced the same."

"No, but you've experienced grief. Dreams being dashed. And the expectations of a church to be perfect while your life is falling apart."

"Oh."

Once again, it startled her to think someone might find her friendship of value, but Arilee resolved to follow up the Valentine's date by inviting Violet Alexander over for tea one morning soon.

As they drove to the Georgian Terrace, the two couples conversed pleasantly. The Terrace was about a decade old, modeled after the "Grand Dames" of Paris in an exquisite Beaux-Arts style. Arilee gave a small gasp as they stepped inside through the columned terrace and took in the soaring ceilings with crystal chandeliers and heard the strains and swells of an orchestra playing from the dining room.

"This sure is swanky for a small-town fellow like me," Adam said as the liveried bellman directed them to the restaurant which held their reservations.

The Alexanders, equally delighted with the grandeur of the location, sat at their own table nearby, which gave each couple privacy for their own conversations. It occurred to Arilee that they would never have been able to afford such a treat on a small church salary.

"Thank you for doing this for them," she told Adam, voice low. "I wish all church members would invest in their pastor's marriage and family as much as they expect them to be the models for everyone else."

"Pastor Andy has helped me a lot," Adam replied. "He's discipled me and talked me through a lot of hard things. It's fair to say I wouldn't be here with you tonight if it weren't for him."

She contemplated this but didn't ask more right now. She desperately didn't want to talk about the war or any difficulties. Tonight, she wanted to be young and pretty and in love and happy for these fleeting moments.

The meal consisted of several courses, all delicious, and they were finishing a delectable strawberry mousse when the musicians started up a fresh round of music and several couples began dancing.

"Some Georgia Tech student named Arthur Murray teaches dance lessons here," Adam said. "Couple of the fellows at school were talking about bringing their girls. Do you dance?"

She laughed softly. "Not really. Daddy forbade it, growing up. Said it was sinful. At college, the girls taught me to waltz so I wouldn't embarrass myself at Myra Roberts's graduation party. I stood serving punch, but Myra felt sorry for me and sent her brother over to ask me to dance. I was so nervous, I spilled punch all over my dress to have an excuse to say no."

"And he's probably never gotten up the courage to ask a woman to dance again."

"*He* probably doesn't remember the event at all." She considered Adam for a moment, enjoying how distinguished he looked in his evening wear. "What made *you* see me differently?" she asked softly. "Not just as your former teacher?"

"I told you I had a crush on you back then. When I returned from the war, I tried to look you up, but you had vanished. This summer when I saw you at church . . ."

"Surely you weren't thinking *then* I'd be your valentine someday."

"I hoped and prayed you would."

She shook her head in disbelief. "Then why did it take you six months to say something?"

He raised his eyebrows at her. "Why do you think? Maybe you didn't spill punch on your dress, but you did about everything else. When I gave you the Shakespeare plates at Christmas, and you were so adorably confused and didn't go all teacherly on me, for the first time I thought maybe you had feelings for me too."

"'Go all teacherly' huh? I think I would be honored to have you be my first dance."

He smiled tenderly at her and took her hand. They rose from the table. The musicians struck up "Song of Love," and they waltzed to the lovely Schubert tune while the tenor sang of a fairy tale prince and the spell lifted by his true love. Arilee couldn't put her feelings into words yet the way Adam could. It still felt unbelievable that he wanted her knowing full well the muddle of her family and the sorrows and secrets of her life.

The last week of February, Arilee finally finished reading through the old family letters. She threw the nasty hatbox into the fire and carefully arranged the letters in a folder, then put them in the safe built into the wall of bookcases. There were a few pieces of Grandma Luella's jewelry there and a stack of worthless Confederate bills, along with the deed to the house and Grandma Luella's will.

In the end, after all her searching, she had more questions than answers, such as the heart-rending letter written by Luella in 1867 to her family back in Maryland.

Dear Mother,

In disbelief I write to tell you of the passing of the Colonel's oldest daughter, Celeste, the widowed Mrs. James Jones, found murdered this week.

After the war, she took up teaching at a Negro school, to help the younger blacks learn to read, write, and cipher. A woman of impeccable Christian character and kindness, of virtue, courage, and fortitude under affliction, she was the light of our home even in the darkness of her early widowhood.

Horrified students found her body outside her school, and we do not know who has done such an unspeakable crime. We have a few suspicions, but speculation will not bring her back, and the official investigation has yielded nothing. That such a loving soul should be taken from us in the prime of life—there are no words. Our already-tenuous joy has grown dim, and I fear this blow will be more than the poor Colonel can endure. Never have I known one man to face such loss.

It is impossible to describe to you the deprivation and desperation here. The hostility and hatred. The Yankees have come in as a conquering foe and demand a false allegiance or a slow death. While I rejoice that the evil of slavery has been removed from our land, I fear it will be as the spirit cast out of the house that brought back seven stronger spirits. The hearts of men must change, and how will that happen if there is peace at gunpoint, loss of our civil rights and local governance, and punitive action for all who disagree with the victors of the war?

This loss leaves Odessa alone of all her mother's children, and she is the one who does not remember her. For the Colonel, it feels as if his first wife has died again, for now there is no one left alive who knew her but himself. I feel I can see him sinking every day. He loves little Tommy, whom he often calls "Stonewall," and I think sometimes it is only this child who has kept him alive.

Yours always,
Luella

Though the safe was closed and locked, her heart remained open to the legacy of the women of Wisteria House. "Oh, God," she prayed, "grant me the courage and resilience of Celeste for the tragedies behind me and whatever heartaches yet lie ahead."

CHAPTER 28

Saturday, March 18, 1922

E very Saturday, Adam and Arilee had a standing date to take in a movie or grab a bite to eat. Davis waved away the idea of a chaperone, but he always wanted to know their plans and waited up the few times they came back later in the evening.

Adam, in the midst of end-of-winter-quarter exams and spring pruning, had started considering when and how he might propose. He planned to talk to Davis about the possibility of living at Wisteria House while he finished medical school and got established in his practice. He'd have to find a part-time job to help pay for his schooling; he wouldn't expect his brother-in-law to support him, even if he did keep working on the place. It was all a little sticky, but not insurmountable.

But the conversation he needed to have before he proposed made his blood pressure rise every time he thought about it. Only the thought that Pastor Andy was praying for him and would hold him accountable kept him grimly focused.

He had finished exams yesterday. On this mild Saturday afternoon, he and Arilee went downtown to the Carnegie Library for her to get a few books and then to Lambert's Cafeteria for pie and coffee. As they walked back to the automobile, she chatted about the kids and the house; he grew sweaty thinking about how and when and where to tell her what he needed to say.

"Harrison!"

He turned at a familiar voice to see a large fellow swaggering toward them. His heart began to pound.

"Sims." He tried not to grind his teeth.

Sims slapped a thick hand on his shoulder, too hard. "How in the world are you? You're as ugly as you ever were, you old mug. Who's this lovely lady?"

Adam began shaking as memory after memory that he'd carefully locked away was tossed out into the open consciousness of his mind. He could hear the whistle of incoming shells. Feel the mud caking his fingers and oozing into his boots. He could *smell* the trenches again. All in the leering face of this man he'd prayed he'd never see again as long as he lived.

Adam spoke tightly around the strangling feeling in his throat. "Arilee, this is Grover Sims. He was in my platoon. Sims, this is Miss Arilee Rutledge."

"Well, your luck has improved, Harrison. I'd say she's a fair sight better looking than that whore in Pigalle, eh?"

Sims kept talking, but Adam didn't hear another word. The world rushed around him like the men running past him to battle as he stooped beside his brother's body. He heard Arilee's soft intake of breath next to him and felt her questioning gaze upon him. Saw the light fade from her face like the sun setting and was as powerless to stop it.

Sensations swirled around him, spinning as if in a cyclone. The burn of alcohol in his throat. The sting of needles tattooing his arm. The scent of cheap perfume and the scratch of rough, gaudy lace.

Profanity directed at Sims shot through his mind, but he stood there mute, wishing the earth would open and swallow him whole. He couldn't speak. Arilee said nothing either. Finally, Sims muttered something unintelligible and went on his way.

Somehow he and Arilee were back at the car. He had no memory of walking there.

She had grown pale and deathly *still*. Sims's one careless remark had brought her into his nightmare. The thing Adam had planned to painstakingly explain, Sims had set off like a grenade and walked away. And now Adam's secret past had wounded her just like her fath—

Behind the car, he vomited the contents of his stomach.

"Are you all right?" she asked, voice trembling, coming up behind him. He shook his head.

"Let's go home. I'll fix you some ginger ale."

He nodded. He was going to lose her. God help him, he would rather die.

"D-do you w-want me to drive?" she asked.

"I will."

They were silent. He tried to think of the right words to say, but there were no right words. If there had been, he would already have said them. He tried to think of *any* words. But the pictures, the feelings, kept washing over him. Barbed wire. Rats. A tinny piano playing ragtime in a smoky room. The flavor of a freshly-rolled Bull Durham cigarette.

Back at Wisteria House, Arilee told him to lie down while she fixed the drink. He wandered out to the front porch instead, the cool breeze better than the stuffy indoors. He sat on the porch swing, startling Woodrow who had been napping there; with a yowl of protest, the cat jumped down and ran into the yard. Adam ran his finger through the pollen coating the arm of the swing. Nothing at all came to his mind except a wordless prayer, over and over, an ache begging God for mercy and for the ability to say to Arilee what he'd never yet been able to verbalize to anyone.

She handed him a glass of ginger ale with ice. He took it and sipped it slowly.

"Are you ill?" she asked quietly, concern lacing her tone.

He shook his head. "Not exactly. Seeing him brought back memories more vivid than any nightmare. Are the kids around?"

"No. Davis took them to the park." Softly she asked, "It's true what he said, isn't it?"

"I was going to tell you."

"When were you going to tell me?"

He stared ahead at the roses beginning to put out new shoots and new thorns. "Today" sounded too unlikely. He gave the other answer: "Pastor Andy told me to tell you three months ago."

"He knows?"

Adam nodded. "Some. Would you let me explain?"

"Yes."

He exhaled, glanced at her once, and almost lost his nerve. Her trusting eyes were already filled with tears. He'd already hurt her, and she hadn't even heard his story.

"I saw Joshua die," he began, voice low, words forced out one after the other. "The St. Mihiel Offensive. Shot through the chest. I couldn't stop the blood. So much blood. My sergeant kicked me forward. Told me to do my duty. Said the medic would take care of Joshua. I stumbled forward a couple steps, then looked back, and he lay dead, his eyes fixed on me. No last words. No goodbyes. He was alive, then he was dead, and his last sight was me leaving him behind. I left my brother behind."

He almost puked again. He could not imagine any moment in his whole life being worse than that, although this moment, reliving it, wasn't much better.

"You had no choice, Adam. If you'd disobeyed an order, you could have been court-martialed."

"Then I should have been court-martialed! When I finally saw his body again, after the battle—the rats had gotten to it."

Arilee gasped. A few tears spilled out onto her cheeks.

"I was really messed up. I couldn't eat or sleep or even speak."

She placed her hand on his back, rubbing gently. She brushed his hair off his forehead, her hand soft and cool against his clammy skin. "I can't even imagine what that did to you," she said gently. "To lose any sibling is a deep wound, but your only sibling and your twin—" Emotion laced every syllable. "I used to marvel at how you and Josh could communicate without words. It seemed you always knew what the other was thinking. You must have felt as if part of yourself had died."

He nodded, grateful for her putting words to some of it. "Yeah. Yeah, exactly. My commander got me a few days' leave to try to help me. But he sent me with Sims. Told him to help me get my mind off the war.

"Sims was already a real man of the world. He knew where and how to get things. Took me to Paris, where we weren't supposed to be. Kept me liquored up. The first night we smoked opium. The next night, I went with him to a brothel.

"I'd never been with a woman before. Mother and Dad taught me right. But I was half-drunk and Sims kept egging me on. That's not an excuse; I wasn't tricked into it. I was so angry with God for letting Josh die, I thought I'd show Him by doing all the worst sins I could think of. I was such a fool, Arilee.

"The woman was probably twice my age. I let her do—what she did —and it was grotesque. Like tasting something you think is going to be delicious, and instead, it's bitter poison. I glimpsed what a beautiful gift

God *meant* intimacy to be, but what I experienced left me more alone and lost than before. A body without a soul. She even mocked my burns from the mustard gas, said no wonder I had to pay to get a woman."

"Oh, Adam."

He glanced at her. "It's not only the one on my side. There's one on my— inner thigh too." Since he was telling her all the bad stuff, he might as well get that out of the way.

Her tears spilled over again. Of course they did. Arilee, so tenderhearted even mockery brought on by his own stupidity elicited her compassion. How he wished she could be his first and only! At least, he thought grimly, she had been his first kiss; the prostitute had not given even pretend affection, only a heartless exchange of her body for his money.

"In three days' leave, I broke every principle and biblical code of conduct I'd ever held. I dishonored my parents, my country, my Savior. I hated myself and determined to end it all. It was easy there in the trenches if you didn't want to live anymore. I'd seen men throw themselves into no-man's- land, preferring death by a hundred bullets to another minute of that hell. But when we got back to the front lines, the 82nd went into battle again."

"The Meuse-Argonne?"

"Yeah. The Distinguished Service Cross because I tried to get killed. They said I was fearless. But I was hopeless."

"What changed for you?" she asked as she rubbed his back again.

"A few weeks of fighting later, at a field dressing station for a minor wound, I met a chaplain from the First Division. Pastor Andy as you know him. The medic told him I was about to self-destruct, and he talked with me, most of one night. The next morning I prayed, 'God if what he says is true, and You really will forgive me and give me another chance, please show me some kind of sign.' That day I got the letter from you. That it should get through at all, let alone in good time and to the hospital, stunned me. Only God could have made that happen."

He heard her soft intake of breath.

He wondered if she remembered what she'd written. He certainly did.

Dear Adam,

I heard the tragic news about your brother. I also lost my brother about the same time. When the pain of it overwhelms me, I use it as a reminder to pray for you, as it seems impossible to imagine you without Joshua. I have thought much on these words lately, "There is a friend that sticketh closer than a brother." Whatever you face right now, "thy best, thy heavenly Friend through thorny ways leads to a joyful end."

Until that Joyful Reunion on the Other Side,
I Remain Your Friend,
Arilee Rutledge

He supposed that when she'd written it, she hadn't been able to imagine there could ever be any more joy in this life, and neither had he thought it possible. But they had been wrong. Despite all the pain, they had found joy. Joy in going deeper into Christ's love. Joy in knowing each other. Joy in caring for the children and watching them grow and learn.

Joy now lost in a murky no-man's-land of questions and pain.

"I don't know how you knew what to write except God must've given you the words, for they were exactly what I needed. I sat in the metal cot at the field hospital and read the Bible, hour after hour, as if my life depended on it."

He cleared his throat.

"I didn't contract a venereal disease. I feared I would because I deserved it. I deserved the beating you sure didn't. I don't know why God protected me from the consequences I should've had, why He showed me mercy. Only Pastor Andy and Sims know about that night. And now you."

"When were you going to tell me?" Her simple repeated question stabbed him. "Or rather, Adam, *why* couldn't you?"

"I couldn't bear for you to think less of me," he finally admitted.

She nodded and dabbed at her wet eyes. "I had put you on a bit of a pedestal," she admitted. "Of unparalleled integrity and heroism. It turns out you are a sinner too. I don't hold that against you."

He nodded, unable to speak further. She took his hand and squeezed it.

"But Adam, my good opinion of you can't be more important to you than the truth. Or else you have put *me* on a pedestal where I don't belong. I can forgive you, but I don't know if I can trust you."

He sucked in his breath. She was right. He had worshiped her esteem. He deserved this. Every horrible minute of this torture.

The silence stretched long between them. The late afternoon shadows had grown cool.

"Where—where does this leave us now?" He stood before the firing squad, waiting for the final bullet.

"I don't know."

He nodded. None of the words he thought of now meant anything. None of them could fix this.

CHAPTER 29

Saturday, March 18, 1922

A rilee studied Adam's profile in the shadows. How excruciating and humiliating for him to tell her these secrets. She wished—

Well, she wished she could say it didn't matter. Could kiss him and let it all be right between them again. Even more, she wished she could comfort the tremendous pain radiating from his every look and word.

He rose. "I need to go."

"Please don't leave."

"I owe my parents a visit. I'll spend a couple days out there during my school break."

"Adam." She took a deep breath and tried to keep the desperation from her voice. "Please don't abandon me. I need some time to think and pray about all this. I don't condemn you. Not at all. But the old fears about what my father—" Her voice faltered.

He nodded. "I'll be back. I don't deserve you, darlin', and I understand if you're done with me, but I sure as heck won't ever *abandon* you."

He looked at her, finally, and his eyes brimmed with tears. She knew it was too much for him to weep in front of her when he'd already bared his soul. She nodded resolutely. "Give your mother my love." He nodded again, squeezed her hand, and strode off the porch.

She wandered upstairs to her balcony spot and shook the pollen off the settee cushions, getting some in her already teary eyes. Several minutes later, watching him walk down the driveway, satchel in hand and broad shoulders slumped, she muttered, "Et tu, Brutè?" Everyone in her life disappointed or betrayed or left her. Why had she thought he would be different? Would he *really* return?

Had it been nearly five years ago now? That summer of '17. She'd finished her first year of teaching and was excited to be home for two whole months, the longest since Daddy had sent her away. Not having to spend her summer at Wisteria House with Aunt Odessa relieved her so much, she'd ignored the unnamed tension at home.

At Davis and Muriel's house one evening, she sat on the floor playing with two-year-old Nathaniel. She chattered away about her students, wondering if any of them would be going overseas to this so-called "Great War." Without warning, Brax came bursting into the house, panting and sobbing.

"I saw them!" he declared. "Daddy and Edith Souder. In the church."

"What on earth do you mean, Brax?" Davis demanded.

Brax's scrawny seventeen-year-old frame shook. "They were—gosh, Davis, I can't even say it, it's too terrible. They were committing adultery."

Davis stepped over and laid a hand on Brax's shoulder. "Are you sure? What —were they kissing?"

"No, Davis. Everything. They didn't have on their clothes. It was—" He cried too hard to speak any further, but nothing else could be said. Davis grabbed his hat and put his arm around Brax, then opened the front door. Arilee jumped up.

"Stay here," Davis told her.

"I need to be with Mama." Arilee hadn't cried then. Not yet. Shock, uncertainty, these were good buffers for tears.

Davis nodded. They went back to the church, but found it empty, so they walked to the parsonage where Daddy and Mama sat eating supper. Arilee would never forget that scene, hauntingly normal, as Mama passed Daddy another slice of homemade bread, warm and buttered the way he liked it.

The three of them filed in mutely. Davis cleared his throat. "Dad," he asked. "Are you having an affair with Mrs. Souder?"

Mama gasped and dropped the butter knife. She started to say something in Daddy's defense, but when Daddy didn't answer, she grew silent. Thirty agonizing seconds passed. Though Arilee stood behind her brothers, she had a view of her father's face. Regret, guilt, and finally defensiveness played across his countenance.

"Of course no—" Daddy began, but Brax's broken sobs started up again.

"What's the use?" Daddy rose and left, slamming the door behind him.

At the time, she'd mourned how Daddy hurt Mama, Brax, and Davis. Having the ones she loved most destroyed by each other had stung worse than her father's whip. She'd not considered the pain eating at Daddy's own soul, keeping him distanced from God and his family. She hadn't realized the heaviness of the secret sin he carried.

He'd tried to bear his burden alone. Finding out he wasn't whom he believed he was, he'd tried to manage the grief and betrayal on his own. He hadn't let anyone in, not even Mama. He'd hidden the truth from everyone. This was the Rutledge way. Don't let anyone know your weaknesses. Don't speak your doubts. Hide your fears. Handle it and keep being a smiling, good example for the watching world.

Adam *was* different than Daddy. He had acknowledged and repented of his sin. He hadn't persisted in it. He'd found a wise mentor in Pastor Andy. He wasn't shutting out the truth—but would he have told it to her if it hadn't been forced on him by that horrid man?

She wept now for a young man still in his teens who'd been snatched from an idyllic childhood and thrown into a whirlwind of death, violence, and senselessness and expected somehow to make right choices when part of himself was ripped away before his eyes. The weight of his pain physically ached within her core.

Yes, it had been his own fault, his own decisions. But looking into her own heart, she could never judge him for it. For years, she'd wondered: if Daddy hadn't interrupted her kiss behind the barn with Walt, would she have given in to him completely? If not then, perhaps another time when he pushed her for *more*? And she hadn't been in the throes of grief then, but a naive girl who didn't know how to say *no*.

Daddy's voice echoed in her head along with a vision of him pounding the pulpit as he shouted: "'Whoremongers . . . shall have their part in the lake which burneth with fire and brimstone . . .'" and "'No whoremonger . . . hath any inheritance in the kingdom of Christ.'" She could see him holding his Bible in the air and declaring, "'Shall I then take the members of Christ, and make them the members of an harlot? . . . he that committeth fornication sinneth against his own body.'"

She'd always heard those warnings as coming from an angry Almighty ready to smite those who dared to dishonor His commands, as Daddy had physically smote her when she had tasted of the forbidden fruit.

But what if those pronouncements were rather a loving Father warning His sons and daughters away from what would bring them heartache and pain? Adam had done something he could never undo, something that had sent him spiraling into guilt, fear, and despair on top of his crushing grief. God would have spared him all that. Adam's sin hurt *her*. This heartache wasn't God's idea. The blessing of the Lord came without sorrow. But Satan always came to steal, kill, and destroy, and in yielding to his temptations, Adam had suffered immensely and needlessly.

Still, he should have told her before now. She shouldn't have heard it from a stranger.

Lost, she went inside.

She picked up her Bible and moved through the pages till she found it. The postcard Adam had sent her from France. The picture on the front was not of some famous Parisian site, but a simple landscape that could have been a field and house in Canton, Georgia. On the reverse side he'd written:

Dear Miss Rutledge,

Thank you for your letter. You saved my life. Your prayers mean everything to me.

Yours always,
Adam Harrison

He'd been much more literal about the saving his life part than she'd supposed. She'd put the card in her Bible as a reminder to pray for him whenever she came across it. Though in recent months, she hadn't needed a reminder. She traced his round, even script with her finger.

Yours always.

Except when she wasn't his because he was giving himself to a French prostitute.

Oh, God, she groaned. *What do I do?*

When Daddy had betrayed them, when Brax had died, when Mama had died, when Muriel had been taken away, always she'd faced the darkness alone. She'd not let anyone see her doubts and despair. Ever the preacher's daughter, she must not have problems, needs, failures, uncertainties.

Except she had them all, and they weren't going anywhere.

If only she could talk to someone.

Why couldn't she?

She wasn't the preacher's daughter anymore, and Daddy wasn't here to tell her to put all her pain back inside and let no one see it. That hadn't worked for him anyway. It had come out in a lot worse ways than telling someone the truth about his struggles.

Davis and the children were noisily coming in downstairs. She made her way down and picked up her purse and hat from the hall chair where she'd left them. She hugged the children and shooed them up to the nursery, then asked, "May I borrow the car? I need to pay a visit."

"On a Saturday evening? You've been crying. Where's Harrison? You two have an argument?"

"No. He's gone to visit his parents."

"What then?"

"Just some things we have to figure out."

"Did he break your heart?" Her brother's voice held an edge and his golden eyes narrowed.

She sighed. "Life and love aren't that one-dimensional, Davis. As you well know."

He grunted. "I've been hoping your life could be less complicated than mine."

"Not likely. I'm fine. I need to talk to Pastor and Mrs. Alexander."

"Really? You're going to talk to a pastor? With our history? You can talk to me, you know—"

"No, I don't know, Davis. *You've* never told me what it's like to have the woman you love locked away and unable to get her out. *You've* never asked me how I felt left alone, everyone dead or gone, with two babies who needed me every hour of the day, living in the house of a woman who hated us. For almost three years, we've never talked about our parents, our brother, none of it. You told me I wasn't *bound* to stay here raising your kids, that you could hire someone till Muriel recovers. As if some hired woman would love them the way I do. You didn't ask me what *I* wanted. As if I could abandon them, Davis! I could as easily cut off my own hands.

"Adam's the first and only person who's understood that I love them, and I can't leave them, and he loves *me* anyway. He listens to me. So maybe he has his own hurts and secrets. Same as us. And I'll be hanged if I'm going to discuss *any* of it with *you*."

"Fair enough." Predictably, Davis wouldn't let her anger get to him. Fine. He could keep on alone if he wanted, but she refused to live that way anymore.

"Macy's been unwell," Arilee said woodenly, "Have sandwiches for supper, and be sure she gets to bed early and has some warm milk first."

Davis nodded, brows knit in concern. "Yeah, she didn't run and play much at the park."

"I've already booked an appointment with the doctor this week."

Arilee turned resolutely and walked outside, not bothering with a driving coat or gloves for the short trek to Greenwood Avenue. She had been to the Alexander house once. Violet had invited her and Macy for lunch a few weeks ago. A lovely home, with graceful trees and blooming daffodils, it had clearly been built for a houseful of children—a dream that remained in question for the pastor and his wife.

Violet Alexander opened to Arilee's knock. The house smelled of gingerbread.

"Why, come in, Arilee," she welcomed, smoothing her black curls. "Have you come to see me or Pastor Andy?"

"I would feel better if you were both present," Arilee stammered.

Violet went to get her husband, and the tall, lanky man welcomed Arilee with a smile. Violet offered Arilee gingerbread or something to drink, which she declined. The three of them sat in the living room.

"I'm sorry to disturb you on a Saturday evening and without telephoning first," Arilee began. "I am a pastor's daughter, and I know how inconsiderate I'm being, but I—" she twisted and untwisted her—Adam's—handkerchief and tried to think how to say it all.

"Adam told you then?" Pastor Andy prompted gently.

"Yes," she whispered. "How did you know?"

"You look miserable. And he told me he planned to tonight."

"You mean, he really *was* going to tell me?"

Pastor Andy looked confused. "Yes. He knew it would be the honorable thing to do before he propose— Maybe I'm not supposed to tell you that. Did he propose?"

"No." The tears began again. "But he didn't initiate telling me, either. We ran into an old army pal. Somebody Sims. Adam reacted so strongly—he got sick really—and then he finally told me everything. All about Joshua dying to when he tried to get himself killed. I want to believe him. I do believe him. But I'm also afraid of being my mother who couldn't see for five years that my father was being unfaithful to her because she always believed the best about him."

Pastor Andy exhaled. "Where is Adam now?"

"He went to see his parents."

"That's good."

"I hope so. I didn't even know how to respond to what he told me. Now I see the pieces connecting. I knew he'd had a hard time after Joshua died. He doesn't do well with being alone, and in his brother's absence he easily fell under the influence of a bad companion."

"Adam's commanding officer was a fool. Sending a vulnerable, grief-stricken young man off with that reprobate, Sims. Anyone could have predicted the exact disaster that followed."

"Am I a fool—well, you see—I've admired him for a long while now, but I felt unworthy of him with my messed-up family. But after what he told me today, when I saw his own weakness and flaws, I finally knew for sure that I do indeed love *him*. It doesn't even make sense. My father taught us to despise anyone who fell into sexual sin. But then *he* did." She chewed on her bottom lip and twisted the handkerchief again.

"Christlike love doesn't make a lot of sense apart from the Gospel," Andy agreed. "But the Gospel promises any and every sin can be forgiven and cleansed. First John 1:9, 'If we confess our sins, he is faithful and just to forgive us our sins, and to cleanse us from all unrighteousness.' That isn't for certain categories of sins and not for others, or else the cross is powerless. Meaningless. The same Lord who said 'whoremongers and adulterers God will judge' also told the woman taken in adultery 'Neither do I condemn thee; go, and sin no more.' The same God who said 'Be ye holy; for I am holy,' also placed a harlot named Rahab and an adulterer named David in the lineage of His Son.

"Adam, like a lot of the young men I met in the service, was an untested boy from a good home, one who had professed belief in Christ, but never grown deep in his faith because he'd never had to. I can tell you that from the time he repented of his waywardness, I saw and continue to see tremendous sincerity and growth in his life. And constancy. It is not an entirely bad thing that he had to come face to face with his own wickedness, for it has made him dependent on the Lord in ways that many men take decades to learn. However, as truly as he has repented of his sins, I don't believe he has ever fully allowed himself to grieve his brother's death. He's kept himself insanely busy in an effort to run from something so overpowering and senseless, so close to his heart, that it terrifies him."

Arilee sat silently digesting this information. Violet spoke for the first time, her voice and countenance gentle.

"You can forgive Adam without choosing to spend your life with him, Arilee. But if God has given you true love for each other, think how much help you could be to one another in your Christian walk. The real key to remaining faithful to one's spouse is first being faithful to the Lord."

"I think if he had just told me," Arilee shook her head, "without me having to find out on accident."

"I agree he should have told you before now," said Andy. "But for what it's worth, most of our veterans find it almost impossible to talk about their war experiences. I don't think he intended to be deceptive or dishonorable. He has been upfront with me in our weekly accountability meetings, although he has never told me details about his brother's death. Does he know what you told us about your father?"

She nodded. "And some other hard things about my past."

"Knowing what *you* have been through probably made it that much more difficult for him to tell you of his own failings."

Arilee thought back to the night of their first kiss, to her refusal to talk about her past and her cowardly decision to put the truth-telling off on Davis. Adam may have waited too long to tell her, but when he had, he'd told her more than he'd ever told anyone else.

"Your compassion is not a weakness, Arilee." Violet spoke up again. "Perhaps you are God's gift to Adam to help him learn to accept God's grace in his life. And he is God's gift to you to help you understand God's unfailing care over yours."

Arilee nodded thoughtfully. Why had she ever been afraid of these gracious, genuine people?

"Do *you* know who my father is and what he did?" she ventured.

"I have heard about it," Pastor Andy said, and Violet nodded.

"My parents know about the situation," Violet explained. "When you started coming to church, they told us about it to help us understand how best to minister to your family. Not that I think we do fully understand or have always ministered as you needed," she finished apologetically.

Arilee put her hand over her chin, then made herself pull it away. She always hid her scar when she felt noticed. "I expected censure. That's all I've ever gotten from church. I've never had anyone talk about me to *help* instead of *hurt*. It was Adam who showed me how I sabotaged myself when I shut everyone out."

"It's understandable you would feel that way, given what you've faced," Pastor Andy said. "We endured a rough split at a sister church before coming here to Grace Baptist. Nothing near what you experienced, yet painful for us both in many ways. When our church hurts us, the answer isn't to abandon the Body of Christ altogether, but to find fellowship with others who are living out the Church's biblical mission. Recovery isn't quick or easy, but it is vital. Amputation from the body isn't healing, it's death."

"Yes," said Arilee softly, rising. "Thank you for your kindness and your advice. I am sorry to interrupt your evening."

Violet rose and hugged her. Arilee remembered how she'd first thought the pastor's wife to have such a charmed life with her large, loving family and smitten husband. But there were other things, like losing three babies in less than two years, that weren't obvious at first glance but which had given this younger woman a sincerity that drew Arilee.

"I'm glad you came," Violet said. "Just because it was an interruption doesn't make it unwelcome."

"Thank you for trusting us with your burden." Pastor Andy rose as well. "We can't tell you what to do, but we will certainly pray for you and Adam both to be guided by the Lord."

Arilee knew he didn't say it because he was supposed to. She had no doubt the Alexanders really were praying for them. As she drove home, she thought and prayed through what she should say to Adam when she saw him again. He had promised he would return.

Before tonight, she had been *in love* with an idea.

Tonight, she had chosen truth and love, and in the choosing, she chose *him*.

CHAPTER 30

Saturday, March 18, to Tuesday, March 21, 1922

E mpty. He felt empty. Over and over he saw the horror on Arilee's face when Sims bellowed "that whore in Pigalle." Heard her asking, "When were you going to tell me?"

When indeed? Would he really have gone through with it tonight? How many times had he started to, planned his speech, and then lost his nerve? And now in a strange twist of irony, she could forgive his sin but not his silence.

He took the last train to Canton and arrived around eight that night. He hadn't told his parents he was coming. Awkwardly, he knocked on the door of his boyhood home and hoped he wouldn't alarm them with his unexpected visit.

His mother answered. "Adam!"

"Thought I'd spend my days off here," he explained, setting down his bag and wrapping his mother in his arms. She didn't even reach his shoulder, yet she looked up at him with the same delight that in his boyhood *he* had looked up to see.

"Of course, son, you're always welcome. Everything ok?"

"Sure."

His mother looked at him sharply.

"Do you want something to eat?" The house smelled of cornbread, ham, and greens.

"No, thank you."

"Adam, what's wrong? Did you and Arilee have a fight?"

He wondered if her anger would have been easier to bear than her grief and compassion.

"No," he mumbled and walked into the living room. He looked at the framed picture over the fireplace of him and Josh as boys.

"Son, what's troubling you?" His father appeared now, Mother right behind him.

"Nothing" died on the tip of his tongue. He stared at the picture. "Josh shoulda lived instead of me," he blurted out. "He was a much better man. I'm so sorry God took him and left you with me."

At last, he began weeping, the tears he'd held back from them for nearly three years. His parents sat on either side of him on the sofa. His mother said gently, "You've carried this a long time, son. Too long."

"We could never have chosen between you," his father said. "And it's not your fault Joshua died and you lived."

"But I convinced him to join. He was only there because of me. If one of us had to die, it should've been me." He cleared his throat and added, "After I saw Josh die, I tried to get myself killed."

His mother gave a sharp gasp. "Adam, why would you ever think you were less valuable to us than he was?"

"You didn't make me think that. But if I had been the one killed, he woulda stayed the course. Trusted God, shared the Gospel, been all the more honorable in my memory. But I—I lived wicked."

They listened to his sordid tale, and he told it all, from the details of Joshua's death that they deserved to know to his conversation with Arilee tonight. Through her tears, his mother said over and over, "Thank God."

"Why are you thanking God?" he asked. "Haven't you been listening? I went off the rails. Josh never would've."

"Maybe he would and maybe he wouldn't. We can't ever know. He was a good boy, Adam, but he wasn't perfect. But don't you see the mercies of God all over your story?"

"I guess."

"Oh, Adam. *Look.* You were reckless, but God protected you from yourself. You fell into sinful doings, but they disgusted you and never became habits. When you were going to take your life, He protected you in battle, then sent Pastor Andy, a God-fearing chaplain who knew what to say to you. And then He prompted Arilee to write to you, and her letter came at the perfect time. Sweet Arilee, who listened to this story and offers you forgiveness."

"I don't know how to make things right with her again."

"Seems to me if she never wanted to see you again, she'd have told you so," his mother said. "'Stead of asking you not to abandon her."

"Praying can fix a heap of things we don't know how," Dad added.

"I don't deserve a life with her. I don't deserve a life at all."

"It's hard to accept grace, isn't it?" Dad clasped his shoulder. "We're so used to earning everything."

"Josh would've done better."

"Suppose that's true," Mother replied. "Maybe God chose to leave the one who needed to learn from Him most. But you can't carry this burden anymore. You are our son, and we love *you*. I thank God He spared you to us, Adam, and we didn't lose you both."

"It's all right, son." His father would never spout off paragraphs like his mother, but his hand on Adam's shoulder, the way he looked him in the eye, said as much. Adam sat soaking in their acceptance and forgiveness, allowing it to heal hurts from which he'd thought never to recover.

That night he slept in his old room, in the lower bunk—Joshua's. All night he had nightmares about the war, his days in Paris, and seeing Josh die. Sunday morning, he sat at the breakfast table feeling as numb and exhausted as after a physical battle.

He went with his parents to church and greeted the old home crowd, who were always happy to see him. Thankfully, his parents didn't linger after the service, sparing him from endless questions about how his studies were going and did he have a girl yet.

As they were finishing up Sunday dinner, his father turned to him. "I wondered if you'd like to go fishing this afternoon?"

Fishing had always been Josh's thing with Dad. Adam didn't like being quiet and still for that long. He'd rather help Dad on a construction site. Yet he craved the time with his father, and in his exhaustion, maybe he *could* sit for a bit. Maybe his father needed it.

"Sure, Dad."

They settled down at a shaded pool off the Etowah and waited for a catch. The sun shone warm, and the scent of damp earth and honeysuckle eased his tension. After a moment, Dad chuckled and said, "I don't really expect you to be quiet, son."

"Guess I'm all talked out after yesterday."

"Thank you for telling us what happened. I know it wasn't easy to say."

Adam fiddled with the tackle box, startled when Dad spoke again.

"I want you to know, I'm sorry I didn't prepare you better for what you might face over there. I told myself you and your brother would help and encourage one another. I refused to consider the possibility one of you might lose the other.

"When we got the telegram about Josh, I couldn't sleep for weeks. I'd wake up in the middle of the night and be overwhelmed with a burden to pray for you. It felt like a physical weight, pulling me to my knees. I thought I must be reacting to one loss by fearing another. But after what you told us last night, I reckon it was the Lord, waking me and burdening me to pray for you when you needed it most."

"Thank you. And you don't need to apologize to me. You and Mother gave us both the best childhood and the best example boys could have."

"The Scripture says a father should do more than be a good example. He should *teach* his sons diligently. I didn't. I told myself that's what church was for. But the Lord says it's what *I* was for. My purpose shouldn't have been just to give you a good childhood but to prepare you for godly manhood. You'll do better with your sons, I'm certain. I'm proud of the man you've become, Adam, despite where I didn't live up to my calling. You are seeking the Lord for yourself, you are walking with Him, and He spared your life because He has good works that He has foreordained for you to walk in."

"Thanks, Dad." He wanted to say much more, but he didn't trust himself to speak right now. Instead, he let his father's affirmation sink down into his heart, turning the words round and round, examining and treasuring them, and letting them give him a challenge for the days ahead.

"Well," Dad drawled after a few minutes, "It's been bothering me a while now, but I figured last night when you had the courage to say all that to your mother and me, I ought to man up and say this to you."

Sunday night the nightmares returned, and he rose early on Monday to enjoy Mother's pancakes. He and Dad checked on Dad's current build, a new grocery store. For several hours, they drew up and tried out mock versions of display shelves, finally landing on a design that provided optimum strength, stability, and visibility of goods.

Yet despite the honest, hard work, once again, in the wee hours, Adam woke to nightmares. Jingle-brained, he got up and staggered to the sofa; too tall to stretch out on it, he folded into fetal position. Even with the picture over the mantle, Josh's consuming absence didn't seem quite as overpowering as in their boyhood room.

In the morning, he padded back upstairs but found his mother standing in his bedroom, looking about as though she were seeing it for the first time.

"It's the room, isn't it? Why you're having the nightmares?"

He shrugged. "Maybe, maybe not. I have them other places too."

"But you have them every night here, don't you?"

"Yes."

"I'm sorry. I don't rightly know what to do with Joshua's things. It pains me to get rid of them."

He stepped over and hugged Mother. She wept a little into his chest, and he held her. "You shoulda told me," she scolded him.

"I thought maybe you needed it to stay like it was."

"I need *you* to be OK."

"I'm doing better. I think it's knowing Arilee that finally gave me strength to face the grief."

"I wish you'd left things a little clearer between you two."

"Yeah, me too. I'm going to spend some time today thinking and praying about it all."

He hiked along in the woods by the Etowah River, finally stopping at a spot beside some small falls. The sun glinted on the water, and wild violets carpeted the shady spots. He sat down with his back to a tree and picked up rocks and threw them in the river. The trees were putting out small green leaves; some wild jonquils bloomed in the woods.

Arilee would like this spot, he thought, then groaned. He couldn't go five minutes without thinking about her. How could he ever regain her trust?

My good opinion can't mean more to you than the truth.

Truth. Her father had lived a lie for years. Only truth could build trust.

He'd told her the truth, and it had been the most agonizing conversation of his life.

"Lord, I don't know what it's going to be like when I go back," he murmured. "I've been trying to be patient like she needs because of her own hurts, but how do I build our relationship on truth?"

Sanctify them through thy truth: thy word is truth . . .

. . . that he might sanctify and cleanse it with the washing of water by the word . . .

God's Word, the ultimate truth, had some kind of sanctifying and cleansing power that he didn't fully understand but had certainly experienced. If ingesting God's Word had rebuilt his soul after he'd fallen away, couldn't it also rebuild Arilee's trust, and give their future marriage a firmer foundation than merely their feelings for one another?

Peace stole over him; this was the right path forward. Running his hand over the soft moss, listening to the endless swish of the falls, he accepted *rest*. Rest for his mind, exhausted from study. Rest for his soul, long burdened with shame and guilt, both real and imagined. Rest for his heart, that in its desperate quest for Arilee's affections had neglected its first love for the Savior. He didn't have to prove anything to anyone. Didn't have to justify his existence because he had lived and Josh had died.

He dozed, catching up on physical rest denied him for three sleepless nights, and woke stiff but filled with peace. The shadows were lengthening, and his stomach growled; he hadn't realized how far he had hiked this morning, and dusk had descended by the time he got back to the house. His mother stood in the kitchen, pacing with her wooden spoon.

"You fixin' to paddle me for being late for supper?" he teased.

"At last you're back!"

"What's wrong?"

"It's Arilee. She called here for you about an hour ago. She sounded terribly upset. Something about Macy being ill."

His stomach knotted. He remembered her saying she was going to take Macy to the doctor this week, concerned over how thin and tired the girl had been lately, but he'd thought the appointment wasn't until tomorrow.

"May I use your telephone?"

"Of course."

It took a few minutes to make the long-distance call to *Hemlock 8194*.

"Hello?"

"Arilee, darlin', what's wrong?"

"Adam!"

How two syllables could convey such heartbreak, he wasn't sure, but his

237

own heart twisted at her voice.

"It's Macy. I'm s-so afraid she's going to die. I've never s-seen anyone this s-sick except Mama right before influenza took her."

"What's happening?"

"She can't keep anything down. Not even water or ginger ale. She keeps passing out and talking crazy. Dr. Smith came and said it's a stomach virus and I'm overreacting, but it's s-something worse. *I know.*"

"Is she feverish?"

"Off and on. She's finally sleeping right now. I called Dr. Harper whom some of the church folks recommended. He stopped by and said she should be fine by the morning, that these things have to work themselves out. Suggested some soothing teas for her stomach. Do you think I'm crazy?"

"Of course not. They might know medicine, but you know Macy. Is Davis or Brax there?"

"No, no one but me and the kids. I'm s-scared, Adam."

"I'll be there as fast as I can."

"There's not another train tonight."

"I'll find a way. Take her to Grady if she gets any worse. I'll be there tonight, I promise."

"I'm s-sorry, I shouldn't pull you away from your family."

"*I love you*, Arilee."

After they ended the call, he briefly explained it to his mother, his father coming in partway through the conversation.

"I'll drive you in the truck, son," Dad offered. "I can leave whenever you're ready."

Adam hesitated. His father's Ford Model TT maxed out at about 15 mph. At that rate, it would take him all night to get to Atlanta.

"Oh, give him the flivver," Mother said. "We can come get it later. Won't hurt me a bit to walk to town and church now that the weather's nice. 'Sides, everyone thinks we're putting on airs, what with two automobiles."

Adam doubted anyone had ever thought his parents pretentious, especially since his father's truck transported lumber and building supplies for his business. By the time he had stuffed his things into his bag and thrown the bag into the Model T, Mother had a large basket of food on the front seat, and Dad had topped off the gas tank. "Thank you for this," he told them, waving at the car. He hugged his mother and kissed her cheek.

"We love you, son," she said fiercely. "Don't you ever forget that. We're praying for you. And Arilee. And Macy."

He nodded and shook his father's hand, but Dad pulled him into a tight hug. Adam blinked rapidly.

"You go take care of your girl," Dad said. Then he stepped beside Mother and put his arm around her waist.

Adam watched their simple interaction with a deeper gratitude than he'd ever known. Their love, forgiveness, and acceptance gave him the courage to lead, to persevere in his quest to be the man God had made him to be.

And the man Arilee Rutledge needed him to be, which right now was fast and focused. As soon as the Model T hit Highway 5, he eased it up to 40 mph and began to pray.

CHAPTER 31

Tuesday, March 21, to Wednesday, March 22, 1922

A dam turned into the driveway of Wisteria House at about 10:00 Tuesday night. Arilee met him at the door, eyes puffy from crying, startling him by throwing her arms around him and exclaiming, "Thank you for coming back."

"I told you I would, darlin'." He held her a moment, breathing in her lavender scent, running his hand over the messy braid down her back.

"Macy's upstairs sleeping. No fever, but she's so weak, and she can't keep anything down but a little camomile tea."

"You said both doctors say it's a stomach virus. Tell me why you think they're wrong." He began up the stairs as he spoke.

"For one thing, Nat hasn't caught it, and you know how these things are among kids."

"True." Anytime he or Josh had gotten sick, the other had invariably caught it within hours.

"Nat's been in Davis's room for sleeping but keeps sneaking in to see Macy. Tonight he's over at the Macdonalds' house; Alannah came and got him for the night in case I had to take Macy to the hospital."

"I'm glad you're letting her help."

Arilee nodded. "I've never known a stomach bug to go on this long getting worse instead of better."

"Did you tell all this to the doctor?"

She nodded. "Yes, but Dr. Smith said not to worry. That *mothers* know this is how these things go. As if *I* couldn't possibly understand because I'm not really Macy's mother."

"Phonus balonus." Adam bent over Macy's sleeping frame now. He felt her pulse and listened to her breathing. He sat staring at the tiny child, silently praying for wisdom.

"I'm not a doctor, Arilee."

"But you will be. And you care about Macy. What do you think?"

He saw no reason to doubt the physicians who had already given the same diagnosis. But Arilee didn't panic like this. He'd seen her behind the eight ball numerous times. She might worry or fear or cry too much, but she never *panicked*.

"Have there been any other things? Anything at all strange. Even if it seems irrelevant?"

Arilee stared into space, thinking. Then: "Ever since Christmas, she's been a bit off. I thought at first she'd merely eaten too many rich foods and sweets. But she's raided the pantry for candy or sugar cubes frequently. Maybe they've hurt her tummy."

Something in him jolted. He did not want to ask the next question.

"Has there been anything different in her thirst?"

Arilee wrinkled her brow. "Yes, now that you mention it, she *has* been quite thirsty lately, even before she got sick. I thought it a reaction to the weather warming up. She's wet the bed more nights than not for the past few weeks."

"Do you have any of her wet sheets you haven't washed yet?"

"Yes. From a little while ago. What is it, Adam?"

"Let me see a sheet."

She brought him the urine-soaked sheet she'd set in the bathroom till she could take it down to wash. He saw her eyes go round as he put it into his mouth.

It tasted sweet.

He dropped the sheet and met her eyes. "We need to go to Grady right now."

"What is it?"

"I pray to God I'm wrong. Because everything points to diabetes."

The next morning Arilee and Adam sat facing a doctor in a small, spartan office in the main building of Grady Hospital. Arilee gripped a sodden handkerchief in one hand and Adam's hand in the other.

"You are Macy's parents?" Dr. Miller asked. He had thinning white hair and a pointed nose, atop which were wire-rimmed spectacles.

Arilee shook her head. In her current state of sleep deprivation and emotional devastation, trying to come up with an explanation for their family felt like trying to explain Shakespeare to a first grader. Thankfully, Adam spoke up.

"Miss Rutledge is Macy's aunt and has been her caregiver since infancy. She is the only mother Macy knows. Macy's father is a pilot and gone Monday through Friday each week."

Whatever curiosity the doctor had about who and what Adam was, he apparently came to his own conclusions from seeing their linked hands.

"Macy does indeed have diabetes. Her condition is severe. At her age and size, I do not expect her to live past three months even with the best care."

"Jesus help us," Arilee breathed. Though Adam had guessed correctly, to have it confirmed and stated so bluntly destroyed any remaining hope. Adam squeezed her hand, the strength and firmness of his own somehow imparting courage to endure this horrific conversation.

"There is a group of doctors and researchers in Toronto who have developed a tincture of sorts. A pancreatic extract. It is said to replace what the human pancreas cannot produce in a diabetic patient. But they are still in the experimental stages of administering this. They have seen some successes and some failures. I telegrammed Dr. Banting up there about another diabetic patient in severe condition and received a reply from his associate that they have none of the extract available right now and not to come.

"There is a possibility this substance could help Macy, but we have to keep her alive without it until they can get a steady supply. It likely will take too long; I don't want to give you false hope."

Arilee couldn't see *any* hope.

"The best way to prolong her life is through the Allen Starvation Diet. An extremely limited diet of specially chosen proteins and fats. A few vegetables."

"But she's too thin already," Arilee protested. "How can she lose more weight and be healthy?"

"She won't be healthy. Her skin will dry and crack, her hair will fall out. She will be hungry and weak all the time. But it is the sole chance of prolonging her life."

The only way to prolong her life was to make it unbearable? And she wasn't yet even four years old. How could they explain any of this to her? How could they rationalize why they weren't *feeding* her?

"What do we need to do?" Adam asked.

"I recommend she stay here; her care will be complicated, and she will be miserable. At home, the temptation will be too great to give in to her cries for foods she likes. Our nurses will watch over her, I will personally oversee her case, and you can visit twice a week."

"No," gasped Arilee.

"Miss Rutledge," the doctor intoned. "I understand this is difficult, but it will be best for her."

"Best? Her mother and grandmother are gone. Her father never saw her till nearly her first birthday. I held her and rocked her and fed her and changed her and got up in the night with her and taught her to speak and comforted her when she got hurt and read her stories and sang to her and —best for whom? For you and your staff? I'm supposed to *abandon* her now when she's dying and needs me most?"

The doctor looked at Adam. "Perhaps you can help Miss Rutledge to see reason? A hysterical female will not help the situation."

Arilee wanted to leap over the desk and tear the man to pieces. Adam's steady voice stilled her.

"Sir, if I may? I work at the Rutledges' home and have lived in their guest house since this past summer. The child is ferociously attached to Miss Rutledge. To rip Macy from the only mother she's ever known will surely depress and frighten her, and the psychological effects will shorten her life more than any perceived advantage to the separation will lengthen it."

"And what do you propose?" Dr. Miller asked sharply, adjusting the spectacles on his mousey face.

"What if Macy has a private room, allowing Miss Rutledge to be with her at least during daytime hours. Let's get her able to keep food and water down and figure out the correct diet for her. Then we can see about bringing her home where she will be more comfortable and happy."

"I see little chance that child will ever return home," Dr. Miller replied grimly. "Miss Rutledge, you need to prepare yourself to face the worst. However, having Macy removed from the other children in the ward who are receiving more desirable food would be advantageous. I'll try to accommodate your request for a private room and daytime access to the patient. Perhaps in the Butler Building."

Arilee nodded her agreement. "Her father will want to be with her when he's here."

"If you'll move to the waiting area," Dr. Miller concluded, rising, "I will see about a transfer and let you know when you may see her."

They walked to a wooden bench in the Lysol-scented waiting room. Arilee leaned against Adam as she had for most of the night—a blur of tests and Macy's heart-rending cries as the medical staff drew blood and tried to rehydrate her through a rectal infusion of fluids. A night of endless waiting and wondering only to have their worst fears confirmed.

As Dr. Miller strode by without a glance, she muttered, "I don't know why someone becomes a doctor when they have so little compassion."

"Some men become doctors because they love medicine and some because they love people. I'd put Doc Miller in the medicine camp."

"You'll be in the people camp for sure."

He smiled and squeezed her hand. "I know he's not pleasant, but this is a good hospital. Last year they performed an open-heart surgery. Sockdolager! Opening up someone's chest, fixing his heart, and closing him back up again. And next year they'll be opening the first cancer center in the world. Right here in Atlanta."

"But it sounds like we need to be in Toronto."

"I will talk to the medical professors at Emory and see if anything can be done to get her this extract."

Arilee nodded numbly. "Thank you," she whispered. "For everything."

The massive brick structure of Grady's main building reflected the Victorian years during which the institution was built, but in the companionable silence between them, she noticed sounds of life and motion around her: voices of nurses giving directions, the squeak of a wheelchair, an infant's cries, morning traffic outside on Butler Street.

"Did you have a good visit with your parents?" she asked.

"It was what I needed. The Lord really spoke to me out in the woods yesterday."

"I'm so glad. Adam, I know we need to talk about—"

"Shh, darlin', not now. Just let me be here for you and help you, OK?"

"OK."

"Once we see Macy, maybe you'd let me stay with her while you go home and rest. I'm worried you're going to collapse on me."

She started to answer, but a tremendous yawn interrupted.

"I went to see Pastor Andy after you left Friday," she murmured sleepily.

"And?" he prompted when she forgot to go on.

"He said it's OK for me to love you."

"And do you?" Hope tinged his voice.

She meant to look at him. She meant to say a great many things. She didn't remember any of what she had practiced. Her eyelids would not stay open.

"Yes." She yawned again. "So very much. 'I would not wish any companion in the world but you.'"

As she murmured the words from *The Tempest*, he put his arm around her, and she fell into exhausted sleep, her head cradled against his chest, close to the steady beating of his heart.

CHAPTER 32

Thursday, March 23, to Sunday, April 9, 1922

Later that morning, they stepped inside Macy's room in the Butler Building to find her awake, her tiny body still receiving fluids, thankfully subcutaneously now.

"Aun'Ari," she cried, her voice small as a baby kitten's.

"Hey, baby. How do you feel?"

"I wanna go home."

"I know. We'll go as soon as we can, but you've got to feel better first."

Her big blue eyes filled with tears.

"Aunt Ari is going to go home and get your favorite things." Adam jumped in. "What do you want her to bring?"

"Can Woodrow come?"

"No, cats hate hospitals."

"But he's sick."

"I talked to him last night," Adam said, "and he told me he felt swell. Maybe you have some toys or books you'd like?"

"Can Small Baby come?"

"Yes, of course," said Arilee. "And I'll bring your storybook and tablet and some new crayons."

Macy offered a tentative smile.

"While Aunt Ari gets those things, I'm going to stay here and tell you the story of when Woodrow dressed up in his best suit and went downtown to eat at the Georgian Terrace," Adam began.

Macy giggled. Adam launched into his tale, gesturing wildly and raising and lowering his voice. Never had she appreciated his acting skills so much.

Never had she appreciated *him* so much. She wanted to tell him, but her heart felt turned inside out.

I see little chance that child will ever return home.

And they still had to tell Davis. She'd attempt now to reach her brother with a telegram, but he might or might not receive it before Friday anyway. What would this new sorrow do to him? He already lived locked inside himself. Would she lose both Macy and what she had left of her brother too?

∞ ∞ ∞

"Mr. Adam?"

Adam looked up from the hedge to see Nathaniel standing before him. The beauty of the spring day with newly-blooming dogwoods and twittering birds contrasted sharply with the misery on the boy's face as he shifted from one foot to the other.

"Hey, Nat. You wanna help?"

Nathaniel's eyes filled with tears. "Is Aunt Ari back?"

"Not yet." Adam checked his army-issue wristwatch. "Shouldn't be too much longer, though." Over the past week, their lives had become an elaborate coordination of his and Nathaniel's school schedules, Davis's flying schedule, and keeping someone with Macy as often as possible. Nathaniel not being allowed at the hospital complicated things.

"Did your brother *really* die, not like Uncle Brax?"

"Yeah." Adam could only imagine how confusing the situation with Brax must be to a child.

"Is Macy going to die?"

Adam set down the trimmers and pulled Nathaniel close. The boy began crying. Adam led him over to the porch steps, then went inside the house and got them both some lemonade.

"I don't know," he finally answered Nathaniel. "Something in Macy's body isn't working, and that's making her very sick."

"Will Macy be like those bones you found in the basement and go be in the ground in the place with all the flags?"

"Macy . . . if Macy dies, the real Macy, who laughs and loves and plays and sings, will go to heaven to be with Jesus. And God will give her a brand new healthy body."

"Sometimes I teased her and made her cry. If I tell God I'm sorry and pray really hard and don't do anything naughty, will He make her better?"

"Oh, Nat, Macy being sick isn't your fault at all. We definitely can pray and ask God to heal her or bring the right cure to help her get well. But we have to trust that God has a good plan for Macy's life and each of ours. He already knows exactly how many days each of us is going to live on this earth."

"Do you miss your brother?"

"Every day."

"I'm scared."

Adam hugged the boy again. "I know, Nat. Me too."

Nat regarded him with wide, amber eyes. His chin quivered a little.

"When I'm missing my brother," Adam said slowly, "it helps me to remember that Jesus is with him, and Jesus is with me. We're still connected that way, even though I can't see him right now. And Jesus has promised to never leave us."

Nathaniel considered this and then in a small voice asked, "Will *you* be here?"

Adam could hardly speak around the burning lump in the back of his throat. "Yeah, kid," he said, resting a hand on Nathaniel's shoulder. "I promise, for as long as I'm able."

∞ ∞ ∞

Macy's room at the hospital became so inviting that the nurses looked for excuses to come check on her. Davis bought a portable wind-up phonograph, and Arilee kept cheerful music playing. Uncle Brax sent colorful balloons. Nathaniel's school class gave Macy three new coloring books. Arilee checked out stacks of children's books from the public library.

Pastor Andy and Violet came a few times a week. On one Saturday, while Davis visited at the hospital, the young minister anointed Macy with oil, and he and two deacons in the church prayed over her.

Mrs. Sweet and Mrs. Macdonald came regularly. Katie Sweet, the Little Lambs teacher at church, sent a black crocheted cat, which Macy immediately named Woodrow and spoke to as if it were her real cat. "It seemed odd to me," Mrs. Sweet said, "but I've learned not to question Katie's cleverness about gifts or creating things." The soft squeezable toy became inseparable from Macy, and Adam created volumes of make-believe stories about the adventures of Woodrow.

Toward the end of the second week, Arilee sat half asleep in the chair beside Macy's bed while the child napped. She startled at a tap on the door and looked up to see Mrs. Harrison.

"Oh, Arilee, I'm sorry it took me so long to get into Atlanta, and I am terribly sorry for what you are going through."

Arilee rose. She wanted to welcome Adam's mother warmly, or give an intelligent update on the situation, but instead, she burst into tears. Mrs. Harrison held her close and rubbed her back. "It's all right to cry," she soothed. "It's OK, sweetie." When Arilee's sobs had subsided, Mrs. Harrison sat beside her and took Arilee's long, thin hands into her own plump, dimpled ones.

"Adam told us about the possible solution in Toronto. We are praying that might become available for you."

"Thank you. I thought nothing could be harder than losing my mother or brother, but this . . ."

Mrs. Harrison nodded compassionately. "Nothing's harder than losing a child. How are Macy's spirits?"

"She cries in hunger and cries to go home. I can distract her with books and paper dolls and such for a while, but she grows restless and misses her brother."

"I'm to be here for a week," Mrs. Harrison said. "And then I've got to be home a bit, but I will come again when I can. Adam said the church ladies are bringing meals?"

"They've been wonderful. Look at all the cards they've sent." Arilee pointed to the lovely display she had pinned to the wall where Macy could see them easily. "Davis has stayed in town the past few Sundays, and I've been able to go to church. Adam promised that when Davis can't be here, he and I will switch off, one going Sunday morning and one Sunday evening. I don't want to ever be without true fellowship again. The way they pray for me when my mind is too scattered to even think what to say—"

Her dependence on this body of believers was far removed from Daddy's insistence that they must never be beholden, must never be needy, must always take care of their own problems. That independence had not brought freedom, but loneliness and captivity to perfection she could never achieve.

It was OK for her to cry in Mrs. Harrison's arms.

To tell Violet that she didn't understand God's purposes and her faith wavered.

To neglect cleaning the house and accept meals from near strangers who wanted to help.

To not be pressed and polished and put together, but tired, rumpled, and confused.

To sit with Macy, hour after hour, day after day, while she still had the chance.

Now she abruptly blurted out to Mrs. Harrison: "I love Adam. I haven't told him properly. I said so after we were up all night when Macy was diagnosed. We haven't had a real conversation since all this." She waved at the bed where Macy slept.

"No, I reckon not. It's like that in marriage too. Sometimes you don't talk for an awful long time about the most important things. But there's something sweet about having someone you know is there for you, no matter what. If you've given that boy of mine even a smidgen of hope you like him too, you just see if you can ever get rid of him now."

Near an azalea bush sporting a riot of pink blossoms, Davis sat with Muriel in the asylum garden. Shrilly, she berated him because he had not been there the past two Sundays. He stood from the bench and turned his back to her, looking at the high brick wall, ignoring the shrieks of patients inside the Powell Building and his desire to shriek too.

A psychiatrist from Johns Hopkins had come, recommended by the famed Dr. Meyer. The expense had been considerable, and the expert changed Muriel's diagnosis from schizophrenia to a progressing manic depression. But his report concluded that while the asylum might not be helping Muriel's condition, neither was it harming her. Davis had told no one of the report, for once he said the words, they would become irrevocably *real.*

"Macy is deathly ill," he said when Muriel at last settled into moody silence. "I needed to be with her."

He had told her this already. Twice. But the longer she stayed here, the more disconnected she became from the outside world, including a mother's natural care for her own children. No matter how much he talked to her about Nathaniel and Macy, they were strangers to her, their needs and concerns far outranked by her own.

"So, your sister can't take care of her either. Took my child from me, and now she can't even keep her healthy."

"Arilee has been caring for her to the point of wearing herself out. I am Macy's father. It was right for me to be with her."

"You love her more than me."

He forced himself to go back to the bench, to look at Muriel. "Macy needed me more than you needed me. Please, Muriel. Don't you care at all about your daughter?"

"Your sister took her. She's not mine anymore."

"Arilee didn't *take* Macy, she had to *take care* of Macy or send her to an orphanage. She protected her and raised her so that when you are better you can know and care for her too."

"I will never leave here."

He had thought this possibility was his greatest fear. For the past few years, it had been. But everything had changed when he'd come home from his mail run Friday night two weeks ago to see Arilee with swollen, dark-rimmed eyes and a pallor over her face. Adam had been urging her to eat, but the simple plate of food before her had been untouched.

"What's happened? Is it Brax?" he had asked.

He couldn't even remember now if it had been Adam or Arilee who had told him. He'd heard "diabetes," "Macy," "not long," "Grady hospital," while something inside him sputtered and died like a failing engine.

He'd tasked Adam with looking after Arilee, and he had been there when the hospital opened Saturday morning. He'd brought Macy flowers. Watching her scream at the nurses and gag as they forced her to eat a boiled egg, hearing her crying for toast and to go home—it had felt eerily similar to a visit with Muriel. And just as desperately, wretchedly hopeless.

CHAPTER 33

Mid-April to Mid-May, 1922

Adam saw in Arilee's countenance the single focus and grim determination of a soldier in the heat of battle. Often he found her staring into space, or he had to plead with her to eat and rest.

The meals from the church women helped tremendously, and he and Nathaniel took over dish duty each evening. Nathaniel became his shadow, though Arilee, worried over how Macy's illness affected the boy, still made sure she took Nathaniel to school every morning and tucked him in bed every night.

In the evenings, Adam, Arilee, and Nathaniel would gather around the radio from seven to eight to hear the musical selections of the brand new WSB station. It might be a choral group from one of the schools or toe-tapping music by local Fiddlin' John Carson. Arilee would use the time to catch up on the ironing, then afterward put Nathaniel to bed while Adam got his notes and books to study. While he studied, she often worked on a new little surprise to take to Macy at the hospital—felt dollies to dress, a box of colored sand with shells buried in it, stamps and an ink pad.

When the clock chimed ten, Adam would take her hand, read a psalm aloud, and pray over her, Macy, Nat, and Davis. He would kiss her cheek, say, "Good night, darlin'," and force himself to go to the carriage house where he'd toss and turn for a few hours until he could finally sleep.

In late April, his mother came again for a week. On a rainy evening, the three adults were in the library. He was working on a paper due next week; Arilee was knitting a sweater for Macy, now always cold in her emaciated state. Mother, meanwhile, tackled some much-needed mending. Suddenly,

Arilee rose and threw the knitting to the floor.

"I can't," she exclaimed.

Adam leapt up and came over to her, putting his arms around her. "Darlin', could we go sit on the balcony and talk about it?" he asked gently.

"I can't."

"You're exhausted. Why don't we pray and you try to get some sleep?"

"I can't, Adam. I can't pray again. I can't. I can't talk to you, and I can't talk to God, and sometimes I can't even breathe. I'm sorry. I'm so sorry. I can't."

He held her close and smoothed her hair, and after several moments, she whispered, "I need to go to bed."

"OK. I love you, darlin'."

She nodded but did not reply. He watched as she walked through the hall and up the stairs, but she never met his eyes.

He sat back down in the library and sighed heavily. "What am I doing wrong?" he asked his mother, folding and unfolding a page of notes from anatomy class.

"Looks to me like you're not doing anything wrong. You can't fix this."

He exhaled. "But that's what I do. I've fixed up this house. I've tried to fix Arilee's problems with how she feels about her father and brothers and church."

"Adam, she's a person, not a project. Do you love *her* or do you love what you want her to be?"

"I love her. As she is. But I ache seeing her hurting so much. Again."

"And she hates seeing Macy hurting. You can't fix Arilee any more than she can fix Macy."

"But she won't talk to me about anything. I mean, sometimes I wonder if she'd even notice if I disappeared. I don't know how to help if she shuts me out."

Mother looked at him compassionately. "You see Arilee's mettle and her weaknesses. You know how she will respond to tragedy. You could choose a young lady who hasn't a past full of pain and loss. A young woman who doesn't come with two children who see her as their mother but won't ever see you as their father. It would be easier, but you wouldn't know how an untested woman will measure up to the worse, sickness, and poverty you pledge to stay with each other through. What do you really want, Adam?"

"I want her," he answered without hesitation. "I've known from the start it would be hard. That's not what's bothering me. It's that she won't let me share it with her."

"I don't think she's keeping you out, son. I think she doesn't know herself how to walk through this." Mother's eyes misted over. "You know you have a sister in heaven. Four years before you and Josh. Our little girl was stillborn. Your father and I were devastated. Loss can drive you together or apart. And unlike with Josh, that loss nearly did separate us."

Adam wondered why he had naively assumed his parents always effortlessly loved and supported one other. "How did you fix it?"

"We stopped trying. Stopped trying to fix each other. Stopped trying to fix the situation, which was harder for your father than for me, because one way you're like him is you both want to solve problems, including ones that can't be solved. We learned to hold tight to Jesus and each other, and after a while, we were able to talk again. And finally, even to laugh. You and Josh were a comfort to us."

Adam studied his mother. She didn't speak of the loss of her daughter as something from decades ago, but as pain still as present as Josh's death.

"She would be twenty-six now," he mused, thinking of the sister he'd never known. "The same age as Ar—that's why you're drawn to her, isn't it?"

"It's not the only reason, but it has occurred to me." She pulled a small box out of her bag. "My mother gave me this ring, and I never had a daughter to give it to, but if you'd like to give it to Arilee when the time is right, I would be honored."

"Oh, Mother. Thank you." He took the ring, a beautiful aquamarine, flanked with a diamond and a pearl on either side. He couldn't have selected anything more perfect.

"You said back in March you didn't know how to earn her trust," Mother said. "But this, Adam. Being here day by day and not demanding anything of her. Being a person she can talk to *or* be silent with. Putting your own needs aside. If anything can build trust, selflessness sure can."

He nodded thoughtfully. "You're pretty wise, there, Mother," he said at last, rising and stretching.

"I knew you'd discover that someday," she returned lightly. "And in return, I'll say you're going to make Arilee a fine husband. God is at work, son, in bringing you two together. He's going to finish what He started here.

Be patient and let *Him* lead *you*, so you can best lead Arilee."

∞∞∞

On a Saturday, when Davis was at the hospital with Macy, Arilee heard the front doorbell. The church folks all used the back door, closest to the kitchen, for delivering meals. She couldn't recall the last time she'd heard the buzzer, and she opened the door to find Mrs. Margaret Rose Woodhouse standing there.

"Miss Rutledge," she said cheerily. "Good day."

Immediately, Arilee understood Davis's irritation with this too-perfect woman. *Her* eyes weren't rimmed in dark circles from lack of sleep, and *her* clothes didn't hang loosely because she grew thin, unable to eat while her tiny niece starved to death. Even the pleasantness of her greeting unreasonably annoyed Arilee.

"Hello, Mrs. Woodhouse," she forced herself to say. "Do come in."

They sat in the elegant old parlor, Arilee in her frumpy green-and-white gingham house dress across from Margaret Rose Woodhouse in her elegant drop-waist lavender chiffon number. A look completed by a charming braided and be-feathered hat with an off-the-face brim.

"I hoped you might have had a chance to finish going through the family letters or that you might allow me to do so." Mrs. Woodhouse got straight to the point.

Had it been just three months ago she'd found that awful letter? It seemed like a lifetime ago. At this moment, she didn't really care if her grandparents had been cannibals or crooks.

"Are you quite all right, Miss Rutledge?" Mrs. Woodhouse inquired when Arilee did not answer.

"No, I am not all right. I am in no way all right. My niece is dying of diabetes, and they say there's a tincture in Toronto that can save her, but none is available right now. We have to try to keep her alive by starving her to death until they can figure out how to make more of this miracle potion. We're out of time. So, to be perfectly blunt with you, Mrs. Woodhouse, I don't give a rat's rear end about who the skeleton in the basement was or why he was there. If you really want to be an influential journalist, why don't you use your investigative skills to find ways to save the living instead of trying to dig up the sins of the dead?"

Mrs. Woodhouse paled a little. "I am shocked to learn this about sweet Macy," she said. "I assure you, I will do all in my power to help."

This wasn't the response Arilee had been expecting. She sat speechless while Mrs. Woodhouse gave her a brief embrace before showing herself out.

"Well, Davis, you'd be proud of me," she muttered, "but I'm pretty ashamed of myself right now."

Four days later, the *Journal* ran this piece:

Local Girl Needs Miracle Tincture to Live

by M. R. Woodhouse

Macy Jane Rutledge, the almost four-year-old daughter of Mr. Davis Rutledge of Atlanta, is fighting for her life against the dreaded diagnosis of diabetes. Doctors in Toronto have developed an extract from animal pancreatic glands that could potentially save the lives of diabetic patients around the world. But right now, this extract is experimental and not available.

The article went on to describe what Arilee had already heard about experiments performed on dogs last summer and a few children receiving successful injections of the tincture this winter only to have the manufacturing of it come to a grinding halt in March.

For Macy Rutledge and thousands of children like her, the delay could indeed be deadly. Pray this miracle extract may soon be available to all in need.

"Do you think Davis will have a fit over it?" Adam asked as he finished reading the piece aloud over breakfast (strategically waiting till Nathaniel had run off).

"I'm not going to tell him. It can't hurt anything, can it? I'll certainly take all the prayers we can get."

"Good point. I can't imagine it will be noticed outside of town and the people who already know anyway. Maybe Woodhouse'll leave us alone now."

"Maybe. But I doubt it."

$$\infty \infty \infty$$

The following Saturday evening, the twentieth of May, they were eating supper together. Davis had spent most of the day with Macy and come back more taciturn and grumpy than usual. Mrs. Cantrell from church had brought over a roast chicken dinner, and they sat in the dining room pushing food around their plates, appetites dulled with a looming sense that it would not be long.

"Daddy, guess what, I learned how to whistle. Wanna hear?" Nathaniel looked up from his plate hopefully.

"Nat, not at the table," his father chastised without glancing at the boy.

Nathaniel scooted out of his chair and stood beside it to begin whistling. Arilee saw Adam hide a smile at Nathaniel's literal interpretation of "not at the table."

"Nathaniel!"

At his father's tone, Nathaniel returned to his seat, head down and tears filling his eyes. Arilee glared at Davis in annoyance, but they'd had this argument too many times for it to do any good to start again.

"Sorry, Daddy," the boy said after a few minutes.

"Please use your manners and eat your food."

"Yes, sir."

They finished eating in silence, the clinking of utensils and Nathaniel's sniffling the only sounds.

"May I be 'scused?" he asked Arilee dejectedly when he had mostly cleaned his plate.

"Yes, love," she replied before Davis could insist he take the last few bites. He scurried from the table and ran outside.

"I thought Brax was here." Davis looked about as if just noticing the absence.

"He did come by earlier, asked after Macy. I thought he'd join us for supper. I can't imagine why he doesn't want to spend time with us; it's so pleasant here."

Davis scowled at her sarcasm. "He's a selfish creep, Arilee. Why does that continue to surprise you?" He rose abruptly; a moment later, they heard static as he turned on the radio in the library.

She pushed back her chair, ready to flee upstairs to her balcony.

"Arilee." The authoritative calm of Adam's tone stopped her.

"No, Adam, I can't talk about anything right now. I can't."

"Arilee."

She met his eyes finally. His gray-green eyes looked at her with concern and compassion. But also something else.

"We have to stop this. We've both done it. Walking away—literally or figuratively—when it hurts too much to face the truth. We have to learn to stay and work it through or at least stay and be with each other in the pain."

"Adam—"

"No. Please. Go for a walk with me. Please."

For twenty seconds, she remained frozen, feeling that maybe their entire future together hinged on her answer.

"All right." Her concession came at a whisper, and she almost changed her mind before they were out the door.

He took her hand, and she appreciated his steady strength. For a while they walked in silence, the pleasant spring evening filled with the scent of the newly-blooming wisteria.

"Have you come to terms with the past? About your grandparents?" Adam's choice of subject surprised her a little, and she took a moment to answer.

"I don't know. Sometimes I think it makes sense, and my grandmother was brave in her own way. Other times, I think my existence and all of my family's is based on sin and a lie."

"Do you feel that way about Nat and Macy?"

"No."

"God is a Redeemer, and He brought something good out of something evil. And I don't know how, but I believe He will also do that in this situation with Macy."

"What about you? Have you been able to see God's redemption in your own past in France?"

"Fair enough." He rubbed his thumb in circles over her hand. They were at a lazy creek that ran through the back of the property. Frogs croaked to one another in a harmonic blend and dragonflies flitted over the water, their gossamer wings golden in the looming sunset. The scent of honeysuckle hung in the air. Arilee plucked a blossom and sucked the nectar out of the end, a long-forgotten girlhood pleasure.

"I can't change it. I'll always regret my rebellion and sinful actions. I'll always grieve Josh and the senselessness of his death. But all of it has shaped me, grown me, broken and remade me. God's grace—and yours—have humbled me and helped me be less self-centered."

"For what it's worth, I think you are very selfless, Adam. I know I haven't been the least attentive to you these past several weeks . . ."

"I'll be here, darlin'. Through this, and when it's all resolved."

Resolved. When Macy died, he meant. Only the thought that he would be there for her kept her from complete panic at the loss looming before them.

She stepped closer to him, and he put his arms around her and held her. She rested her head against his chest. That she, always too tall and awkward for a girl, could feel small and protected in his embrace still amazed her. He rubbed her back, and she relaxed, content, and yet wanting. She looked up and reached a hand behind his neck.

He took the cue. He lowered his head to kiss her, and she tingled with anticipation. They had been through so much since that lover's kiss over Shakespeare. All the revelations of her past and his, all the agony over Macy, all the learning to communicate and to stay.

For a moment, the memories of Walter and the barn and Daddy came rushing back, but instead of pulling away, she leaned in and thought about other memories. Including the fact that for the past several months, Adam had never done more than put his arm around her or give her a quick peck goodnight, even when she knew perfectly well he longed for more. He'd respected her. He'd demanded nothing of her. He'd waited for her to be ready. And she was.

His lips had barely touched hers when she heard, "Aunt Ari! Daddy says to come! The hospital called."

Adam grabbed her hand, and together they ran to the house.

CHAPTER 34

Saturday, May 20, to Wednesday, May 24, 1922

"The doctor asked if we want to bring Macy home to die," Davis said to Adam and Arilee as they hurried into the main hall. "He doesn't expect her to be conscious much longer."

Adam leaned against the banister, seeing past Davis's unreadable expression to his clenched fists and hard features.

"Harrison, you spend a lot of time with Nathaniel. What do you think would be best for him?"

"I think losing his sister will devastate him either way. But seeing her first will help him to understand what's happened better than us telling him."

"Have they talked to the doctors in Toronto?" Arilee demanded.

"Dr. Miller wired two days ago and got no response. Last week, they said not to come."

"But maybe if we *went*—"

"Macy can't survive travel anyway, Arilee. It's too late. There's no guarantee the serum would work even if they had it."

"But we have to try—"

"Arilee! They've asked and asked. All they hear is 'not yet.' It's too late for Macy, OK? It's too late. Don't make this harder than it already is."

Adam moved to put his arm around Arilee.

"Are we in agreement to bring her home for the end?" Davis looked from him to Arilee. She nodded.

"Did the doctor say how long?" Adam gently rubbed Arilee's shoulders.

"Probably a week at the most." Davis strode to the kitchen to call the hospital. They heard him arranging for an ambulance to bring Macy home in the morning. Adam and Arilee spent the rest of the evening moving Nathaniel into Davis's room and arranging the nursery to be comfortable and peaceful for Macy.

The next morning they all missed church, and Davis didn't go to Milledgeville. Macy came home. Davis carried her upstairs, and she smiled faintly at her room and her toys. Then she beamed at Nathaniel.

"I missed you, Nat. Wook, see the cat Miss Katie made me. It wooks wike Woodrow."

"I missed you too, Macy." Nathaniel, for perhaps the first time in his life, seemed at a loss for words. His sister's altered appearance and the knowledge she was dying were heavy burdens indeed for a seven-year-old.

"I'm tired," Macy said. "Now can I have strawberries, Aun'Ari?"

"I'm afraid we don't have any," Arilee answered. "The hospital sent home instructions about exactly what sort of food you are to eat."

Horrible stuff, all of it, Arilee thought. Celery and turnips and a bit of bland chicken.

For a moment, Macy's chin quivered. Then she snuggled down in her bed and dozed.

∞ ∞ ∞

On Monday morning, Arilee was fixing breakfast when Davis came down, duffle bag in hand.

"Where are you going?" Arilee dropped the spatula.

"Where do I go every Monday?"

"Good God, Davis, your daughter is dying and you're going to work?"

"I can't do anything to help her."

"But you can be here with her."

Davis swallowed his coffee, scalding hot. "I'll see you Friday night," he muttered and headed for the hall.

She followed him. "Are you out of your mind? Jefferson Davis Rutledge! How—"

"Call me a coward or whatever you want. But I can't watch her die. I saw Brax die, I thought, and it destroyed me. Then every week for the past two years, I've gone to see Muriel, and every week, it's like losing her again. At first, I hoped. Maybe she'll have turned a corner. Maybe this time she'll be a little better. Maybe we'll be a family again. I know now it's not going to change. I've lost her, and I'm left with a sick caricature of the woman I married.

"But this. My sweet, innocent baby girl? The only thing good to come out of all the mistakes I made and all the loss? No. I can't do it, Arilee. I won't."

She froze, speechless, as he headed out the front door. A moment later, Adam came in the back to find her still standing, staring at the door. Briefly, she told him what had happened.

"I agree he *should* be here, darlin', but he's not lying when he says he *can't*. I ran from Josh's death by working as hard as I could, as much as I could. His leaving isn't about how little he feels this, but how much."

Adam walked Nathaniel to school on his way to Emory, and Arilee went up to Macy's room. The child had become too weak to take interest in her favorite stories or dressing her dollies. She looked out the window at the roses now in bloom and birds flitting from one branch to the next. For most of that day and the next, Arilee sat cuddling her in the rocking chair, singing hymns to her as she had when infant Macy had first been given to her.

Wednesday morning, after looking at Macy, Adam stayed home from classes. Though she knew he should go, Arilee didn't protest. Early in the afternoon, the girl slipped into a diabetic coma.

"How much longer?" Arilee asked Adam wearily.

"I'm not sure. About a day. I have one idea."

"We aren't taking her back to the hospital."

"No, not that. If I gave her subcutaneous fluids, though, it might lengthen her life by several hours, staving off dehydration. Is it cruel to prolong the inevitable?"

Arilee looked at the still form, eyes and cheeks already sunken.

"No. She's not in pain now. We could try to reach Davis. Just in case he changed his mind and wants to hold her one last time. Several extra hours might give him time to get here."

"OK. I have the supplies, though only doctors are supposed to—"

"It doesn't matter, Adam. If you know how, I trust you to do what's best for her."

While Adam administered the fluids, Arilee made a long-distance phone call and left a message with Davis's supervisor, who assured her he would do his best to get word to her brother as soon as Davis landed from his current flight.

Then she sat down stupidly at the kitchen table. Adam came in, reporting that Macy was hydrated and resting. He began fixing himself and Arilee tea and the spice cake that Mrs. Sweet had brought over the day before.

"Macy brought us together, you know," Adam said. "If she hadn't run from you that day last June, I don't know if I would've seen you. If it had been another week or two before I met you at church—"

"That's assuming I even came back," Arilee interjected.

"True. Another week or two and I might have found a job elsewhere, and I never would have come here to work. Considering your proclivity at the time to bolt out the door and not talk to anyone at church, we would have been 'ships passing in the night.'"

"A literary reference instead of slang? I'm impressed."

"Now that I'm nearly a college graduate, I have to talk highbrow like you." He kissed the top of her head as he handed her the snack. She hadn't had lunch and couldn't remember if she'd eaten breakfast.

Arilee drank the tea and managed two bites of the cake. It looked and smelled delicious, but now everything tasted like sawdust in her mouth. She picked up a pamphlet from Barclay & Brandon Funeral Directors. Adam sat beside her, his arm resting comfortingly around her shoulders, as she looked at pictures of tiny caskets and tried to think what a service for Macy should be like. Brax, who'd spent the night in the circuit rider's room, came in and helped himself to a large wedge of cake. He stood silently eating and watching them.

They were startled by the sound of someone pulling in the driveway in a great hurry and a car door slamming, followed by the door buzzer a moment later. Adam rose and went to answer, while Brax, ever elusive, moved to the hallway.

A moment later, Adam reentered the kitchen, a look of apology on his face and Margaret Rose Woodhouse trailing him.

"Mrs. Woodhouse," said Arilee, meaning to rise, but not quite succeeding. "I'm afraid you've come at a bad time. Our Macy hasn't much longer."

"That's why I'm here." Mrs. Woodhouse looked about suspiciously. Her hair looked a bit askew and her chiffon dress bore a wrinkle in the skirt. "I could lose my job and more for telling you this. I lay awake all last night wrestling over what was the right thing to do."

She took a deep breath. "I know in the strictest confidence that a boy in Rochester, the son of a former congressman, has received the diabetes extract."

"There is some available then?" Adam dropped the cake knife he'd just picked up. "Insulin. They are calling it insulin now."

"This boy was in his final days, and received the tincture under orders that there be no press. I know the family through my deceased husband's relatives. There's not enough of the extract for all who need it, but there *is* some again. You need to *go*. Now. To Toronto."

Arilee looked at Adam.

"It's too late, isn't it?" she whispered.

"The Cincinnati-Atlanta Express takes all night, and then we'd still have over halfway to go. It would probably be a full twenty-four hours to get to Toronto. The odds aren't good."

"What about ten hours?" Brax stepped in from the hall. "Do you think she'd last ten hours?"

Adam leveled his eyes on him. "It's more likely."

"What if we flew there?" Brax looked at Arilee.

"Davis isn't due in till Friday night," Arilee said. "I'm trying to reach him, but I don't know how long it will take. Are *you* offering, Brax?"

He shrugged. "I'm flying out this afternoon." He glanced uncertainly at Margaret.

"This is our friend, Mrs. Woodhouse," Arilee said, not wanting to scare Brax away with details of the woman's profession.

Brax gave the smallest nod of acknowledgment. "If we left right now, we could be in Toronto before tomorrow morning. My plane has lights. I fly night or day."

Arilee exhaled.

"I'll fly with him and hold Macy," Adam volunteered. "If you want to try this, Arilee."

"No," said Brax. "You're tall and you weigh, what? Sixty pounds more than her, at least. I've already got the plane loaded with my deliveries. I'm going to Cleveland, a few hours across the lakes from Toronto. If I do this, I'm only taking Sis and Macy."

"I don't want Arilee in that kind of danger!" Adam slapped his palms on the kitchen counter.

"It's up to her, but I've given my conditions."

Arilee knew *she* had to make the decision, even as she'd had to make every other decision regarding Macy since she was four months old.

She rose and walked over to the kitchen shelf. She picked up a framed picture of Grandma Luella, Aunt Celeste, and Aunt Odessa, with Jewel in the background, as she'd had to be her whole life. These were the women of Wisteria House. Arilee might not be related to all of them, but she knew their heartaches intimately.

War.

Loss.

Scandal.

Shame.

Desperation.

Sacrifice.

She'd lived all those things.

"I'd rather die trying to save her than sit back bitterly bemoaning someone else taken from me. What do I need to do, Brax?"

"First off, have a little faith in me. I've flown hundreds of flights, and I'm not going to get you killed. I've got an extra helmet, goggles, and flying suit, but you'll need warm clothes on underneath. Borrow some of Davis's overalls. Extra socks, thick. Dress Macy like she was going out to play in the snow. We'll keep her wrapped up in blankets, and she'll have your body heat. Harrison, if you drive us to the airstrip, it'll save a heap of time."

"I don't mind driving," Mrs. Woodhouse piped up.

"No," replied all three of the others in chorus.

Brax disappeared out to his room to get the pilot gear. "I don't want you to do this," Adam protested again. "I don't care what Brax says, it's not safe, and the conditions will be harrowing. Please, convince him to take *me*."

"He won't be convinced. You know that. It has to be me. You know that too."

He didn't answer, but pain and fear warred across his countenance.

Arilee stepped beside him and took his hand. "*You* said, love doesn't mean shielding someone from heartache and hardship but trusting them to God when you can't be with them."

"You shouldn't listen to idiots."

"I'm sorry that my life is as tangled as those wisteria vines out front. I love you, and only you, as a woman loves a man. But there are other kinds of love and—"

"And you wouldn't be the woman *I* love if they weren't all a part of who you are. I understand, darlin'. I adore you for it. But I'd rather go back to the trenches than send you to the skies."

The moment between them evaporated as Brax returned with the flying accessories. He handed Arilee the helmet. "Figure this out with your hair, and I'll put the suit and goggles in the car."

She turned to Adam. "Will you telephone Mrs. Macdonald and see if she will pick up Nathaniel from school and keep him till—I don't know?"

"I'll call now," Adam assured her. "And I'll pick up Nat from their house tonight."

"Mrs. Woodhouse, would you help me?" Arilee asked, suddenly registering that the woman had stood there overhearing the entire conversation between her and Adam.

The journalist looked surprised but not displeased as she followed Arilee up to her bedroom. "Please call me Meg," she said. "We must be close in age."

"I need you to bob my hair," Arilee explained when the bedroom door was shut. "So it will fit inside this helmet."

"What will Adam say?"

"We'll find out." Arilee pulled out her hairpins, shaking free her waist-length tresses. She sat down in a straight-back chair and shut her eyes; three times she heard the metal twang of the scissors opening and closing and felt the sudden lightness as she was shorn.

"If we had more time, I could shape it up better," Margaret said apologetically.

"I'll worry about it later." Arilee refused to look in the mirror. Seeing the nut-brown swathes lying on her bedroom floor already turned her stomach. She began stuffing a change of clothes and her Bible into an old valise. She pulled cash out of a drawer, as well as the passport she'd secured after Macy was first diagnosed and they'd hoped to hear from Toronto any day.

"There's a large suitcase in the attic," she directed Margaret. "After we leave here, I need you to rummage through my dresser and wardrobe and pack all the things I might need for an indefinite stay in Toronto. I'd rather a woman packed for me than Davis or Adam. Davis can bring the suitcase when he comes, if he comes, you know, because by some miracle this all works."

"I have two sisters. I'll take good care of getting what you need."

"Davis would have a conniption if he knew I'm leaving and giving you unfettered access to the house," she muttered.

"Arilee." Margaret's tone made her stop and meet the woman's chocolate brown eyes. "I would never profit off someone else's misery. I am here as your friend."

"Thank you." Arilee again thought that in different circumstances she could be great friends with Margaret Woodhouse.

Arilee took a pair of Davis's clean overalls out of his room. They were too long and broad, but she cinched them at the waist with a belt and put a heavy knit sweater over the top. She stuffed a cloche in her bag, added in extra clothes for Macy, and shut it. Then she dressed Macy in long underwear, a woolen dress, her coat, mittens, and extra socks. The girl hardly stirred.

Arilee stood in the hall when Adam came up the stairs. He stared at her, his face unreadable.

"Please say something," she said. "Are you very angry at me?"

"No. I'm not a little bit angry at you. It is something of a mystery to me how the perfectly proper Miss Rutledge became a bobbed-headed, trouser-wearing barnstormer."

He winked at her roguishly, and she smiled a bit in spite of herself. Adam went into Macy's room and gently lifted her. He tucked the crocheted cat in her arms, and Arilee picked up the valise.

"You ready?" he asked.

She wasn't really, but she nodded and bade Margaret goodbye. She glanced back at Wisteria House as she climbed into the automobile. When and under what circumstances would she see it again?

No one said much on the drive to the old racetrack, now Candler

Field, which was planned for the city's future landing field and operated somewhat informally as an airstrip already. Adam parked on the field where Brax directed them, near a small wooden shed and a biplane painted khaki. Arilee lay Macy across the backseat and got out of the auto, as did the men.

"That's the largest wingspan on an airplane I've ever seen," Adam commented.

"This is a De Havilland DH-4, with a 400 horsepower Liberty Engine," Brax said, proud as a new father.

Arilee, perspiring in her heavy clothes, looked at the contraption of metal, wood, fabric, and leather. This would transport her and Macy across the country in a night? She shook her head and chewed on her bottom lip. Her brothers had flown in planes similar to these in dogfights, she reminded herself. *She'd* been on a Ferris Wheel once.

"Don't worry, it's been modified quite a bit since the days these were nicknamed 'the flaming coffin.'" Brax picked her up so unexpectedly she squealed.

"I'm going with 125," he said. "Even with those heavy clothes. You've gotten too scrawny, Sis, and lost your dimples. With the flying suit and Macy who's hardly a whisper, we're around 160."

"I have a satchel," she said, handing it to him. "And blankets." Brax frowned in thought, then strode over to the plane and began moving and unloading things into a small outbuilding. Arilee turned to Adam, who stood leaning on the roadster, scowling at the plane.

"Come here," he said and opened his arms to her. His embrace helped still her trembling.

"You're the bravest woman I know," Adam whispered after a while. "I promise I'll be praying for you all the way, all night long. I love you, darlin', with all my heart."

"Adam?" Her mind swirled with all the things she needed to say to him. In case.

"Hmm?"

She stepped back a bit, needing to see his face. "Thank you for loving me enough to let me go. To try this crazy thing. For being my anchor these past two months and showing me Christlike love when I had nothing to give you in return." She blinked. "I hope we get a chance . . ."

He pulled something from his pocket and met her gaze with gentle certainty.

"I know this isn't the time or the place or the way. But I want you to have something to see, to feel, to constantly remind you while we are apart that I love you and you belong to me. Would you wear this ring, and would you be my wife?"

This was *that* moment. The one she'd locked away in her heart with other hopeless dreams. The moment others might have, but she never would. Only now, at nearly twenty-seven years old, on the verge of doing the scariest thing she'd ever done and risking the future he offered her . . . now standing here hot and sweaty in these hideous clothes with her hair chopped off . . . now this good, true man who knew the entire mess of her family and the complication of her life *wanted* her. Loved her.

She nodded her head, incapable of speech.

He slipped the ring on her finger; it fit perfectly. "It belonged to my mother, a gift from her mother many years ago," he said. "She loves you too, and she wanted you to have it, to know she welcomes having you as a daughter."

"It's beautiful," Arilee whispered. "I'm proud to wear it. So very honored to be yours. Thankful to become part of your family."

"Let's go," called Brax, oblivious, as he came around from the far side of the plane.

Arilee stepped into and fastened the flying suit and tried to figure out the hideous leather helmet.

"Let me help," said Adam. "I think you're supposed to do this first." He bent and kissed her lips tenderly, then gently caressed the sides of her face.

Brax climbed into the cockpit and secured his harness. Adam helped her up into the deep but narrow second seat. Then he gently lifted Macy from the car, kissed her forehead, and handed her up to Arilee.

She secured the harness around herself and Macy, then Adam handed her the blankets. She cocooned Macy in them, making sure the child could breathe yet remained shielded from the wind. The valise sat at her feet in the deep, narrow well of a seat.

Adam moved to spin the large wooden propeller as Brax directed him. Brax started the engine and Adam moved over to watch by the Stutz.

"I love you," she called over the clacking of the engine.

"I love you, Roberta Edwarda Lee Rutledge!" he yelled back, succeeding in making her laugh in spite of everything.

The plane began to move. Faster and faster, bumping down the grassy airstrip. And then they left the ground and headed for the sky.

CHAPTER 35

Wednesday, May 24, 1922

U nnatural stillness greeted Davis as he rushed into the house at five o'clock Wednesday evening. None of the usual creaks of floorboards or chatter of Nathaniel's unending questions met his straining ears.

He'd been barely able to function all Monday and Tuesday. This morning when he'd nearly crashed his plane after foolishly forgetting to refuel, instead of being lambasted by his boss, he'd been given a message about Macy's impending death and sent home. A fellow pilot, Tucker, agreed to take some extra shifts for him, and everyone offered their sympathy and concern.

Now he wandered through the empty rooms until he found Adam sitting at the kitchen table, face lined with a weariness that reminded Davis of the soldiers he'd seen shuffling out of the trenches after a battle.

"Where's Macy? Am I too late?"

"She slipped into a coma. She has hours left." Adam turned an empty mug over and over in his hands.

"She's at Grady?"

"No. They took her. Arilee and Brax."

"Took her where?"

"To Toronto. To see if they could get insulin. Mrs. Woodhouse came and told us she'd found out confidentially they have some again."

"That Woodhouse woman! She always causes trouble."

"She risked her job to tell us."

"Why didn't you take them?"

"I can't fly."

Davis felt like something fell out of his middle.

"Fly? What the devil?"

"Brax took Arilee and Macy in his plane. I tried to get Arilee to let me take the risk, but Brax wouldn't agree, because I weigh more, and he already had the plane loaded with cargo. And Arilee can see to her care, and I can't because I'm not her blood kin."

"Brax took them in his plane?"

"Yes."

"You didn't stop this?"

"I helped them."

Davis grabbed Adam by his shirt front, hauled him out of the kitchen bench, and slammed him into the wall, pinning him with his arm.

"Are you out of your mind? Brax? You let Brax fly them to Toronto? Halfway in the dark? In his plane full of bootleg liquor?"

"Liquor? I don't know anything about that. His plane was on the outskirts of Candler Field, so he couldn't have been—"

"Right, Adam. Because there's never any corruption in the city of Atlanta. Brax can't be happy unless he's on the wrong side of the law. The signs are all there. I'd bet my life he's involved in some illegal operation, probably with gangsters."

Adam met his eyes, blinking. "There was no other chance for Macy, anyway."

"You said Macy is going to die. But it's not enough I have to lose my little girl, have already essentially lost my wife and both parents, you thought it would be a good idea to finish off my sister as well? How about Nathaniel? Did you invite him to play with matches on the roof or splash in the stream with a live wire?"

"Nat is with the Macdonalds. Arilee wanted to do it. She knew the risk. She made her own decision."

"And you were OK with that?"

"Of course not! We all know the odds are it won't work and Macy will die on the way. But before God, Davis, we couldn't stay here and watch her die if *anything* could be tried to save her. We couldn't ask God for a miracle and then not do the one thing we could."

"You're a fool, Harrison. They're flying straight into a massive storm formation."

"Is Brax a good pilot?"

"Was he pie-eyed?"

"No."

"He's a better pilot than me, when he's not full of hooch or horsefeathers." Davis finally released Adam and paced the kitchen, running his hands through his hair, muttering profanity. Adam shook himself and started for the door.

"Where are you going?" Davis demanded.

"Wednesday night prayer meeting at church. I plan to stay all night or till we hear from Arilee. I'm asking God for a miracle."

"Yeah, sure, fine. Maybe God will listen to you. God doesn't do good things for me."

Adam spun back around, and now he got in Davis's face.

"Doesn't He? Is it really that God doesn't do good things for you, Davis, or is it that you've shut yourself off from God and His people and become too bitter and stubborn and sorry for yourself to see His goodness anymore?"

"You're an annoying mustard plaster, aren't you?"

"You think God's abandoned and failed you because your father did, but that's not who He is."

"Since you know it all, how do you explain—"

"I don't and I can't, but I'm sure as heck not gonna figure out anything talking to you. As you told me once about Arilee, man up and say how you feel. Take up your dogfight with God. He's the only One who can help you."

Adam slammed his Panama hat on his head and slammed the front door shut behind him.

Davis wandered out to the back porch. Arilee's annoying cat came meowing, in what sounded like a demand for something. A cool mist fell from the overcast sky.

Somewhere above, his sister attempted to warm fragile Macy with her own body and his brother attempted to fly through God-knew-what weather, and Davis couldn't help any of them. It was not rain soaking his cheeks as he bent over double on the back steps.

"How can I hope? But how can I bear to lose my child? Oh, God, why won't you let me die instead?"

But he couldn't die. He had to live and work and provide for everyone. Though he conveniently blamed Brax for drawing him into the army, the offer of a pilot's wages to better support his wife and abandoned mother also had enticed him. Now there were medical bills and legal bills, besides providing for the family. Not to mention he might have to repay the government thousands of dollars for Brax's life insurance policy. He'd become as much a machine as his plane. Work. He kept working and didn't let anyone see the no-man's-land of his own heart.

"Oh, God," he moaned.

Go to church.

He gave a short laugh. What kind of man ignored God for years and showed up at the house of the Lord only when he desperately wanted something out of Him? A hypocrite, that's who. A hypocrite, just as his father had been.

As the plane leveled off, Arilee's stomach settled back into her gut instead of her chest, and she opened her eyes and looked around with appropriate awe. No wonder Davis did this week after week. Did he ever lose the thrill of seeing the world from above? Trees and farms dotted the landscape below, punctuated by creeks and hills. Entranced, she took it in, heedless of the passage of time until gradually the view to their right grew shadowy, while to their left the lowering evening sun gilded the plane. She wished Adam were seeing this wonder with her. She fingered the precious ring.

Brax saw these things regularly too. How could he look at this magnificence and deny the One who had created it? *Oh, God, open His eyes to the truth. Use even this situation with Macy to help him see who You are.*

As they flew over the Appalachians, she thought of the Scripture:

I will lift up mine eyes unto the hills, from whence cometh my help.
My help cometh from the Lord, which made heaven and earth.
. . . The Lord shall preserve thy going out and thy coming in
from this time forth, and even for evermore.

The God who had made this beauty before her held and helped her now. Macy still breathed, still clung to life. Arilee rubbed the girl's limbs, whispering, "I love you, baby. Hang on just a bit longer."

A flash illuminated the western sky. Brax turned the plane a few degrees east. Still, rain began to pelt them, and the clouds thickened. The plane bounced as the wind picked up, knocking Arilee this way and that. Despite her many layers, cold seeped in. But under a waterproof canvas, Macy remained dry and safe, her tiny body cushioned between Arilee and quilts Mama had made years ago.

As abruptly as it had started, the storm passed, or perhaps they passed through it. The fading sunlight illuminated a field below, and she heard Brax yell. He began circling the plane, taking it lower with each lap. They jolted across a landing strip with such force Arilee expected to find bruises later.

Blessed silence filled the air when Brax shut off the engine.

"Almost missed it," he said, tearing off his goggles and hopping out of the plane. "This is where we refuel. There's not another good place for 100 miles."

Arilee took off her own headgear and noted an outhouse and a tent but no people at this field. Brax got a large metal can out of the De Havilland and began refueling the plane.

"This is gonna take a minute," he advised. "I suggest you get out, stretch your legs, visit the outhouse."

Making sure Macy was safely settled, she ungracefully climbed out of the plane, thinking of Adam helping her into the seat a few hours ago and blushing as she considered exactly where he'd placed his hands to bolster her up and in.

"Here." Brax threw her a flashlight. "Don't fall in the hole."

She nodded and went to take care of her personal business, which took a while with both the flying suit and overalls to undo and redo. Nonetheless, Brax still stood refueling when she returned. She stood watching him, glad to stretch after the cramped hours of the first leg of their journey.

"You OK?" he asked, handing her his canteen in exchange for the flashlight. "You haven't said anything since we landed."

"It's breathtaking one minute and treacherous the next. I can see why you and Davis love flying. And why you get paid so much. I'm glad to have this glimpse into your world."

Brax smiled. "Yep. Watch out, or it'll get in your blood too."

"No, thanks. Where are we anyway?"

"Near Lexington, Kentucky."

"Kentucky! And it's only been a few hours."

"Three. Pretty remarkable with the load we're carrying. You're flying with an ace, Sis, and *Unseen Things Above* here is a workhorse of a plane. Next stop, Cleveland. You want anything to eat?"

She shook her head. She would likely lose it.

"All right, then. Let's fly 'for the night is coming.'"

Davis walked through the rain, the cold drops pelting him, hitting the warm ground, and making mist rise. If only the rain could cleanse his soul and soften the hardness of his heart.

In the gray, light shone invitingly from the church windows. He slipped inside and stood at the back. A man he did not know prayed aloud. "Lord, guide the pilot, whether he believes in Your guidance or not. Protect our sister Arilee and that precious child and bring them safely to their desired haven. Place friends along their way to aid them, and may there be effective treatment to heal Macy and restore her to life."

The prayer was punctuated by "amens" and "yes, Lords" throughout. Davis drew nearer. Adam knelt near the front, lips moving in silent prayer. Billy Sweet sat in a pew, his walking stick beside him, holding hands with a red-haired young woman Davis assumed to be his wife. There were over two dozen people here; though a few looked familiar, Davis didn't really know anyone other than Billy and the minister. Yet voice after voice rose on behalf of Arilee and Macy.

He sat down heavily in an empty pew. After several folks had prayed, Pastor Andy said, "Amen" and walked over to Davis. He put his arm around him and offered a simple: "Welcome, Davis, I'm glad you came."

"I—I'm Macy's father." Davis felt he owed the watching crowd this explanation, then waited for looks of censure that it had taken his daughter's impending death to get him here.

"Daddy!" Nathaniel's head appeared from where he'd been lost among the pews, and he ran to Davis who caught him in his arms. Soon they were surrounded by people praying over them and for Macy; others clapped him on the shoulder and promised they would be up throughout the night praying for Macy's safe arrival in Toronto and for the miracle cure to save her life.

A woman he vaguely recognized came over to him. Her hair was as red as Billy's wife's, and the resemblance strong enough that he figured she must be the younger woman's mother.

"I'm Alannah Macdonald, Arilee's friend. Nathaniel is welcome to stay with us anytime, for as long as you need. If you need to go to Toronto, and want him here to finish school—however we can help, we are happy to do so. It's all boys at my house now that Cornelia's married—and had a boy." He noticed then that Billy's wife held a child who looked about two years old.

"Thank you, ma'am," he answered, as Nathaniel wriggled down and ran after a red-haired boy. "I'm much obliged for your help."

She waved her hand. "He's a sweet boy; it's no trouble." She glanced over at where Adam sat in the front pew. "Oh, good, Andy's talking to him," she said. "Poor young man is distraught."

"He seemed plenty confident when he told me off earlier," Davis remarked drily.

Mrs. Macdonald looked at him curiously. "Oh, but he promised himself he would always protect Arilee, and he let her go into danger. It's eating him up."

Davis supposed he'd been rather unfair to Adam. As ill-advised as the plan might be, it had been done in hopes of saving Macy, and letting Arilee go had to hurt. Not to mention that Arilee and Adam appeared to have suspended whatever personal plans they had to focus on his little girl's care over the past several months.

He was moving toward Adam when a man who looked about fifty clapped him on the shoulder, the same man who'd been praying when he entered.

"John Sweet," he said, offering his hand. "I'm glad to meet you, Davis. You don't know me, but my wife and I went with our former pastor and his wife, Rev. and Mrs. Curtis Wood, to visit your mother after your father left."

Davis stiffened. The man's tone, though tinged with a bit of a Northern accent, sounded kind, yet Davis wondered if his greeting would be followed with the "sins of the fathers passed down to the children" warning or the "be sure your sin will find you out" interrogation as to if he had been covering for his father. He'd heard both more times than he could count.

"Your mother was a saintly woman. And clearly you and your sister were a great comfort to her. She told us what you did in giving up your own savings and selling your own home to repay what your father had stolen."

Mr. Sweet cleared his throat, and his distinct blue eyes shone with unshed tears. "Rarely in my life have I heard of such principle and integrity, son. I want to encourage you—God sees you. He sees the quiet, selfless acts of valor. And He will reward you for your faithfulness."

"The only thing I want is the life of my child," Davis said hoarsely, in shock over this near-stranger's blessing. "But I don't have enough faith to pray for that."

"Then let us all pray it for you. I have been in a similar position. During the epidemic, I nearly lost my oldest daughter."

He nodded toward the dark-haired young woman who stood beside Pastor Andy, his arm around her waist.

"The doctor had given up, had called the coroner. I prayed like the father in the Gospels, 'Lord, I believe; help thou mine unbelief.' It takes faith to hope for healing. And it takes even greater faith to accept as His goodness if He chooses not to heal."

Davis nodded. He needed someone here to be angry at him, to condemn him. It would be more comfortable.

A middle-aged woman holding the hands of two toddlers came up beside Mr. Sweet. "Sarah, I was telling Davis about when we went to visit his mother. Davis, this is my wife Sarah, and our two youngest children."

"I was heartbroken to learn of your mother's passing," Mrs. Sweet said so sincerely Davis believed her. "What a lovely Christian woman. Your sister favors her not only in looks, but in character. We certainly have loved having Arilee and the children here. Please know you are welcome any time your schedule might allow."

Another person saying it might have sounded reproachful, but Mrs. Sweet's tone held warmth and regard. "Thank you, ma'am," he murmured.

Most of the congregation had shuffled out of the church by now, but

Pastor Andy came back over. "I will be back to pray with you and Adam," he said, "but I want to take my wife home first. She's not feeling quite well." Mr. Sweet added that he would return later also.

Davis started to say no one had to come back but instead murmured, "Thank you." He needed others with stronger faith to bolster his.

∞ ∞ ∞

Within an hour, nothing remained in view except occasional lights on the ground. The temperature dropped as night fell and they continued northward. Clouds covered the sliver of moon. After a while, fat, angry drops began pelting them. The wind picked up and began whipping the plane around. This time, they weren't in and out of the storm quickly. It seemed the storm was flying them, rather than that they were flying through the storm. Arilee shook from more than the cold.

The plane rose on the wind and tilted so far to the left Arilee thought they would be inverted. She'd been to one of those barnstorming shows once with Davis and the kids, about a year after he'd returned. Of course, Nathaniel had been completely enamored. She'd watched the wing walkers and the pilots rolling the planes and decided adventures on the ground were quite enough for her.

A jagged streak of lightning to their immediate right sizzled down to earth. Pea-sized hail hit the exposed part of her face, icy bits pinging against her goggles and the body of the plane. She heard Brax yell profanity into the wind.

Adam had said he would pray all night. Recalling the look on his face, she knew it hadn't been empty talk. He feared for her.

She feared for him. He'd lost his brother, and now he was going to lose her too. She'd left him for a desperate fool's errand, but he might wrongly assume guilt for her death as he did for Josh's.

Why would God give them Macy only to take her after such a short time? Macy's birth had sent Muriel into a tailspin from which she had never recovered. Caring for an infant had overwhelmed Arilee. And yet unconditionally loving this helpless, motherless child had saved her from sinking into the bitterness of Odessa or the madness of Muriel. She had had to keep going because Macy needed her.

She could never view this short life as a mistake. Loving Macy had kept her soul alive. Somehow the daily pouring out of herself for both the children had become a spiritual discipline, an act of worship that had kept her tethered to God in the raging winds of her own doubts and fears.

"Oh, Jesus, this child is Yours!" she screamed into the wind. If God's purposes for Macy's life—and her own—were completed, she would not cling to their lives in desperation.

But Brax, who claimed not to believe in God at all, if he perished—

"Oh, Jesus, help us!"

CHAPTER 36

Wednesday, May 24, 1922

After the church cleared out, Nathaniel lay across a pew, covered up with Davis's jacket, and fell asleep. Davis sat with him for a while, then wandered over to Adam on the front pew and lowered himself beside him.

"You OK?"

Adam shrugged. "Are you?"

"Not really."

"I wouldn't say everything's jake." Adam folded and unfolded a discarded church bulletin. "Brax said he'd get them there in ten hours. Arilee promised to send a telegram as soon as she could. They should be over halfway now."

Davis felt his chest tighten.

"I don't know if I did the right thing," Adam admitted, voice low. "But it wasn't my place to tell Arilee what she could and couldn't do. I tried to be the one to go. I hope you know, I would have done it without a second thought. I love Arilee with all my being, and right now reminds me of being stuck in the mud of a rat-filled trench taking fire."

"I'm mad at myself." Davis exhaled. "I should have been here. Macy's my daughter. I should be the one taking her to Toronto right now . . ."

He didn't add his ever-present fear: he was failing his children as his own father had failed him. Sure, he stayed faithful to their mother, and he provided for them. But from a distance. "I'll go up there as soon as we hear something."

"Can I come with you, Daddy?" Nathaniel popped up suddenly, startling

Davis and making him wonder how much of the conversation the boy had heard and understood.

"Yeah, squirt. But we'll take the train. No airplanes for you yet."

Davis walked over to the pew to settle Nathaniel. Unexpectedly, the boy snuggled into his lap. "I love you, Daddy," he murmured sleepily and soon dozed off again. Davis stroked the blond hair back from the child's face. How long had it been since he'd just held and loved on his boy?

How long had it been since he'd allowed himself to be held and loved by his Heavenly Father? How long since he'd trusted the wisdom of God's sovereign plan with the same acceptance of his boy trusting Davis's own uncertain plans?

He thought of Christ's postponement in coming to heal the dying Lazarus. His slowness in getting to Jairus's home to save his desperately ill daughter. The delays had not been accidents. They had led to a greater miracle and more glory to God. Perhaps Macy's condition was not retribution for his own sins "but that the works of God should be made manifest" in her.

"Oh, God, show Yourself to me, whether by her life or her death," he whispered. As Davis sat staring into Nathaniel's sleeping countenance, awash with the peace born of innocence, Adam began to sing:

"Be still, my soul: the Lord is on thy side.
Bear patiently the cross of grief or pain.
Leave to thy God to order and provide;
In every change, He faithful will remain.
Be still, my soul: thy best, thy heav'nly Friend
Through thorny ways leads to a joyful end."

The anguish that had shadowed Adam's face all night had been replaced with a look of rest not unlike that on Nathaniel's face. Davis still struggled to find the words for prayer, the faith to believe for Macy's healing. But one thing he knew. Unlike his father, the Lord would never leave him. And Davis clung to the One who was holding him as surely and as tenderly as Davis held his own beloved son.

As the storm raged about her, into Arilee's heart came words of a song she hadn't thought of in years. The speech class she'd taught at Canton High School had also encompassed voice for several weeks, and she had chosen this obscure hymn for the high school chorus because of its beautiful lyrics.

Now she began to sing at the top of her lungs, her words snatched up by the wailing winds and drowned out by hail banging against the metal plane.

"Be still, my soul: the Lord is on thy side . . ."

She loved the description of God as "thy best, thy heav'nly Friend." He had never left her desolate.

"Be still, my soul: thy God doth undertake
To guide the future, as He has the past.
Thy hope, thy confidence let nothing shake;
All now mysterious shall be bright at last."

She sang it into the wind, loud and strong, concluding with:

"Be still, my soul: the waves and winds still know
His voice Who ruled them while He dwelt below."

He could find nowhere to land.

Brax had never flown through wind like this. He lowered their altitude until they were barely clearing the treetops. But he couldn't see a break anywhere. Not that he could see much at all, the danged rain blowing in all over his goggles and instruments, his airplane's lights like tiny star specks against the black firmament.

They were going to plunge to gruesome deaths below.

He had one parachute. If he took *Unseen* back up . . . ? But Sis would never leave Macy, and she couldn't jump out with her. And he couldn't abandon them.

They were all going to die.

He hadn't made ace in six weeks without facing his mortality repeatedly. Defying death had been a thrilling game to his eighteen-year-old self. His world-weary twenty-one-year-old self longed for some meaning to his life to make sense of his death.

Brax had heard people speak of voices in the wind, and for a moment, he thought terror had driven him batty. Then he realized the voice he heard through his leather helmet and the cacophony of the storm was his sister's soprano. Despite being dubbed "The Walking Hymnal" by the fellows in his squad, he didn't recognize the song she sang now. The seats on the DH-4s had been designed too far apart to allow for communication between the pilot and the passenger, but a moment later, he caught snatches of "It Is Well," and the familiar hymn jolted something in him.

He wasn't really an atheist. He longed to be. He *wanted* it all to be fairy tales. But his reflex right now was to cry out to the God to whom Arilee sang.

The hail dissipated, though the lightning and rain continued. Sis kept singing. "He Will Hold Me Fast," and "From Every Stormy Wind," and "What a Friend We Have in Jesus." The rain lessened. Brax pushed off his spattered goggles and squinted through the dark. Lights from a city dotted below. The compass showed they were headed due west, and he needed to adjust their course, but in what direction? The wind had blown them so fiercely he had no idea where they were, and they were out of time to figure it out. The engine sputtered, its fuel gone.

And then before him were the lights of an airstrip that looked like—

He began trembling.

He saw the tents and shacks and ramshackle outbuildings. There was Mill Creek. Part of the transcontinental mail route, the Cleveland airfield in Woodland Hills Park was unmistakable. Under perfect conditions, it should have taken them three hours to arrive here. But it had been only two and a half. The storm had blown them in the right direction faster than he could have flown here on his own.

His feet eased the rudder to hone in on an empty grassy spot, and he brought *Unseen* to a jolting but successful landing. He cut the engine off and sat staring into the darkness.

They should be dead now. For multiple reasons.

"Brax?"

"Are you OK?" he asked, turning to look at Arilee, glad she couldn't see his tears in the dark.

"The Lord brought us through."

"I don't know how else we didn't go down."

"Oh." She shivered. "I'm glad I thought it was just what you pilots do every day."

He gave a shaky laugh and climbed out. She handed Macy down to him and climbed out herself.

"Before I refuel and unload, there's a shack over there with coffee and simple food. You want anything?"

"Coffee sounds good."

He handed Macy back to her and strode to the concession shack. Trembling and nauseated from the flight, he plunked money on the counter, then leaned against the wall and closed his eyes while he waited for the Hungarian attendant to pour two mugs. He mentally played "It Is Well" on the piano, his fingers moving as if they could touch the keys, until his shaking finally stopped. But at the sound of men yelling outside, he glanced out the window and swore.

A dozen men in suits and fedoras surrounded Arilee and Macy.

Prohibition agents?

Capone's men?

Either way, could this night get any worse?

If he disappeared right now, slithered into the shadows and ran—

One of the men pulled out handcuffs. Arilee still clung to Macy, pointing at the child and gesturing at the plane.

Over his dead body would they arrest Arilee in his place. Maybe they knew that. Maybe this was all a setup to get to him, but if so, they'd found his Achilles' heel. Because now he was eleven again and begging Dad to stop beating his sister and let him take her place.

He jogged over to the plane. "What's going on here?"

"Are you the pilot of this craft?" A large man with a nasally New Jersey accent poked a finger at his chest.

"Yes." Strike one.

"You've got quite a load of liquor. Enough to put you and your *sister* here behind bars for a very long time."

Strike two.

"Listen," Brax snapped, "she doesn't have anything to do with this. You see the child she's holding. The girl is dying, and the cure is in Toronto, and I told my sister she could ride along, and I'd get them there. That's the God-honest truth. Why else would we bring a half-dead kid through the night and a storm in an airplane, for Pete's sake?"

"Funny how you needed a plane full of tiger milk to get her there."

"I loaded the plane before Sis decided to come. She has nothing to do with my business. She doesn't know anything about it."

A tall, mustached fellow snorted.

"Who are you and what do you want?" Brax ground his teeth.

"Pretty sure we're holding all the cards here. Now maybe your sister is innocent, and maybe she isn't, but that'll be for a judge to decide."

Brax swore again. "Then the blood of this child is on your hands."

"She looks more dead than alive to me. Miss, what's your name?"

Well, they didn't hold *all* the cards.

He shook his head slightly at Arilee and spoke up instead.

"What if in exchange for you letting her go without question, I give you information about a notorious deserter of the U.S. Army and an international rumrunning operation led by Nicho Bazán?"

"And agree to plead guilty to the charges?"

"The ones I'm guilty of."

Arilee started to speak, her distress palpable, but he shook his head at her again and nodded toward Macy in her arms. She needed to worry about Macy and herself, not him. Sweet Beulah Land, Arilee would be eaten alive in a prison. Thoughts of what the other inmates and the guards would do to his innocent sister made him sick to his stomach. If she went there for even an hour because of him, not only would Davis and Adam never forgive him, he would never forgive himself.

"Call the boss," the mustached man said to one of the others. Brax still wasn't sure if they were truly Prohibition agents or on the payroll for Capone and his gang.

A smallish man with overly greased hair disappeared. Brax stood by Arilee. The New Jersey fellow kept a rifle trained on them, while the others began pulling the plane apart.

"Seems a bit of overkill," Brax remarked drily to Arilee, voice low. "Do you want me to take Macy for you?"

She shook her head and rearranged the blankets around the child. Something flashed on her left hand, and he held it for a moment.

"He finally proposed?"

"Tonight. Before we left."

"He'll be good to you, I reckon. You deserve to be happy for a change."

Arilee studied him. "What about you, Brax? Are you happy?"

He lit a cigarette and stared off into the distance. "I don't deserve to be."

At last, Greasy Hair returned. "Boss said take him in and let the dame go on a sworn statement. If she's lying, or if he doesn't cooperate, we'll arrest her for perjury later."

"Miss," said New Jersey Fellow. "Will you swear under oath you did not know the contents of this plane?"

She nodded, eyes round. "I have a Bible in my satchel," she volunteered, nodding at the bag they'd thrown to the ground as they pawed through *Unseen Things Above.*

Greasy Hair reached for the bag, and everyone filed inside a shack lit by an overhead lantern. Mustache Man wrote up a statement, while Greasy Hair rifled through Arilee's things. She flushed as he dumped her clothes and cash all over the floor and unfolded her passport.

"Looks like we have a Miss Roberta Rutledge of Atlanta, Georgia," he announced. At last, he pulled out her Bible, which Brax recognized with an ache as their mother's well-worn copy of the Scriptures. He rejoiced Mama couldn't see what he'd become; it would break her heart more than his supposed death.

Mustache Man slammed the hastily-written statement atop the Bible. Arilee—pale, almost gaunt, battered from the storm—signed it with one hand, still holding Macy with her other arm. He'd never seen a picture of greater strength and beauty.

"You are free to go now, miss." Greasy Hair practically pushed her out of the way.

"Go where? How am I to get to Toronto?"

"That's your beef, while we put the bracelets on this hood and take him to the Big House."

She knelt to gather her possessions with her free arm; the agents stood above her watching, but none offered any assistance. Brax crouched beside her and began carefully putting everything back in the valise.

"Thank you, Brax," she whispered around a sob.

One of the agents kicked him in the back and swore. He ignored it.

"Davis has an attorney, he will help." Arilee gave him a quick hug as they rose. Her eyes said all the rest: love, gratitude, and concern she couldn't speak before these watching wolves.

She picked up her satchel; he held out his wrists. Then handcuffed and surrounded by his captors, he stepped out into the dark.

CHAPTER 37

Thursday, May 25, 1922

A rilee watched Brax glance back at her once, regret etched over his handsome face. He had done the most heroic, selfless act of his life. What would happen to him now? Worse than a bootlegger, he was a deserter. He could be put to hard labor, or spend years in prison, or even be executed. If she hadn't been in his way, he could have escaped. Yet he had been trying to outrun God for a long time, and maybe he needed more than even a life-threatening storm to get his attention.

And now what was she to do?

She sat down on the floor of the shack, holding Macy's still form that lingered somewhere between life and death. She didn't even have the strength to cry. It was around midnight. Could she get a cab to take them to the train station? And how long would they have to wait for a train to Toronto? Then how long would that journey take by rail?

"Jesus help us," she whispered. The God who had allowed men to discover how to make this insulin, Who had enabled Brax to get them through a deadly gale—He would not abandon her now. He simply wouldn't. "Show me what to do."

"Miss Rutledge?"

She looked up to see a man about her own age in pilot's garb, looking at her with concern.

"Yes, I'm Miss Rutledge."

"Are you Davis's sister?"

"That's right."

He exhaled. "Name's Oliver Tucker. I know your brothers. We served together in the 22nd Aero Squadron, and then Davis and I have flown the mail these past few years. He saved my life in France at the cost of making ace. Because of him, I lived to come home and get married and have a daughter myself." He cleared his throat. "Is this Macy?"

Arilee nodded and brushed Macy's hair from her white face.

"Davis told us about his little girl dying and the medicine in Toronto that could save her but wasn't available yet."

"We heard they have some now."

"If you want to get to Toronto, ma'am, I will take you right now in my plane."

Overcome, she could barely force words past the lump in her throat. "Yes. Yes, we'll leave as soon as you can."

In less than ten minutes, they were flying in a clear sky with a crescent moon, Lake Eerie sparkling beneath them like a sea of black diamonds. Three hours later, Captain Tucker landed the plane in Queen's Park, Toronto.

"I don't have permission to land here," Tucker said when he'd shut off the engine. "I apologize for leaving you alone in the dark, but I've got to refuel and get out of here before the police come asking me questions. This is a government plane that I flew unauthorized into another country, so . . ."

"I understand," said Arilee. "I thank you more than words can say for what you have done for us."

"Your brothers and I trained here, during the war, so I remember my way around a little. Head down the street here." He gestured as he spoke. "The hospital is about a mile down, on the left."

"Thank you," Arilee repeated. "So very much." She shed the heavy flying suit and some of the extra blankets; the night was cool, but not bitter. Picking up Macy and the valise, she walked as briskly as she could, glad she'd chosen her old gardening boots over more stylish footwear.

Fifteen minutes later, she stood before a massive four-story, Victorian-styled building, the Toronto Hospital for Sick Children. In the dim moonlight of predawn, it looked as creepy as a haunted castle, but exhaustion rather than reluctance slowed her pace through the arched entry. The night guard let her in without question.

"She needs insulin," Arilee gasped to the nurse on duty and collapsed on the floor.

"Oh goodness," cried the woman, rising. "Is she—"

"She is in a diabetic coma."

"We've not had one recover from a coma yet," the woman said compassionately. "But knowing Dr. Banting, he'll certainly try. Let me telephone him."

Arilee sat numbly on the floor, cradling Macy. An orderly wheeled a gurney over and helped her lay the girl across it. Macy was taken to a small, bare room, and Arilee followed. In less time than she had dared hope, a scruffy-looking man in his mid-thirties entered carrying a tray of supplies.

"How old is she?" he asked Arilee.

"Four, in a few weeks."

"When was she diagnosed?"

"March. She was small to begin with, and the starvation diet hasn't done much to help her."

"Her weight?"

"Twenty-four pounds, at least it was."

Without warning, he stuck Macy in the leg with a large syringe filled with a brownish-colored liquid.

"That will work or she will die," he said, adjusting his spectacles. "Where have you come from?"

"Atlanta. We left last night and flew."

"You brought this child in an airplane?" He looked up and down at Arilee, who still wore the ridiculous overalls and a scarf about her neck.

"Yes."

"You saved her life. If this works." He checked over Macy, listening to her heart and breathing. "She needs an infusion of fluids immediately. You must understand, Mrs.—?"

"Miss Rutledge. I am her aunt but have been her caregiver since she was an infant."

"You must understand, Miss Rutledge, this is all new and experimental. It is a miracle, yes, but some patients do better than others, and we don't know all the reasons why. Some recover and some die. Some develop abscesses where the shots are injected. Some are allergic to the extract. Sometimes the insulin is more or less potent, and determining the right amount is a matter of trial and error. Too much and the patient goes into hypoglycemic shock because the blood sugar is too low. Sometimes a batch goes bad. And we never have enough."

"But there is insulin now?"

"At the moment. For two months there was practically none. An American company, Eli Lilly, is working to create the vast quantities needed. Till then we do what we can for who we can."

He jotted down some notes, then left to get the infusion. Arilee sat by the gurney, Macy's tiny hand in her own. She rested her head on the side of the mattress. Every muscle in her body ached, and she felt dizzy from hunger. When she closed her eyes, she rocked as if she were still in the plane.

Unsteady.

Vulnerable.

Surrounded by darkness.

This will work or she will die.

They had starved Macy, taken her on a perilous journey, and jabbed her with a painful shot of an experimental tincture, all for one purpose. To save her life. Well might Macy in her young mind question their kindness to her, even as Arilee had long questioned her Heavenly Father's in her own life.

And yet she saw now: the pain had been necessary to change her from an idealistic, idolizing girl to a woman who depended on Him to do hard things. She fingered Adam's ring. Adam. Wisteria House. Grace Baptist Church. Nathaniel and Macy. The best things in her life, the things that gave her purpose and courage, had come from the most painful ministrations. As a skillful doctor, the Great Physician had allowed drastic, sometimes heartbreaking measures to bring about His "joyful ends."

Whatever happened here now, she would not question His goodness again.

Arilee opened her eyes to see Macy looking at her.

Looking at her.

"Aun'Ari, I'm hungry," she whispered.

Arilee began to weep.

Dr. Banting, coming back in, smiled, and said, "What would you like to eat, little girl?"

"I want strawberries, but Aunt Ari says they will make me sick. But I wike strawberries and cream."

Banting nodded slightly at Arilee. "You shall have them. You shall have whatever you want for being so brave."

The girl smiled wide, and Arilee thought her heart would burst.

Adam and Davis arrived back at the house at 6:30 Thursday morning after a sleepless night at the church. True to their word, Pastor Andy and John Sweet had come back to the church and prayed with them; later Jim Macdonald and Billy Sweet had come. Adam appreciated these faithful, godly men, examples of what he aspired to be himself.

Silently, Davis began cracking eggs and Adam buttering toast. The kitchen smelled of Arilee, all lavender and vanilla. Her blue apron lay folded across a chair. He thought he might be sick with waiting. Nathaniel, well-rested, asked incessant questions that the men ignored.

The doorbell rang. Davis went to answer it; Adam froze, suspended in time. He heard Davis thank someone gruffly and close the door.

He walked back in with a telegram, opened it, and spread it out on the kitchen counter.

FROM TORONTO ONT 517A MAY 25 1922

WISTERIA HOUSE RANDOLPH ST
ATLANTA GA

BRAX ARRESTED STOP MACY RECEIVED INJECTION REVIVED EATING
TALKING PRAISE GOD LOVE ARILEE

Davis woke with a start at the sound of a car tearing down the gravel driveway. He'd sat down in the library armchair to finish his coffee and must've fallen asleep. The softly ticking mantle clock showed nearly ten in the morning. With Adam and Nathaniel at school and Arilee gone, he ought to be preparing for his own trip to Toronto.

The door buzzer sounded. Stretching, he rose, praying it wasn't bad news to contradict the good report of a few hours ago. Perhaps Pastor Andy had decided to come by in response to Adam telephoning him earlier with the update. But through the leaded glass of the front door, Davis saw the outline of a woman and groaned. That Woodhouse woman.

He hadn't shaved and was dressed in the same old cotton shirt and suspenders he'd had on since yesterday morning. Between sleeplessness and high emotion, he remained addled and didn't want to see anybody right now, least of all her.

He opened the door. She had on a straw cloche over her cropped golden hair and a white shirtwaist and vest with a silk tie. Though her skirt was long, he didn't like the look of a woman in a tie, infringing on masculine territory.

"Mrs. Woodhouse."

"Good morning, Mr. Rutledge. I could hardly sleep last night for wondering about Macy and the flight."

Sighing, Davis shut the door behind him and stepped out onto the front porch, squinting at the sunlight. The air bore the fragrance of blooming roses and mimosas. He waved Mrs. Woodhouse to a rocking chair and sat down on the porch swing heavily, its suspension chains rattling. From his pocket, he pulled the telegram and passed it to her.

She read it and exhaled. "This is wonderful news. It pains me I can't report it. Yet."

"I understand I am in your debt for the information that saved Macy's life."

She shrugged. "It seemed the right thing to do to tell you. I hope you didn't get too angry at your sister and brother and Adam. They had to make a quick decision on what was best."

"Since you like news: Arilee and Adam got engaged."

"Then congratulations to them. I trust you are in favor of the match?"

"Quite."

"Do you know why your brother might have been arrested?"

"I'm afraid what little I know I cannot share till I speak to my attorney." She pursed her lips.

"I know I owe you a great deal, ma'am. But there's a lot of things about my family that are complicated, and sometimes my silence is to protect the ones I love."

"Like your wife in Milledgeville?"

"You know about that?"

"I've known since last fall. What kind of a journalist would I be if I didn't?"

He quirked his eyebrow and managed to reply, "Thanks for not printing it."

"Mr. Rutledge, I may be an independent woman, but I am not a heartless one. My husband was 'presumed dead,' his body never found. His family entertains false hopes he will yet return; they will cut me off from all support if I remarry. My family threatens to cut me off entirely if I *don't* remarry a wealthy politician's son of their choosing. I throw myself into my work as an escape from the complexities of my own life and in hopes I can someday make my way without any of them."

"I understand escaping into work a lot more than I care to admit. Truth is, it took all this with Macy to remind me God hasn't forgotten me. I guess I tried to forget Him for a long time."

She shifted. "And I understand that more than I care to admit."

Davis looked at her and instead of seeing the annoying "Woodhouse woman" who wreaked havoc on his life, he saw an echo of his own pain. What could he say from all he'd recently rediscovered that might bolster her faith?

"I'm resolved to embrace the life God has given me right now and leave the future with the One who will be there to see me through it."

She nodded and idly doodled on her notepad with the pencil stub. When she looked back up at him, her eyes shone with unshed tears.

"What about your wife? How is it you are faithful to a woman who can give you nothing in return?" Her tone held a desperate curiosity, not condemnation.

"The Lord's been faithful to me when I've given Him nothing in return."

The rocking chair creaked as she shifted again. "I appreciate your fidelity, Mr. Rutledge. My husband was unfaithful to me the entire five years of our marriage. Some believed him justified because of our particular circumstances. I can't quite fathom a man who would choose to be faithful in a situation such as yours when a divorce would be granted him on a silver platter and free him from a wife who might never get better."

"She isn't going to get better," he admitted quietly. "But loving her even when she's this way has made me a better man."

Mrs. Woodhouse dropped the pencil. She swallowed and from her handbag pulled out a starched and monogrammed handkerchief and dabbed at her eyes. Her facade of perfection didn't annoy him today, because he saw it for what it was—part of her running and hiding from an unbearable reality.

She cleared her throat. "Well, then. I also needed to tell you that I packed a suitcase for your sister and left it in her bedroom. She requested it be sent up to her. Unless you are going yourself?"

"I leave on the 5:10 Cincinnati-Atlanta Express."

She rose. "Excellent. Give Arilee my regards. She may have beat me to riding in an airplane, but I shall have my day."

Davis nodded respectfully as he rose. "Thank you, again, Mrs. Woodhouse. I pray the Lord rewards you for your kindness and courage in helping us."

"I believe He already has." He almost missed her quiet statement as she stepped down the porch steps and took her leave.

●

CHAPTER 38

Friday, May 26, to Sunday, May 28, 1922

Washington, D.C.

Brax stepped off the train, surrounded by agents, but thankfully not handcuffed. His cooperation thus far had earned him a surprising amount of respect. He followed the suit in front of him away from the smoke and crowds of the station to a waiting motor car, and they drove through the streets of Washington, D.C.

He had already told them what he knew about Torrio and Capone's operation, as well as the empire of Nicho Bazán. And he'd told them about his desertion in France. Left to the tender mercies of the United States government or to those of either group of bootleggers, he supposed Uncle Sam would be the more merciful. And while he didn't relish jail time, he'd probably be safer behind bars. He had no doubt Bazán would come after him; his greatest wish now, besides hoping Macy had made it, was that his boss wouldn't find his family.

They arrived at a government building he didn't recognize, and Brax followed his captors inside and through a maze of hallways smelling of stale coffee and cigarette smoke. A rather homely fellow in his mid-twenties sat behind the desk but came around to stand before Brax.

"Mr. Rutledge," he said, "I am John Edgar Hoover, Assistant Director of the Bureau of Investigation."

He held out his hand, so Brax shook it. Why on earth had they brought him here? Wasn't this the division of the Justice Department that hunted down subversive activity? Surely he wasn't being charged with conspiracy too?

When they were seated, Hoover began. "I'll shoot straight with you, Rutledge. We have enough on you to put you behind bars for at least the next ten years. Leavenworth for desertion and fraud. The Federal Pen for bootlegging. I'm sure we could find more with even a quick survey."

He paused, waiting for Brax's reaction. Brax had learned a thing or two in dogfights; he knew better than to show fear to the enemy. When he remained nonplussed at the assessment, Hoover looked satisfied.

"However, prison and manual labor seem a waste of your exceptional talents. Not just your impressive skills as a pilot, but the ability to appear and disappear, to know things and forget them.

"How would you like for the charges to all go away? You stay dead as far as the military is concerned. Your family keeps your life insurance money. We burn up your plane, make sure Bazán gets word you crashed and died, and no one's coming after your sister or anyone else you care about. And then you fly for us."

"Us?"

"The Bureau. You fly my agents wherever they need to go. You see things, and you learn what to remember and what to forget. We'll take care of you, and we'll own you."

Brax considered. It wasn't coming clean, restoring his name and identity. Truth be told, down deep, he'd been thinking he wanted to be himself again, even if it meant prison time. To simply live an honest life like Davis and Arilee, no matter how difficult.

Hoover wasn't offering him that. But he was offering him piloting as opposed to prison. And the best chance of protecting his family.

"If I serve you well, will I ever be able to, I don't know, do something else?"

"Sure. We have lots of jobs. You could be an agent someday. I don't think you're the sit-behind-a-desk type, but there are office jobs too."

The United States Government would own him till the day he died.

"What if I betray you?"

"Your sister will be arrested for bootlegging, your brother for theft and conspiracy in accepting your army-issued life insurance, and you will be shot on sight by the next one of my agents who sees you."

Maybe he'd been wrong. Maybe they weren't more merciful than the gangsters but more subtle in their entrapment.

"All right," he said, meeting Hoover's snaky eyes. "I'll work for you." This time he initiated the handshake. He shuddered as a typewriter in the next room dinged the end of a line. For a split second it had sounded exactly like a prison door banging closed.

He wasn't free, but maybe in saving Arilee and Davis from the danger he'd created for them, he could find a measure of atonement.

∞ ∞ ∞

Toronto, Ontario

Friday morning, after Macy's third insulin injection, twenty-four hours of fluids, and eating every few hours, the girl had grown remarkably happy and talkative. Arilee began to believe her niece no longer teetered on the edge of imminent death.

However, having spent Thursday night sleeping on a hard bench in the hospital waiting room, Arilee knew something must be done immediately about lodgings and personal hygiene for herself.

"Macy, we don't want to live in the hospital; Aunt Ari is going to go get us another place to stay."

"I wanna go to 'steria House."

"Me too, baby, but first we have to get you all better and have lots of medicine to take home with us. We might be here in Toronto for a while. It's all a grand adventure. I'm going out, and I want you to take a nap, and then I'll be here when you have supper. Can you be brave for Aunt Ari?"

Macy's chin quivered, but she nodded and clutched her yarn cat close. Arilee kissed her forehead and promised to bring her back a surprise.

She went first to Athelma Apartments over on Grosvenor Street as recommended by Dr. Banting. The complex was close to his practice, which would enable him to make house calls twice daily to administer insulin to Macy once she recovered enough to leave the hospital. Having secured a furnished flat, Arilee telegrammed the address to Wisteria House, not knowing if Davis was there now or still out on his mail route.

Next, she bought food, consulting with the list Banting had given her for Macy's new diet. Then she returned to the hospital, seeing Macy through her next injection. Right before she left to go back to the apartment for the night, a nurse brought in a telegram from Davis, sent yesterday afternoon, and stating in its entirety: "On the way."

"Chatty as ever," she muttered, but since she hadn't expected him to leave Atlanta till Saturday evening at the earliest, she rejoiced at the news he was already en route.

A long soak in the tub refreshed her, but though exhausted after two nearly sleepless nights, she heard every sound in this unfamiliar place and slept fitfully. She dreamed of Brax and woke up panicked. She did not know how to find him or get news of him. She hoped Davis would know what to do.

Anxiety from the dream led her to worry over Nathaniel. Her poor nephew, already terrified about losing his sister, had been abandoned by her as well and without warning. It relieved her that Adam had promised to look out for the boy.

Adam. Had it been mere days? It felt like a lifetime. She ached with missing him. She had his ring. She knew he would wait for her till she could come back. He'd been patient all year waiting for her. But how could she bear what would no doubt be *months* of separation while they waited for insulin to become plentiful and readily available?

Saturday morning, she found a barber shop and asked the barber to do something about her hair. The older gentleman looked at her severely, doubtless ready to lecture her on her horrible fashion decision. Instead, she blabbered out the whole story to him while he wet her hair and trimmed it.

When he turned her to see the mirror, she gasped. Darling natural waves framed her face. If she added a beaded headband or be-feathered ribbon, even Margaret Woodhouse would approve.

The barber shop stood two doors down from a dress shop, and on impulse, she entered. She bought a new white cloche-style hat, a blue dress embroidered with a silver art deco design, and silver pumps. She took her purchases back to the apartment to wear for something special, such as Macy's release, and returned to the hospital in the one wrinkled dress and sensible brown shoes she'd brought up.

Macy sat in bed eating bread and cheese, ham, and strawberries.

"Dey are da best strawberries in the wor-word, Aun'Ari," she exclaimed. "Are we far 'way from 'steria House? I wanna see Daddy."

"Your Daddy is coming to see you." Arilee smoothed the girl's hair, smiling at her fondly. "Yes, we are very far away from home. You'll never guess how we got here. You and I flew with Uncle Brax in his airplane."

"In da sky?"

"Yes. You were sleeping, baby, but you rode the whole way in my lap."

"And Woodrow too?" asked Macy, eyeing the crocheted cat beside her.

"And Woodrow too."

"Was it high?"

"Yes, but Jesus got us safely here so you could get the medicine you need to get better."

"And have strawberries?"

"And have strawberries."

The nurses changed shifts, and the evening nurse explained to Arilee the things she watched for at night. At any time, Macy's blood sugar could drop too low. "Once she's released to your care, you'll have to check her every few hours through the night," the nurse explained. "Have candy or a sugar cube handy in case she exhibits symptoms such as rapid heartbeat, shaking, sweating, or nausea."

Arilee nodded as if she were competent and confident, but the burden of Macy's illness weighed heavier than when four-month-old colicky Macy had been thrust into her arms. How could she keep this child alive? It was all fine and well to decide to *not sleep*, but already she felt thick-headed with fatigue. What if she made a stupid mistake that set Macy back? The insulin could enable her to live, but it couldn't cure her. She would be dependent on this substance, and on the elusive perfect balance of it, for the rest of her days.

How could Arilee manage to go to the grocer's or any sort of errands once Macy was released? The girl wasn't strong enough to come along yet without being carried. Perhaps Davis could help her find some kind of wagon. And what about Nathaniel? He needed her too. Should he come up here and stay with her? But if he did, how would she manage his exuberance and desire to play outdoors with Macy's delicacy and need for care?

She kissed Macy and promised to see her in the morning. Then in a daze, she began the walk back to the apartment, the beauty of the spring evening completely lost to her senses.

"Jesus, You saved her life, You saved all our lives, I know I can trust You for all these other things. But You've shown me this past year not to shut everyone out, to be a part of the Body, giving and receiving. Here I am not knowing a soul or how to even manage daily life all alone again. I know You will never leave me nor forsake me. You never have, through all the thorny ways. Show me how, help me . . ."

The sound of the apartment door closing behind her echoed in her head, causing her to renew her prayer. She should eat. But in her exhaustion, she didn't even realize she sat on the floor staring into space until a knock startled her back to the present.

She cracked the door to see Davis and Nathaniel. Her brother embraced her warmly and Nathaniel clung to her. She knelt to his level and hugged and kissed him.

"Our train arrived an hour ago, and we went straight to the hospital," Davis explained. "They let me see Macy for a few minutes and told us we'd find you here. We must've just missed you at the hospital."

Then she caught a whiff of citrus and sandalwood and looked up sharply to see Adam in the doorway. With a cry, she jumped up and flew into his waiting arms.

He held her. Possessively. His strong arms completely enveloped her and upheld her as Davis brought in the luggage.

"Arilee," Adam said gently. "You look like you need to sit down. There's a lot happening all at once."

She nodded, and they all sat in the living room. "Sorry it took so long to get here," Davis said. "We left Thursday night but missed the connection in Cincinnati. Flying really was the only way you could have gotten here in time. Thank you for what you did for Macy. To see her smiling and talking, *living*—" Davis's voice broke, and he couldn't go on.

She nodded, a burning lump in her own throat. "Did you hear from Brax?"

"No. What happened?"

She told them the story of the trip up. Adam held her close the whole time, squeezing her shoulders at some of the harder parts of her account. When she had finished, he cleared his throat. "It appears I came close to losing you twice—once to a storm and once to prison. You sure know how to wreak havoc on a man's heart. And now you look ready to collapse.

Please, let us look after everything, and you go *rest*."

"Thank you for coming. I—"

"You can tell me all your sweet nothings later," he teased. "Go to bed."

She slipped into the bedroom, stripped down to her chemise, and lay down. Adam's love for her had taken on a new level of selflessness. As much as she knew he wanted to talk to her, he was giving her what she needed more. How could he even *be* here right before finals and graduation? She needed to figure it out, but before she could, she fell asleep.

∞ ∞ ∞

Arilee woke slowly, confused. Morning light filtered through the curtains. Mid-morning light.

She bolted upright, which sent strange flashes into her vision. Quickly, she dressed, thankful Davis had brought her suitcase. The kitchen smelled of some sort of meat and butter; clean plates were stacked and drying by the sink. Adam sat reading *The Curious Case of Benjamin Button*, and she wondered why he had Fitzgerald's new release instead of a medical text. Davis and Nathaniel were nowhere to be seen.

Adam dropped the book. "Hey, hey, slow down."

"Macy—"

"Is fine. I saw her myself this morning and met the famed Dr. Banting. Davis is there with her now, and then he's going to take Nathaniel over to the park."

She looked at the clock. "Why did y'all let me sleep till ten? *Why* did I sleep till ten? Is something wrong with me?"

"How long you got?"

"You're not funny."

"I'm the funniest person I know."

She shook her head.

"You've been not sleeping, not eating, and living in a state of high anxiety for the past several months, but especially the past week. Your body has had enough of this mistreatment. It's the perfect makings for shell shock or illness, but I don't aim to let either of those happen."

"I'm fine now. I—"

He rose and gently seated her in the chair he'd abandoned, his hands resting on her shoulders.

"Sit down," he instructed. "But don't let my residual body heat make you have unchaste thoughts. I'm here to take care of you."

She opened her mouth and shut it. The Lord had always been with her and sustained and strengthened her, through all the hardships. But even so, human arms holding her and the audible voice of the man she loved soothing her both comforted and broke her at the same time. He could be the answer to the prayer she'd prayed last night, except, of course, he couldn't stay.

"Let me get you some breakfast."

"You can cook?"

He shrugged. "One summer it rained every day, and Mother got tired of me and Josh underfoot all the time. She taught us some basics. The best chicken and dumplings you ever ate and big fluffy pancakes drenched in butter are my specialties. You ever had maple syrup?"

"No."

"It's popular up here. I got some, and without being disloyal to the South, I have to say it's better than sorghum."

"I guess I could eat."

"I think you'd better, or Dr. Banting's going to get confused about which emaciated patient he's supposed to be treating."

She sat and watched as he reheated the griddle and poured the already-prepared batter on it. Soon her mouth watered at the aroma of melted butter, heated syrup, and crisping pancakes.

His cooking skills were not exaggerated. She had never had such light, buttery pancakes, and she licked the maple syrup off her fingers so as not to waste a drop. She ate two stacks and meat that Adam said Torontonians called "peameal bacon," a sort of fried pork loin slice with a cornmeal edge. Adam watched her with satisfaction while polishing off a second breakfast plate for himself and serving them both endless coffee.

"Now get your hat, we're going to take a walk in that huge park. I need to talk to you. Then we'll go see Macy."

Adam offered his arm to Arilee, and they strolled about Queen's Park. He and Davis had discussed the plan at length while on the journey, but Arilee was so battle-worn, he knew he had to present it carefully lest she feel behind the eight ball about their ideas. He didn't want to push her into something she wasn't ready for. On the other hand, seeing her last night had made him that much more certain he needed to be here with her. He had enough medical training—and plain common sense—to be deeply concerned about what the stress of the past months had done to her own well-being.

He led her to a bench, and they sat taking in the vibrant greens of the oaks putting out their leaves, the bold rainbow riot of tulips, and a white, three-petaled flower with a gold center that the locals called trillium.

She spoke first. "Thank you for being here. I'll sure miss you and Davis when you head back home. Speaking of which, shouldn't you be there for final exams?

"I went and took them all this past Thursday."

"Took them all?"

"All my finals."

"What? Five exams? You took them all in one day?"

"Sure. Long day, but here I am, still the goat's whiskers."

"But you can't have done your best taking them one after the next. What about your perfect A and summa cum laude? Wait a minute. You didn't really stay up all night Wednesday praying and then take *all* your tests on Thursday, did you?"

Her gaze required an answer. Not wanting to admit to it or lie, he at last nodded.

"Adam Harrison! What on earth?"

"No fancy Latin words on a graduation program mean anything to me without you. I talked to my professors Thursday morning and under the circumstances, with where I was headed and why, they agreed for me to take all my exams at once. Of course, they are expecting a full report of my observations here."

"I don't understand."

"I'm moving to Toronto to help you as long as you and Macy have to be here. I'll get a job at the hospital or for Dr. Banting. I want to learn as much as I can about how to care for diabetic children and then take that knowledge back to Atlanta. Everyone can't fly to Toronto, you know."

"But it's not fair to you. You've worked so hard. What about your bachelor's degree and graduation? What about next quarter? You can't throw away your whole future—"

"Didn't you do what other folks considered throwing away your whole future for Nat and Macy? There are different dreams, darlin', and sometimes you have to figure out which ones mean the most to you. A few years from now, who will care what my undergraduate grades were? What will that matter compared to if I loved my wife well?"

"I don't feel I merit that sort of devotion."

"Have you figured out yet I love you?" He ran his fingers through her short, wavy hair.

"But where would you stay?"

"Did you hear me just say 'wife'? I was hoping you were serious when you agreed to marry me a couple days ago, and maybe you'd let me live with you as your husband."

"Yes, but—"

Instead of finishing her protest, her mouth found his, and she kissed him. He knew what it meant for Arilee Rutledge to initiate this kind of kiss, and at first, he froze, too shocked to respond. But quickly, he pulled her close and held her while his lips explored hers, soft and full and still tasting faintly of maple syrup.

He wasn't sure which of them pulled away first, but he felt himself grinning like a kid at Christmas by the time they did. "You must've really liked those pancakes," he murmured into her hair, still holding her close. She laughed softly. Her musical laugh. He would never get tired of bringing some joy to her shadowed life.

"I really like you," she admitted, a little shyly for someone who'd just kissed the sense out of him in the middle of a public park with Queen Victoria's statue staring down in disapproval. "While I've been obsessed with keeping Macy alive, you've been steady and unwavering, even when I kept ignoring you and our future. I feel like I should nobly resist your gallant offer to be here with me, but I've come to depend on you entirely. I guess what I'm trying to say is—"

She kissed him again. It didn't take him as long to respond this time. His hands cupped her face, the sweet countenance he wanted to see every day for the rest of his life.

"I think you've said it really well, darlin'," he said huskily when she shifted slightly back. "I understand you, though I might need a bit more clarification." And with that, *he* kissed *her*, running his lips down the side of her face and her neck and her ear, then finding her mouth again and kissing her till she melted into his side.

Then he reached out and gently traced the scar along her chin. "I sure do love you."

She nodded. "I know you do. And I love you, Adam. I kept wondering all spring, could that really be enough. Enough to last a lifetime. To not end up like my parents. I heeded all my fears. But on the flight up here, wondering if I would even live another minute, I realized I only need to take the next step. Live the next day. Trust the Lord for the next moment. Obey right now and let Him hold on to our future."

"Are you ready for the next step to be the big one? While Davis is here with Macy, we'll go across to New York and stand before the justice of the peace."

"What about your parents? Won't they be upset for us not to have a wedding at home?"

"They'll be so happy you agreed to marry me, they won't care if it's on the moon."

"Then—yes!" Tears shone in her aqua eyes, making them as luminous as the gem in her ring. "A year ago if anyone had told me I'd be getting married at all, let alone to *Adam Harrison*, I would have said they were 'loaded to the muzzle,' to use some of your crazy talk."

"I'm sure I'm far different than what you imagined for your life."

"Indeed. You—us—oh, Adam, it's so very much *better*."

CHAPTER 39

Monday, May 29, to Tuesday, May 30, 1922

Niagara Falls, New York

In the morning, they took the train to New York state.

She wore her new dress and hat. Adam had on his best suit. They filled out the paperwork for the marriage license, and the justice of the peace agreed to meet them in an hour at a small rose garden with a view of Bridal Veil Falls. Perusing their application, he said to Arilee, "Never would've thought you were older than he is. Must be the hair."

"Guess you'll never grow it out now, huh?" Adam teased after they stepped outside.

"Oh, we'll see. You haven't said what *you* think of it."

"It's growing on me. Or I guess, it's growing on you, but if you like it, it's jake with me."

"Who are we going to get to be witnesses?"

Adam shrugged. "Guess we can ask a random tourist."

"It ought—" she started and stopped herself.

"I know. I wish they were here too. All the people who helped us get to this point."

She nodded and willed herself not to cry. Though right for their situation, this wasn't the wedding she wanted. She didn't feel like a bride. All the friends from church who had become her family should be here. And Davis and the children. Brax.

From a florist's cart, Adam bought her a nosegay of fragrant roses. "'By the roses of the spring, by maidhood, honor, truth, and everything, I love thee so,'" she quoted softly. He smiled and took her hand, and they walked together to meet the justice of the peace. A couple on their honeymoon agreed to act as witnesses.

A portly man in his fifties, the officiant gave the usual words with no homily or personal remarks such as Pastor Andy would have spoken. He called her "Roberta," in accordance with the marriage license.

A quick proposal, no engagement announcement, no wedding, no Scripture or exhortation at the ceremony. She told herself it didn't matter; she was married either way. How dare she be disappointed or ungrateful. She looked at Adam and focused on him. He smiled tenderly at her. His hands holding hers were strong. Half in a trance, she repeated the "I do" and the "love, honor, and cherish, till death do us part." She heard, "You may kiss the bride." Adam cupped her face and took care of that thoroughly. With three complete strangers looking on, she stood stiffly, unable to reciprocate, hoping Adam didn't take her lack of response for reluctance. "I present Mr. and Mrs. Adam James Harrison," the officiant announced with no particular enthusiasm, then stood with his hand out for Adam to give him the fee. The witnesses signed their names, offered their congratulations, and disappeared. Adam and Arilee stood looking at each other.

"Food?" he asked, and she nodded.

They visited a local eatery called Simon's on the Canadian-United States border and ate in companionable silence. Such momentous changes had happened so fast. She wondered if he felt nervous too. The possibility strangely comforted her.

After the meal, they strolled hand-in-hand over the recently renovated Lower Arch Bridge which spanned the Niagara River. Leaning against the railing to gaze at the powerfully rushing water below, Adam placed his arm about her waist.

"Kinda makes me want to sing." Arilee snuggled into his side. "'I Sing the Mighty Power of God' or something."

"The night you were flying up here, I was praying; well, me and most of the church. Pastor Andy focused the Wednesday night meeting on prayers for y'all to make it here and Macy to live. After everyone went home, Davis and I stayed—"

"Davis went to church?"

"Yes. He talked to people there, and they welcomed him. I think he might go back, you know, when he can. He was crying and everything."

"Davis cried?"

He nodded. "Yeah, you and Macy flying rattled him bad. He and I stayed up at the church, and then Pastor Andy and some of the other men returned at different points throughout the night to pray with us. Anyway, I don't remember exactly what time it was, sometime after ten, I think, I started singing a song I hadn't thought of in years, but I remembered all the verses."

"'Be Still My Soul'?"

"Yes. How did you know? Did Davis tell you?"

"No, he didn't tell me. I didn't know. But it came to *me*, in the storm. I sang it out loud into the wind."

Their eyes met, the awe she felt mirrored in his expression. "I know all of this has been unconventional," he said at last, "but I think there's a bigger plan here than we can see. I think we're doing what the Lord wants us to do, even though it's not the circumstances we would've picked."

He hummed a bit of the song, and then they sang it together. Arilee loved how their voices blended as if created to fit together.

"'Through thorny ways leads to a joyful end,'" Adam quoted. "When I first came to Wisteria House and saw all the thorns and overgrowth and how hard you'd had it, I imagined myself the prince coming to tear through the thorns, win your heart, and awaken you from the spell with a kiss. Speaking of kisses . . ."

"Let's not speak of them, let's share them."

He grinned. "Shall we go to the cottage then?"

She took his hand, and they walked back through the early evening shadows to the tiny but clean honeymoon cabin they'd rented for the night. It boasted a bathroom, a neatly made bed, and two armchairs before a fireplace. Adam carried Arilee over the threshold. "I don't know why, but I think I'm supposed to do this."

He took off his suit and sat down on the bed in his undershirt and shorts. She stared at his tattoo, tracing it with her finger. "I think this should stand for 'Adam and Arilee' now instead of 'All American.'"

He laughed.

"That evening you got stung by the yellow jackets, I, uh, started thinking of you differently," she admitted.

"Oh? What kind of differently?"

"I didn't feel about you with your shirt off the way I thought I would."

"And just what were you feeling, Mrs. Harrison?"

Heat washed over her face. "I think I'd better change for bed."

"Most sockdolager idea I've ever heard."

Not as comfortable with the idea of undressing as he was, she stepped into the bathroom and took off her dress and stockings and all her underthings. She had but one nightgown packed, a sleeveless, ankle-length cotton gown, loose-fitting but pretty with its lace yolk and blue embroidery down the front. She grabbed her blue wrapper and tied it over the thin gown, then went and sat beside Adam on the bed.

"It's strange to think that a few hours ago what we are about to do would have been sinful, but now it's what God wants us to do," he mused.

"Mmm-hmm."

He wiped his hands on the bedspread. So, he *was* nervous. She exhaled. She wanted him. And she wanted to be loved by him as completely as a bride should be loved by her groom. Would her old fears and his old guilt come between them still?

"May I take off your robe?" he asked softly.

She nodded and untied it, letting it fall from her shoulders. His eyes studied her. "You are so beautiful," he breathed, his hands lightly trailing over her arms, up to her shoulders, down to rest on her waist. She closed her eyes and relished in his touch, then opened them at his gasp.

"What is it?"

"Your back."

The nightgown plunged low in the back, showing some of her scars. He traced them with his finger. "It hurts me that this happened to you. I want always to protect you. I wish I—"

She heard the regret creeping into his voice and covered his mouth with her hand.

"There's been more than enough difficulty, I think. We love each other, and it's our wedding night. God is a Redeemer of all the broken past, and He has brought us together. I'm glad to become yours—in every way. But I don't exactly know what to do. How to please you and all."

"I don't really, either. Davis pulled me aside last night. He said it takes time to learn each other and not to expect to get everything perfect at first but just enjoy the education."

He ran his fingers lightly over her arms again, sending delicious shivers down her spine. Then he pulled her into his lap, kissing her neck, fingering her hair. Abruptly he stopped. "Do you like that? Is it—"

"Use your mouth for kissing and not talking, please," she said in her most "teacherly" voice.

He laughed softly and started to say something more, then shook his head. "Yes, ma'am," he whispered, eyes sparkling with mischief. He kissed her lips and slipped her nightgown off her shoulders.

∞ ∞ ∞

They got back to Toronto Tuesday night. Nathaniel had fallen asleep on the sofa, and the adults sat around the kitchen table with mugs of tea. Amiably, they discussed how they'd split the bills, where Adam might find a job, and how soon Macy might be released from the hospital. Davis explained his plan to fly up to visit them once a month. Then he yawned and picked up a piece of paper from the side table.

"A telegram came for you, Adam," he explained. "I apologize, I opened it by mistake, but I'm not exactly sorry I read it."

"Everything OK with my parents? I did let them know Arilee and I were getting married."

"It's not from them. It's from Emory. Seems they are expecting you."

He shrugged. "They'll be fine. To be honest, I really would prefer not to go to graduation, even if I was in Atlanta."

"I'm sorry to hear that, because I already made the necessary arrangements. They want you to give a speech."

"Ha! Horsefeathers." Adam snatched the telegram from Davis. Arilee leaned into his side to read it over his shoulder, and he moved it so she could see. His exam scores had lowered his final grades for the quarter to a B, but the faculty were so impressed with his involvement in Macy's diagnosis and care, they wanted him to give a speech at commencement.

"Whatta ya know?" he muttered.

"Oh, Adam, you've got to go now," Arilee exclaimed. "Is it because it's on the sixth that you don't want to?"

He nodded, wishing she weren't so perceptive even as he appreciated her intuition. The sixth was his birthday. His and Joshua's birthday. He'd refused to acknowledge the day for the past three years.

"You should be there for the reward of all your hard work." She laid a hand on his arm, her eyes so hopeful his resolve began to waver.

"I worked hard to win you, and that reward is a lot sweeter." He winked and made her blush. Memories of last night and this morning overpowered the issue at hand. Could anything be more exhilarating than waking up next to *his wife*?

Davis cleared his throat and raised an eyebrow. "In all your making eyes at each other, I don't think you caught what I said. I've already made arrangements. I've taken additional time off from work and bought two tickets to Atlanta. You'll be leaving on Thursday. I also telegrammed Mr. and Mrs. Harrison to let them know you are coming."

"Oh, Adam, surely you'll agree?"

"I'm not good at saying no to you, even if I wanted to. Thank you, Davis."

"No. I owe Sis a lot, and whenever I get a chance to make her happy, I need to take it. I owe you a lot too, Adam. Not many men would be willing to start their marriage taking care of another man's desperately ill child. You've been a brother to me when we both needed one."

Adam swallowed and nodded. At that moment, Nathaniel came stumbling into the room, half asleep.

"Mr. Adam, did you really marry Aunt Ari?" he yawned.

"Yep. You can call me 'Uncle Adam' now."

"You're not going to take her away from us, are you?" Nathaniel narrowed his eyes in suspicion.

"No. We're going to live in Toronto till Macy gets better, then as soon as we can come home, we will, and we'll all be together at Wisteria House."

The boy threw himself at Adam and hugged him. Adam thanked God his marriage to the woman he loved carried the added joy of bringing some happiness to the sorrowful life of this precious child; of bringing his own parents a daughter and God-willing, grandchildren; of making him and Davis brothers; of establishing a new home within their church. Family, though hard and even heartbreaking sometimes, remained infinitely better than being alone.

CHAPTER 40

Tuesday, June 6, 1922

Atlanta, Georgia

A week and a day after becoming *Mrs. Adam Harrison*, Arilee sat in the audience watching the commencement ceremony at Emory University. All had been set up outdoors, none of the buildings of the school sufficient to hold the crowd. Her now twenty-three-year-old husband not only received his Bachelor of Science degree, but was introduced with accolades by Dr. Elkin, the Dean of Medicine:

"A decorated hero from the recent war, Mr. Harrison not only completed four years in three, but his final year of his B.S. has also been his first year of medical school. He gave up graduating with honors to go to Toronto and study the new miracle extract for solving the problem of diabetes, after being the first to correctly diagnose his young niece's condition. This is a young man who has a bright future in medicine, and we are proud to have him as an alumnus."

Adam didn't stammer standing before hundreds of people, his peers and professors and parents. He spread out the notes he'd written up late last night but barely glanced at them as he spoke to the crowd.

"Scripture tells us 'Hope deferred maketh the heart sick: but when the desire cometh, it is a tree of life.' Shakespeare reflected this when he stated, 'The miserable have no other medicine but only hope.' Recently, a doctor in Toronto, a veteran of the war, with the assistance of a medical student the age of many of us here, discovered a pancreatic extract that is giving hope to the families of dying children everywhere. Diabetes Mellitus will soon no longer be a death sentence. And why? Because one man refused to rest until he found hope for the sick and miserable.

"He couldn't do it alone, and neither can any of us. But by finding others who also want to bring hope to the world and refusing to give up until we have taken hold of that tree of life, we can change a life or even history itself. The scope of a man's success matters far less than his faithfulness. Whether you graduate today to enter ministry, medicine, or management, your call is to bring hope to the desperate and despairing. That is the measure of a successful man who is a credit to his family, this institution, and his Savior . . ."

Arilee's clapping may have been muffled by her proper white gloves, but she thought she might burst with pride and gratitude. This man belonged to *her*. This was *her husband*. Next to her, Mrs. Harrison wiped tears from her eyes, and Mr. Harrison patted his wife's knee. When the ceremony ended, the three of them stood talking under the shade of an oak, waiting for Adam.

Arilee felt she owed her in-laws an apology. "He could have graduated very top of his class. He gave it up to come to Toronto, and I fear I'm responsible—"

"Sure are," said Mr. Harrison. "We think you're real good for him, Arilee. You've helped him settle down and focus on what matters a lot more than this degree has."

"Of course Adam needed to be with you." Mrs. Harrison swatted away a mosquito with a paper hand fan.

"But I worry I've taken him far away from you, Mrs. Harrison, and you didn't even get to see us wed."

"In some ways, you've restored him to us, dear." Mrs. Harrison laid a hand on her arm. "It's wonderful to see him happy again. You don't have to call us parental names if you don't want to, but I don't need to be 'Mrs. Harrison' to you anymore."

"*May* I call you 'Mother' and 'Father'?"

"We would love that, dear girl." Mrs. Harrison hugged her and held her.

Adam met up with them and they took pictures, then Mrs. Harrison announced, "The folks from your church have been setting up a bit of a celebration back at Wisteria House while we were here. We'll head there now."

Arilee looked at Adam, but he shrugged. Despite the warmth of the day, she snuggled up against him in the back seat of his parents' flivver, and he put his arm around her. But Mr. Harrison had something to say before he started the car.

"Adam, your mother and I have talked, and if you aim to continue on with medical school, we'd like to pay for it."

"No, Dad, y'all don't have that kind of money. I've got a little saved up, and I can work."

"Sure, but you've married into the family, so now you have to work for them for free." He winked. "And we have your brother's life insurance money."

Adam stiffened beside her. He put his fist to his mouth and stared straight ahead. "That's for your retirement," he said at last.

"Oh, but you're going to be a successful doctor and take care of us in our old age." Mrs. Harrison fanned herself. "I think this is the perfect way to honor your brother's memory. It's what Joshua would want. You know it is. Think of it as a birthday, graduation, and wedding gift from him. Did he ever discourage you in any of your plans?"

"No, not even when he should have," Adam murmured.

"Just think on it, son," Mr. Harrison urged. "It would enable you to focus wholly on your studies and your wife without the added burden of trying to provide. She'll never see you if you try to work a job *and* complete medical school, and we want her to be happy."

"You really know how to push a fellow into a corner," Adam remarked, but a slight smile played about the corners of his mouth. "I'll think on it."

"And by the way," Mrs. Harrison added. "If Davis is all right with it, we'd love to have Nathaniel come spend the summer with us. Might make it a little easier on the two of you and give him some special attention. And help your father and I wait a respectable length of time for our own grandchildren."

"As if the pressure isn't already on to produce an heir to the Harrison legacy." Adam rolled his eyes.

As they pulled into the driveway at Wisteria House, Arilee noted several cars parked on the lawn by the carriage house. In front of the main house, wooden folding chairs were set on the lawn with an aisle between them. The chairs faced an arch adorned with climbing roses.

"This doesn't look like any birthday or graduation party I've ever seen," Adam remarked.

"It's your wedding." Mrs. Harrison smiled. "I mentioned to a few of the ladies from your church that you'd gotten married before a justice of the peace, and they wanted to do something special for you now while they have the chance. It seems you're both quite loved."

Arilee stepped out of the car, and her eyes filled with tears that overflowed onto her cheeks. She'd never spoken this dream aloud, had died to it as frivolous and unimportant. Yet before her, what she'd envisioned in unguarded moments of wishing had materialized.

Adam pulled her close. "Hey, now, is it already so awful being married to me that you cry at the thought of doing it again?"

How did he always make her laugh? "I can't believe it," she whispered. "To think all these folks did this for us."

Andy and Violet Alexander stepped over.

"We hated the thought of the two of you gettting married among strangers when we all wished to rejoice with you at what God has done," Violet said. "It gave us such delight to plan a celebration for you, and with so many helping, it came together easily."

"Thank you doesn't seem adequate." Arilee choked back more tears.

"Thank *you*," said Pastor Andy. "You gave us a chance to come together in prayer for Macy and in support of a new Christian home. You've both honored the Lord, and it is our great joy to honor you."

"Come, Arilee." Violet rested a hand on her arm. "Let's get you dressed as a bride."

After the ceremony and meal, the same church ladies who had prepared everything cleaned it up, while Adam and Arilee spoke to each of their guests. Besides most of the church families celebrating with them, many of Adam's friends from school, and even several of the Harrisons' friends from Canton attended. Mr. and Mrs. Harrison were the last to say goodbye, and as she embraced them, Arilee thought, startled, that she had parents again.

Then she and Adam went into Wisteria House and closed the door, quite alone. The credenza in the front hall was covered with gifts to open. Arilee supposed they could do that tomorrow, but she stepped over at the sight of two telegrams and opened the first:

Wish we could be there. All our love and gratitude always, Davis, Nat, and Macy.

Arilee blinked rapidly. Something had softened in Davis recently, making him stronger rather than weaker. She had missed his true self more than she even knew.

And the second:

Congratulations, Sis, from your baby brother. P.S. I am safe and OK. Try not to worry. See you when I can.

She gasped and showed it to Adam. "More lives than a cat and always lands on his feet," Adam muttered. "I can't even imagine how he finagled his way out of that mess or what 'see you when I can' means. Or how he even knows about our wedding."

"I will try not to worry about him, but he won't stop me from praying for him every day." She placed the telegrams back on the credenza and noted a postcard in the stack of mail that had accumulated in her absence. Turning it over, she gave a cry of delight.

Dearest Arilee,

I may not have written, but I have prayed for you every day this past year. Keep looking to Jesus to make all things right in His own time and way.

Love always,
Jewel

"He has, Jewel, He is," she murmured, running her hand along the script and wishing she could hug Jewel instead.

Then she looked up and her eyes met the portrait of the Colonel staring down at them. She froze, overcome by the tragedy of the Rutledges that had shadowed her own life. For a moment she was sixteen again, homeless and terrified, sent here by her father to beg Aunt Odessa to take her in.

Adam switched off the lights and rested a hand on the small of her back.

"Let's go upstairs," he murmured.

She was a Harrison now. She belonged to Adam.

They sat together outside on the small settee on the second-floor porch, his arms about her, her hands rubbing him gently. He'd shed his suit coat, collar, and tie, but she still wore the elegant ivory gown she would keep for the rest of her life.

"We never did find out who the skeleton was. Or find the treasure," she said abruptly.

"I think *I* found the treasure."

She smiled up at him. "I know. But I wonder if the family legend is real. If the treasure is lost forever, or if we'll stumble upon it one day by mistake. I know this sounds silly, but I wanted to find it so something Daddy believed about our past would be true."

"I think what you're really wondering," he said gently, "is if you'll see your daddy again."

After a moment of struggling not to cry: "Your diagnosis is correct, not-yet-a-doctor Harrison."

"I missed Josh so much today. It was his birthday too. He shoulda been graduating with me. Shoulda been my best man. Every time the ache grew unbearable, I prayed for you going through all these things without your parents and separated from your brothers. It must have been a hard day for you."

"Hard, but still good. I'm part of your family and the church family. They gave us such a gift, and it wasn't even a need, just grace. And you, you are a gift of God's grace to me too. I'm so happy to be yours."

"I'm glad to hear it." He locked his arms behind his neck, gave an exaggerated sigh, and looked at her sidelong. "I thought when I came here, I might have to fight through a few thorns and overgrown bushes. I had no idea what lay ahead: bats, rats, roaches, and skeletons, plus old letters about scandals, back-from-the-dead brothers who give wicked black eyes, and a woman determined to see me as her student or kid brother no matter how many ways I tried to show her I was crazy about her. Ah, well. The Bard long ago warned us, 'The course of true love never did run smooth.'"

"I'm thinking of another Shakespearean quote." Arilee arched her eyebrows.

"If thou rememb'rest not the slightest folly
That ever love did make thee run into,
Thou has not loved."

"'Love comforteth like sunshine after rain,'" he replied.

"You'll not out-quote Shakespeare to me, Adam Harrison, no matter how *sockdolager* you are."

"I wouldn't dream of it, Roberta Rutledge."

She started to pounce on him, but he fended her off, protesting:

"What's in a name?
That which we call a rose
By any other word would smell as sweet."

"I'm Mrs. Harrison now."

He moved his arms back around her, settling her. She picked up his hand and traced it, too shy to look into his face as she murmured:

"[Love] . . . is an ever-fixed mark
That looks on tempests and is never shaken;
It is the star to every wand'ring bark . . ."

"That's swell, but didn't he write something about kissing?"

"No," she lied.

"You think I don't know anything. 'Teach not thy lip such scorn, for it was made for kissing, lady, not for such contempt.'"

"'A thousand kisses buys my heart from me, And pay them at thy leisure, one by one.'"

"All right, that's it." He picked her up and carried her inside to her room—*their* room—at Wisteria House, while she giggled between his many kisses.

This neglected house had been restored and made beautiful under Adam's care. And their broken, sinful hearts had been transformed under the loving care of the great Redeemer. He had restored them not only for

Himself, but for each other, and even, incredibly, to be a part of this family of believers surrounding and supporting them.

Though much remained mysterious, these things she did know gave her the confidence to go forward living and loving with all her heart.

∞∞∞

That night, Margaret Rose Woodhouse sat down and wrote up the following for the Atlanta *Journal*:

Recently, a most unique wedding took place at the historic Wisteria House on Randolph Street. Miss Arilee Rutledge, daughter of Thomas Rutledge and the late Susanna McEnnis Rutledge, was wed to Mr. Adam Harrison, son of Mr. and Mrs. Joseph Harrison of Canton. The bride is a graduate of Agnes Scott and a beloved local schoolteacher; the groom is a recent graduate of Emory University and a decorated veteran of the late war.

The front lawn of Wisteria House, as lush and fragrant as Eden at the dawn of the world, bloomed with flowers of every hue. Classical music was played on a phonograph. In the absence of the bride's father, her new father-in-law presented her to his son. The bride's veil, the "something borrowed" from Mrs. William Sweet II, featured embroidered flowers and scalloped edges. The bride wore an ivory dress of silk and chiffon, fashioned by Mrs. Andrew Alexander, the pastor's wife of Grace Baptist Church, where the newlyweds first met. Rev. Alexander performed a touching ceremony, with many personal words of encouragement to the young couple for whom he obviously feels the affection of friendship.
The wedding was a complete surprise for the bride and groom, planned and executed entirely by their church. Having been called out of town for a family emergency, Miss Rutledge and Mr. Harrison were married before a justice of the peace in New York one week prior to their Atlanta wedding.

Mrs. John Sweet baked the delicious yellow cake and frosted it with white almond-flavored frosting. Her daughter Miss Katherine Sweet decorated the confection with fresh roses and a charming topper of miniature bridal figures. Other ladies of the church provided various dishes for the wedding meal, and the joy of the bride and groom was shared by all.

Many prayers and well wishes were offered for the happy couple. May their joys be many, their sorrows few, and their love undiminished through a long life together.

As she hit the final period on her Remington portable typewriter, Meg Woodhouse bowed her head.

"Lord, I know we aren't exactly on speaking terms, and I never intend to marry again, but I would make an exception if Davis Rutledge ever became free."

The End

AUTHOR'S NOTE

*"To help divert my mind from such incessant brooding over my sorrows,
I am writing a new book. . . . I trust it may do some little good; at least
I would not dare to write it, if it* could *do none. May God bless it!"*
—Elizabeth Prentiss
More Love to Thee: The Life & Letters of Elizabeth Prentiss

In the course of crafting this book, I have had Covid, back issues, the flu, an unexpected move to a smaller house that was on the market and being shown, the ongoing challenges of parenting and homeschooling four children ages 5-10, financial stress, and finally a second move to a new area and a house God providentially provided for us. Writing this story has been a healing outlet and a gift from God to me personally as I've wrestled through many of the same questions as my characters, albeit in different circumstances.

Like my characters, I've also lived through my share of church drama since my early teens, from hurtful division to proud and misguided spiritual leaders. If you've been hurt by a church or a Christian leader, I would love to talk to you more about how you can find hope and healing within the Body of Christ again. I would encourage you to go deeper into God's Word to really understand His heart for you and for His bride, the Church.

The description of **Wisteria House** is loosely based on the Archibald Smith Plantation and Bulloch Hall, both in Roswell, Georgia. These antebellum homes each have a fascinating story of their own. Bulloch Hall is the girlhood home of Teddy Roosevelt's mother, Mittie. The Smith Plantation is more of a farmhouse than a mansion. As a volunteer tour guide there, I became acquainted with the *The Burial of Latané* print, the Victorian need for numerous chairs, and threads of life in the Reconstruction Era South. A trunk full of Civil War artifacts really was found in the attic of the Smith Plantation. Much like the Rutledges, the family never recovered from the upheaval of the war.

Of course, **Emory University** is not only still around but now a huge and prestigious institution with its own hospital. The Emory of 100 years ago would hardly be recognizable today, both in size and scope; at that time it was a distinctly Christian school.

It was fun to write about **Canton, Georgia**, where I lived while writing this book. The original high school building still stands. It served the entire (and enormous) Cherokee County, some students taking the train daily, others boarding in town to attend.

The **Georgia State Sanitarium, aka Milledgeville,** is a real place. You can still see the mostly abandoned buildings and unmarked graves today, eerie memorials to the thousands who lived and died at what was once the largest insane asylum in the world. Built in 1842, it went through several names and phases. In the late 1800s, there was about a 40% return rate of patients to normal life. By the 1910s, that number had dropped to a mere 11%. This was due to poor administration, overcrowding, and understaffing. Also, attitudes toward mental illness shifted in the early 1900s through the Progressive Movement and the so-called science of eugenics. Many families saw the free state asylum as a way to dispose of a problem they couldn't solve.

Things would get worse before they got better. In the mid-twentieth century treatments included insulin shock therapy, electric shock therapy, and even lobotomies. My own great-grandmother was a patient at Milledgeville, diagnosed with pellagra, now known to be caused by a nutritional deficiency. Currently called Central State Hospital, the complex was set to close in 2010, but a small population of mostly prison inmates remains, while the majority of the buildings on the enormous campus sit empty.

The discovery of insulin is truly miraculous. A team of doctors and researchers began working together (and sometimes against one another) at the University of Toronto in the sweltering summer of 1921. Dr. Frederick Banting was the primary discoverer and set up a private practice near the Athelma Apartments to administer insulin to desperate patients who came to Toronto. One notable patient was Elizabeth Hughes, daughter of eminent politician Charles Evans Hughes. She had survived three years on the Allen Starvation Diet and at 15 years old weighed only 45 pounds when she first received insulin. She went on to lead a full and normal life. The former congressman's son that Mrs. Woodhouse referred to was James Havens. He had lived for seven years on the starvation diet and was within a week of death. Through insulin he was able to recover and lead a happy adult life, becoming well known as an artist—a skill he first developed during the long years of illness. Teddy Ryder was just five years old and weighed under 30 pounds when Dr. Banting treated him. And Elsie Needham was the first child to recover from a diabetic coma through the use of insulin. (Note that what was described at the time as a diabetic coma was severe ketoacidosis from a too-high blood sugar, not to be confused with hypoglycemic shock from a too-low blood sugar.)

It was not until an American pharmaceutical company, Eli Lilly, stepped in that the vast quantities of insulin needed were able to be manufactured and a somewhat consistent product developed. In the 1920s, the thought of a doctor gaining financially from his research was considered unethical and unprofessional. The discoverers of insulin faced multiple moral dilemmas in the early administration and manufacture of their miracle discovery. For a fascinating inside look, I highly recommend the book *Breakthrough: Elizabeth Hughes, the Discovery of Insulin, and the Making of a Medical Miracle* by Thea Cooper and Arthur Ainsberg.

The hymn **"Be Still My Soul"** was published around 1752 in German by Katherine von Schlegal and translated into English around 1855 by Jane Borthwick of Scotland. The beautiful melody "Finlandia" was not paired with it until 1933 in the United States. The original tune of "St. Helen" has been all but lost to us.

The 82nd Division is well known from the Second World War as the "82nd Airborne." But in World War 1, they were but a lowly infantry division made up of regular men from every state in the Union. The nickname "All American" was picked through a local competition in Atlanta (the division trained at Camp Gordon). Once in France, the 82nd faced some of the most harrowing and exhausting battle conditions of the war as well as great losses: over 15,000 casualties between the Saint-Mihiel and the Meuse-Argonne. Sergeant Alvin York of the division received the Medal of Honor and was the most famous citizen soldier of the war.

A few of the **slang expressions** I have used cannot be found in published material until later than 1921, but I have taken the view that slang lives in spoken language, especially on college campuses and among enlisted soldiers, well before it finds its way to print. A 1926 article listed *nertz* as one of the ugliest words in the English language, a Cornell professor lamenting that it fairly curdled his blood to hear it!

The romance of **flight in the 1920s** can hardly be overstated. Pilots were popular heroes like sports figures. People flocked to air shows to watch daring tricks or to pay for a few moments of flight themselves. In 1922 there were very few airports, night flying was extremely risky, and flight in general was dangerous and unpredictable with frequent crashes. The transcontinental mail route began in 1920, but it took several years for it to expand throughout the country and for the landing strips needed to become available.

I hope you'll join me for *All Now Mysterious*, book two in the Wisteria House series. Until then, if you'd like a closer look at the Sweet, Alexander, and Macdonald families who served as minor characters in this book, check out my *Sorrow & Song* series. And for updates, giveaways, behind-the-scenes stories, historical tidbits, and more, sign up for my newsletter at jenniferqhunt.com and follow me on Instagram (jennifer.q.hunt.author) or my Facebook Author page (Jennifer Q. Hunt, Author).

Heartfelt thanks to my beloved beta readers and fellow authors: Bethany Cox (authorbethanycox.com), Kelsey Gietl (kelseygietl.com), Heather Wood (heatherwoodauthor.com), Liz Chapman (theworshipdesk.com), and Dani Renee (danireneewrites.com). I cannot say enough about your support. From messages back and forth with Bethany when this was all but an idea, to prayers back and forth with Elizabeth on the other side of the world, from detailed notes from Heather and Kelsey and encouragement from Danielle—y'all are *the best*. You're also some of my absolute favorite writers.

Thank you to **Kelsey Gietl** for another *sockdolager* cover. Before this, I couldn't imagine loving a cover without a person on the front, but this may be my favorite one yet. Your imagination and ability to take my very vague ideas and make them into something meaningful never ceases to amaze me.

* Thanks to my brother-in-law, Chaplain Avram Powell, for tips on a military funeral.
* Thank you to Kaylee Johnson with the Cherokee County Historical Society for her marvelous information on the original Canton High School.
* Thank you to talented author and artist Alisa Hall (alisahall.com) for transforming my rough sketch into a lovely diagram of Wisteria House.
* Thank you fellow Mommy Writer Stefanie Lozinski (authorstefanielozinski.com) for helping me bring Toronto to life.
* Thank you to Jennifer Doggart for initial insights into the life of a diabetes parent, and for the recommendation of the book *Breakthrough*, which really made this story.
* Thanks to Latisha Sexton for creating beautiful promotional graphics. Romantic suspense readers, check out latishasexton.com!
* To all of my dear fellow Christian Mommy Writers, I cannot say enough. You've taken writing from a lonely pastime to an incredible fellowship.
* Thanks to Mom for watching my youngest every Tuesday morning to give me an uninterrupted block of time to write.
* To my sweet oldest daughter, Ellie, thank you for always asking me how

my writing is going and wanting to hear about my stories.

* To Christopher, I enjoyed talking old house structure and remodeling with you. Never in a million years would I have dreamed when I started this book that a year later at its release we would be living in our own hundred-year-old house! I'm so grateful for you, my own handyman hero!

* For the Lord's sustaining grace and bringing ideas together and allowing me the opportunity to write stories for His glory, I am profoundly grateful.

Sorrow & Song Series

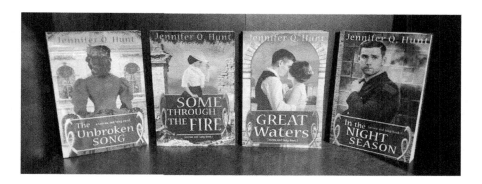

This family saga begins in 1895 (*The Unbroken Song*) and traces the lives of three generations of the Sweet family and their friends. *Some Through the Fire* tells how Violet learns to trust the Lord through the Atlanta Fire, World War 1, and the influenza pandemic. In *Great Waters*, Katie and Russell's marriage is tested during the Great Depression. And in *In the Night Season* Cal fights for truth—and his family—during World War 2.

"This series is going down as one of my favorite of all time."
—Author Latisha Sexton

"It was hard to say goodbye to these wonderful and endearing characters. Prepare to be swept away in a range of emotions in this compelling, page-turning Christian historical romance from a must-read author." —Goodreads Reviewer

About The Author

Jennifer Q. Hunt

Jennifer Hunt lives in the North Metro Atlanta area, a happy wife to her husband Christopher and grateful mama to two girls and two boys.

Jennifer has over twenty-five years of experience writing and editing for churches, Christian ministries, and the Christian fiction market. She is the author of the Sorrow & Song series, historical fiction with faith and purpose.

When she's not busy homeschooling her children or writing her next book, Jennifer enjoys talking to her fellow Mommy Writers, reading, long walks, hot tea, and antique shops off the beaten path.

Printed in Great Britain
by Amazon

40166022R00192